Carol Marinelli recently filled in a form asking for her job title. Thrilled to be able to put down her answer, she put 'writer'. Then it asked what Carol did for relaxation and she put down the truth: 'writing'. The third question asked for her hobbies. Well, not wanting to look obsessed, she crossed her fingers and answered 'swimming'—but, given that the chlorine in the pool does terrible things to her highlights, I'm sure you can guess the real answer!

Fiona McArthur is an Australian midwife who lives in the country and loves to dream. Writing Medical Romance gives Fiona the scope to write about all the wonderful aspects of romance, adventure and medicine, and the midwifery she feels so passionate about. When she's not catching babies, Fiona and her husband Ian are off to meet new people, see new places and have wonderful adventures. Drop in and say hi at Fiona's website: fionamcarthurauthor.com.

ONE MONTH TO TAME THE SURGEON

CAROL MARINELLI

HEALING THE BABY DOC'S HEART

FIONA McARTHUR

MILLS & BOON

First published in Great Britain 2024
by Mills & Boon, an imprint of HarperCollins*Publishers* Ltd,
1 London Bridge Street, London, SE1 9GF

www.harpercollins.co.uk

HarperCollins*Publishers* Macken House, 39/40 Mayor Street Upper, Dublin 1, D01 C9W8, Ireland

One Month to Tame the Surgeon © 2024 Carol Marinelli

Healing the Baby Doc's Heart © 2024 Fiona McArthur

ISBN: 978-0-263-32149-4

02/24

This book contains FSC™ certified paper
and other controlled sources to ensure responsible forest management.

For more information visit www.harpercollins.co.uk/green.

Printed and Bound in the UK using 100% Renewable Electricity
at CPI Group (UK) Ltd, Croydon, CR0 4YY

ONE MONTH TO TAME THE SURGEON

CAROL MARINELLI

MILLS & BOON

For Rosie.

Thank you for being a wonderful friend.

C xxxx

PROLOGUE

PIPPA WESTFORD HAD learnt to make the school library her haven.

Here she could catch up on her homework or do some uninterrupted study.

She didn't make friends easily.

Well, as a little girl she had, but her family had relocated so many times that by the age of sixteen Pippa was used to being the new girl—and always the outsider.

She had vague memories of nursery and infant school in the small village in Wales where she'd been born. Then they had moved to Cardiff, to be closer to a major hospital. As her older sister Julia's condition had deteriorated, they had moved again, to make the endless appointments in London more manageable. Then, when Julia had been placed on the transplant list, they had moved again, to ensure the tight four-hour window to get her to the hospital should a heart and lungs become available could be met.

Now, with Julia's transplanted heart failing, the library felt like her only refuge.

The chairs were heavy and comfortable, and there were lots of little nooks in which to hide. It was May—not that you could tell. The library had small, high windows that let in little light, and dark mahogany furnishings. Though the table had lamps, it felt as if it could just as well have been midwinter rather than approaching summer.

Pippa sat in a small recess, coiling her dark curls around

her fingers as she read the sparse notes she'd made with the careers counsellor.

Hearing the thump of a bag, and someone taking the seat opposite her own, she took a calming breath and didn't look up. The peace she'd come here to find had been broken.

What *did* she want to do with the rest of her life?

Removing her fingers from her unruly hair, she picked up a pen, determined to tackle the blank form that had plagued her for weeks. She filled in her first name in full—Philippa—and then sighed—at only sixteen years of age she felt more than a little overwhelmed at the prospect of choosing the A level subjects that would shape her future.

The careers counsellor and her teachers had all said that the decisions she made, though important, could be changed, depending on the results of her GCSEs.

Pippa was rather certain that the results were not going to be the ones she hoped for.

She turned to the front page of her school diary and looked at the study schedule she'd meticulously mapped out when she'd started the new school year at her latest school.

Her hand tightened on the pen she was holding and she was tempted to scribble angrily all over it, or simply tear the pages out, because she'd barely managed to meet a quarter of the hours she'd allocated.

There was always something...

'Pippa, can you stop at the shops...?'

'If you can meet us at the hospital and bring in Julia's dressing gown...'

'Go and talk to your sister, Pippa. She's been home alone all day...'

Somehow she'd managed to work around all that, and then the news they'd been waiting for had come.

'There's a donor!'

Was she the worst sister in the world, because she'd sat in the waiting room with her parents as the hours had passed, wishing she'd brought her homework?

Mrs Blane would understand if her homework was late.

Pippa knew that. She wouldn't be in trouble. Just permanently behind....

And now, as hope faded for her sister, Pippa felt as if her own heart was in decline. Far from being jealous of Julia, she loved her more than anyone in the world.

She wasn't just losing her sister; Pippa was losing her best friend.

'Having trouble deciding?'

Pippa looked up and blinked when she saw that it was Luke Harris sitting opposite her and, what was more, he was asking her a question.

She tried to think of something suitably witty but only said, 'A bit.'

It was hardly a dazzling response, but it was all her sixteen-year-old voice knew how to say when she was under the gaze of his brown eyes.

Everyone had a crush on Luke.

A slight exaggeration, perhaps, but certainly amongst Pippa's peers he was the most popular boy in school. Two years older than Pippa, Luke Harris was the one they all cheered on at school sports day or whispered about in assembly if he gave a speech or some such.

He was good-looking, with straight hair that was a softer shade of brown than his eyes, and he was good at everything. He had the Midas touch and, really, he was just...gorgeous.

'How did *you* decide?' she asked, both curious and wanting to prolong this small conversation.

She expected to be fobbed off, or given some vague answer, but Luke really seemed to consider her question before responding.

'I think it was decided for me, before I was born,' he said with an edge to his tone.

'You're going to be a doctor?' she asked, because she had watched the senior school's Speech Night online with Julia, and his father had presented some awards.

'A surgeon,' he corrected.

She finally looked up and saw his red eyes in the lamplight.

For a stupid moment she thought that Luke—effortless Luke—had been crying, but then she realised he'd probably just come from the pool. Naturally he was good at swimming too.

Then, embarrassed to be staring, she dragged her eyes from his and saw a little graze on his strong jaw. It made her smile just a little that perfect Luke must have cut himself shaving.

He returned her smile, though his was a curious one, as if wondering what might have amused her. 'I'm Luke,' he introduced. 'Luke Harris.'

'I know,' Pippa said, smiling. 'I do pay attention in assembly. Well, sometimes...'

His smile widened and her heart seemed to do a small somersault, almost escaping the confines of her chest.

He looked at the upside-down form she had started to fill out. 'Philippa?'

'Yes, but—' She'd been about to tell him she usually went by Pippa, but then found she didn't want to get into names.

Especially if it led to surnames.

Westford wasn't a particularly unusual name, but there was just one other at their school.

Julia.

And in that moment Pippa didn't want to be recognised as Julia's sister.

They looked nothing alike—Julia was petite and blonde, with huge blue eyes, whereas Pippa was all wild, dark curls and more sturdily framed. As for her eyes... Well, last week's art homework had been to find the closest hue to your eyes on the colour chart. Try as she might to match something wonderful, like jade or malachite, Pippa's had discovered that her eyes were plain old army-green.

And even more awkward than comparing their looks, whenever anyone found out who she was there was always an uncomfortable pause, a flicker of sympathy, a particular weighty hush or an enquiry as to how Julia was doing.

Always.

Luke was in the same form as Julia, and even if she had been too unwell to attend much school this year, he'd know her.

He would also know, as everyone did, that Julia had cystic fibrosis and that her heart and lung transplant hadn't been the success everybody had hoped for, and he would naturally enquire how she was...

Pippa knew she was the lucky one.

Sometimes, though, all she felt was invisible.

The one who could take care of herself. The one whose problems really didn't matter.

What was a pair of broken glasses when your sister had been admitted to hospital that very day? What was getting your first period when your sister had just been given the news that she'd been placed on the transplant list? And why on earth would you cry over a few spots, even a face full of them, when your sister was dying?

Pippa had felt guilty, rubbing in the cream she'd bought to try and get rid of the spots. She'd clearly used far too much cream, because the peroxide had turned the long strings of brown curls on her forehead into an odd shade of orange.

Though she didn't want to admit to being Julia's little sister, Pippa loved her very much, and was terrified at the thought of a world without her. But Pippa had no one to go to with her fears, because her parents were consumed by enough fears for all of them.

It was nice, for a moment, to sit in the quiet library and talk about herself.

'The careers guidance wasn't much help,' Pippa admitted.

She had tried to discuss it with Julia, who had been happy to do so, but her mother had ushered her away and then scolded her in the kitchen.

'Have some tact, Pippa,' she'd told her, reminding her that Julia didn't have the luxury of planning a future.

And so another topic had been added to the forbidden conversation list. She certainly hadn't felt able to ask her parents about subject selection, and the fifteen-minute interview with the careers counsellor had been confusing rather than enlightening.

'What GCSEs are you taking?' Luke asked, and Pippa told him.

'I like French,' she said. 'But I don't think I could make a career out of it.'

'So you're not looking to be a translator?'

'Gosh, no. I think I'll just save it for holidays.' Pippa smiled. 'It's the same with art,' she admitted. 'I like sketching and ceramics—' she chewed on her pen for a moment '—actually, I love art. Well, I did until last week…' She suddenly smiled.

'What's so funny?'

'Nothing. Just…'

'Just what?'

He persisted, and it felt new and unfamiliar to have someone persist, to have someone other than her sister truly wanting to know her thoughts, or wanting to know the reason a smile had flickered across her face.

It was so pleasing that Pippa readily told him about the homework assignment, and the rather disappointing conclusion that the colour of her eyes was army-green.

'It's not very exciting.'

'Better than brown,' he said. 'You clearly enjoy art.'

'I do, but…' She shrugged tightly in a manner that usually would have closed a conversation, and yet he waited…waited for her to elaborate. 'It's the same as French, though: I can't see myself making a career out of it…'

'You could always combine the two and be a pavement artist in Paris…'

Pippa laughed at the very notion. 'I think I'd feel ripped off if I was in Paris getting my portrait done and I got me as the artist.' She realised that probably didn't make sense, and began to explain better, but he just smiled.

'Anything?' he asked. 'If you could be anything?'

She turned the question to him, 'What would you be?'

His head moved to one side, as if he'd never actually considered it.

'Anything?' she insisted.

'Rock star,' he grinned.

'Guitar?'

'Oh, no.' He shook his head. 'Drums.'

'Drummers are the wild ones,' Pippa mused. 'Can you play the drums?'

'I've never tried,' he admitted, and Pippa started to laugh.

'Shh!' they were told by the librarian.

Luke came around the table and sat beside her. She could feel him next to her, reading through the notes she'd made during the career counsellor's session.

'The police?'

'Detective.' Pippa pointed to the clarification. 'That was her suggestion,' Pippa said. 'I stay calm in a crisis and I'm big on trust.' She shook her head. 'I don't think it's me, though...'

He looked at her for a long moment. 'No,' he agreed.

'You have to be in uniform first, and I can't run.'

'You can't run?'

Pippa shook her head.

'Can't or won't?' he asked.

'Both,' Pippa admitted, and then watched as he went back to the odd little notes she'd written.

'Cake?' He frowned at the single word. 'Are you into baking?'

'No.' Pippa shook her head. 'It was just... I was explaining to the careers counsellor that I'd thought about nursing.'

'But what does that have to do with cake?'

'I just...' Her voice trailed off.

Pippa knew she couldn't tell him without sounding a little selfish. She hadn't considered nursing for altruistic reasons; it was actually because of something nice that had happened. On the day she had been turning seven she had woken up excited, yet when she'd gone downstairs it had been a neighbour in the kitchen who had explained that Julia had been taken ill in the early hours.

That evening Pippa had been taken to see her sister, who by then had thankfully stabilised. Pippa had hugged her, just wanting to climb in bed beside her, but it had been all masks and gowns for adults, and she'd been told to stay well back.

Pippa had felt guilty for her own disappointment that nobody had even wished her a happy birthday, but then a nurse had come into the side ward, carrying a cake. Everybody had sung 'Happy Birthday' and for a short while she had felt remembered.

'Why does nursing appeal?' Luke persisted, dragging her back to the present.

Pippa realised then that it wasn't just his dark good looks that made him popular—he listened, and he engaged with people—with *her*—fully.

'I just think it's something…' Pippa didn't really know how to elaborate—and not just because she didn't want to mention Julia. That nurse had made such a difference. Had made her feel like an important part of the family, even if just for a little while. 'Something I might like…'

'So what do you need for that?'

'Two or three A levels, one in science. I know I want to do biology and English…' Pippa spoke in a low whisper and thought how nice it was to actually talk it through with someone. 'I really want to do art, but…' She shrugged.

'But…?'

'I don't think I'm *that* good.'

'My mother paints. She's dreadful at it…' His voice faded, as if he was lost in thought for a moment, but then he quickly regrouped, and his gorgeous brown eyes were back on Pippa. 'You really enjoy it?'

'Very much,' she admitted. She'd been taught to hold in her emotions, or to handle them herself, but in art class she felt she could let them slip out. 'I find it peaceful. Ceramics especially…'

'Then do it.'

Their heads moved closer together and she expected to smell chlorine, given that he'd just been at the pool. Or rather, given that his red eyes had made her assume he'd been swimming.

She looked up and in the lamplight saw again his reddened, slightly swollen eyes. She swallowed.

He had been crying.

Was it possible that Luke Harris was also hiding from the world in the library?

Just as she didn't want to reveal her surname, Pippa knew he wouldn't want her to probe.

Still, she did enquire a little with her eyes.

There was just a moment when each stared at the other, and Pippa forgot about the tape on her glasses and that her fringe was streaked with orange.

It was as if both knew that behind the smiles and easy chatter there was hurt.

'Don't give up art if you enjoy it,' he said, still staring at her.

'It might be a waste. Maybe I should just focus on two...'

'But it's your favourite subject.'

'Yes.' She nodded. 'It's really relaxing. It's not like being in a class.'

'Then don't let it go.'

Pippa knew he was right—knew he was confirming what she'd wanted to hear, that she should do a subject she enjoyed—and so she nodded. 'I think I will do it.'

'Good.'

But now her dilemma was a little more solved, Pippa found that she didn't want to leave the path of his gaze. His eyes were more than chocolate-brown. She wanted to go back to her colour charts and try to identify it. Yet, despite their beauty, she could not ignore the redness of the whites and the slight puffiness of his heavy lids.

'Are you okay?' she asked.

He didn't answer straight away. Nor did he query why she might ask such a thing.

People were packing up, the end of lunch bell was ringing, and activity was all around. Yet for a moment they remained there, her question still hanging in the air between them.

'I will be,' he finally said, and then gave her a sort of down-turned smile.

'Can I help?' Pippa asked, and then blushed. Because as if she could offer Luke Harris advice on anything! 'I just—'

'I'll be fine.' He stood up. 'Better get back. What have you got now?'

'Double art,' Pippa said, and his smile turned a little upwards. 'You?' she asked as they walked out of the library together.

'Double sport.'

Her art class flew by, as it always did, and as well as glazing a pot she'd made Pippa worked on a little ceramic heart to go into the kiln.

'Is that for Julia?' the art teacher asked, because she often made little ornaments for her sister.

Pippa didn't answer.

She walked home, stopping to pick up the new pair of glasses she had ordered, and also to get some groceries her mother had asked her to fetch. And then she went on to the chemist to pick up the special lotion Julia needed for her skin, now that she was spending most of her time in bed.

All the while, though, Pippa was replaying her time in the library with Luke, and then, as she turned into her street, she found herself in a daydream. One where the bell hadn't gone and she and Luke had been locked in the library for hours, days… A convenient siege situation or a blackout or something. And, given it was *her* daydream, she'd been a year or two older, and not wearing taped-up glasses with flares of orange in her hair. But what about the loo…? There were none in the library!

That tripped up her fantasy, but she decided to ignore that issue for the moment. She returned to her daydream.

When she got home, Pippa thought, Julia could give her the inside gossip on him. Perhaps she could work Luke into the conversation and find out more about him? Or even tell Julia that the totally normal crush she'd had on Luke had been massively upgraded to full-blown infatuation…

She took a breath before she turned the key in the front door. It was something she'd only recently become aware of: a certain nervousness as to what she might come home to.

'Hi?' she called out, and then saw her mum coming out of the kitchen. 'I got the shopping.'

'How was school?'

'Good. We had to think about A-level subject selection—'

'That's nice.'

'I'm thinking about—'

'Julia's got something exciting to tell you,' her mother interrupted, without waiting to hear any more about Pippa's day. 'It's good news!' She prompted an appropriate response as Pippa put down the groceries. 'But I'll let her tell you herself.'

'Sure,' Pippa said, and then headed up the stairs.

'Hey…' Pippa knocked on the open bedroom door and smiled at her sister, who was sitting propped up in bed and just finishing a nebuliser. Pippa took the mask, and was hanging it up when Julia's breathy voice came.

'Guess what?'

'What?' Pippa asked, and sat on her sister's bed.

'Luke called. He's *finally* asked me out.' Julia smiled. 'Luke Harris!'

It was selfish, Pippa was sure, to have such a painful sinking feeling…to be jealous of her sister's happiness when she had so little in her life.

'We're going to the school dance,' Julia elaborated and lay back on the pillow, her cornflower-blue eyes shining and a smile on her dusky lips.

'He just called,' their mum said, coming into the bedroom, all smiles. 'Said that he'd missed seeing Julia at school.'

'Oh.'

For a few seconds it was all Pippa could manage. She'd known, deep down, that he'd just been being nice this lunchtime and had *never* been going to ask her out. But it was such a painfully abrupt end to her daydream, to her little escape.

She forced out a more suitable response. 'That's brilliant.'

Luke came to the house a couple of times, although Pippa stayed in her room. But at school Luke looked straight through her the one time she passed him in the hall. She consoled herself with the likelihood that he was either going in or coming out of an exam.

On the night of the school dance she helped Julia with her

make-up, and thought her big sister looked gorgeous in her pale silver dress.

'You look beautiful,' Pippa said as she added a little more blusher. 'Are you excited?'

'Nervous,' Julia admitted. 'But excited too!'

It had taken weeks to get Julia well enough to attend the dance. Her medications had had to be tailored for this one precious night, and there was oxygen set up in a private room at the hall should she need it. But for now she looked simply perfect.

'He's here!' Their mum came in. 'Dad will carry you down the stairs,' she asserted, 'so you can save your breath for dancing.'

'I don't want Luke to see me being carried,' Julia warned.

It was Julia's night, so Pippa stayed upstairs as her sister was carried down. She knelt on the bed, fiddling with the little ceramic heart she'd made on that special day, now on the window ledge. Since then it had been fired, and she'd painted it the closest shade she could find to match Luke's eyes. The next week she'd glazed it and it had been fired again.

Now she watched Luke walk Julia to the waiting car and felt guilty for wishing that she was the girl on his arm.

For the first time ever, she wished that she was Julia.

CHAPTER ONE

'WOW!'

On a cold November morning, when she should be dashing to get to hand-over, Pippa stood at the hospital entrance, take-away coffee in hand and mouth agape…

'It looks like a space ship.'

May, the emergency department's nurse manager, had been walking ahead of Pippa, but she too had stopped to take in the new paediatric wing at London's Primary Hospital.

For the past couple of years the east wing of the post-war concrete building had been undergoing a facelift and extension, and now the scaffolding had been removed, revealing gleaming white arches and an awful lot of glass.

'I'm getting dizzy just looking at it,' May said in her strong Irish brogue. 'I can't imagine walking along those corridors.'

'I can,' Pippa said with a smile. As a paediatric nurse at The Primary, she was thrilled at the long overdue upgrade. 'Where's Paediatric Emergency?' Pippa asked, and May let out a hmmph.

'It's the same old Emergency,' May said, rolling her eyes, 'just a fancy new entrance and a few more bays. Basically, we'll be filling up that whole place with barely any extra staff…'

'Surely not?' Pippa said, laughing.

'Well, a few extra,' May conceded. 'What's happening with your ward?'

'We'll be moving to the first floor of the new building, taking acute admissions only…'

'It won't be the same.' May voiced Pippa's thoughts. 'Anything half interesting will be admitted to its own special-ised unit.'

May was right.

At the moment, the paediatric ward took everyone from ba-bies right up till fifteen- or sixteen-year-olds, and there was an eclectic mix of patients, from planned admissions to emergen-cies and anything in between.

Once the new wing opened they'd be more of a short-stay ward, or a holding area before the patient was moved to a more specialised unit.

'Look at the time,' May said, flustered. 'We're both going to be late…'

Perhaps so, but before she entered the old building Pippa took one more look. She had pored over the plans that had been posted, and read all the notes about the new units, and there was one that had captured Pippa's interest.

She hadn't told a soul, but next week Pippa had an interview.

Times were changing…

And so was Pippa.

'Sorry!'

The apology wasn't aimed at him.

As Luke Harris stepped out of a side ward, a blur of dark curls and a grey coat was dashing past, trailing a scarf, apolo-gising to the staff waiting to hand over.

She brought the chilly autumn air in with her, but there was the scent of summer too. Perhaps it was her perfume—or was there just something about her that drew the eye?

'I'll just get changed!' she called to the gathered nursing team, and he turned his head and watched as she ducked into what was presumably the changing room.

Yes, there was something about her that drew his eye—something familiar.

Given that he'd spent the last two years in Philadelphia, Luke was more used to unfamiliar faces. Of course on his travels he'd crossed paths with the occasional former colleague, and even the occasional ex… Now that he was temporarily back in London, he expected a lot more of the same.

He couldn't quite place her, though.

There was something about the loosely coiled dark curls that made him lose the thread of his conversation with Nola, the ward's unit manager, as she took him and his junior doctor for a brief ward round, while also showing him the layout of the paediatric unit.

'As well as the cots and isolation rooms, we've twelve general beds and eight high-dependency beds, both medical and surgical.' Nola gestured to the two glass-framed four-bedded wards that were closest to the nurses' station. 'The new wing opens soon, but for now your paediatric surgical patients—'

Then she laughed.

Not Nola.

Nor Fiona, the rather eager junior doctor who had been a third-year med student at St Bede's when he'd last seen her— and an annoying one at that.

No, the sound of laughter came from the nurses' station, and Luke knew—simply knew—that it came from *her*.

Her?

Luke glanced over. Despite his rather wild reputation with women, he did at least remember all his exes, and she was not one of them. Her dark hair fell in long coils, which she was tying up as she chatted and laughed. She had taken off her coat and scarf and she stood there, solidly built, yet curvy, in pale blue scrubs. Luke was absolutely certain that he knew her.

Perhaps she'd worked at his old hospital? He'd known most of the staff there.

Indeed, that had been part of the problem. In the end, he'd felt he had no choice but to leave.

It must be from there that he knew her, Luke decided.

And if that was the case, he certainly wouldn't be acknowledging the connection.

Luke let his mental search go as they made their way down the ward and he met the patients and parents.

'Chloe James, seven years old,' Nola informed him. 'Fell

five metres from playground apparatus on Friday and suffered a lac liver. No surgery…'

Luke listened as he read through the notes and then introduced himself to the anxious mother.

'A locum?' Mrs James frowned. 'So you're just standing in? How long have you worked here for?'

'I'm just starting today—' Luke began to explain, but his attempts to reassure the anxious mother were hastily interrupted by Nola.

'Mr Harris was a surgical consultant at St Bede's, so we're very lucky to have him at The Primary.'

Luke felt his lips tighten a touch—not just at the interruption, but because the Unit Manager clearly knew his work history.

Then he glanced over to the junior doctor, and as he met her eyes he saw her go a little pink.

Ah, so Fiona must have told Nola where he'd worked. He wondered what else Fiona might have revealed…

'Mrs James.' Luke addressed the concerned mother. 'I'm sure you've seen more medical staff than you can keep track of, but I'm currently standing in for Mr Eames while he's on extended leave. I'm a general surgeon, with a specialist interest in trauma, and I'll be overseeing Chloe's care from here on.'

'So you're not just here for today?'

'No, I'm here for a month—and, judging by the look of things, Chloe will be long since home by then. How has she been?'

'Better,' Mrs James said. 'Well, she's starting to say she's hungry, and she's asking to play games on my phone.'

'I see that,' Luke said. 'Can I take a look at you, Chloe?'

'Am I allowed to have breakfast?' Chloe asked, lifting her blonde head from the game she was playing.

'I think it's a little too soon for that,' Luke admitted, 'but I'll know more when I've had a look at your abdomen—your tummy,' he corrected himself.

'I do know what an abdomen is,' Chloe said, putting down the phone and lying back. She gave him a smile that displayed a lot of missing teeth.

'Well, I'm sorry for talking down to you,' Luke said as he lifted her gown. 'I take care of adults too,' he told her as he felt her abdomen. 'Some of them say stomach…some say belly—'

'Or guts!' Chloe said with relish.

'Chloe!' her mother warned.

And Luke laughed at the clever, cheeky young girl, very pleased that her abdomen remained soft as she too laughed at her chosen word.

'Can you sit up for me?' he asked, giving Mrs James a little shake of his head as she went to assist. He was pleased when Chloe moved well and required only the slight support of his hand to sit up.

'She couldn't do that before,' Mrs James observed.

'I'm sure.'

Chole, having terrified everyone, was clearly a lot better than she had been when she'd arrived in the emergency department on Friday afternoon.

'They bounce back a lot quicker than us,' he said, with raised brows. 'Emotionally too.'

'Yes.' Mrs James gave a half-laugh and held out a trembling hand. 'I'm still shaking while she's begging to have breakfast. Can she have something to eat?'

'Clear fluids only for today,' Luke said. 'We don't want to rush things. I'd like to organise another ultrasound.'

'But I'm hungry,' Chloe whined, looking up at him with a glum expression.

'So am I,' Luke responded.

The little girl smiled. 'Didn't you have breakfast?'

'I didn't.' He shook his head. 'We'll get some more pictures of your abdomen and then see how you are.'

And then *she* came in.

The mystery nurse.

'Hey, Chloe…' Her voice faded when she saw that the doctors were with them.

'Oh, sorry to interrupt,' she said quickly. 'I'll come back.'

'No problem,' Nola responded. 'We're finished here.'

He knew that voice, Luke thought as he left Chloe's room and saw the nurse replacing the IV fluids.

A memory stirred...a name, a moment in time demanding to be placed.

Still, as they left the side ward, it was the patient that was discussed.

'I'd like to be paged when she goes down to imaging. If I'm not available, David?' He glanced at his registrar, who was looking at his pager.

'I need to go down to the ED,' David said.

'Sure.'

With David out of the way, Luke addressed Nola. While the polite thing to do might have been to excuse Fiona from the conversation, there was a very good reason he did not.

'I can reassure the patients and their carers as to my qualifications myself,' he said, rather curtly.

'I just thought—' Nola swallowed and glanced at Fiona, who was positively scarlet. 'Well, Mrs James was clearly worried that it was your first day and...'

'As I said, any concerns as to my professional abilities I'll deal with myself. Please don't speak on my behalf when I'm standing right there!'

Luke knew he was being blunt, but it was essential he made his position clear on this point from the start. The cloud of scandal hanging over him when he'd left St Bede's, more than two years ago, clearly hadn't dispersed completely and he didn't want it to poison his new role here.

They took the elevator up to the adult surgical units, and he walked in silence with his junior. He silently berated himself for the way he had handled the situation, because he was in no doubt that Fiona would soon be sharing far more of his past with her colleagues than just his résumé!

Gossip spread in a hospital more rapidly than any virus.

He considered trying to address it here and now, but how?

Should he *order* Fiona not to repeat what she had seen and heard a couple of years ago? Or *ask* her, maybe?

But wouldn't that just add fuel to a fire that he had fervently hoped, after two years, had gone out?

Who was he kidding?

It wasn't just Fiona.

As they made their way to Surgical Unit One he nodded to *another* familiar face—a theatre tech he'd worked alongside at St Bede's.

'Jimmy!'

'Luke!'

Pleasantries were exchanged, and they had a brief catch-up in the highly polished corridor that ran between Theatres and Surgical Unit One, but he could see the flare of interest in his colleague's eyes.

'Back in London?' Jimmy asked.

'Yes.' Luke nodded, though he could almost hear the question that wasn't voiced—*Avoiding St Bede's?*

'I went out the other week with the old mob,' Jimmy told him. 'Well, a few have moved on, but we keep in touch. Ross is a cardiac technician now.'

'Good for him.'

'And Shona moved to the ICU.'

Just for a moment Luke felt relieved at Jimmy's casual mention of her name. Maybe the world really had moved on. But then Jimmy cleared his throat and mumbled something about needing to get on, and Fiona started checking her pager, which hadn't even gone off, and Luke could feel the sudden awkwardness caused by the mention of Shona's name.

'Good to see you,' Luke said, and knew then, for sure, that he was in for a month of hell.

His…*active* sex life and his refusal to commit had been popular topics for gossip at St Bede's. Luke had always carried his reputation well—this leopard was happy with his spots and his care factor was zero when it came to gossip. For the most part his short relationships ended amicably, because he chose his partners wisely and always spelt out from the start that things would not be progressing further than a casual liaison. He would *never* settle down—and he made sure they knew that.

A couple of years ago, though, his reputation had caught up with him. Assumptions had been made about him and Shona, a married theatre nurse at St Bede's. Rumours had started to spread—as they undoubtedly would here at The Primary.

They had, however, been completely unfounded.

But Luke, for reasons he would never reveal, had been in no position to correct them.

And it was for those same reasons that he was only in London for a month or so. He was here to sell his apartment—or at least get the ball rolling on the sale of it—and then get the hell out.

This time for good.

Pippa didn't notice the surgeons leave.

She collected the charts the junior doctor had updated and then spoke at length with Mrs James, who was upset that Chloe couldn't eat.

'Why don't you go and have some breakfast away from Chloe? When I've finished doing the drugs I'll come and have a chat with her,' Pippa suggested. 'She's a clever little thing; she needs to know why she's not allowed to eat.'

'But I don't want to scare her,' Mrs James fretted. 'I need to go home for a few hours and get some milk expressed. I can't relax enough here, and—'

'And you need to see your baby.'

'Yes, but if Chloe gets upset I won't be able to leave her.'

'I'm not going to upset her. Go home and have a shower and some breakfast,' Pippa suggested again. 'Like I said, she's a bright girl. Chloe knows you need to go home this morning.'

The little girl just didn't like the fact!

As Mrs James went to collect her wash things Jenny, one of the RNs, rolled her eyes. 'She needs to learn to say no to her. Honestly… It's "Chloe this…", "Chloe that—"'

'Chloe's got a new baby brother and she's had a nasty accident,' Pippa interrupted. 'It's no wonder she's a bit clingy and her mother's anxious. Gosh, I pretended to break my arm when

I was seven just to get my mum's attention—at least Chloe's reasons are real.'

Pippa left a grumpy Jenny and made her way to the drug room, where she started preparing the morning medications for her patients.

'There you are,' Nola said as she came in.

'Just in time,' Pippa replied with a smile. 'Can you check these with me?'

'Of course,' Nola said, but rather than get on with checking the drugs she took a moment to discuss something else. 'Pippa, you know that applications close today...?'

Pippa frowned.

'For my maternity leave position,' she prompted, patting her bump affectionately. 'You often fill in for me, yet you haven't applied...'

'No.' Pippa felt a little flustered. She'd been hoping not to say anything just yet, but now Nola had specifically commented on the fact that she hadn't applied for the role she knew now was the time to tell Nola everything. 'I've put in an expression of interest for a unit manager role when the new paediatric wing opens.'

'You didn't say.'

'Because I wasn't sure if I even stood a chance. It's a big leap. I've only been a fill-in here. It's for the PAC Unit.' There were so many new specialities coming to The Primary that she wasn't surprised when she saw Nola frown at the terminology. 'Paediatric Acute with Comorbidities.'

'So, looking after chronically ill children?'

'Yes, with an acute illness or undergoing routine procedures. It sounds like a really interesting role but, like I said, I didn't know if I had a hope when I applied. I've been invited for a preliminary interview. I was going ask if you'd mind being a referee for my application?'

'Of course,' Nola said. 'But Pippa...' She pressed her lips together for a moment in slight exasperation.

'What?'

'Why didn't you say anything before?'

'I told you. I wasn't sure if I'd even get to the interview stage.'

'We've been talking about the new paediatric wing for months. All of us have been working out what positions we want...' She looked at Pippa and gave a slight shake of her head. 'Not you, though.'

'Is that a problem?'

'Reference wise, no,' Nola said, and didn't elaborate as she was called to the phone.

Pippa was left standing, and knew she'd been told off—just a little.

She was friendly enough at work, and got on with her colleagues for the most part. She'd held several nursing positions over the years and, apart from her training, her time here at The Primary was the longest she'd spent anywhere. But because she didn't bring her private life to the break room, or the handover desk, she was considered a little aloof and standoffish.

It wasn't just her private life where she held back, though, Pippa acknowledged. She *hadn't* joined in with discussions about careers and promotions either. She simply wasn't used to discussing her decisions with others or debating her options. She had grown up dealing with her emotions on her own, or keeping them in check so as not to upset anyone.

Nola was right—all the staff had been excitedly discussing the options and opportunities that the new paediatric wing had created for weeks. And while Pippa had been present during a lot of those chats, she hadn't told anyone about her interest in the PAC Unit.

When Nola returned, Pippa could tell she was still a bit offended, and decided an apology was in order. 'Nola, I'm sorry I didn't say anything earlier.'

'It's fine.'

'No, I should have told you. To be honest, I'm not a hundred percent sure it's the right role for me.'

'Isn't that what colleagues are for, Pippa? And managers?' Nola sounded a bit exasperated. 'We could have spoken about it.'

That was the issue in a nutshell. Pippa wasn't sure she could explain her reasons for wanting to work with chronically ill children without getting upset and teary.

She hadn't told her colleagues about Julia.

By the time she'd finished her training, attached to another hospital, Pippa had worked out that she couldn't speak about Julia without tears coming into her eyes. Her emotions when it came to her sister had been silently forbidden as a child and as a teenager. Now, as an adult, breaking down was the one thing Pippa dreaded the most, so she avoided the topic entirely.

It was one of the reasons she was nervous at the prospect of an interview.

'You're really good with the chronic patients, Pippa. I don't doubt you'd be brilliant.' Nola gave a tight smile. 'And, had you asked, I'd have told you that.'

'Thank you.'

'Do you want to run through some interview questions with me? We can do a mock-up, if you'd like.'

'I think I'm as prepared as I'm going to be,' Pippa said. 'But thanks.'

'Well, if you change your mind…' Nola offered. 'Anyway, your lac liver is going for an ultrasound sometime today.'

'I'll put it on the board,' Pippa said, and also made a mental note.

'You can tell he came from St Bede's,' Nola added. 'He's so arrogant!'

'Who?' Pippa asked.

'The locum consultant. All I did was try to reassure a patient and he snapped at me!'

'Snapped?' Pippa checked, tapping out the bubbles from a syringe.

'Oh, yes,' Nola said, and put on a haughty tone. '"*I don't appreciate you speaking for me.*" I was just trying to tell Mrs James that he wasn't some guy we'd dragged off the street taking care of her daughter and that he'd once been a consultant at St Bede's.'

There wasn't any rivalry, but St Benedict's—or St Bede's

as it was affectionally known— was a renowned and highly esteemed teaching hospital.

'Can you update the board when you get a minute?'

'Sure.'

'Mr Harris,' Nola told her, clarifying the new locum's name. 'Luke Harris. We've got him for a month.'

Very deliberately, Pippa didn't react. With the drugs checked, Nola signed her name and then left Pippa, and she stood alone for a moment in the small annexe.

It couldn't be the same Luke Harris, surely?

Well, of course it very well could be.

She'd known that Luke hoped to be a surgeon, and had long ago gleaned that his father was a professor of surgery at St Bede's.

But if it had been Luke on the ward then she'd have recognised him, wouldn't she? After all, there was still a picture of him on her parents' mantelpiece, standing beside Julia on the night of the school dance.

Pippa cast her mind back twenty minutes or so. She'd recognised Fiona—she'd been here for a couple of months—and David, of course, but as for the dark-haired doctor in scrubs, all she'd seen was his tall and rather broad back.

Luke Harris had been her first crush—she cast her mind back—wow, almost fourteen years ago now.

Her very guilty first crush.

Her memory didn't just take her back to the warm glow of the library…instead it shot her straight back to the pain of the past.

To a time when she'd had a sister.

And then to a time when she no longer did.

Pippa closed her eyes for a moment.

Instead of being curious, or even excited at the prosect of seeing Luke again, she felt a surge of annoyance at this intrusion in her life. The jumble of emotions from the that time had long ago been sorted and put away.

Well, not exactly *sorted*.

Luke still occasionally flitted into her mind, and she blushed at the thought…

Not that anyone needed to know that!

As far back as she could remember, Pippa had learnt to keep her feelings in check for fear of further upsetting her parents—particularly her mother. And when Julia had died, Pippa had felt as if there was no one she could share her feelings with.

She'd been to see the school counsellor but, too used to holding things inside, had been unable to open up to a stranger. Julia had been the sole person she'd been able to talk to, the one person who had understood her. And, ironically, she was the only one who would have been able to comfort her in her grief.

The very person she'd needed the most had no longer been there.

At first Pippa had buried herself in art. Later, through university and beyond, instead of working through her confusing emotions she had bundled them up and shoved them into a box labelled *Too Hard to Deal With*, and Pippa did *not* want them brought back out.

And she did not want Luke Harris here, churning up and muddying waters that had taken years to settle.

Heading to Chloe's room, Pippa couldn't help but smile when she saw the little girl, purple ear muffs on and fine blonde hair sticking up, her face pouty as she lay on the bed, looking completely fed-up.

'Hey,' Pippa said, and gestured for her to take off the ear muffs—which, with a dramatic sigh, Chloe did.

'Those babies are so noisy!' she moaned, though Pippa rather thought it might be more to do with the breakfasts being given out. 'Why can't I eat?'

'Because we don't want to do anything that might upset your tummy.'

'It's upset now because it's hungry!'

'I can hear that it is.' Pippa smiled, because it was gurgling loudly as she sat down by the little girl's bed. 'It sounds very cross.'

'Have you had breakfast?' Chloe asked, and Pippa gave a less than honest shake of her head.

'No.' Pippa chose to fib, deciding her almond croissant on the way to work was something Chloe didn't need to know about! 'I was in a rush.'

'That doctor hasn't had breakfast either. He said I might be able to sit out of bed later, but I just want something to eat...'

She started to cry, and Pippa comforted her. Really, apart from letting her organs rest and recover, one of the reasons that Chloe was being kept on clear fluids only was in case she suddenly started bleeding and had to be rushed to Theatre. There was no need to scare the little girl with too much information but, almond croissants aside, Pippa had learnt early on in life from her sister, and then later at work, to be as honest with children as she could be.

'Do you remember on Friday how they thought you might have to have an operation?' Pippa checked, and Chloe nodded. 'Do you remember being asked when you'd last eaten?'

'No,' Chloe said, but then, as Pippa gave her some tissues, she gave a little nod and wiped her tears. 'I think so.'

'The reason they asked was because if you have to have an operation then it's better if you haven't eaten. You wouldn't want to be sick while you're asleep, would you?'

'No—but I'm getting better.'

'You are.'

'I don't need an operation now.'

'It doesn't seem so. You've been resting so well, and the drip is allowing your tummy to rest too. We're going to get some more pictures of it today, and if you keep improving it won't be long until you're able to eat.'

Mrs James came in then, and gave Pippa a tentative smile. 'Is she still asking for food?'

'I think she understands why we can't let her eat just yet.'

'In case I'm sick,' Chloe said, a touch happier now things had been explained, and willing to negotiate with her mother. 'Can I play on your phone?'

'I've got a game you can play,' Pippa said, when she saw

Mrs James' tense expression. 'Mummy needs to go home for a little while.'

'No!'

'Yes,' Pippa said in a very calm voice. 'And Mummy needs to have her phone with her so I can call her if necessary.'

'You mean, call her about me?'

'About you,' Pippa agreed.

'I don't want to be here on my own.'

'Chloe,' Mrs James said, 'George has hardly seen me since Friday.'

'He's just a baby,' Chloe dismissed. 'He doesn't know.'

'He does know,' Pippa said. 'And as well as that, Mummy needs to feed him. If she has a nice quiet morning then she can make extra milk.'

'And then come back?'

'Of course I'm coming back,' Mrs James said.

'But what if I have to get my X-rays while you're not here?'

'Then I'll come with you,' Pippa said, and looked at Mrs James' torn expression. 'Chloe, nobody's going to forget you.'

Chloe looked anxiously over to her mum. 'Promise?'

'Of course I'm not going to forget you, silly,' Mrs James said as she kissed and hugged her daughter.

There was plenty to do before Pippa got around to updating the board—erasing *Locum* and writing *Mr Harris*, while explaining to her nursing student that doctors who had completed their fellowship for the Royal College of Surgeons were to be called Mr.

'What if they're a woman?'

'Still Mr,' Pippa said, and then, seeing the student frown, she smiled. 'I was joking—they're called Miss.'

'What if they're married?' the student asked.

'Still Miss,' Pippa said, answering the questions easily and not letting anyone glimpse how unsettled she felt—a skill she had honed to perfection.

Luke Harris had been the beat of her heart for months.

No, make that years!

Even before that conversation in the library she'd had a crush on him, just as most of her friends had, but after the day in the library…after he'd arrived to take Julia to the dance… When things had got hard at home, she'd used to picture herself in a silver dress, being led to a waiting car.

She could still, with absolute clarity, remember the thrill of him speaking to her that long-ago lunchtime. Taking the time to really listen to her.

She recalled it now.

Not so much the conversation they'd shared, but how she'd felt listened to—how it had felt to be in the spotlight of another's attention, rather than constantly on the periphery…

Luke Harris had made her feel as if her thoughts, her opinions, really mattered. And even if she hadn't told him she was Julia's sister, he'd made her brave enough to share other little parts of herself.

The memory of the library made her want to cry, for some reason, and crying was something Pippa simply did not do.

Certainly not at work.

Nor with family—heaven forbid!

Not with anyone.

Not even herself.

Her last relationship had ended with a dash of bitterness.

'The thing is, Pippa, I don't know you any better than I did the first night we met.'

Another relationship fail.

Another round of being told that, despite her friendly demeanour, there was nothing behind that wall.

Because she never let anyone in.

Oh, sex was okay—ish. Though she took for ever to be seduced into bed, and then very quickly decided she ought to go home, or wished that he would…

No pillow-talk for her!

She wasn't a superficial person—in fact, her emotions ran deeper than most people's. Pippa just preferred her relationships to be that way: on the surface. She didn't know how to share her feelings, let alone her private thoughts. Just as she didn't know how to drop Julia into the conversation, and neither did she know how to tell someone she was dating that she was a carrier for CF.

At the age of twenty she'd made the decision to get tested, to find out if she was a carrier, and the counsellor at the clinic had asked if she had support…

'*I do,*' Pippa had replied. '*I just want to know.*'

She had the same support she'd relied on since she was a little girl: herself.

'And you understand that even if you are a carrier, it doesn't mean your child will have CF. The father would have to be a carrier too, and even then…'

She hadn't told her parents the result.

They'd never asked, but then they so rarely asked anything when it came to her.

Instead, even though she hadn't been dating anyone at the time, Pippa had gone on the Pill, and was always careful to make sure her lovers used condoms.

There had never been an accident.

Sex had never been exciting enough for breakages!

CHAPTER TWO

IT WAS A typical busy day on the paediatric ward, yet an extremely untypical one for Pippa.

She felt as if she was on heightened alert and kept glancing at the corridor, or towards the nurses' station, where doctors often gathered. It was a relief when the day neared its end—especially when Mrs James called to say she was half an hour away.

'I'm just about to take Chloe down to Imaging,' Pippa informed her. 'I'll let her know that you'll be waiting for her when she gets back to the ward.'

'The porter's here,' called Kim, the sister on late duty. 'If Mrs James isn't back in time then I'll send someone down to relieve you,' she assured her.

Escorting Chloe, Pippa was simply pleased to have made it through the day without seeing Luke. She wanted to get her head together before facing him.

Still, even if she was aching to get home and somehow process the fact that Luke was actually working here at The Primary, she kept her smile on for her patient.

'Do you remember being in here on Friday?' Pippa asked Chloe as she and the porter wheeled her to Imaging.

'Not very much,' Chloe said. 'They gave me an injection. It made me sleepy.'

Chloe had had a CT on Friday, with contrast, but today it was an ultrasound.

Just as the procedure was about to get underway, the radiologist looked up and smiled. 'Hey, Luke.'

'Mike! I didn't know you worked here.'

Pippa felt her throat go tight. Even before she glanced up, just hearing his voice confirmed her worst… Was it fears? Her worst fears? Or actually her deepest wish?

She wasn't sure. All she was sure of was that it was most definitely him.

Luke.

She glanced over and found she couldn't tear her eyes away. Age had *not* wearied him.

Gosh, he'd been a stunning teenager, but as a thirty-something man he was far beyond stunning. That straight hair was superbly cut now, and he looked incredible in his dark navy scrubs, but she couldn't comment on his dark brown eyes because Pippa found that she dared not meet them.

He was big—or rather tall—his shoulders were broad, as if all those years of swimming had paid off, and the slender youth was now a very solid man.

'Hey.' He gave her a brief smile. 'You're from the ward?'

'Yes.' She nodded, but then abruptly looked away, as if it were her heart on the monitor, about to be examined and exposed. 'Chloe was a bit upset about coming down to Imaging without her mum.'

'You'll be fine,' Luke said to the little girl. 'It's not going to hurt at all. It may be a little bit uncomfortable, but we just want to take a good look.'

'How was America?' Mike asked as he washed his hands.

'Incredible,' Luke said.

'You've been to America?' Chloe asked, and Pippa was very grateful for a nosy seven-year-old who could ask any question she chose to when her little tummy was about to be examined. 'Did you go to Disneyland?'

'I didn't,' Luke replied.

'Why not?' she asked, clearly appalled that he'd go all that way and not go to Disneyland.

'I was in Philadelphia. That's a long way from the theme parks.'

'But you could have gone on the way,' Chloe insisted. 'My

friend Sophie went to New York, but they stopped at Los Angeles on the way.'

'Why didn't anyone tell me I could do that?' Luke said, smiling at her idea of geography.

'We're going to Disneyland Paris. Mum promised me on Friday.'

'Oh, I'll bet she did,' Luke said with a grin. 'What else did you wangle?'

Pippa found that she was smiling too, because he'd clearly worked with children before and knew their ways.

'I'm getting a new lampshade for my bedroom, and Daddy bought me these earmuffs—' she held up her bright purple fluffy present '—so I don't hear George crying all the time when I'm at home.'

'Sounds like you're being very spoilt,' Luke said, distracting Chloe as the radiologist probed her abdomen. Yet while he chatted easily his eyes were hawkish as he stared at the screen and Chloe's liver was examined, the laceration measured, and her abdomen was checked for any free fluid. He seemed pleased with the findings, and soon the sheet was back over Chloe's stomach.

'Thanks, Mike.'

He glanced over to Pippa and gave her a very brief smile—the same bland smile he had given to the radiologist—and it was clear to Pippa that he didn't remember her at all.

She had to wait thirty minutes for porter to arrive and take Chloe back up to the ward.

'Oh, sorry.' Kim glanced up when Pippa returned to the ward. 'I forgot about you. Mrs James is here.'

'It's fine,' Pippa said.

'Can you settle Chloe back into bed?' Kim asked. 'Laura's taking care of her tonight, but she's in with Cot Two. His drain is blocked again.'

'Sure.'

It was actually Mrs James who needed settling. 'Surely someone can tell me how the ultrasound went?' she said.

'The staff are a little tied up, but I'll remind them to come and talk to you.'

Pippa knew that the evening meals would soon start to be given out, and mealtimes were particularly difficult for her patient right now. She could see the very active little girl was starting to feel better and her mother was going to have her work cut out to keep her quiet and resting. 'Chloe… Do you like jigsaws?'

'No.'

'We've got some Disney ones.'

Her face lit up, and by the time Pippa had found a couple of jigsaws to keep the little girl amused she was almost an hour past the end of her shift.

Not that she minded, because when her phone buzzed, and she saw that it was her mother, she actually breathed out a sigh of relief that she was still at work.

She often dropped in on a Monday, if her shifts allowed, but today Pippa really wanted a night to herself.

'I'll come over at the weekend,' Pippa told her. 'Well, I'll try.'

'You haven't been to the cemetery for a while.'

Pippa could hear the slight accusatory tone of her mother's voice and ducked into a treatment room to continue the call.

'No,' she said. 'Work's been busy.'

She could hear her own excuses, her own lies. Her mother went to visit Julia's grave most days, but the truth was that Pippa drew no comfort from going.

'We're flat out…' she started to say, but then paused as the overhead chimes went off. They weren't for Pippa's ward, but she was thankful for them all the same.

Once she'd called her mother from home, pretending to be at work. A neighbour had knocked at the door and Pippa had felt caught in the lie. Another time, she'd been in the Tube station on her way home and an announcement had given her away. She felt guilty for not going to see her parents, but relieved at the same time—and wishing it didn't have to be this way.

This evening Pippa knew she couldn't face them. She really just needed to be on her own.

She glanced up and felt a blush spread across her cheeks as Luke came into the treatment room and started going through the drawers.

'We're really short-staffed,' Pippa said to her mother once the emergency chimes had gone quiet. 'So I'm staying back. I really do have to go. Love you…'

She let out a tense breath and then pocketed her phone, relieved that was over—at least for now. But then she looked up and saw Luke turning on the light over the treatment bed. Her sharp intake of breath was just as tight when he spoke.

'Would you be able to give me a hand?' he asked. 'I need to reposition a drain and I'm going to bring him in here.'

'Cot Two?' Pippa checked. 'I think Laura's taking care of him. I'm actually finished for the day.'

'Oh! I thought I just heard you say you were staying back…'

She gave a small laugh, albeit through gritted teeth. Weren't private conversations that you were forced to have in a place where you could be overheard supposed to be politely ignored?

Not only that, but Luke persisted. 'Tut-tut,' he said as he located the alcohol swabs and tape.

'Sorry?' Pippa did a double-take, a little unsure as to what he was referring to.

'Pretending to be stuck at work… I find honesty a much better policy.'

'Not when it comes to my parents.'

'Oh!' He smiled. 'My mistake.' He took a handful of saline flushes and added them to the dish he was filling and then looked right at her. 'In that case, I totally get it.'

It was an odd conversation, being pulled up for a white lie and at the same time meeting his eyes properly.

They were still the same beautiful kaleidoscope of shades of brown. He still had the same thick, dark lashes that barely blinked as he held her gaze. She stood in silence, trying to decipher if the flare of interest that had ignited between them was recognition or attraction.

Pippa knew that in her case it was both.

As for Luke, she wasn't sure.

'I'll let Laura know you need a hand.'

'No need.' He gave her a small smile that perhaps meant he wasn't really in need of a hand after all.

He stared right at her and Pippa felt flustered. For once, she was worried that she might actually be showing it, because she could feel heat spreading up her face.

'I'd better go,' Pippa said, although her feet refused to obey and she stood there, still facing him, trying to think of something to say. 'Oh, and Mrs James wants to know what's happening after the ultrasound.'

'Yes,' he said, his eyes never leaving her face.

It would seem that Luke Harris was either trying to place where he knew her from or blatantly flirting.

Or both!

'Do I know you?'

Pippa didn't answer. She didn't want to be evasive, but his words hurt—like a boot stomping in those muddied waters she'd fought all her life to clear, and she wasn't quite sure of the strength of her voice even if she were able to find the right words.

His eyes narrowed a little, as he obviously kept trying to place her, yet Pippa found she was looking at the dark shadow of his jaw, and the loosened tie around his neck. His jacket was off, sleeves rolled up, and his citrussy scent was somehow morning-fresh, because it cut through the antiseptic smell of the treatment room.

It was hell to know she was attracted to him all over again.

He seemed to take her silence as a game. 'I'll work it out,' he said, and then turned away and carried his tray of items over to the treatment bed, to prepare for his patient's arrival.

She felt as rattled and jolted as the Tube that took her the couple of stops to her home, and the feeling refused to leave her as she went up the stairs to her tiny and very cold flat.

Pippa turned on the electric throw, which she carried with her between the living room and bedroom, before stripping off.

It was so nice to have a shower and pull on her dressing

gown, and then, for the first time in…well, in a long time, she went to take a certain photo album from the shelf.

Pippa's mother had had every single photo of Julia printed for her, as well as other family shots and ones that the school had given them.

Her parents had an almost identical album, but unlike Pippa they went through it most days—at least most of the days that Pippa was there. It sat on the coffee table, or in the kitchen.

Pippa's album was tucked away on a low shelf, not at eye-level. Present, but not immediately visible. And even though her hand went to it straight away, as she took it from the shelf she paused, and her fingers closed over the little ceramic heart she'd made in art that long ago day.

Gosh, she'd been crazy about Luke Harris then.

Now, sitting on the sofa, with her warm blanket wrapped around her, Pippa went slowly through the album.

Julia's first, second and third birthdays. She'd looked so chunky and healthy then, but already she'd been sick.

Pippa knew that Julia had been in hospital even on the day Pippa was born.

Her mother had once proudly stated how that night she'd been wheeled from Maternity down to the children's ward, to stay with her fretful toddler. Newborn Pippa had been left alone with the other babies on the ward.

She turned the page and there was a photo of the two of them on a beach. Julia, ever the big sister, was holding Pippa's hand. Then there was the first day at infants school, junior school, new houses, another new school…

God, she missed Julia so much.

She felt so very cheated on her behalf for the life her sister had never got to live.

More than a few times her mother had shamed Pippa by accusing her of being jealous of the attention given to Julia.

Had she been?

Pippa sat quietly, finally asking herself a question she'd buried deep down inside her.

Maybe? she ventured. *Sometimes*, she admitted. Especially when she'd been a little girl.

Yet for the most part, especially as Julia's condition had deteriorated, *jealous* wasn't quite the right term to use.

Their parents had done all they could to cram so much into Julia's too-short life—trips to theme parks, swimming with dolphins and grand days out—almost willing her to live on for a few more months. And for eighteen years Julia had obliged.

Living, but slowly growing almost translucent.

After the dance, Luke had faded away too. Pippa's mum had said that Julia didn't want him to see her so weak.

So weak…but in other ways so incredibly determined and strong.

One night Pippa had padded out of bed and climbed into Julia's…

'Clever you!' Pippa had said, because Julia had found out that day that she had been accepted into the University of St Andrew in Scotland.

The prestigious university had been Julia's first choice, and despite a failing heart and lung transplant, and endless stays in hospital, as well as multiple procedures and appointments, Julia had made schoolwork her priority.

Pippa had always been in awe of her sister, and never more so than that day.

Julia must have known for some time that she hadn't a hope of going to Scotland and St Andrew's, yet she'd studied incredibly hard and had got the most amazing grades.

Pippa had known that if it had been her she'd have given up long ago, or decided there was no point, yet Julia had pushed herself, living as if she wasn't dying, grabbing on to life and making the most of every precious moment, even if it led nowhere.

'How does it feel to get in?' she'd asked her.

'I made it…' Julia had breathed.

'You did.'

'Go and see it for me.'

'You'll go yourself.'

'*Stop,*' Julia had said huskily. '*I do the happy-clappy routine for Mum and Dad, but I don't want to put on an act with you.*'

'*You don't have to.*'

It was true. Though their mother had done her level best to police their conversations, they'd always found time to talk—really talk—as only siblings could.

'*Will you go and see it for me?*' Julia had asked.

'*I don't know...*'

She'd lain beside her sister, and Julia had stroked her hair. Her wonderful sister had comforted her as Pippa had let a sliver of her fears out.

'*I think it would be too much. I mean, I can't imagine going anywhere without you.*'

'*I'm so tired, Pip.*' Julia was the only one who had called her that.

'*I know.*'

'*Tired of fighting...just to breathe. I'm ready.*'

'*I don't want to let you go,*' Pippa had whispered.

She'd paused and taken a deep breath, because she'd known her mother would forbid this conversation if she knew.

'*Are you scared?*'

'*No,*' Julia had said, but then she'd hesitated. '*Pip, everybody gets scared at times. I just tell myself I'll let myself be scared tomorrow.*'

Pippa hadn't known what she meant, but then Julia had asked, '*Are* you *scared?*'

Pippa hadn't wanted to upset her sister, but her answer had been honest. Almost. '*Sometimes.*' The truth was that she'd been petrified. '*I don't want to be on my own.*'

'*You've had a lot of time on your own,*' Julia had said, wise beyond her years. '*Really, you've always been on your own.*'

'*I've had you,*' Pippa had stated, though she'd known Julia was referring to the disparity in the way their parents treated them. It was the first time it had properly and openly been acknowledged between the girls.

That truth had opened the door for Julia to reveal her real fear. '*I'm worried about them. How they'll be when I'm gone...*'

Pippa had wanted to reassure her sister, to tell her that things would be okay, to say she'd be there for their parents, but Pippa had been worried about that too, and had known in her heart that she wouldn't be enough to fill the gap.

She could never come close.

'They'll keep on loving you, the way they always have,' Pippa had said.

And absolutely her parents had.

At home, even now, it was almost as if Julia had never left. Her bedroom lay untouched; her clothes still hung in the wardrobe. Pippa's old bedroom, on the other hand, was now her mother's sewing room.

Fourteen years on, Pippa looked at the picture of her sister in her silver dress and ran a finger over her pretty face.

Translucent. That really was the word for Julia, because even in the photo it looked as if she was fading.

But not Luke. He stood bold and confident, wearing a suit as if he'd been doing so for a lifetime.

Even if he didn't know it, Luke had helped Pippa a lot, emboldening her to make choices she might not have otherwise. She would never regret taking art.

Returning to school after Julia had died had felt so odd. People had avoided asking her about Julia, or simply avoided her altogether. And there had been no Luke Harris to daydream about bumping into. He'd been off on his gap year. Her one solace had been the chalky, papery smell of the art room. It had become a haven from the despair of life at home.

Back then Luke Harris had still popped into her thoughts, into her daydreams and dreams. But now Luke was back in real life.

In real time.

Grown-up time.

He'd asked where he knew her from and she'd hesitated to answer. He'd taken it as a tease, but she'd actually been completely tongue-tied.

Was it ridiculous to be hurt that he couldn't place her or recall the precious hour they'd shared?

He'd forgotten.

And forgotten was how Pippa had felt all her life.

His question '*Do I know you*?' had catapulted her straight back to the agonising times of her youth.

I loved you! she'd wanted to shout.

Yet that would have been her teenage self responding to him.

Teenagers knew nothing about love.

Now she turned over the little heart she had painted that day in art class. Kobicha-brown, copper and russet—all the shades of his eyes as she'd gleaned in that precious hour alone with him.

Pippa managed a little laugh at the intensity of her own teenage emotions, then tried to rationalise their long-ago conversation.

He'd simply been being nice. Doing his polite Head Boy duty and helping a younger student.

Apart from attending the same school and having one conversation in the library, they didn't share a past.

Julia was really their only connection.

That was all.

CHAPTER THREE

PIPPA WASN'T THE only one to notice Luke.

It wasn't just his effortless charisma and dark good looks that had people talking, nor his clear skill as a surgeon. It wasn't even the slightly detached arrogance that ruffled some of the staff.

Luke Harris had come to The Primary with scandal attached!

Louise on Maternity had once briefly dated him—or so one of the midwives had told Laura when she'd gone to borrow a breast pump. And on her return had gleefully spread the word.

Oh, and one of the domestics had worked in the residences at St Bede's when Luke had been a medical student there.

As for Jimmy, the theatre tech, he seemed delighted to tell tales of a decadent past.

Rumours swirled in abundance.

Now, on the eve of Pippa's interview, as she sat at the nurses' station in a brief lull as they waited for the late staff to arrive, Luke was the topic of conversation. Pippa was trying not to listen, and to focus instead on that morning's patient discharge papers. She was tempted to ask Chloe if she could borrow her earmuffs as the conversation again turned to Luke.

Jenny was feeding little Toby his bottle at the nurses' station, as his parents hadn't come in yet, as well as providing updates on the sexy new consultant. 'He was just made consultant and then suddenly he threw it all in.'

'I'd hardly call studying trauma in Philadelphia throwing

things in,' Nola responded. 'With all that experience he'll be scorching hot and snapped up wherever he goes.'

'Yes, but that wasn't why he left. He was sleeping with one of the senior theatre nurses and it all blew up.'

'Who *hasn't* he slept with?' Nola sighed, and then let out a soft laugh. 'Aside from us!'

But that wasn't all the gossip Jenny had. 'She was married; her husband worked on the ortho—'

Jenny halted abruptly and, glancing up, Pippa knew why the conversation had been so rapidly terminated. The man being discussed was making his way down the corridor towards the unit.

'Sorry to interrupt,' Luke said drily, as if he knew he'd been the subject of the conversation. 'Martha wants to discuss a patient with me.'

Martha was the paediatrician.

'She's in the ED,' Nola said.

'Is Fiona here?'

'No,' Jenny said, shaking her head. 'She was a short while ago, but she got paged to go to Surg One. They sound busy.'

'Then I'm hiding here,' Luke said, and took out a wrapped canteen sandwich from his pocket.

'Why aren't you eating in the consultants' lounge?' Nola asked.

'That's a very good question,' he replied, nodding, though Pippa noticed he didn't answer it. He looked at baby Toby and said, 'Somebody's hungry.'

'You are, aren't you?' Jenny cooed to the baby.

Pippa glanced over and couldn't help but smile. Jenny might be a dreadful gossip, and to Pippa's mind somewhat abrupt with the parents, yet the babies and children adored her.

Even Toby, a little 'Failure to Thrive' and known to be a fussy feeder, was taking his bottle and gazing up at Jenny in adoration.

'Toby knows better than to not drink his bottle,' Pippa teased. 'He must know you like your charts to be neatly filled in.'

'Absolutely, I do,' Jenny agreed.

When Nola took herself off to the office, Jenny looked at Luke.

'I was in the army for ten years,' she told him.

'Paediatrics?'

'Mostly.' She nodded. 'A couple of years on Maternity in Germany.' She sat Toby up to burp him. 'You were at St Bede's, weren't you?'

But Jenny's fishing expedition ended as Toby's father arrived, and her rather brusque tone returned as she addressed him.

'I thought you were going to be here to give him lunch, so that I could observe.'

Pippa glanced up and saw Luke's subtle eyebrow-raise as Jenny headed off with the somewhat sheepish father.

'Is she always so approachable with the parents?' he asked.

Pippa didn't reply to his sarcastic question, just turned back to her work. But she could feel her neck turning pink and knew his attention was on her. In the days since their paths had first crossed she had occasionally felt his eyes on her, just as they were now. She felt his gaze rather than met it, and it was the most deliciously unsettling feeling she'd known—a flutter of nerves dancing through her veins as she quietly thrilled at his long assessment.

'I do know you,' Luke said. 'I just can't work out how.'

'Because I'm so unforgettable?' Pippa teased. Or was she flirting? Or just covering up how much his vague remembrance hurt when *she* could repeat their conversation verbatim?

'Pippa, I'm saying that I know you from somewhere—not that I've slept with you. I'd certainly remember if I had.'

She actually laughed.

'So,' he persisted, 'where *do* I know you from?'

She was about to tell him, but for one teeny second she was back there, in the library, being listened to for what had felt like the first time in her life. Feeling important. Not an important person, just important enough for someone to listen to her...

'That's mean,' he said, taking her silence as refusal. 'Come on, Pip…'

'Pippa!' she warned, just as she did with anyone who called her that, because only Julia had ever called her Pip.

'Then it's lucky for me that I don't have a speech impediment.'

Pippa couldn't help her reluctant smile at his unsuitable joke as she filled in her paperwork. 'If you want to be precise, my name's actually Philippa.'

'Oh, I'd love to be precise.'

His words were delivered in a low voice, for her burning ears only. Burning because a roar of heat had moved from her throat to her scalp. It seemed he was taking their little *Where do I know you from?* game up a notch.

She should possibly warn him that he was wasting his time. Pippa was the last person to get involved with someone at work—especially some visiting locum who came with a side dish of scandal.

But this scandalous visiting locum was Luke Harris.

And for Pippa that changed everything.

Still, she was saved from responding as Jenny and Nola returned.

'Still here?' Jenny asked him in her blunt way.

'Yes,' Luke answered easily. 'I'm trying to work out where I know Pippa from.'

'Do you two know each other!' Jenny gaped.

'I'm sure we do.'

'How?'

Pippa chose to put him out of his misery. 'We went to the same school.'

'Did we?' His eyes widened as he took in the news.

'You two were at school together?' Nola was clearly delighted by this snippet of news.

'Hardly together,' Pippa said. 'He was two years above me.'

Should she remember that? Pippa pondered. If she hadn't been so crazy about him, would she recall that detail? But then she came up with a good excuse as to why she might.

'He was Head Boy in his final year.'

'Did you have a crush on him?' Nola teased, from the safety of being six months pregnant and in a happy marriage. 'I know I would have.'

Pippa casually shrugged. 'Everybody did.'

'Get out!' Luke refuted.

'Come off it,' Pippa said with a smile, stapling the discharge papers and standing up to file them. 'It's true and well you know it.'

'Were you on the swimming team?' he asked, clearly still trying to place her.

'No.' She looked over, and with her eyes willed him to remember their one conversation, that lunchtime in the library, when the world had stopped for a slice of time.

He looked at her lanyard, clearly to read her surname. The recognition obviously startled him and he looked up in shock.

'Westford... So you're Julia's sister?'

Of course that was how he would remember her.

She swallowed down the hurt and nodded.

'You have a sister?' Nola asked with a hint of surprise and also some confusion. 'Julia?'

'I... Yes,' Pippa managed, unsure how to voice the fact that her sister was dead and uncertain how to handle the fact that she had never mentioned her. 'I *had* a sister,' she added, unable to say outright that Julia had died, watching Nola's smile fade as she heard Pippa place her sister in the past.

'Oh, Pippa...' Nola said as she stood. 'I had no idea.'

'It's fine.' Pippa put up her hand to stop Nola from coming over, but Nola just kept on walking towards her.

'I'm so sorry.'

'Thank you,' Pippa said automatically, feeling her nose pinch and terrified of breaking down. She got up from her seat.

Damn you, Luke, Pippa thought. *Damn you for resurrecting these feelings in me.*

She'd hoped to leave all that pain and confusion in the past. But rather than discuss the agony of loss, it felt easier to voice a different hurt, and so, as Pippa walked off, she threw over her shoulder, 'Luke used to go out with her.'

Luke was about to correct Pippa, and say that he had never gone out with her sister, but then he halted himself. Because this certainly wasn't the place. He could see that her face was on fire and knew that she was upset. It was clear her colleagues hadn't known about Julia and that he'd just revealed something she had carefully kept to herself.

Boy, he'd messed that up, Luke thought, seeing Nola and Jenny exchanging quizzical looks and then turning to him.

'Luke?' Jenny said, clearly hoping for more information.

But Luke would not be enlightening the two nurses further, nor offering any explanation. Instead, he followed Pippa down the corridor.

He had been messing about... just making light conversation, Luke told himself. His stride briefly faltered, because *of course* he'd been flirting. He'd been determined to avoid all that during his brief time here. But then attraction had flared from the moment he'd locked eyes with Pippa. Before that, in fact. For awareness had been there from the moment she'd dashed past him that first morning, her scarf trailing behind her and bringing with her the scent of summer. He'd wanted not just to remember her name and where he knew her from, but to get to know her some more.

No, it hadn't been idle conversation—and he was the one who'd brought the private game they'd been playing right up to the nurses' station...

In fact, he'd been pleased to have an excuse to take a quick break on Paeds. He'd tried to tell himself that Pippa wasn't the only reason he'd taken his lunch there. But he knew he'd been hoping to suggest meeting up away from work. And now their discreet little flirtation had got out of hand.

His eyes briefly shuttered in self-recrimination, because he'd clearly not only hurt her, but in bringing up her sister he'd been indiscreet—and that was most unlike him...

He knew from bitter experience the damage careless words

could cause. Loose lips didn't just sink ships—they torpedoed relationships, changed the course of careers, capsized lives…

He thought back to his old hospital, to those last painful weeks at St Bede's and the conversations that had abruptly halted when he'd walked into the break room—people had acted the same way Jenny and Nola would undoubtedly act now, when Pippa returned to the desk…

Only on this occasion it was entirely his fault.

'Pippa,' said Luke, as he caught up with her in the kitchen. 'I'm so sorry about that.'

'About what?' Pippa asked, pouring hot water over a tea-bag for a drink she didn't even want—it had just been an excuse to get away.

'If I spoke out of turn about Julia.'

'You didn't.' Pippa attempted a nonchalant shrug, but her neck and shoulders were so rigid that all she did was slop her tea. 'It's not as if it's a state secret or anything,' she said, mopping up the little spill on the bench, glad to have something to focus on rather than look at him.

'It's clear they didn't know.'

'Only because it's never really come up,' Pippa responded, picking up her mug and intending to walk off. 'Unlike most people here, I don't bring my personal life to work.'

'Whatever the case, I was indiscreet,' Luke said. 'And for that, I apologise.'

His voice was both serious and sincere, so much so that it stilled her, and instead of brushing past him Pippa turned and met his eyes. They were serious and sincere too, and also concerned. She hadn't expected him to follow her, and certainly not to confront things so directly and apologise.

'It's fine,' Pippa said, but she knew there was a raw edge to her voice as she accepted his apology; there was still hurt there. 'Thank you.'

'I knew I remembered you.'

'Well, mystery solved,' she said, forcing a smile as her heart seemed to crumple.

After all, *that* was exactly what hurt, though she didn't want to draw any more attention to it with Luke standing there.

She was back to being Julia's sister all over again.

That conversation in the library—that precious hour which had meant so much to Pippa—had clearly meant nothing to him. He couldn't even recall it.

'I've got to go and do hand-over.'

'Hold on a moment.' He halted her attempt to leave. 'Do you want to catch up?'

'Catch up?'

'I should be finished by six.'

'Are we going to sing the school song?' She attempted a joke, but her voice came out just a little too bitter, and so she checked herself. 'Catch up about what?' she asked, a little bewildered, because his eyes were still on hers, and she had the ridiculous thought that his hand was going to move to her cheek.

The fantasy of him had not just returned, it had been remastered, and it was in full Technicolor now, as she looked into those eyes whose colour she'd once faithfully attempted to capture. Not just Technicolor, though—this fantasy came with the bonus of a citrussy bergamot scent and the bizarre feeling that he was going to take her mug of tea and place it down, so that he might hold her and better apologise with a kiss.

But his next words popped the bubble of hope in which she was floating.

'I don't think work is the place for a private catch-up…'

His voice trailed off and with a sinking feeling Pippa thumped back down to reality. She guessed he wanted to talk about Julia, and her final days.

He hadn't been at the funeral. Her eyes had briefly sought him. In the depths of her grief, she'd wanted just a glimpse of him, to know he was near. Pippa had later heard that he'd gone off on his gap year almost the minute his final exam was over.

His request for more information about Julia now took her right back to the days, weeks and months after her sister had died—to the funeral, to the endless albeit well-meaning conversations in which people had asked after her parents and pressed her for details as they attempted to probe the family's grief.

Pippa had soon had it down pat.

'They're getting there.'

'She died at home, as she wanted.'

'It was very peaceful.'

That was what she'd said, because it had always seemed the right thing to say.

She hadn't added that she *hoped* it was peaceful—her parents hadn't thought to pull her out of school to give her a chance to say goodbye.

Pippa had felt ill that entire day.

She'd even been to the sick bay and had been given two headache tablets, wishing she could be sent home.

The day had gone on for ever, and when she'd finally got home she'd turned the key in the door with familiar dread to find her aunt standing there.

'Pippa...' her aunt had said, and then she'd guided her into the kitchen.

There, her aunt had told her that just after nine that morning Julia had died.

It had made no sense. While she'd been doing biology, eating lunch, sitting in the library, followed by an art lesson, Julia had been dead...

'Where is she?'

Pippa had turned to run up the stairs, but her aunt had told her that as she'd been walking home from school, her headache pounding, for once not daydreaming about Luke Harris, Julia's body had been being taken away by the undertakers.

She'd never shared that part...nor how her parents had sat on the couch, holding each other and sobbing.

'She's gone...' her mother had said, barely looking up. 'Julia's gone.'

They hadn't followed her when Pippa had gone into Julia's room. Hadn't checked on her as she'd lain on Julia's bed...

Damn you, Luke Harris, for coming to work here and making me remember everything I've tried to forget.

She looked up and saw he was awaiting her response, and even though going for a drink to talk about Julia's death was the last thing she wanted, she certainly did not want to discuss it here. So she ignored the effect of his gaze and the close proximity of him in the small staff kitchen and managed a casual, 'Sure.'

'How about The Avery?' Luke said, naming a nice pub with a great menu that was close to The Primary.

'Sure.'

The Avery was also close enough that she could go home and change, rather than meet him in the jeans she'd worn into work.

That wasn't just vanity.

Just that he was in a gorgeous dark suit with the palest blue shirt.

Okay, it *was* vanity that later had Pippa leafing through her rather boring wardrobe and taking out the nice grey wrap dress she was intending to wear tomorrow for her interview. She moved to put it back, but then, given it was just a quick drink and this was the nicest outfit she had, she decided to wear it.

The dress was versatile—it could be either dressed up with heels and make-up, as it would be tomorrow, or made last-minute smart-casual with boots.

For this evening she chose the latter.

She was soon back on the Underground, on her way to meet him.

For a catch-up.

Breathe...

She wasn't a gawky sixteen-year-old now, with her first crush.

Instead, Pippa reminded herself, she was about to turn thirty, and, if anything, was a little averse to relationships. Anyway, this wasn't a date. Luke just wanted to find out what had happened to Julia.

As the Tube rattled her towards her destination there was time for another honest appraisal.

She liked this.

Going out.

Whether on a date, or out with friends, Pippa preferred a nice noisy bar where you couldn't really talk too much. It was deeper conversations she avoided—and not just at work, but in all areas of her life...

Still, even if it was Luke Harris, at least she had the conversation down pat.

Died peacefully...yada-yada...

He stood out.

Even in the crowded bar, Pippa saw him straight away. He really was divine, and it made her confident stride falter. If they'd never met—if she'd had no idea who he was—she'd still have noticed him first.

She pushed out a smile and walked over to where he stood at the bar.

'Just in time,' he said. 'What will you have?'

'A grapefruit juice,' she said, and then added, 'Yes, please,' to the offer of ice.

As their drinks were being poured, she glanced around and saw the pub was pretty full, but that there was a high table free in the middle.

'Shall I go and grab it?' Pippa suggested.

'No need.' He shook his head. 'I've got us a place in the lounge,' he said, gesturing beyond. 'It's quieter.'

Her heart sank.

It was indeed quieter.

There were couches and low polished tables that allowed for more intimate conversation. Thankfully he was making his way to some chairs, and Pippa took off her coat, placing it on a hook before taking a seat beside Luke but far enough away to feel opposite to him.

'So,' Pippa said, attempting the dreaded polite small talk, 'you're here for a month?'

He nodded.

'How are you finding it?'

His response was non-committal. 'I'm really just back in London to tie up loose ends.'

'Loose ends?'

'Yes. I want to sell my flat before I head off.'

'Back to America?'

'I'm not sure,' he admitted. 'I was hoping to have a break and get the flat ready to go on the market while I worked out where to go next, but then this offer of a month's work at The Primary came up. It's a great trauma centre, and I couldn't resist… I've left the flat to the estate agent to pretty up.'

'You mean, remove its soul?'

Luke laughed at her perception. 'You could say that. I now have cushions everywhere, as well as rugs I keep tripping over, and this bottle of wine on the counter with two wine glasses and a corkscrew that I'm not allowed to touch.'

'Did they place a cheeseboard in the kitchen?'

'How did you guess?'

'I love looking at houses for sale,' Pippa told him. 'I had vague ideas of being an interior designer once—' she started to say, but then halted, reminding herself that they were here to talk about her sister.

Might as well get it over and done with.

'You wanted to know about Julia?'

He frowned, and she didn't quite know why.

'It was very peaceful,' Pippa told him, and then she gave a practised, reassuring smile. 'She died at home, as she wanted—'

'Pippa.'

He halted her, perhaps a little too abruptly, and in the silence that followed Luke found he was unusually uncertain as to how to proceed. Julia wasn't the reason he had asked her out tonight, but to tell Pippa he wasn't here for a Julia update might sound cold.

Was it cold?

He didn't really know, but there was something he wanted to make very clear.

'I didn't date your sister.'

Her green eyes almost flashed a warning as they met his. 'Yes, Luke, you did.'

'No,' he said. 'I took her to the school dance. That was all.'

'You came over to the house,' Pippa disputed. 'More than a few times.'

'Because she was too unwell to attend the information nights. But we were never dating. Julia wanted to go to the school dance and I was...'

As Luke's voice trailed off she felt foolish as realisation hit. He'd been Head Boy, after all, and no doubt there had been certain duties that came with the role.

'Were you told to ask Julia?'

'It was my pleasure to escort her.'

For someone so arrogant, Pippa thought, he was supremely polite—and his cautious answers gave little away. Yet Pippa wanted clarity.

'But you *were* asked?' she persisted, and he gave a slight nod.

Pippa felt a sudden giddy rush of relief.

They hadn't dated. Luke had just been doing his duty.

'I thought...' She ran a hand through her thick curls, unsure herself how to proceed, and torn because she was still loyal to her sister, who'd clearly had a crush on him too. 'I just assumed the two of you were dating.'

'Pippa...' he said, leaning forward in his chair. He was so tall that, despite the distance between them, their knees and arms brushed. 'I never saw her after the dance. Or visited her in hospital.'

Pippa could feel that she was blushing as he spoke—not just at her own misconceptions but because the heady whoosh of relief she'd felt at the news wasn't abating. If anything, it was heightening...

'I know my relationships are all short lived,' he went on, 'and that at times I can be a bit ruthless, ending things, but even I wouldn't be bastard enough to break up with someone who was terminally ill.'

Pippa blinked as he spoke out loud the words that had been forbidden in her home.

'Sorry.' Pippa reclaimed her knee and moved slightly away, then took a sip of her drink to cover her confusion. It was hard to look back on that time in light of his revelation with him here. 'I was sixteen,' she said. 'I guess at sixteen you think everyone's getting it on.' She gave a hollow laugh. 'Except you.' It was she who frowned now. 'I mean except *me*.'

'I know what you meant,' he said with a smile. 'God, who'd be sixteen again?'

I would, Pippa thought, but didn't say.

The year she'd turned sixteen had been glorious—at least the start of it.

Julia had received her new heart and lungs, and Pippa's birthday and the Christmas that had followed were the happiest weeks Pippa had known. She and Julia had gone Christmas shopping and out for lunch, and then looked at make-up, painting the backs of their hands with lipstick rainbows. Then they'd gone on to a fashionable jewellery shop, where they'd tried on rings neither had been able to afford.

Or so Pippa had thought.

She twisted the silver ring Julia had bought her, which she still wore on her little finger, recalling the bliss of that Christmas Day, when no one had seen the dark clouds gathering and no one had known that the following year everything would change.

And so she got back to the real reason he'd asked her here.

'She died that September,' Pippa said.

'I'd gone on my gap year,' Luke said, nodding, 'but I do remember hearing that she'd died.'

'She'd just found out that she'd got into the university she desperately wanted—St Andrew's.'

There was that swell in her chest again…that rise, that wave, that feeling…but it had nowhere to go. She recalled her sister receiving the wonderful news, the smile on Julia's face, and the shine of pride in her fading eyes.

'She was so pleased to have been accepted. It was her first choice.'

'Oh, yes,' he said, 'that's *such* an achievement. I got my second choice. I was actually hoping for a reason not to be a student with placements at the same hospital as my father, and being accepted at Cambridge would have been a very polite way to bow out...'

She gave a half-laugh, but then realised he was serious. 'You don't get on?'

'I admire his surgical skills.'

And there it was again, the diplomatic response that gave nothing away. But for Pippa it was what he didn't say that spoke volumes.

'So why—?' Pippa halted.

She was usually the least nosy person. And her personal conversations usually dripped like a leaky tap. With Luke, though, it was as if the pipes were shuddering to life. Drip, drip, and then a sudden burst.

'Why did you select it if the two of you weren't getting on?'

'We were getting on fine when the applications went in.' He drained the last of his drink, but instead of heading to the bar, or summoning the waitress, he said, 'My grandfather was a surgeon there...and my father...'

Now Pippa understood what he'd meant in the library when he'd told her his future had been decided even before he was born. She felt a little as if she had a cheat sheet on him, and had to keep remembering to discard what she already knew.

'Still, I really wanted Cambridge. I missed out by a point.'

'Ouch.'

'I ballsed up in the chemistry exam. I can still see the question.' He grimaced. 'Fragmentation...'

Pippa dragged her mind back to her biology lessons, but unlike the library, which she could recall with detail, biology lessons were in the dim past. 'Parent plant?'

'No, that's biology. In chemistry...'

He attempted to explain, but completely lost Pippa along the way.

'Mass spectrometry. Fragmentation.'

'I don't even know what that means!' She groaned at the memory of her science lessons, and especially the homework. 'Chemistry was a nightmare.'

'I liked it. Don't you remember that old chat-up line?' he asked, and she shook her head. 'Excuse me, have you lost an electron? Because you are positively attractive.'

'That's dreadful!' Pippa started to laugh. 'We definitely moved in different circles. I couldn't get past the periodic table.'

Luke smiled. 'Well, I still dream about that damn exam— sitting there, knowing I should know it...' But then his smile faded. 'My head was all over the place,' he admitted. 'My mother wasn't well at the time.'

She watched the column of his throat as he swallowed, the bob of his Adam's apple, and she thought of his red eyes in the library. But she didn't know how to address that—how to discuss a conversation he couldn't even remember.

So she settled for safe. 'St Bede's is a great hospital, though?'

Luke said nothing to that. He just picked up his glass, but then, seeing it was empty, set it down. Clearly he didn't want to prolong the night.

Instead, he got back to being polite. 'So, how have you been since you lost your sister?'

'It's been fourteen years,' Pippa said, but then realised she didn't really know the answer to that question. 'I've been fine, I guess.'

'How about your parents?'

'They're...' It would take more than the dregs of her grapefruit juice to tell him about that. 'They're well.'

'So why are you avoiding them?' He wagged a finger. 'Don't forget, I heard you on the phone.'

Pippa gave a wry laugh at both the memory and his perception. 'Okay, fine...they're not doing so well. They've never moved on from it and I doubt they ever will.'

'It must be hard...'

'Of course, losing a child—'

'I meant it must be hard on *you*.'

Oh.

Pippa hadn't been expecting that. Seriously had not been expecting that. Because since Julia's death, most people only asked about her parents.

She didn't know how to respond, but her silence didn't stop Luke.

'So how come you haven't told anyone at work about Julia?'

'It's just…never come up.' Pippa shrugged, but she saw the frown that said he didn't believe her.

He wasn't wrong. She was a nurse on a paediatric ward, and her colleagues were friendly.

'I haven't worked there for long.'

'How long?'

'Two years…'

'I rest my case.'

She actually laughed.

'And then I went and put my foot in it.'

'Not really,' Pippa said. 'I guess it came out naturally. I mean…' She took a tense breath. 'I just don't like talking about it.'

There was a stretch of silence, and she let it hang there to see whether he would fill it.

He chose not to. Fair enough.

Their drinks were empty, the subject of Julia had been covered—well, not really—but just when she expected the evening to end, Luke picked up the menus and handed her one.

'I thought we were only having a drink?'

'Just a drink?' He frowned. 'At six in the evening? I don't know about you, but I'm starving. Anyway, like I said, I didn't think work was the right place for a private catch-up.' He gave a wry smile. 'Not that we've ever properly met…'

Pippa took a breath and told herself to simply let it go. She was annoyed with herself that it still hurt this much. That he couldn't remember their short conversation was a ridiculous reason to take offence, and yet she still felt slighted.

'We have met,'

'Oh?' He put his head slightly to the side. 'So you *were* on the swimming team?'

'No.' Pippa shook her head and laughed ruefully. 'You helped me choose my A-level subjects.'

Watching his eyes narrow as he tried to recall something that had meant everything to her—and clearly *only* to her—hurt so much it felt almost like a physical pain.

'We were in the library…?' she persisted.

He shook his head.

'The day you asked—' She corrected herself. 'The day you were asked to take Julia to the dance?'

Luke frowned, and not just because he was trying to place her. There was a flicker of a long-ago memory lying just beyond his reach. He hadn't wanted to take Julia to the dance; he hadn't even wanted to go himself. He'd have rather been studying. But for other reasons entirely the school dance had been the last thing on his mind that day.

He'd found out his father was cheating.

A couple of weeks away from important exams, racing home during a study period to grab his forgotten swimming gear, he'd found out that his father wasn't so perfect after all.

'*Get her out*!' he'd screamed at his father.

After the woman had gone, he'd demanded, '*Who is she?*'

'*It doesn't matter.*'

'*It doesn't* matter?' Luke had roared.

'*I mean it's nothing serious.*'

That had only enraged Luke further, and the argument that had followed had almost turned physical.

'*You've got everything!*' Luke had shouted. '*How the hell could you throw it all away?*'

'*I'm not throwing anything away,*' his father, Matthew, had said placatingly. '*Luke, you have no idea…*'

He changed tack then and followed up with, *'Your mother doesn't need to know.'*

'I am not *keeping this from her. Either you tell her, or I will,'* Luke had warned him.

And, grabbing his sports bag, he'd raced back to school.

His father hadn't told her, of course.

His delightfully dizzy, always vague mother had been all smiles when he'd stepped through the front door after school.

'Darling you're home...' She'd given him a kiss. *'Luke, you simply must call Julia. I know you've got homework, but no more putting it off.'*

And so he'd called Julia and asked her to the dance, but his temper had been bubbling beneath the surface the whole time. Once he'd ended the call, his disgust had returned in full force—not just at the deceit, but at the fact that his father would bring his lover into the family home.

'Don't sulk, Luke,' his mother had scolded him lightly. *'The poor girl needs something to look forward to.'*

'I'm not sulking,' he'd said, and when she'd headed into the lounge, he'd looked at his father. *'I'm going for a walk. If you haven't told her by the time I get back, then I will.'*

He'd had no idea what he'd return to.

Flashing blue lights in the driveway.

His mother being stretchered away.

Luke hadn't been able to understand how willing his mother had been to throw it all away either. He still didn't.

He'd not only sworn off marriage that day, he'd vowed that, apart from at work, he would never let anyone be that reliant on him.

Luke didn't want to return to his memories of that time—and certainly not on a Monday night in The Avery. So he looked at Pippa, who was insistent that they'd spoken in the library.

'I don't remember,' he admitted, and then got back to his charming self. 'Do you want some wine?'

'Sure,' she said quietly.

'Red, white…? Or champagne, given it's a reunion?'

* * *

Pippa was tempted to point out that it wasn't much of a reunion if one person had no memory of meeting the other, but she knew she had to let that go or nurse it in private.

That reminded her... 'I thought you wanted to talk privately...?'

'I do,' Luke agreed. '*You're* the reason I wasn't eating in the consultants' lounge.'

Pippa swallowed and frantically looked at the menu, trying to make sense of his words. Was he saying that he'd come to the ward to see *her*?

'That's why I suggested we come here. I'm sure you'd rather your colleagues don't get wind that there's anything going on between us.'

'There *isn't* anything going on between us,' Pippa said sharply.

Only when she dared to glance up he looked as unconvinced by her statement as she felt.

'Are you sure about that?' Luke checked.

His question was too direct to avoid. 'No...' Pippa admitted.

'Good,' he responded, then gestured to the menu. 'Have you chosen?'

He expected her to choose what to eat after *that*?

'The chicken Provençal.'

He screwed up his gorgeous straight nose. 'I wouldn't have that here.'

'Have you tried it?'

'No,' Luke admitted, 'but if I'm eating French then I want an arrogant French chef preparing it. There's a restaurant near me... You can hear Anton cursing in the background.'

Pippa laughed.

'And the waiters and waitresses all speak only French and pretend not to understand your attempts to communicate. I swear, it's agony...'

'It sounds dreadful.'

'Ah, but so worth it.'

'Well, I'll have the Greek lamb salad, then,' Pippa said, 'and I don't care if it's not authentic.'

Luke had steak with salad, but no chips, and ordered a bottle of red wine, which felt very decadent for a week day.

'Philadelphia was incredible,' he told her as they began to talk about work. 'I think it's the most beautiful city I've ever seen. It has its problems, of course—and that's why I went there, for the experience. I just wasn't expecting to love it so much.'

'I've never been to America,' Pippa said with a sigh. 'It's on my list. I want to go to Colorado.'

'Well, add Philadelphia to that list.'

'So, was it always the plan? To study in the States?'

'Not at all.' He topped up their glasses. 'There's no clear path for a trauma surgeon in the UK.'

'Really?'

'For post-grad qualifications you have to go to the States or South Africa.'

'Why, when there's so much trauma here?'

'Exactly! And when they get around to making a clearly defined role, I'll be ready.'

He shrugged and smiled that slightly arrogant smile that made her knees weak.

'I'm taking a break after The Primary. I'm going to the Outer Hebrides. I want to see a Scottish winter, and certainly no trauma.'

'I wouldn't be so sure. You'll be on air and sea rescue, or something.'

Luke opened his mouth to correct her—to tell Pippa that he wasn't going to Scotland to work. Nor even to avoid the agony of playing Happy Families on Christmas Day with his parents and enduring the endless questions from his mother and sister as to when he'd settle down.

No, he was getting away for a much-needed break.

While he loved his job, Luke was self-aware enough to know that he needed time away. The horror of broken, damaged bodies took its toll—he'd accepted that. But lately the hell of breaking bad news, of watching families fall apart before his eyes, had found him wondering not just about whether his patient would make it, but also, with the uphill battle ahead, would their loved ones survive…?

But he hadn't discussed it with anyone, and he wasn't about to bring the mood down now.

He looked at Pippa's soft dark curls, and though this gentleman generally *did* prefer tall, leggy blondes, he thought Pippa Westford might just be changing his mind. Even when she'd been dressed in unflattering scrubs he'd noticed that she was gorgeous, but he'd underestimated quite how much. Her dress affirmed soft curves, and her pale skin flushed easily and told him more than her guarded green eyes.

She intrigued him. There was an air of independence about her, and when combined with a certain restraint it was a stunning mixture.

Their meals arrived—including chips, instead of the salad Luke had ordered. But he didn't comment, just thanked the waiter.

'Won't you miss London?' asked Pippa.

'No.' He gave a very definite shake of his head. 'That's not to say I'm not enjoying my time here.' He looked right at her then. 'And now.'

He meant them.

This.

Here and now.

She could feel the energy between them.

Now that she knew the truth about him and her sister, she could allow herself to feel it…to look back into his velvety eyes, to enjoy him—enjoy *this*—and to feel those eyes drifting to her lips.

She looked at him. Whatever she felt here and now, he was just passing through—or rather, tying up loose ends so that he could leave.

'Isn't it nice to have a base here, though. Couldn't you rent your apartment out?'

'That's what I've been doing, but it's in a very old building and always needing maintenance. It's too much commitment— and I don't need a base here.'

'But your family—' She halted. 'Sorry, that's none of my business.'

Usually Luke would have taken up her polite offer and shut that line of conversation down. He *never* discussed his family—or at least he kept his responses to questions about them minimal and superficial.

Luke didn't even discuss family with his family...

Not any more.

'How could you, Luke?' his mother had asked two years ago.

As vague and dizzy as she'd appeared at times, she'd known all the theatre staff and all the goings-on at St Bede's, and his sister, Anna, worked there in the ED. When it had all blown up, and Shona's husband had been placed on stress leave, Hannah Harris had looked up at her son, white with fury, but with tears in her eyes.

'I thought you of all people would know better,' she'd sneered. *'Like father, like son.'*

He'd gone to the States, and now he was back, it seemed that all was forgotten. The dust had settled.

Luke still couldn't forgive his father, though.

'It's fine,' Luke said in response to Pippa's apology. 'After all, I just asked about your family. Like you, I'd prefer not to talk about it.'

He gave her a smile that had her stomach feeling as if it were made of jelly, though not in a jiggly, fat way...more as if her insides were wobbling in response to his smile and the darkness of his eyes.

'Have a chip.' He changed the subject and pushed forward his plate. 'You know you want to.'

Pippa smiled—only it wasn't her usual smile. It was a new

smile. And she knew that to be the case because there was
an unfamiliar feeling of her top lip stretching, or pressing, or
pouting... She honestly wasn't sure what it was doing. It was,
she deduced, the smile she wore when she was sitting in The
Avery with Luke and flirting.

She wasn't a flirty person.

Usually.

Yet here she was, pushing her half-empty plate forward
to allow him to stab an olive. Usually Pippa didn't share her
food—didn't share anything, really. Not her deep thoughts,
not her emotions, and certainly not what was on her plate...

Things felt different with him.

They chatted so easily. She even told him about her tiny flat
a couple of stops on the Tube from where they were.

'Is it a flat-share?'

'Gosh, no.' Pippa shook her head. 'I'm way past that.'

'How old are you?'

'Twenty-nine,' Pippa told him. 'But I gave up sharing the
day I finished university. I like my own space too much. What
about yours?' Pippa asked. 'Is it on the market?'

'As of today, it is. I'm hoping it will be snapped up; I really
don't want to be here too long...'

'I thought people ran away *to* London?'

'Who said anything about running away?'

'No one. I...um... I...'

For the first time the conversation faltered, and she stam-
mered over her words, but she was rescued by someone coming to clear their plates.

Luke must have noticed, because as he topped up their wine
he addressed her awkwardness. 'You've heard the gossip?'

'I try not to listen, but...' Pippa flushed. 'God knows I hate
it when they gossip about me.'

'About you?' His eyes widened. 'Do tell!'

'That's just it; there's nothing to tell. But because I don't
drag my personal life into work they assume I'm frigid...or
a lesbian...'

'An interesting combination,' he mused. 'I'd love to debunk both assumptions…'

He gave her such a wicked smile that Pippa couldn't help but laugh.

'So what have you heard about me?' he asked.

'Just the usual. I know I shouldn't listen, but it's hard not to at the moment—you're the talk of The Primary.' She pushed out a smile. 'Breaking hearts wherever you go.'

'Incorrect,' he said, shaking his head. 'I don't get overly involved with anyone and, given I make that crystal-clear from the get-go, nobody gets hurt.'

He must have seen her tiny frown, because he went on.

'That rumour you've heard about a married woman is false. For one thing, I would never get in the middle of someone's relationship.'

'And for another?' Pippa was pushing for more information because she had a burning curiosity to know him more.

'I loathe cheats.'

'Fair enough.' She took a sip of her wine.

'Are *you* seeing anyone, Pippa?'

His enquiry was direct. The preamble that had lulled her seemed to have shifted, and like a skilled interrogator he'd caught her unaware with the simplest of questions.

Pippa held her wine in her mouth, knowing her response mattered.

Yes, she wanted to say, even though it would be a complete and utter lie.

But, given what he'd just told her, it would keep the lion in its cage.

Yes, she was tempted to say, *I am seeing someone.*

Because then they would go their separate ways….

Yes, she decided to say as she swallowed her wine.

It was a single word that failed her.

'No,' Pippa responded, and shook her head. 'I'm not seeing anyone.'

'You're sure about that?' Luke checked.

Given her delay in responding, his question was merited.

'Quite sure,' Pippa said, nodding, and then added, 'I'm not brilliant at long-term relationships.'

Their eyes held and she saw the same flare she had seen there on his first day at The Primary—only she knew now that it was desire. It was at that moment when Pippa realised she might have given a false impression and made it sound as if she preferred short-term flings.

What she'd meant was that even though she wasn't good at long-term, she always went into a relationship with hope. Hope that this time things might be different...hope that she might finally be able to open up and truly be herself with another.

It had never worked out, though. Because she always felt a certain sense of threat as things turned more serious. She was coming to accept that she didn't like people getting too close. She didn't even like getting in touch with her own feelings, let alone allowing someone else in.

Last orders were called, and Pippa blinked when she saw the time—the evening had flown by.

'Excuse me a moment.'

It was a relief to escape to the loo. She stood in front of the mirror and took a breath, trying to digest what he'd said about never dating Julia.

She'd been frozen in her teenage mind where Luke and her sister were concerned, and it felt exhilarating to be freed from the misconception that her parents perpetuated even to this day.

Pippa took a shaky breath, almost feeling the years peeling away. Yes, she liked him still. Of course she did. But in a different way. Fourteen years ago her unblemished, innocent heart had believed in silver dresses and being swept away in his arms... That was all she'd dreamt of really...and perhaps a kiss...

Now, her rather bruised heart knew there was more to it.

Luke Harris was here for a month and no more. He'd made it clear so that she understood this was going nowhere. He was a player, not a partner. Pippa understood his terms.

But the trouble wasn't just keeping the lion caged. Rather, it was the lioness inside her, pawing to get out...

Pippa wanted to know true passion, and she wanted to douse the torch she still carried for Luke Harris.

But wasn't she too serious for a casual fling, though? It simply wasn't her...

And yet that heady gush of relief that he hadn't dated Julia *still* hadn't abated.

Pippa caught sight of herself in the mirror. Her hair was tousled and the grey interview dress somehow looked indecent as it clung to her breasts. Those boring army-green eyes were no more. Now they were black with unfamiliar desire...

She thought of her sister and wished she could call her and ask for advice.

But then she realised she already knew Julia's take on life.

Julia had lived her life as if it wasn't ending.

If her sister could study for straight As, knowing there was little prospect of going to university, let alone making use of the grades, then surely she could live the same way...

Julia had grabbed life and taken every opportunity she was offered—smiling and happy, seemingly carefree—squeezing every last drop out of life all the while knowing it would be over too soon.

Julia had lived her entire life without the promise of a future, she realised. Surely she, Pippa, could manage a month.

If Julia could do it...

'Then so can you,' Pippa told her reflection.

Less than a month, she amended, as she made her way back to the table, given he'd been at The Primary a full week now.

The table had been cleared, the bill paid...

'Ready?' he said, and Pippa nodded and put on her coat.

It had rained while they were in the pub. Now, cars and buses swished past, their headlights casting light tails, the beams from streetlamps highlighting the heavy drops that still fell. They stood under cover and faced each other.

'Thanks for dinner,' Pippa said. 'I had a great night.'

'It hasn't finished yet.'

He took her face in his hands and with his velvet-soft lips he kissed her...incredibly slowly.

It was everything she had ever thought it would be.

Actually, it was better—and not just because it was real.

As his tongue slipped in, she could taste the wine they had shared, only it seemed sharper and more potent, and the soft stroking of his tongue evoked a different, unfamiliar type of hunger...

Luke Harris had been her teenage dream, but now he was here, and he was kissing her, and she did not want to let the dream go.

Not just yet...

She thought of her sister—how she'd lived without fear, following her goals and passions.

And that made her brave.

Their kiss ended, but his hands were still cupping her face. She wanted to run her tongue over her lips, if only to taste him again.

'We could have a very nice month, Pippa...'

A month.

Perhaps she should feel offended that he'd named the end date of their affair as it was only just bursting into life, but instead it sent a shiver of excitement through her.

No promises that could never be kept.

No false hope.

Just a chance to live her dream.

And no recriminations over her refusal to open up her heart. Luke didn't want that part of her.

Wanton and emboldened, she released the lioness.

'So,' Pippa said, 'are you going to show me this flat of yours?'

CHAPTER FOUR

LONDON LOOKED ALL SHINY, as if wiped clean by the rain.

'Right you are,' said the taxi driver, when Luke gave him their destination. 'That was some storm!'

'We didn't see it,' Luke said, and turned to resume their kiss.

But the driver had other ideas. 'All the traffic lights went out and…'

He carried on talking and didn't seem to require a response.

Pippa felt all shiny too, like the city, and she was laughing at the press of Luke's hand, and the nudge of his knee, because they'd somehow landed the chattiest taxi driver in the world.

They passed St Bede's, the gorgeous old hospital with its beautiful arches, and then turned down a very narrow cobbled street. This was old, old London, Pippa thought, as Luke paid the taxi driver. His apartment building was very close to the hospital. He'd really had a whole life here, and it bemused her that he could so readily leave it all behind.

Why?

It wasn't as if he denied his reputation—indeed, he seemed at ease with it. Why would he run from some rumour he'd said was false? It didn't equate to the confident, self-assured man who now moved up the steps with her to the heavy entrance doors of the building. As he opened them up, she glanced at a row of doorbells and saw *LH* near the top.

'It's quite a climb,' Luke warned, as he led them into the foyer.

Pippa looked up at the gorgeous swirl of a circular stone staircase with polished banisters, and as she gazed higher, to the incredible domed skylight, he caught her unawares and lowered his head to kiss her throat. His mouth found hers and he guided her to the wall, never breaking the kiss for a second.

'Sustenance,' he said as his hand slid inside her coat and pulled her hips against his. 'We could have a *very* nice month,' he said again, lifting her hair and kissing the side of her neck.

'It's only three weeks,' Pippa gasped, as he pulled her so close that she could feel how turned on her was.

'Haven't you enjoyed it so far?' Luke asked, kissing her as she had secretly wanted him to.

'Yes…'

'So, a month,' he said.

But then they heard footsteps and politely parted, Luke nodding and smiling to a woman who passed them with the cutest little dachshund puppy.

'Hi, Luke,' she said as she passed.

'Hey,' he said. As she opened the door and took the little dog outside, Luke rolled his eyes at Pippa. 'Can you believe she called him Sausage?'

'It's cute.'

'She hardly put a lot of thought into—'

'I think,' Pippa suggested, 'we should go up before she gets back.'

'Agreed.'

They almost flew up the stairs in their mutual race to get to the top, but they held hands the whole way, unable to drop contact. It was as though they were tied together in some new version of a three-legged race.

Not once had she felt like this—laughing, practically running up flights of stairs just to get behind closed doors. Never had she felt so at ease at the prospect of sleeping with a man for the first time.

He opened a large dark door and as he kissed her and moved them inside he shrugged off his coat, then slowly removed Pippa's.

He showered her with kisses that made her breathless as they attempted to undress each other. The bedroom was apparently too far away and buttons were too complicated.

She felt the roughness of his unshaven chin and the probing of his tongue, and there was the ever-present thrum of demand as his kiss changed tempo and they sank to the hardwood floor.

Pippa kissed him back hard, more passionately than she'd thought herself capable of, lost for a moment in the bliss of him. His hands were parting her dress, pulling at her opaque tights, and she lifted her hips with the same urgency his hands communicated. It was Pippa who was pulling her tights and knickers down as he slipped a condom on. She attempted to pull off her boots, but they were too desperate for intimate contact to negotiate even that.

'Ow!' he said as her closed knees pressed into his stomach, but neither of them cared.

'Yes…' she moaned as he pulled her hips down onto him and ground into her. 'Oh, my…'

She must have the female equivalent of premature ejaculation, she thought, because she was starting to come. Not that it mattered; Luke was more than ready to reciprocate.

Her hands were flat on his chest, and she was enjoying the delicious sight of Luke coming. One breast was exposed, her tights were wound like a lasso around her thighs, and he was still inside her…

She was panting, stunned at her own body's rapid response. His hand was on her red cheek as she now attempted to gulp in air.

'Bed,' Luke said, in a voice that told her they'd only just started.

CHAPTER FIVE

'MORNING,' LUKE SAID lazily as his phone bleeped them awake. At least, it had bleeped him awake. Perhaps used to being summoned immediately, he propelled himself to sit up. 'Do you have to be at work?'

'No…' Pippa, still half dozing, tried to peel her eyes open, then remembered she'd fallen asleep in her contact lenses and promptly closed them. 'I'm not back till tomorrow.'

'So you're off today?' he asked, already up and out of bed.

'Mmm…although I've got—'

She stopped herself from telling him about her interview this morning. Because this interview, even if she was trying to play it down to herself, was the most important of her life.

She wanted this job.

It was everything she wanted in her career.

So it didn't make for good idle conversation with a new lover.

Pippa had thought about telling him about the interview. Simply because he was wise. It was an odd thing, to stare at a self-confessed playboy who was just passing through and think about how wise he was.

But he was the one who had talked about how he didn't like to get involved. Surely that kind of conversation would be the definition of *involved*? Talking about the interview would also mean mentioning Julia, and she couldn't do that without crying.

Which would not be a good look at six a.m. after their first night together.

'Got what?' Luke persisted, with a yawn.

'Places I need to be.'

Her response was evasive—the perfect casual lover reply. She peeled her itchy eyes open and wished for twenty/twenty vision, because the sight of a naked Luke stretching and yawning was one she'd rather not have missed!

'Were you in the army?' she asked.

'No—why?'

'I've never seen anyone get up so fast.'

'If I hit snooze…' He shook his head. 'It's a dangerous path. Especially as I've got seven a.m. ward rounds,' he added 'Coffee?' he offered.

'Please.' Pippa nodded as he wrapped a towel around his waist before striding into the lounge. 'Two sugars!' she called to his departing and very attractive back. 'White.'

Sitting up, she shivered and pulled at the throw blanket placed over the headboard. She wrapped it around her bare shoulders, then blinked as the world according to Luke came into focus.

She looked at the rumpled bed with its navy sheets and pillows that she hadn't really noticed last night. Then she gazed at the polished hardwood floors, whose beauty was hidden beneath too many scattered rugs, then up to the very high ceiling, with its cornices and intricate central ceiling rose spoilt by a surprisingly modern light. Above the very beautiful and rather neglected fireplace was a very large print of two buses in Oxford Street; it seemed a rather odd choice for a bedroom.

'Awful, isn't it?' Luke said as he came back into the bedroom with two mugs. 'The estate agent's handiwork, to cover some bumps in the walls. Did you see the one he put up in the lounge?'

'I wasn't really paying attention,' Pippa said, laughing. 'You could dress up the fireplace instead of covering up the walls,' she added. She looked at the huge windows, and then up again at the ceiling. 'And a chandelier in here would be nice.'

'In a bedroom?'

'A small one.' Pippa nodded her thanks as he handed her a mug.

'Sorry, I don't have any milk.'

'It's fine,' Pippa said. 'Your flat is even colder than mine.'

'I've put the heating on, though it takes for ever. I'm meant to leave it on all day.'

'Why?'

'Potential buyers,' he said, sighing. 'Not my idea…' He looked at her and smiled. 'That blanket you're wearing is for display purposes only.'

'Oh? And there I was thinking how thoughtful you were,' Pippa teased. Taking a sip of her coffee, she screwed up her nose and placed it on the bedside table, deciding to stop at her favourite coffee shop on the way home. 'I'm going to get going,' she said.

'Have a shower?' he offered. 'I'm going to.'

He gave her a smile that invited her to join him, but all her bravado from last night seemed to have left.

'I'll wait till I'm home.'

'Pity,' he said.

Pippa bit her lip. She wanted to ask when they might see each other again, but didn't want to sound needy.

So, instead of making a complete fool of herself by asking, or following him into the shower as she'd *really* like to, Pippa got dressed, and was just putting in some fresh contact lenses, which she always kept in her purse, just in case, when he came out.

'I don't sleep in them usually,' Pippa told him, trying to ignore his big, damp body as he hastily dried it. 'I'd really better get going.'

'Pippa!' He called her back. 'I'm on call for the next few nights, and I don't know how busy I'm going to be. I might not be the best company for a while.'

'It's fine.'

'Come on, Pip, give me your number.'

He'd called her that again, not noticing the press of her lips as he took out his phone.

She couldn't quite believe she'd slept with someone who didn't even know her phone number.

But she knew that was the game she'd signed up for, Pippa

thought as they exchanged contact details, and she shook it off as she closed the door of his flat behind her.

And she knew something else—something she dared not admit...

She'd only ever have dared to play this game with him.

Pippa wished she'd taken Nola up on her offer of a mock interview, because the real one wasn't going very well.

'Philippa?'

She'd been introduced to a panel of three people.

'Pippa Westford,' she had said, shaking hands with the formidable trio.

One, Miss Brett, had been the manager of a hospice Pippa had once worked at, although clearly she didn't recall Pippa, because despite her initial correction she kept calling her Philippa.

Pippa had intended to wear the grey dress, but after last night it needed a trip to the dry cleaner's, so she wore a navy suit and low heels instead. She had straightened her wild hair and put it up and, while she knew she looked smart, she feared she didn't sound it!

The first part had been okay...*ish*. Pippa had been given an imagined scenario: an anorexic thirteen-year-old who had taken an overdose but was too acutely unwell to be admitted to Psych—or rather to the new eating disorder unit that would be opening in the new wing.

It had all gone downhill from there.

She'd been expecting a question about how she dealt with conflict, but instead of asking about conflicts with patients or parents, they'd just asked about conflict between colleagues.

'I generally get on well with my colleagues,' Pippa responded, and then kicked herself, because it was a pretty poor effort. 'I always try to see the other side.'

'But as Unit Manager you won't be able to sit on the fence,' Miss Brett pointed out.

Later, she would blame it on lack of sleep, or the night spent with Luke, but she knew that would just be making excuses.

'What do you think you can bring to the PAC Unit, Philippa?'

'Well, I've worked in a lot of different areas. Not just on general wards—I've worked on Oncology, in a hospice, as well as on a renal unit.'

'Yes…' One of the trust directors looked at her sternly. 'You've moved around quite a bit.'

'I have,' Pippa agreed, hearing the slight barb behind the words.

It was true; she had moved around rather a lot. A year here, eighteen months there, two years now at The Primary…

'I'm very happy at The Primary. I just feel…' Her voice trailed off.

She'd been so logical in making the decision to apply, but logic seemed to have gone out of the window since Luke's return. Old wounds were resurfacing, and an interview wasn't the place to rip off the plaster and express the raw feelings that were churning inside her. 'I think that my experience, though varied, is all appropriate for the PAC Unit.'

'What would you like to achieve?'

This one Pippa *had* prepared for!

'A higher-level management role, eventually, but—'

'I meant for the PAC Unit,' Miss Brett said, and Pippa realised she'd misunderstood the question. 'What goals would you set for the PAC Unit?'

Pippa stumbled through the rest of the interview and knew she'd done dreadfully, though it was all pleasant handshakes and 'Thank you for your time,' when it concluded.

As Pippa made her way down the corridor to head for home, she saw Nola.

'How did it go?'

'Awful.' Pippa rolled her eyes. 'There's a reason I didn't want to tell anyone I was applying. I flunked it.'

'Don't worry,' Nola said kindly. 'I won't breathe a word.'

Pippa didn't believe her for a moment.

The day only went downhill from there.

Luke didn't so much as text.

Rather than waiting for him to call, Pippa kept busy, and

even went over to her parents' house—something she'd been putting off.

'I thought you'd be here earlier,' her mother reprimanded as soon as she came in. 'It's been ages since you've been to the cemetery.'

'I might try and go in the week,' Pippa said as she took off her coat. 'Hi, Dad.' She gave him a kiss. 'Or on my birthday.'

'That's weeks away.'

'It's two weeks away. I'm on an early shift,' she ventured, just in case they were planning anything.

Sure, Pippa thought wryly. *As if they would.*

Birthdays were practically a *verboten* subject, and Christmas remained a teary affair.

And even though Pippa was trying not to think about Luke, even at her parents' there was no chance of escape, because there on the mantelpiece was that photo of Julia and Luke, staring back at her.

'You'll never guess who's working at The Primary,' Pippa began.

'Who?' her mother asked.

Yet even as she opened her mouth to respond, she glanced at the picture and knew it would upset them. 'Miss Brett. I worked with her at the hospice.'

Her mother stared at her blankly.

'Briefly,' Pippa amended. 'She was the manager there. She's one of the big bosses at the hospital now. I had an interview today and she was on the panel.'

'That's nice.'

Conversation with her parents felt like hitting the 'Print' button, knowing full well that the printer was switched off, or out of paper, or not within range.

There was no enquiry as to how her interview had gone, let alone any interest in what it might have been for.

Just the usual, 'That's nice.'

Thank goodness she had the excuse of having to leave to get to her art class. She stopped on the way and brought wine, as well as some crackers and cheese, and she felt the familiar relief as she stepped in to the studio.

The same relief she'd felt in the art room at school.

Tonight it was open studio time, and although Pippa had intended to work on her charcoal sketching she found herself mixing oils instead, with the wine and cheese forgotten. She was soon absorbed.

'What are you working on, Pippa?' asked her teacher, Cassie.

'Light beams.' Pippa looked at her effort, thinking back to last night, and how the car lights had reflected on the wet streets, but also how she'd felt as she stepped into the adventure. 'I can't seem to capture them, though...'

The same way she could never capture Luke.

Pippa knew better than to dream, or even try to hold on to him. It would be easier to hold light in her hand.

She didn't regret their night together, even if she wasn't usually that bold or effervescent.

She was, Pippa knew, too serious by far.

A little dreary, even.

Yet last night she'd felt golden and bright and, yes, for the first time, a little radiant, and she wanted more of the same...

As the teacher guided her to blur the lines, to be bolder with her strokes, Pippa watched her work start to come alive.

'Just have fun with it!' Cassie suggested playfully, and moved on to the next student.

Pippa looked at the shimmering lines she'd created, proud of her work, and took a breath, replaying Cassie's words but with Luke in mind...

'Just have fun with it...'

CHAPTER SIX

PIPPA WOKE UP the next morning annoyed that not only was she thinking of Luke, she had even dreamt of him!

And that was *so* not Pippa.

It hadn't been a sexy dream, or anything like that... In truth, as she took the Tube to work, Pippa couldn't really remember what it had been about. She simply wasn't used to having another person so constantly in her thoughts.

And while last night she'd felt emboldened as she'd painted, now she was back to wondering if she had what it took for a casual fling.

It was all very well to 'just have fun with it', but Pippa knew she still needed to guard her heart.

She stopped for her regular coffee and chatted to the barista while it was being made.

'We had a food truck on the river for Diwali last night,' Rohan explained as he made her milky brew. 'You know— the festival of light.'

'One of the mums at work told me about it.' Pippa nodded. 'I should go and have a look.'

'Do,' Rohan agreed, putting the lid on her coffee. 'They're lighting up the London Eye in the colours of the Rangoli tonight.'

'Sounds wonderful. I will go!' Pippa said, collecting her drink and dashing off, because she really didn't want to be late for work.

Very deliberately she didn't pause to look at the brand-new extension. She was still disappointed at how the interview had gone yesterday. Even though her ward would be moving into the new wing, it was the PAC Unit that she wanted, and she was certain she'd blown it.

Oh, why hadn't she asked Nola for help in preparing?

She was mulling over that, rather than Luke, as she walked down the corridor, overheating in her long scarf, when she heard his voice.

'Excuse me, have you lost an electron?'

Pippa laughed. 'That really is the worst line. And I know I'm not positively attractive this morning.'

'Me neither.'

Pippa chose not to debate the point—he was wearing navy scrubs and had a theatre cap tied on, and he was looking incredibly sexy.

'What did you get up to last night?' he asked.

'I had my art class,' Pippa said. 'Well, *class* might be stretching it a bit. Really it's a weekly "Paint and Sip..."' He frowned, but there wasn't time to elaborate, and anyway she wasn't sure how to play this. 'I'm late...'

'Not too late to stop for coffee,' he pointed out.

'They know my usual order,' she said, and couldn't help adding, 'And they always have milk!'

Instead of responding to her little jibe he said, 'Can I steal it?'

'Not a chance.'

'Seriously... I'm dead on my feet. Just a few ward rounds and then I'm crashing—hopefully until tomorrow.'

'Busy night?'

'Yes.' He nodded, but didn't elaborate, because his pager went off then—and not just his pager, but the overhead chimes too, asking for the trauma team to come to ED. 'Damn,' Luke said, looking at his pager. 'Multi-trauma on its way.'

It was a horrible time to be called—just before the pagers had been handed over to the day team—but it happened all too often.

'Here,' she said, handing over her precious brew, then rolled her eyes at herself as he took it and sped off.

Honestly, there wasn't anyone else she'd have done that for.

Not that he could ever know that, Pippa told herself, determined to keep things light between them, to be the woman she'd hoped to be—the one who grabbed life...

She walked on to the children's ward, and had barely taken off her scarf before Jenny chimed up. 'So, you've applied for the Unit Manager position on the PAC?'

So much for Nola's discretion. Pippa just rolled her eyes again and headed to the kitchen to make a horrible cup of the hospital's instant coffee, still surprised she'd given her own away—even to Luke.

Thank God Pippa had given him her coffee.

It was warm, sickly sweet, and nothing like the strong black he preferred, but it was incredibly welcome after a long night that wasn't even about to end soon, judging by the alerts coming in regarding a major RTA—Road Traffic Accident.

Fiona arrived, breathless from her run through the hospital, just as May, the ED Nurse Manager, was giving a briefing, giving the staff the latest update from the scene.

The accident was on the A4, and although there were other hospitals closer, some casualties were being flown in by helicopter or driven with lights and sirens to The Primary, which was a major trauma centre and covered a vast area.

'There are eight casualties in total; we're accepting three.' May held up three fingers to the gathered teams. 'First one's a traumatic chest. Med flight eight minutes. Gino's got him.'

Luke knew there were teams already at the helipad. Gino, one of the senior surgeons from the first on team for the day, would take care of this young man from one of vehicles, though as the patient was wheeled into Resus, Luke could see he didn't look good.

'Go and assist,' Luke told Fiona—and not just because they were short-staffed. Fiona needed the experience, and David, Luke's registrar, had just arrived.

A second patient was rushed past, screaming for her children. She had a displaced hip and, from what Luke could see, a nasty lower leg fracture.

The emergency team took over her care and then May pointed to Luke as he drained the last of Pippa's coffee. 'Four-year-old male, multi-trauma, unconscious. ETA five minutes. I'll go and meet him.'

As she went to meet the patient Luke began checking drugs as the nursing team set up for a paediatric trauma patient. Remi, the anaesthetist, was selecting various-sized endotracheal tubes, preparing for all possibilities.

When he came, it was clear that the patient was small. It was the first thing Luke noticed as the paramedics wheeled the stretcher in—as well as the fact he'd already been intubated at the scene.

'Darcy!' The paramedic said the child's name very specifically, and soon Luke understood why. 'Identical twin...'

The grim features of the paramedics and trauma team told Luke that what they'd seen had been upsetting. He didn't ask about the other twin, deliberately keeping his focus solely on the patient he had.

'He's four?' Luke checked. The information was important for drug doses and such.

'No, turned five last week,' he was told by the paramedic.

A doctor who'd happened to be on the scene described the life-saving procedures that had been performed. 'Hypovolemic shock, became bradycardic...cardiac massage commenced, then intubated.'

His pyjamas had been cut open, revealing a skinny frame and a distended abdomen which Luke palpated and then percussed, tapping it and eliciting dull sounds that indicated fluid. When the anaesthetist confirmed the airway inserted on scene was patent and secured, the boy was carefully rolled and examined. Luke made the decision to get him straight to CT, and if that wasn't clear then up to Theatre.

'Is CT ready for him?' he called out to May, who came in then. 'Or is the other patient still...?'

'It's clear,' she said, and shook her head.

When Fiona appeared, coming to assist him, Luke knew the young man must have died.

'They're ready,' May said. 'I've let them know you're on your way.'

They were indeed waiting, and soon images were coming through that, mercifully, showed no sign of serious head injury. But his torso had taken the blunt force, and he had a ruptured spleen and a lacerated kidney; this little boy needed Theatre now.

'Let's get him straight up,' Luke said, and saw that May had now joined them, carrying paperwork and a phone. 'Was that the mother in the ED?'

'Yes. They've had to sedate her.' May briefed him as they walked at pace through the corridors. 'They're reducing her hip in the ED.'

'What about the father?'

'He's coming from Heathrow. They'd just dropped him off there.' She grimaced.

'Can someone try and get him on the line for me? If I can get verbal consent...?'

'I've got the father on hold now—Mr Williams,' May said, but before she handed him the phone she brought him up to speed, 'Identical twins,' she informed Luke, in case he didn't already know.

'I'm aware.'

'Just check for any identifying features. Best to confirm we've got the right twin. The mother was hysterical on scene. The other little boy's still trapped.' Luke said nothing, just listened as May spoke on. 'The father's first name is Evan; the wife is Amber. Darcy's twin brother is called Hamish.'

Poor man, Luke thought, and took a steadying breath before taking the phone as he walked up to theatre.

'Mr Williams,' he said, introducing himself, but he didn't get any further.

'The police are bringing me there now. We're fifteen minutes away,' the panicked man said. 'Is there any chance I can see Darcy before you operate?'

'I'm sorry, no. I can't wait.' Luke was firm in his decision and he listed the boy's injuries. 'Every moment is vital. Now, Mr Williams, before you give your consent, we need to be as sure as we can that we have the right twin.'

Mr Williams was clearly used to the question, and as Luke put the telephone on speaker he said, 'Darcy has a strawberry birthmark behind his left ear.'

May halted the trolley and did the brief check. 'He does,' Luke said.

But after Mr Williams had given consent he started to break down. Unfortunately there wasn't even time for that.

'The anaesthetist wants to have a brief word.'

He handed the phone to the Remi, whom he'd been working with a lot these past few days. She was an elegant redhead, and she spoke calmly to the man. 'So he has asthma?' she checked and then asked if he'd ever been intubated before.

'I'm going to be with your son,' Remi assured the father. 'I'm not leaving his side.'

She was very, very kind as she told the anguished father she had a daughter the same age.

Then, 'You can tell him that yourself,' Remi said. 'He's intubated, so he can't respond, but I'll put the phone to his ear. Your daddy's on the phone, Darcy...'

Luke was so grateful for Remi. He could not bring any emotion into Theatre, and snapped his focus to the operation ahead. He always felt great responsibility when operating, but especially when it was a child. Knowing the child's father wasn't even here, Luke felt the trust placed in him fall heavy on his shoulders this morning.

Remi feels it too, Luke thought, looking thoughtful as she spoke with the rest of the theatre staff while he raced ahead to scrub in. She remained close to the little boy, stroking his hair and talking to him.

'Where's David?' he asked, when Fiona arrived alone.

'Still in Emergency,' Fiona said, and he could hear the slight trembling in her voice. 'A fourth patient was brought in. They only got notified last-minute.'

'You'll be fine,' Luke said reassuringly.

He was such a small fellow, Luke thought as Darcy was moved over. His ribs were visible. But the thing that twisted Luke was his little knees, one with a bruise and the other covered with a plaster. Though they were quickly covered by green theatre drapes, it was that brief glimpse of a normal little boy who must have recently tripped and fallen that got to Luke. And then there was the thought of a father racing across the city to get to his son…

He couldn't think of that now.

Very deliberately, he hadn't asked for any updates on the other twin. He simply wouldn't allow emotion into the operating room, but he was grateful that his anaesthetist did.

'Daddy's coming,' Remi told the boy, over and over, and, even though he was now under anaesthetic, she was still stroking the little boy's dark hair and reassuring him. 'And Mummy's here at the hospital.'

How he needed his upcoming break, Luke thought. It was getting more difficult with each passing day to push emotion aside and focus on the job.

'Let's start.' He glanced at the scrub nurse. 'Good to see you.'

They'd done a couple of cases together before, and he knew she was excellent, but apart from the brief greeting he said little. Gone were the days when he'd chatted at work, or spoken easily with the other staff.

Well, with one exception… But there was no space in his mind for anyone other than Darcy Williams right now.

'Splenectomy,' he said, as soon as the abdomen was open. What he saw confirmed his decision to remove the spleen, because it looked as if it was beyond saving, and any attempt to do so would take precious time from the other injuries. 'Perforated bowel.'

He surveyed the damage with a practised eye and was so grateful for his time in Philadelphia and the lessons passed on to him there—the main one by Carl, the chief under whom he'd worked: *Do what you have to, then what you can…*

Fiona did an incredible job—the whole team did.

David, his registrar, was already with his patient when Luke got to Recovery—the unexpected fourth arrival.

'Motorcyclist,' David explained. 'Looked like minor injuries at the scene but, given the mechanics of the injury, the paramedics brought him in.'

He went through the motorcyclist's injuries and the surgery that had been performed with Luke, and as David went to speak with the man's family, Luke made his way to a separate waiting room.

It was this part that he was finding increasingly difficult.

He gave it his all in Theatre, but lately, when dealing with a family, he tended to adopt a polite, professional distance, telling himself it was his surgical skills they required, not his personal ones.

Luke knocked on the closed door and went in.

Given that his wife and children had just dropped Mr Williams off at the airport, Luke had expected a businessman around his own age, in a suit, but instead an incredibly young-looking man dressed in a high-vis vest was pacing anxiously.

'Mr Williams?'

'Evan,' the man said. 'Is it bad news?'

'Darcy's in Recovery,' Luke told him straight away. 'Shall we sit?' he suggested as the young man almost dropped in relief. 'Soon we'll be moving him to the ICU.'

'Is he awake?'

'The anaesthetist did rouse him briefly at the end of his surgery, but we're going to be keeping him sedated for the next few days. However, he responded appropriately, fighting the tube and moving all his limbs. That's good news,' he added, and then carefully he went through the boy's injuries, both the good and the bad. 'He doesn't appear to have any serious head injuries,' he finished.

'He was unconscious, though. They said his heart stopped!'

'His heart didn't stop. It slowed to a dangerous level because he'd lost a lot of blood,' Luke explained. 'I had to remove his spleen.' He saw the father wince, then bury his face in his hands as Luke mentioned the bruised kidney. 'In Theatre, we found a small perforation to his bowel. It closed nicely. We've avoided a colostomy.'

Mr Williams swallowed air a few times. 'What about his legs?'

'His legs are fine.'

'Someone said…' He pressed his fingers into his eyes. 'No, I'm getting mixed up.'

'Your wife has leg injuries.'

'I know, but…'

Mr Williams was clearly overloaded with information.

'Darcy has a couple of old bruises on his knees. I saw a plaster on one,' Luke said, and watched the father's mouth stretch into a pale smile.

'He loves plasters.'

The bad news hadn't ended yet.

'Darcy's had to have a lot of blood. We're still transfusing him.' He didn't want to overwhelm the father, but the volume of the blood transfused was of great concern. 'While he desperately needs the blood, we need to monitor him very closely in case he runs into complications.' Luke decided that was enough for now. 'You should be able to see him before he's moved to the ICU.' Then he asked the question he'd been avoiding prior to operating. 'Have you heard how your other son is—Hamish?'

'He's in Intensive Care at St Bede's.'

'Okay.' Luke took that in. 'Do you know any more than that?'

'He's awake, but they're talking about sedating him.' Urgent eyes looked to Luke. 'I don't know where I should be.'

'Would you like me to call St Bede's and find out what I can?'

'Please.' He nodded. 'I was at work…'

Luke found out that Evan was an aircraft cleaner at Heathrow and had been just starting his shift when the news had hit.

'Amber drops me off at six. We have to wake the boys…put them in the car in their pyjamas… You think you're doing the right thing… They'd have been safer in bed.'

Luke had heard similar words many times from loved ones. Had they done the right thing? He'd asked the same question of himself over and over after his mother's emotional collapse. He'd insisted his father tell her about the affair…had been so certain he was right.

It was one of the reasons he found offering personal advice to families difficult. He always second-guessed himself.

'Let me find out what I can,' he said now.

Luke headed back into Recovery and checked in on the little boy, and from there he called St Bede's to find out what he could about his brother.

He was quickly transferred to the ICU.

'Sister Adams.'

'Shona.' Luke was too tired to care who it was on the other end of the line. 'I'm calling about Hamish Williams.'

'You've got his brother, I hear?'

'Correct,' Luke said. 'He's about to be moved to the ICU.' He went through the injuries and prognosis. 'Still too early to say—he's had a lot of blood.'

'DIC?' Shona asked, knowing that there could be serious issues with coagulation.

'I hope not,' Luke said. 'How's Hamish doing?'

'The main injury is a small subdural haematoma,' Shona informed him. That was a small bleed into Hamish's brain. 'He's conscious, but restless. They're talking about sedating him. Horace is with him now. I can get him to speak with you?'

'Don't pull him away,' Luke said, pleased that Hamish was under the care of such a brilliant neurosurgeon. 'I really just want to know what to tell the father. If he's needed more here or there.'

'Give me a moment. I'll see what I can find out.'

'Thanks.'

It was a long moment.

Luke didn't like Shona. In fact, he actively disliked her. But he knew she was good at her job, and very thorough, and would be speaking with Horace now. Professionally speaking, he trusted her.

He could hear the sounds of the ICU at St Bede's, and familiar voices in the background. It felt odd to be miles away...

Shona returned to the phone. 'I've spoken to Horace. He thinks having Dad here might help settle Hamish, and at least he can be there as they sedate him.'

'Thanks,' Luke said. 'I'll let the father know.'

Without further ceremony he ended the call and headed back to Mr Williams.

'Okay.' Luke stayed standing while talking this time. 'I've spoken with St Bede's and I think it would be a great comfort to Hamish for him to have you there.'

'I see.'

It was clear Evan Williams was torn. 'The staff here will call you if there is any change, but for now Darcy's as stable as he can be.'

'So you think I should head there?'

'I do,' Luke said, knowing there was no easy answer. 'See Darcy before you leave, but then head over.'

'What about Amber? If she's awake she'll be frantic.'

'I'll go down there now and talk to her if I can. Or let the ED staff know what's happening so they can inform her when she's awake.' It did sound as if St Bede's really did want the father there. 'You go and be with Hamish.'

As the theatre nurse led Mr Williams in to see his son, Luke made his way to Emergency and updated Mrs Williams, who was awake but said little. Her face was pale with shock and pain, and she was clearly terrified for her sons. 'I need to see them.'

'I know,' Luke said. But she was about to go to theatre to have her lower leg pinned. 'It's simply not possible yet. Evan will soon be with Hamish, and Darcy is sedated.'

He came away from the grim conversation and saw the flushed face of May.

'There's a debriefing for all the personnel involved in the RTA at two.'

'I'll hopefully be asleep by then.'

'There's another one at eight for the night staff.'

'And I'll hopefully *still* be asleep then,' Luke responded.

But May tutted. 'You ought to go.'

'Are you going?'

'I have a deaf husband,' May chuckled. 'He knows when to nod and when to shake his head.'

Luke smiled, and then headed up to deal with the patients he'd been about to see before his pager had gone off, who were no doubt still waiting for him.

Luke's patients were indeed waiting for him, but Pippa knew he would come when he could.

'Where *is* Mr Harris?'

Mrs James was up at the nurses' station and agitated. She'd been hoping to take Chloe home, but there had been no early-morning ward round.

'He's still in Theatre,' Jenny said. 'It might be a while.'

'You said that two hours ago. How much longer is he going to be?'

Jenny shrugged and walked off, and although Mrs James was being prickly, Pippa knew it wasn't without reason. She was exhausted, Pippa could see that, and on top of a sick child she had a new baby at home and other concerns too—such as how she was going to manage her usually active and demand-ing daughter, who really needed to have a very quiet few weeks.

'There were several emergencies brought in this morning,' Pippa explained.

She knew about the multi-trauma not only from being with Luke when he was paged, but because it had been on the news during her break. She didn't go into any sort of detail with Mrs James, though, just explained things as best she could.

'The operating theatres are really busy. I know it's frustrat-ing, but emergencies have to come first.'

'I know they do.' Mrs James closed her eyes. 'They were talking about taking Chloe to Theatre at one point.'

While Mrs James clearly irked Jenny, she didn't bother Pippa. In fact, she thought it nice that the woman was so worried about her daughter and her little baby, and how to juggle her young family.

Had it been the same for her own mother when she'd been born?

Pippa had spent a lot of time at her aunt's house…

A lot.

She knew how delays and emergencies upended so many things in a hospital, and even if it was true that emergencies had to take priority, it still caused inconvenience and upset.

'He's not going to recognise me,' Mrs James said with a sigh.

'George?' Pippa checked, referring to Chloe's new brother.

'I wanted to breastfeed, but that's starting to fall by the wayside.'

'Whether it's today or in a couple of days' time, you'll soon be home,' Pippa said.

But she knew getting Chloe discharged from hospital wasn't the only problem Mrs James faced.

'How am I going to keep her amused? I know she's a bit spoilt, but we thought we were just having the one child. She's already a bit jealous of the new baby.'

'I'll get the doctor to speak to her, and I'll talk to her too.' Pippa paused when she saw Luke and Fiona arriving. 'Here he is now.'

As Mrs James went to sit with her daughter, Luke and Fiona came to the desk. They both looked pretty grim—understandably so, given they had been on call all night and then operating this morning. With the added emergencies they must be dead on their feet.

'How's the child from this morning?' Pippa asked him.

'On the ICU,' Luke said, but didn't elaborate. Instead, he looked over to Fiona, who looked as white as he looked grey. 'Why don't you go and grab some lunch?' he suggested. 'And could you get me something to eat and a coffee?'

'I was going to go to the…' She paused. 'Sure.'

Fiona walked off, no doubt exhausted, and it was then that Luke pulled a face.

'Damn, she probably wants to go to the debriefing.' He brought his attention back to his patients. 'What do you have for me?'

'Just the one. Chloe James.'

'How's she been?'

'Bored. Mum's worried about her following directions at home.' Pippa smiled at Jenny as she came over with a drug sheet for Luke to sign. 'We're just about to go and see Chloe.'

'Well, remind her mum she's not the only one on the ward,' Jenny said. 'And that it's the NHS. We don't have private chefs!'

Luke didn't know exactly what Jenny meant, but guessed that Chloe wasn't happy with the food. He'd expected, perhaps, for Pippa to roll her eyes, for her to ignore Jenny's statement and simply get on, but instead Pippa turned around and looked straight at her colleague.

'Give her a break,' Pippa told Jenny.

Jenny said nothing, just took the chart, and then they went in to see Chloe.

'Take your earmuffs off, Chloe,' Mrs James said as they walked in to the small side ward.

'Sorry for the delay,' he said.

'Where have you been?' whined Chloe.

'Busy,' Luke said. 'How are you?'

'Better!' Chloe said. 'I want to go home.'

'Then let me take a look at you. You've been eating?'

'I had a takeaway last night.'

Luke turned sharply to Pippa. 'I specifically instructed that she was to be on a low-fat diet.'

'She didn't like the dinner,' Mrs James hurriedly explained.

But Luke shook his head. 'I don't want her eating takeaway. Not until she's been seen in Outpatients.'

'But we're getting pizza tonight,' Chloe protested.

'Do you want to go home?' he asked.

'Yes.'

'Okay, then let's take a look at you.'

Having examined her, he sat on the chair by her bed. Pippa

could almost feel his weariness, but he smiled at the little girl
and her mother.

'Chloe will need to come in to the clinic in two weeks' time.'

'Can she go to school next week?'

'No school until we see her at the clinic, and then it will be
a modified return.'

'What does "modified" mean?' Chloe asked.

'No sport for a while,' Luke said.

Now might not be the right time to tell her she wouldn't be
able to go out at playtime for a little while yet, so he qualified
his words.

'Or anything like that. We'll talk about it at your Outpatients
appointment. I need to have a private word with your mother,
but first I want you to listen to me. You are going to have to
do everything your mother says for the next few weeks and eat
what she gives you. No takeaway, no pizza. Just plain food.'

She pulled a face.

'It's very important, Chloe. If you don't, I'll find out at the
clinic and tell your mum that there's to be no Disney.'

'No!'

'Yes,' he said. 'That injury in your tummy is getting better every day, but I don't want you falling or getting knocked
over and having to come back here. This is very important.'

'Okay...'

'You've had a nasty knock and I don't want you climbing or
playing roughly with anyone for a while. No jumping up and
down on the bed or the sofa. You might be bored, but you can
manage that for a couple of weeks, can't you?'

Chloe gave a reluctant nod.

'I'll see you in the clinic, then, unless I hear from your
mother before.'

He hoped he was stern, but kind, and knew the clinic appointment in two weeks would take a lot of pressure off Chloe's
exhausted mother.

He spoke to Mrs James outside the ward and told her to use
his name as a threat as much as she liked. 'If she wants to play,
or eat something unsuitable, tell her you're going to call me, or

that you already have and that I've said no. Mrs James, this isn't a punishment. This is about her recovery from a serious injury.'

'Yes, I understand.' She closed her eyes. 'Thank you for everything.'

'My pleasure. I'll see both in two weeks. Take very good care.'

They shook hands, but before Pippa could follow Mrs James back into the side ward, he looked over to her.

'Nurse, can I have a quick word?'

'Sure.' She smiled at Mrs James. 'I'll be in with you in a moment.'

Pippa and Luke stood by the linen trolley, which was hardly private, but it would look as if they were just discussing work.

'Thanks for the coffee, earlier,' he said.

'My pleasure,' she said, and smiled begrudgingly. 'Sort of.'

'Well, it was much appreciated.'

'It sounds as if it was pretty grim...'

'Yep. Poor kid. He had this plaster on his knee...'

And even though he halted, Pippa understood exactly what he meant.

'It's the little things,' she ventured. 'They get to you sometimes.'

Luke said nothing, but he gave a small, weary nod.

He looked at her then. 'It seems a long time since that night.'

Pippa gave a soft, slightly ironic laugh. It felt like an *eternity*, and while she knew he'd been impossibly busy, they'd parted without any promises or plans and she hated the uncertainty.

'I think tonight's a write-off,' Luke said. 'I'll see, but...'

He'd see?

Had he not been so obviously dead on his feet, Pippa would have shot back a smart retort. Thankfully, he was saved from seeing her pursed lips, because Fiona returned, with a paper bag containing food and a large coffee for her boss.

'Thanks.'

'Do you want me to go to Surg One?' Fiona offered. 'Start the paperwork on the discharges?'

'No,' he said, shaking his head. 'I'll do it. You head off to the debriefing,'

'What about you?'

'I don't need a debrief. I didn't work on the fatality.' Luke shrugged. 'I'll see you tomorrow, Fiona. Thanks for your help—especially in Theatre this morning. You did an incredible job. It was touch and go for a while.'

Pippa had watched the exchange, and as Fiona walked off she saw him pull a face as he opened up the bag and pulled out a Scotch egg and a bag of crisps.

'And I tell the patients not to eat junk!'

'Do as say, not as I do.' Pippa smiled, but it wavered. She could see his mind was elsewhere. 'Nola said there were young twins involved,' Pippa ventured. 'Have you heard how the other one is?'

'I've been focussing on the patient I had.' Luke's response was a touch curt, but then he seemed to check himself. 'The other twin has a head injury. His father's in a taxi on his way to him at St Bede's now. I believe the mother's on her way to Theatre.'

'Gosh…'

'Hopefully they're all going to make a full recovery.' He took a bite of Scotch egg. 'Unlike my arteries.'

'You prefer health food?'

'Not really. I just prefer my eggs not to be wrapped in sausage meat and deep-fried!' He shook his head, and then managed a half-wave as he went to walk off. 'Ignore me. It's been a long night…'

Luke couldn't ignore his thoughts of Pippa, though.

He woke late in the evening in a bed that held the subtle scent of summer on a dark wintery evening. He thought about calling her, but knew he wouldn't be great company tonight.

Instead, he returned a call from his father.

'You called?' Luke said curtly, because when his mother wasn't around they were still barely talking.

'Good to hear from you,' Matthew Harris said, in the cheery

voice that indicated he was at home. 'Your mother wants to talk about our fortieth anniversary.'

'You're not serious,' Luke replied.

'I know it's a way off,' Matthew carried on cheerfully, as if his son wasn't sending daggers down the phone, 'but we want you to pencil in the date. Hold on a moment…'

Luke lay there, looking at a ceiling that needed painting.

'Your mother wants to know when you're coming over.'

'I'll call her,' Luke said. 'It's pretty full on at The Primary.'

'Well, you insisted on crossing to the other side,' his father quipped. 'I heard you got the brunt of that multi-trauma.'

'Yep.'

'We had a couple admitted…'

Luke said nothing in response. He didn't want updates— especially if the news wasn't good.

His father broke the silence. 'So, what are you up to?'

'I'm about to have something to eat and then go back to sleep. I'm back on tomorrow at seven.'

'Come over,' Matthew suggested.

'And go through the guest list for your party?' Luke asked, with more than an edge to his tone, because he knew his mother would insist on his father's colleagues being invited. Who knew whether his latest mistress would be amongst them? 'I don't think so.'

'I meant,' Matthew said, 'come and have some supper. Your mother's about to go into her studio to paint. We can talk…'

'I thought you didn't want to discuss things.'

'I meant come over and get the hospital out of your head for a bit. You know what they say—all work and no play…'

'Don't,' Luke warned, because he did not need one of his father's little pep talks.

And yet behind the jovial tone he knew that, despite appearances, certain patients did get to his father and he was trying to connect. Luke just didn't want to hear it tonight.

'I'm going back to sleep. Tell Mum I'll call her soon.'

Luke ended the call and tossed the phone onto the mattress.

He was still furious with his father—he simply did not get why a man who had everything would risk it all.

No, he didn't get it.

He tried to get back to sleep, but the scent of summer was still on his pillow and in this instance his father was right. All work and no play did make one dull, Luke thought, and came up with his usual solution as he pulled up Pippa's number. He wanted food, and sex, though when he thought of the night they had spent together, possibly not in that order...

'Hey,' he said when she answered. 'I just woke up.' He glanced at the time and saw that it was almost nine. 'I know it's a bit late.'

'It's fine,' Pippa said, though he could barely hear her. 'What do you want?'

'You,' Luke said, because usually it was that easy. 'And food.'

'Then you'd better get dressed.'

Only then did he hear the music in the background. 'Where are you?'

'Thanks, Rohan.' Pippa took two paper plates piled with scented dahl and roti bread and handed one to her late guest.

It was all very well being bright and spontaneous, but Pippa knew boundaries were urgently required if she was to hold on to her heart.

Determined not to be sitting at home if he called, Pippa had made herself go out. As Rohan had said, the Diwali atmosphere was incredible, and whether or not Luke called, Pippa was glad to have come out and seen it.

'You two know each other?' Luke checked as they walked to the river's edge, because he'd seen Pippa had bypassed quite a queue to get their food.

'Rohan works at the coffee shop I use,' she explained. 'That's his father's truck.'

They stood, looking at the London Eye, all lit up in a rainbow of colours that meant good luck and prosperity. They dipped hot roti into fragrant dahl, but all too soon his bread was gone.

Pippa still had a decent bit left, and he eyed it hungrily. 'I'm starving, Pippa…'

'Then line up,' she said, and popped the last piece of roti in her mouth.

They dropped their plates into a bin and then got back to enjoying the music and the lights.

'Any interest in the apartment?' she asked.

'No idea,' Luke said. 'Given that I'd hoped to be in bed, I told them no viewings today. How was your day?'

'It was all right,' Pippa said, even though for the most part it had been difficult. But she was determined not to get into all that.

And this was why, she told herself. Because with his arm around her, watching the lanterns bobbing on the Thames, she was as happy as she knew how to be.

She'd lit one for Julia, before Luke had arrived.

Not that she'd tell him that.

But now she stared at the lights and knew that hers was out there.

'You're freezing,' he said, and turned her to face him.

'I've been here since sunset.' She thought for a moment. 'Luke, I know what you said the other day, but I don't want anyone at work knowing about…' she gave a casual shrug '…this.'

'They won't hear it from me.'

'Good.'

'You don't want them knowing about your wild side?' he asked.

'Something like that,' Pippa said, and then she told him what she'd decided. 'But don't think I'm on call for you, Luke. I won't be waiting by the phone, and nor will I be at your beck and call.'

Luke turned her to face him and looked at her properly. She looked far from wild.

Pippa wore a grey woolly hat, and the curls escaping it were soft from the damp air. Her scarf was double-wrapped, and he ached to unravel it and expose her pale neck. But there would be time for that later.

Right now, it was nice to take in the night and this woman who had dragged him from his bed to civilisation.

The lights from the river and above their heads were reflected in her pale cheeks, and the wind was making her eyes glassy. And, while he would have liked to still those chattering lips with a kiss, instead he took her frozen hands and placed then beneath his coat and pulled her in.

'You're right,' he agreed. 'And I wouldn't expect you to be on call for me,' he said.

He had enjoyed getting out this evening, slightly to his surprise, and it also occurred to him that it felt good to be back in London…

Pippa closed her eyes and held on to his warmth. When she opened them, she saw all the lanterns and smiled. She felt like an imposter in the body of a woman who knew how to let loose and be happy…

She rested her head on his chest, hearing the thump-thump of his heart and blinking back sudden tears as she saw the lanterns floating out of view.

She never cried.

She definitely wasn't about to start now.

Thankfully, he made her smile instead.

'The heating is on at mine,' he said into the shell of her pale, cold ear. 'Come on,' he told her, taking her hand and leading her through the happy crowds.

But Pippa halted him.

'Do you have milk?'

'We can get some on the way.'

He didn't call it home.

Yet.

Ah, but London had her ways…

CHAPTER SEVEN

THEY WERE GOING to be late.

'Go!' Pippa said as she came out of the shower, watching as Luke hastily attempted to make the bed. 'I'll do it. You have to be at work by seven.'

'I do,' he agreed, selecting a tie from his wardrobe and putting up his shirt collar. 'So hurry up and get dressed.'

Pippa shook her head. 'I can take the Tube. I don't have to be there until half-past.'

'Or is it that you don't want to be seen arriving with me.'

'Both,' Pippa openly agreed.

Only her words clearly didn't offend him, because rather than picking up his keys and heading out he crossed the bedroom towards her.

It had been a week since that night at The Avery.

And even without her contacts in Luke in the morning was a very nice sight indeed.

'You haven't shaved,' Pippa said, not because he was close enough for her to see it, but because his farewell kiss was rough and probing and his hand was moving to the knot on her towel.

'When is there time to shave?'

'Go!' Pippa said, even though she'd rather not be the sensible one.

'You're bad for me, Pippa,' he said, reluctantly releasing her.

'I think it's the other way round!' Pippa joked as he walked out through the door.

Or rather, he was by far too good for her, Pippa thought as she heard his footsteps fade on the stairs.

She didn't mean that he was too good for her in a self-deprecating way—more that this week had been the best she'd ever known.

And not just making love—though there had been plenty of that in their busy schedules. As well as the evening they spent at the Diwali celebrations, they'd crammed in a candlelit concert in a gorgeous cathedral, and just last night, though she'd been on a late shift, they'd taken his neighbour's puppy for a walk.

'How did we get roped into this?' Luke had asked as the puppy had sat and refused either to wee or walk. 'It's your fault!'

Pippa had not been able to resist patting Sausage one day in the corridor, and the next thing they knew Luke had been lumbered with feeding it and walking it.

Finally the puppy had weed, and he'd picked it up and carried it home. Then they'd let the puppy back into its owner's apartment.

'"It's just this once",' Pippa had said, mimicking the owner's voice, as they'd given Sausage his necessary treats and then placed him in his crate. 'Mind you,' she'd added as they'd left, 'that's how it starts…'

'And that's how it ends,' Luke had said, posting the keys through the letterbox, clearly refusing to get embroiled.

He had said he didn't like to get involved, and if she'd needed any further proof then this was it.

Now, instead of making the bed, Pippa sat on it. She kept a strip of contact lenses at his flat now, and she popped a fresh pair in. The room certainly looked clearer, and her eyes landed on a couple of packing boxes neatly stacked in the corner, under the large, ugly painting the estate agent had chosen to draw attention away from the bumpy wall.

The bedroom felt silent without their easy chatter—yes, easy, because they didn't really touch on anything deep. Luke refused to bring his work home with him, and neither of them spoke much about family. Occasionally they touched on the past—a teacher they'd both had, or a person they recalled—but nothing too weighty.

And, given they weren't looking to the future, she didn't tell him of her surprise that she'd been called back for a second interview; nor did he mention his upcoming job in Scotland or whatever lay beyond that.

They were happily suspended in the now.

But in the peace and quiet of the morning there was too much space for the thoughts that Pippa had been trying to ignore.

In a couple of weeks Luke would be gone.

You got through it once before, Pippa reminded herself.

Yet she'd been sixteen then, and hadn't known his kiss, let alone anything else.

Now she knew how it felt to touch him, to have him on her and in her... How behind that rather brusque demeanour he was still the guy she'd met that day in the library...

He still had a piece of her heart, and Pippa was doing all she could not to let it show.

'We're expecting an admission from the ICU,' the night sister informed the day staff. 'Darcy Williams, five years old.'

'From the multi-trauma?' Pippa checked.

She nodded. 'Splenectomy, contusion on left kidney, perforated bowel and concussion. He was extubated forty-eight hours ago. GCS thirteen to fifteen.'

The Glasgow Coma Scale was a score given to measure the severity or worsening of a brain injury, and fifteen was the best score, so Darcy was doing well.

'He's opening his eyes, though mainly to verbal command, but he's barely talking. His mother was admitted here, but she's being discharged today. His identical twin was taken to another trauma centre.'

'What about the father?'

'Running in between hospitals, apparently.'

'When should we expect Darcy?'

'I've told them we won't have a side room until lunchtime.' Laura raised her hands skywards. 'But they want to send him up before that.'

'Just tell them we're not ready,' a grumpy Jenny snapped, but thankfully Nola stepped in.

'Pippa, can you see about moving Room Four up to the main ward? She's due for discharge.'

It became a dance of the beds, because Mrs Williams had a serious leg injury, and Room Four was the smallest, so it would be difficult for her to move around in there alongside her son's bed when she visited. But finally Room Seven was ready and waiting, meds and breakfasts had been given, and Jenny was feeding Toby at the desk because his parents weren't in yet.

'Hi, Luke,' Nola said as he came up to the desk.

'Is my admission here?' he asked.

'Not yet.' Nola called over to Pippa. 'Go and have your break before he gets here.'

'Sure...'

As Luke went to check on his other patients Pippa made a mug of—horrible—coffee and found Fiona sitting in the break room.

'Is Darcy here?' she asked. 'The ICU admission?'

'Not yet.' Pippa shook her head. 'They'll buzz if he arrives—that's why I'm on my break.'

It was actually a relief to be away from the ward while Luke was on it. Pippa still felt a blush creeping up when he was around, and he wasn't quite as discreet as her. He often pulled her aside, more than willing to chat or even discuss their evening plans, when Pippa would have preferred things to stay strictly professional at work and to be kept private between them.

'Have you heard how the other twin is?' Pippa asked.

'He's doing well.' Fiona nodded. 'They're talking about moving him to the neuro ward. I've asked Luke about transferring him here.'

'And?'

'He says it's not my decision,' Fiona responded tartly. 'Easy enough for him to say when he's not the one dealing with the parents.'

Pippa said nothing.

'He's brilliant in Theatre,' Fiona elaborated to her silent audience. 'And I know you have to have a certain ruthlessness to do his job. But still, a little sensitivity outside the operating room wouldn't go amiss.'

Still Pippa said nothing. Okay, Luke wasn't all jokes and small talk—and, yes, he was strict with his orders. But it was always with the patient's best interests in mind.

Still, Fiona hadn't quite finished, and now she was giving a dramatic eyeroll. 'He's always been like that...'

'Like what?'

'Straight on to the next one...' She raised her eyebrows meaningfully. 'And not just with his patients.'

Pippa left Fiona to it and returned from her break early. Darcy still hadn't arrived, and Luke was looking at X-rays, his phone tucked into his neck. He was sounding less than impressed.

'Seriously?' Luke's voice was impatient as he spoke into the phone. 'How am I supposed to manage that when I have ward rounds at seven?' He shook his head impatiently. 'Let me get back to you...'

'Trouble?' Nola asked.

'Apparently so.' He sighed, pocketing his phone, and then, perhaps seeing Pippa appear, he asked Nola, 'Do you make your bed in the morning?'

'Of course,' Nola said.

'Jenny?'

'I was in the army,' Jenny answered. 'So yes.'

'And do you tidy the bathroom? Wipe down the shower?'

She nodded.

Then he glanced over at Pippa, who must surely have gone as red as a beetroot.

'Pippa,' he asked, 'do you make your bed in the morning?'

'Of course,' she croaked, knowing full well what he was referring to. Not only had she not made the bed this morning, she'd dressed in a hurry and left his bathroom in morning chaos.

'*Every* morning?' he checked, and she looked up to see his incredulous smile.

'If I'm on night duty, yes,' Pippa amended. 'If I'm on a late, sometimes...'

'What about if you're on an early?'

'That depends.' Pippa shook her head and refused to flirt, but both of them knew they were discussing this morning.

'Well, I've just been told by my estate agent that if I want people brought round while I'm at work I'm to leave my flat inspection-ready.'

'Obviously,' Jenny said.

'I got the golden package. I thought they'd at least—'

'You thought the estate agent would dash around and do a quick tidy?' Jenny harumphed as she walked off. 'Oh, no...'

Luke waited till Pippa was in the drug room and then wagged a finger as he walked in. 'What happened to "I'll do it"?' he quoted back her own words.

'I lost track of time,' Pippa admitted, but instead of telling him she'd been sitting on the bed, thinking how impossible it would be to say goodbye to him, she came up with something lighter. 'I was looking at your walls.'

'My walls?'

'Yes, they need wallpaper. But if you don't have time for that then, like I said, you should dress up the fireplaces rather than put ugly prints on the wall.'

'Says the would-be interior designer? I'll leave it to the experts, thanks.'

'It's okay, Luke,' Pippa said with a smirk, seeing his slight look of horror, as if his latest squeeze had told him she was thinking of moving in. 'I'm not hoping for a trip to IKEA with you, or to pick out bedspreads. I just love old buildings.'

'Luke,' Jenny called. 'Your ICU transfer's here.'

'Thanks.'

Pippa went too, as she had been assigned to care for little Darcy. His father was with him, and he and Luke were clearly on first-name terms.

'Hi, Evan,' Luke said, and then went over to his little patient. 'Hey, Darcy. You're looking even better than you did this morning,'

Dark, solemn grey eyes looked briefly at Luke and then flicked away.

He was recovering well from his dreadful injuries, Pippa heard from the ICU nurse who gave hand-over.

'Luke has said he can start on sips of water, but so far he's refusing. He's really quiet, which is apparently unusual for him. He's barely spoken, except a couple of times to ask for his mum.'

'She's being discharged this morning?' Pippa checked.

'Yes. You know he has an identical twin?'

'I do.'

'They're arranging transport so Mum can visit Hamish, then she'll come here. Darcy hasn't asked for his brother or anything, which Dad says is also unusual. He's really withdrawn.'

Evan, the twins' father, walked over then, and thanked the ICU nurse for her care. When she'd left he spoke to Pippa.

'My wife and I are going to take it in turns to stay with Darcy, but Amber's got a fractured leg.'

'Yes, we've put Darcy in the biggest side room, so that we can put a recliner in there for her, as well as a bed.' She glanced into the side room and saw the anaesthetist had also arrived to assess Darcy, and there was quite a crowd in there now. 'I'll show you the facilities.'

'Thanks.'

Pippa took Evan round and showed him the parents' room and the small kitchenette, as well as the shower and bathroom. 'How's Hamish doing?' she asked.

'Better than Darcy,' Evan said with a relieved sigh. 'He's off the ventilator and talking. A little bit confused... I'm crossing my fingers that he can be transferred here. I've asked Mr Harris if he can look into it, but I haven't heard yet whether it's possible...'

Darcy was indeed very subdued, his eyes barely tracking

as Pippa did his obs late that afternoon, though he did look up when Luke came into the room.

'How are you feeling, Darcy?'

He didn't answer, just turned his head away.

'Who's this?' Pippa asked, tickling the face of the scruffy and clearly much-loved teddy Darcy had tucked under his arm.

'That's Whiskers.' Evan spoke for his silent son.

'Does Hamish have a bear?' Pippa asked as she checked the various drips. Out of the corner of her eye she saw Darcy stir.

'Coco,' Darcy whispered.

'And is Coco with Hamish now?' Pippa asked.

And even though it was Evan who answered, he was clearly pleased at the one-word response from his son.

'Yes. Amber told me to fetch them the day after the accident. The boys hide them when their friends come to play.'

'You hide them?' Pippa gave Darcy a shocked look, then smiled at the little boy. 'I hide my teddy too. Mind you, I'm a lot older than you...'

But Darcy wasn't engaging any longer. He just closed his eyes and held on to his bear and lay there listlessly as he was examined.

'Try and get him to take some fluids,' Luke told Evan, moving away from the bedside.

'He's not really interested.'

'The drip is keeping him hydrated,' Luke explained, 'but if you can encourage him to drink it will aid his recovery.'

Soon it became a bit of an issue.

Unlike little Chloe, who had been begging to drink and to eat, Darcy continued to show no interest in food or fluids.

'He wants his brother,' Nola said to Luke late the next afternoon. 'Can't you speak to Allocations?'

'It has nothing to do with Allocations,' Luke responded tartly. 'His brother is on a top neuro ward and really wouldn't benefit from an ambulance ride across town.' He glanced over as Jenny called his name. 'Yes?'

'Martha wants to speak with you,' she said, gesturing with her head towards the office.

'Sure.'

But as he stood Evan Williams made his way over to ask again if there was any chance of his other son being transferred.

'It would just make things easier all around,' the harried father said. 'And I know it would cheer Darcy up.'

'I do understand where you're coming from,' Luke said.

Pippa was feeding a baby at the desk, so she was able to listen as he explained the situation a little more gently to the father.

'By all accounts Hamish is doing well, but he's had a serious bleed on the brain and he needs to be closely monitored. I don't think a transfer right now is in his best interests. He's where he needs to be.'

'I know he is…' Evan ran a tired hand over his forehead. 'Darcy wants me to take Hamish his bear. I told Darcy he needs it for now, and that Hamish has Coco with him.'

'Probably wise,' Luke said.

No! Pippa glanced up, wanting to intervene. If Darcy wanted Hamish to have *his* bear, then that was probably the right thing.

But Nola was in on the conversation now, and was agreeing with both Luke and Evan. As well as that, the social worker had arrived and Martha, the paediatrician, was at the desk. It wasn't Pippa's place, especially in front of Mr Williams, to disagree.

As they all moved into the NUM's office to discuss things, Pippa not only wanted the PAC Unit job more than ever, she knew she was right for it. Knew she was ready to have more of a voice.

'Luke?' she said as soon as he stepped out of the meeting.

'What?' He was tense and distracted. 'I'm waiting for a consult from Mr Benson. Can you fetch me the moment he calls?'

'Sure,' Pippa said.

'In the meantime, ask Toby's parents to come through to the NUM's office.'

Pippa nodded, but she was frowning, because Toby wasn't his patient.

Then she saw Jenny, standing by the cot, making small talk with the parents—which was unusual for Jenny. It was clear to Pippa that she wasn't letting the baby out of her sight.

Nola came out then, and briefly brought Pippa up to speed: some rather worrying information had come to light regarding Toby.

The social worker wasn't here about Darcy and Hamish, Pippa realised. The moment to talk about teddies and on whose bed they belonged had passed.

CHAPTER EIGHT

EVEN BEFORE SIX in the morning it was already her happiest birthday ever.

Although Luke didn't know that he'd just made love to a thirty-year-old!

Pippa lay facing the wall, with Luke spooning her, both relishing the aftershocks of early-morning sex. The alarm hadn't even gone off yet.

'Sorry to wake you,' he said.

'You can wake me like that every morning!'

Pippa smiled to herself, but it soon faded as she realised there wouldn't be many more mornings like this.

Still, if this was how it felt to be thirty, Pippa thought, then bring it on!

She hadn't told Luke that today was her birthday, and it wasn't just because they were keeping things light. She never made a big deal out of it.

Nor did her parents.

There would be a card with some cash in it waiting for her the next time she called in. Still, given it was a milestone birthday perhaps she hoped they might call and ask her to come over. Surprise her with cake…

Pippa was aware that birthdays were extremely painful for them. Her own eighteenth and twenty-first had barely been mentioned, and on what would have been Julia's thirtieth, her mother had been in bits.

Pippa closed her eyes, trying not to recall the tears and drama and return to the blissful floaty feeling of being wrapped in Luke's arms, feeling safe and warm on a cold late-November day.

Even the alarm didn't intrude on the pleasure, because Luke uncoiled himself from her and turned it off. Instead of rolling straight out of bed, as was his usual practice, he turned on her electric blanket topper, turned onto his back and pulled her into him.

'There is an advantage to staying at yours...' he said.

'Because we don't have to make the bed and tidy up?'

'Well, there's that,' he agreed. 'I meant it's closer to work. We don't have to rush.'

'True.'

There was even time for tea and toast, topped with ginger marmalade from the night market they'd been to earlier in the week. It was fiery and spicy and the perfect winter breakfast.

They were now both 'two toothbrush households'— something he'd said drily when, having first ended up back at hers, morning had broken and there'd been no time for him to go home and wash and change before work. Thankfully, Pippa had found him a spare toothbrush, and now he brushed his teeth at her place with a neon pink one. At his, Pippa had the spare toothbrush from the goody-bag from his flight home from the States.

They weren't yet 'two deodorant households'. So it was Luke's turn to smell of baby powder for the day. Fair enough, given that for most of this week Pippa's usual scent of summer had been rather drowned out by some kind of twenty-four-hour-lasting concoction for 'active men'.

Luke even had a couple of shirts hanging in her wardrobe, still in their plastic from the dry-cleaning service, and as he ripped open one of the covers, Luke couldn't help but think how he usually used the lack of a fresh shirt or a toothbrush or whatever as a good reason to head off early, or even leave in the middle of the night.

Not now.

When Pippa had said she needed to pick up her dry-cleaning, it had prompted him to throw a few clean shirts into the car.

It just made things easier.

Or rather, it made things a little more complicated than he was used to... But then, he reasoned, their affair would be so short-lived that it wouldn't matter. It was good to spend as much time as they had together rather than shuffling back and forth.

He looked at Pippa, lying in bed watching him and wearing a sleepy smile.

'The blanket's warming up,' she said, with all the temptation of a practised seductress.

'That's not fair,' he said, knowing she was naked and warm beneath the sheets. For the first time ever he was considering being late for rounds. 'Have you got your contacts in?'

'No.' She smiled.

'Pity...'

'I'm not blind!' Pippa laughed, and looked down at how turned on he was, and then back up to his face. 'You know you want to...'

He resisted temptation—but with a proviso. 'I should be able to get off at a reasonable time tonight,' he said. 'Maybe we could—'

'I'm not sure I can tonight,' Pippa interrupted. 'I'll let you know.'

'I'm on call tomorrow night,' he reminded her.

It wasn't like Luke to push, but he was getting to the pointy end of his contract and time was fading fast. He'd also had to put a deposit down for a cottage he'd found...

'I've found a nice place in Scotland... Skye,' he told her. 'A stone cottage, with peat fires in both the bedroom and lounge.'

'Estate-agent-speak for freezing,' Pippa said with authority. 'Does it have hot water?'

'I assume so.'

'Never assume.'

'You can take a look tonight,' Luke said.

And then he halted—not just because she'd said she might have plans, but because in recent days he'd been thinking of asking if she would join him for a couple of weeks in Scotland. He'd never done anything like that with another woman.

'Or whenever,' he amended, pulling on his suit jacket and trying to quash the thought of spoiling things by suggesting they extend their arrangement. 'You can make sure I won't be fetching my water from a well...'

Pippa gave him a thin smile, deciding she definitely would *not* be helping him choose the accommodation that would be enjoyed by his next lover...

When he'd left, she checked her phone, hoping for a birthday message—then reminded herself it wasn't even seven yet. Her parents would barely be awake.

They still hadn't messaged when Pippa checked her phone later that morning, when she was on her break.

She didn't get to go to lunch until late, because Darcy threw up in a major way. Evan had gone with Amber to visit Hamish, and Darcy was teary, so Pippa changed his bedding while Laura went to page Fiona to come and check on him.

'It's okay, Darcy,' Pippa told him, when he was tucked up in a clean bed with his teddy. 'Mummy will be back soon.'

'I'll stay with him,' Laura said, coming back into the room. 'Fiona's going to come when she can.'

Eating her cheese sandwich, Pippa went through her messages, but although a couple of friends had texted, as well as her aunt, there was nothing from her parents.

Pippa was more angry than hurt.

Or was she more hurt than angry?

She honestly didn't know how she felt as she headed back to the ward.

Evan was back from visiting his other son, but Amber was staying with Hamish for now.

Fiona had come to see Darcy.

'How's that tummy?' she asked as she gently probed Darcy's stomach.

But Darcy didn't answer her. Instead, he looked over to the more familiar face of Pippa. 'Where's Hamish?'

'He's being looked after in another hospital,' Pippa told the little boy, as she had many times before. 'Darcy, the doctor wants to know if your tummy's sore.'

Darcy just turned his little head and carried on staring out at the grey afternoon.

'Is he drinking anything?' asked Fiona.

'Just small sips,' Pippa said, 'and only with a lot of encouragement.'

'So just the one vomit?' Fiona checked, and Pippa nodded. 'I might speak to David…'

'Thanks.'

It was Luke who came to check on the patient later in the afternoon, but there were no clinical changes.

'I'm going to call the anaesthetist and ask her to come and do a pain review,' he told Pippa. 'And I'll increase his IV fluids. He's very listless.'

Luke was more than aware that he was the bad guy here. Especially as there was an empty twin-bedded room that had opened up on the paediatric ward.

Darcy wanted his twin!

As he sat at the desk checking labs, Nola pointed it out to him.

'So I've repeatedly been told,' Luke snapped.

By several of the staff, by the bed allocations team, and by Darcy's father, who had just brought Amber back to be with Darcy and was now peering into the spare two-bed room…

Luke was well aware of the impact on the family, and had even touched on the prospect of a transfer with Horace. For now, though, both had chosen to err on the side of caution and agreed that, for the time being, it was better that each twin stay where he was.

'Delivery for Pippa Westford.'

Luke glanced up at the delivery man and saw a huge potted plant that surely belonged in some retro musical land on the edge of the nurses' station.

'Good grief,' Nola said when she saw it. 'Who's that for?'

'Pippa,' Jenny said. She peered at the little white card and took it off the plastic stick.

'Jenny!' Nola warned.

'It's stuck down with a heart.' Jenny said, and sighed. She went to put it back, though not quite in time, because Pippa emerged from the office. 'This came for you,' Jenny said.

'Do tell me who it's from,' Pippa said rather pointedly as she took the card from Jenny. But instead of opening it, she pocketed it in her scrubs.

'Who sent it?' Jenny asked.

'I'll find out when I get home,' Pippa retorted, and then looked at the large plant, now taking up a lot of the desk. 'When the two of us get home. Heavens, look at the size of it!'

She stashed it in the office temporarily, and then headed into the drug room.

Luke worried that he was turning into Nosy Jenny, because he was dying to know what was in the envelope.

He was more than used to women and the games they played. A lover had once sent flowers to herself, pretending they were from an ex, in an attempt to make him jealous and nudge him to commit.

It hadn't worked.

This plant, though, must be a triffid. Because even though it had been put away, he could still see its shiny leaves, waving from the office door.

And, given how little time they had left, it niggled him that Pippa had been so vague about her plans tonight.

As her shift was about to end, he caved in and headed to the drug room.

'Your secret lover has terrible taste,' he said, when he found her.

Pippa laughed. 'My aunt sends me a plant every year. I don't know why she doesn't send it to my flat.' She glanced over. 'Don't tell Jenny who it's from.'

'Wait—it's your birthday?' he checked, and did a quick mental calculation, because if she'd been two years below him at school… 'Your thirtieth?'

'Don't remind me.'

'But why didn't you say anything?'

'I just didn't.' Pippa shrugged.

'So what are you up to?'

'I'm catching up with friends at the weekend.'

'But what about tonight?'

'Luke, I really don't make a fuss about birthdays.'

'Maybe *I* want to make a fuss.' He came a little closer than he usually would at work and named the very nice French restaurant just a short walk from his flat.

'I really don't need—' Pippa started, but then she took out her phone and saw that there was *still* no message from her parents. Hell, she wanted to celebrate her birthday—and for once there was actually someone who wanted to celebrate it too. 'I'd like that,' Pippa said.

'What about your plans?' Luke checked.

'They've changed.' Pippa smiled.

'Brilliant. Should I book it for seven?' he asked. 'I should be finished here in an hour or so.' He checked his pager. 'Maybe two. It might be better to meet there…'

'Sounds great.'

It really did.

It was the first birthday she'd dared even hope to celebrate like this, and she was rushing as she pulled off her scrubs and changed into jeans, her head full of what on earth to wear, wondering if she had time to hit the shops…

'Drama, drama!' Jenny said as she came into the changing room. 'Shona just called and asked to speak to Luke.'

'Who?'

'That ICU nurse from St Bede's.'

'You've lost me.'

'Shona—the one he had the affair with.'

'That's just gossip.'

'Oh, no, it's not,' Jenny said, pulling on the vast jumper she'd knitted. 'Fiona told me all about it. She caught them in the break room herself. Shona must have heard he's back in London. You should have seen Luke's face when I told him who was on the phone, asking to speak with him privately.'

Privately?

Pippa felt her heart sink—but then reminded herself how much she loathed gossip. And anyway, Luke had said himself that the rumours were false.

'He asked to take the call in Nola's office,' Jenny elaborated. 'His face was like thunder.'

Sure enough, she could see Luke on the phone in the office. The blinds weren't closed and, even though she tried not to look, Pippa could see the tension in his shoulders as he stood with his back to the ward, his hand raking through his dark hair.

'Told you!' Jenny said, clearly delighted with her gossip. 'Go in and get your plant. You might hear—'

'I've got to dash,' Pippa interrupted, unsure whether she was refusing to engage in gossip, or burying her head in the sand, or just selfish, because she wanted one perfect birthday with this man she had liked for far too long...

She decided she would leave the enormous plant at work overnight, so she could make it to the shops. In the end, she found a lovely lilac dress that was so soft she thought it was wool—but she looked at the label and saw it was silk.

And then she saw the price. Even though it was in the sale, it was still out of her league.

But then she was already playing way out of her league...

Yes, there was a fair chance Luke had looked her in the eye and lied about his past, but Pippa knew she too had been lying all along...pretending she belonged in a world of casual lovers and passion that came with no strings attached.

'Try it on,' the assistant suggested.

Perhaps she should have walked away in The Avery, or should walk away even now, yet she found herself in a cubicle, stripping down to her underwear and pulling the dress on over her head.

It was—unfortunately for her credit card—perfect.

She angled her head in the mirror, hoping she'd look dreadful from behind. But no, it was as if a thousand magical mice had been working on the gown all night.

It wasn't really a gown, but it made her think of Julia, in her silver ballgown, heading out for one fabulous night…

Well, Pippa would have one fabulous birthday!

Back in her flat, Pippa decided she would go all-out tonight and make a real effort.

She put loads of product in her hair, then hung her head upside down and tackled the diffuser. It took for ever, and even then her thick dark hair wasn't completely dry, but she was running out of time.

Pippa put on some make-up, as well as the fabulous underwear that she'd added to her purchase—and even stockings, heels and dangly earrings…

When she checked her reflection she worried that it was too much, and didn't suit her.

Because this night mattered more than any other ever had…

'Madame…' the greeter said, and smiled when she gave her name and then said something in French.

It took a second's delay to work out that he'd asked for her coat. Pippa handed it over and then was shown to a reserved table. A little unsure, she ordered a glass of red wine, but he stared at her blankly, so Pippa dragged out her schoolgirl French.

Her wine came with a little silver dish of nibbles.

The garlicky, herby scent was making her stomach rumble. She looked at the other couples there, and the pair of elderly ladies who were laughing as they went out for a cigarette.

The waiter was back, brandishing the wine bottle.

'No, I'm fine,' Pippa said. *'Non, merci,'* she corrected herself.

And only then did it enter her head that Luke might not be coming.

He wouldn't stand her up on her birthday, would he?

Unless something had come up at the hospital…?

But then surely he could have fired off a quick text?

No, he was a trauma surgeon, Pippa reminded herself. He was hardly going to ask one of the staff to message her; she was the one who had insisted on discretion after all...

There were so many arguments taking place in her head. She wanted to trust him, to believe it was nothing more than work delaying him. But the voice she had been trying to ignore chimed up a little more loudly.

Had the call from his ex derailed his plans for the night?

Finally, there came a text, and it felt as if every pair of eyes in the restaurant were on her as she read it.

Sorry. Talk later.

An apology, but no explanation.

Still, it told Pippa enough, and she signalled for the waiter.

'Could I have the bill, please?' He gave her a non-plussed look. 'You know exactly what I mean,' Pippa snapped, and to the waiter's credit he gave her a little smile, then headed off to fetch a velvet folder.

Pippa paid for the *extremely* expensive glass of red wine, and even added a tip because—well, she was burning with embarrassment.

No, it wasn't embarrassment. It was the disappearance of hope that *one* birthday, just one...

It was a long taxi ride home, with a thankfully quiet driver.

Behind closed doors, she peeled off her shoes and stockings and washed off all her make-up, then donned an over-sized T-shirt. She poured herself a far cheaper glass of wine than she'd had in the restaurant and moved her heated blanket from the bedroom to the sofa and curled up under it.

This was supposed to be fun —and yet it was starting to hurt.

It was close to ten when there was a knock at the door and Pippa knew it was Luke. She was tempted not to open it, but she knew that would be petty.

'Hey,' she said, trying to pretend it didn't really matter.

'I'm so sorry, Pippa, for leaving you stranded on your birthday.'

'Hardly stranded,' Pippa said as she let him in. 'I've been stood up in worse places.'

But then she saw his tense expression and watched as he sat on the couch, picked up her glass and took a drink.

'I got a call from St Bede's.'

'Shona?' Pippa nodded, refusing to skirt the issue. 'Jenny told me.'

'She's working on the ICU now.' He frowned, but then dismissed whatever thought he'd just had. 'Hamish collapsed.'

'Hamish?' Pippa felt a jolt of panic dart through her, but she remained perfectly still. 'You mean Darcy's twin?'

Luke nodded. 'Evan was already on his way to visit, and I had to go and tell Amber that he'd taken a sudden turn for the worse.'

'Oh, my God.'

'Amber was frantic. She didn't know what was happening. And, what with them being identical twins, she wanted me to check on Darcy—bloods, infection...'

Pippa nodded. It had been days since the accident, though, and hopefully the boys hadn't been brewing any infection or unknowingly sharing an undiagnosed condition. Of course it was vital to check, and only right that the doctors would be concerned for the healthier twin.

'Did you find anything?'

'No. Nothing related. It would seem that Hamish's brain bleed had extended.'

Pippa swallowed.

'I heard an hour or so ago that he'd died.'

She watched Luke put his head in his hands and felt goosebumps prickle her arms and even her bare legs as she stood there in nothing but her T-shirt. She was helpless, waiting for Luke to correct himself, to say it had been a mistake, for the world to go back to a more correct order.

Luke must have noted her complete lack of response because he lifted his head. 'Are you okay?'

'I don't know,' Pippa admitted, a little stunned to see his face streaked with tears.

She took a seat on the couch beside him. She felt shaken up inside, but kept her breathing steady. 'Who's with Darcy?'

'An uncle or a cousin arrived to sit with him just as I left, although Darcy was asleep.'

'He knew,' Pippa said through pale lips. 'Darcy knew something was wrong...'

'Pippa—'

'He did.' Pippa was insistent. 'When Julia took a turn for the worse I felt ill all day at school.' She let out a sliver of her hurt. 'No one thought to call me to come home and say goodbye. I found out when I got back from school.' She looked over. 'It needs to be his parents who tell him—not his uncle.' Pippa's voice was urgent. 'My aunt was the one who told me and—'

'Pippa,' he interrupted. 'I'm sure Amber and Evan will tell him together; they just don't want him to be on his own to-night...' He frowned at her pallid face. 'I'm sorry to bring bad news.'

He took her hand, and although she wanted to cling to it, Pippa was scared by her own devastation and the dreadful memories it was unleashing. She wasn't used to sharing her grief, and surely Luke, who was already clearly upset, didn't need his short-term lover to crumple emotionally.

'How was Amber?' Pippa asked.

'I told her well away from Darcy; Nola brought her into the office. I've had to give bad news to a lot of parents, but this one's really got to me.' He took a shaky breath and wiped his cheeks. 'Looks as if I'm like my father after all...'

'Meaning?'

'He's come home upset a couple of times. You'd never have guessed if you only knew him at work. I came downstairs once and found him crying. It scared the life out of me.'

'What did you do?'

'Offered to get my mother...' He looked over. 'She paints too...'

* * *

It was an odd moment for Luke.

To be sitting with the woman he realised he needed tonight.

And, while Pippa wasn't exactly effusive, she wasn't shut away in her studio like his mother. Instead, she sat beside him, pulling her T-shirt down over her knees…

It wasn't the wildest birthday for her.

Pippa lay on the sofa with her head in his lap, while Luke finished the wine.

Both were locked in their own thoughts.

But they were together.

And tonight, that meant the world.

Pippa would have hated to hear this news tomorrow, in hand-over. The dread that gripped her was similar to the way she'd felt when she'd been told Julia had died. She'd panicked when Luke had told her about Hamish, yet he didn't seem to mind.

She felt his hand still in her hair, and then heard his voice, which rarely revealed any uncertainty.

'I should have transferred Hamish. At least Darcy would have been with his brother.'

Pippa thought for a moment. 'And witnessed his collapse? Heard the resuscitation attempts? Seen him die?'

She shook her head, and then turned in his lap so she could see him.

'It would have been dreadful for Darcy. Aside from that, St Bede's is one of the best neuro hospitals. You did the right thing, keeping Hamish there. What if he'd died in the back of an ambulance?' She watched as he closed his eyes and finally accepted her words. 'By not bending to everyone's wishes and moving him, you gave him the best chance.'

'Thank you,' he said, 'for saying that.'

'It's the truth,' Pippa said with conviction. She moved up on his lap. 'You did the best you could—life just doesn't always play fair.'

'No,' he agreed. 'It doesn't.'

* * *

Luke looked at this woman whom he'd stood up tonight—
there'd not been a single text demanding where he was…not
one angry call.

'I'm sorry I ruined your birthday.'

'You didn't.' Pippa shrugged. 'I hate birthdays anyway.'

'Hate them?'

Pippa blinked, about to retract or cover up her statement.
But yes, on this, her thirtieth birthday, thinking of little Darcy
and poor Hamish, it felt safe to say she officially hated them.

'Yes.'

'Why?' Luke pushed. 'Do you mean since you lost—?'

'No.' She shook her head, because it wasn't all about Julia's
death, and he'd been honest about how he was feeling, so she
felt a little braver. 'I always hated them,' she admitted. 'I used
to turn down friends' party invites.'

'How come?' he asked, his hands on her bare thighs.

He looked into green eyes that were finally a little less
guarded than they'd been since the day they'd met.

'Julia couldn't go to parties, you see. Mum didn't think it
was fair.'

'What about *your* birthdays?'

'Some were nice…' she said. 'My parents forgot my seventh
birthday, though.'

'Totally forgot?'

'With good reason.' She told him how sick Julia had been,
and about the nurse who had remembered at the eleventh hour.
'Maybe Julia told her,' Pippa mused. 'I don't know where she
got that cake.'

Luke mulled this over. For all his father's faults, he'd never
missed a birthday. Hell, even though they were still barely talking, he'd called the other night to check on him.

'So they don't bother with your birthday at all now?'

'There'll be a card with some cash next time I go over.'

He thought of her checking her phone in the drug room.
'Do they call?'

'Birthdays upset them,' Pippa said, in her parents' defence. 'No one can know how they feel unless they've lost a child.'

Luke swallowed down a slightly caustic reply, because it would be aimed at Pippa's parents rather than at her. He thought of Amber, about how desperate she had been to get to Hamish, and yet she had never for one second forgotten the son she was leaving behind and had begged Luke to check on him...

'Anyway,' Pippa said, shrugging, 'I don't make a big deal of them.'

He kissed her then, and Pippa kissed him back, chasing away the horrors of the day.

As he undressed, he saw Pippa reach into his jacket for a condom. Knew they were both urgent for escape.

They made love on the sofa, but it was necessary sex, to drown out the noise in their heads. It was passionate, rather than intimate.

But it was in the small hours of the morning that they ran into danger...

CHAPTER NINE

PIPPA WOKE BEFORE DAWN, and although Luke lay still beside her, she could feel he was awake.

'Can't sleep?' she asked.

'No,' Luke said, and then, 'You thought I was with Shona?'

Pippa realised that it wasn't only the sad events of the night keeping him awake.

'Tonight?' Luke persisted. 'You thought I was with her.'

'I didn't know what to think,' Pippa admitted. 'I *don't* know what to think.'

She stared up at the ceiling, asking herself who she was to play judge and jury over his past. But there were things that mattered...that were important to discuss.

'She was *married*, Luke.'

'So was my father...'

Her head turned to face him 'What?'

'It wasn't *me* having the affair.' In the darkness, they rolled over and faced each other. 'It was my father and Shona.'

'So why did *you* leave St Bede's?' Pippa frowned. 'Why did you take the fall?'

'I just knew I didn't want to be there any more. I'd lost all respect for my father. And Shona's husband worked on one of the wards. Nice guy...' He thought for a moment. 'I'd already been looking at studying in America, and that gave me the push I needed.'

He didn't speak for a moment, yet Pippa could feel he was still thinking.

'Truth be told, I was never one hundred percent sure I wanted to work there… That bloody chemistry exam!'

'Fragmentation,' she said, and he laughed and gave her a playful punch.

His hand remained on her arm and she could see his dark eyes shining…knew they were locked with hers. She felt closer to him than she ever had to another. Whispered conversations in the night with Julia didn't count, because this was very different. This was two adults confiding and sharing, being vulnerable, touching and supporting, letting the other in…

'How did you find out? About the affair, I mean?' Pippa said. 'Gossip, or…?'

'No. It would seem they were actually very discreet. That's why people thought it was Shona and me.'

He smiled at her frown.

'It was pure chance,' he explained. 'Just a couple of things. My parents and I didn't live in each other's pockets. When I started my residency, he was setting up a surgical department in a new hospital in the Middle East.'

'Your mother went with him?'

'Yes. They only came back a couple of years before I left St Bede's.'

'Was it odd?' Pippa asked. 'Working with him?'

'We didn't overlap much, though we were certainly operating within each other's orbit. Still, you know how tight-knit Theatre is?'

'I guess…' Pippa started.

But then she thought back to her training and nodded. Theatre, more than anywhere, had been its own separate world. She thought of her shoes squeaking on the sticky mats as she entered, the flap of doors behind her, and how the nursing staff, at least for the most part, even took all their breaks there.

'Yes,' she now agreed. 'Although since my training—apart from handing over a patient or picking them up in Recovery— I've never really been inside a theatre.'

'I'd heard him laughing a bit more vibrantly in Theatre—his

"holiday laugh", I always call it, because he's a different guy when he's away from the hospital.'

'Nicer?'

'Mmm,' Luke affirmed. 'He lightens up a bit. But suddenly he started to seem a bit more cheerful at work.' He ran a hand down to her waist. 'Perhaps the same way *you've* been more cheerful at work of late.'

'No!' Pippa said, laughing. 'I'm hopefully more discreet than that.'

'You are. Though I guess they were discreet too…that was how they got away with it. If I hadn't been his son I'd never have known.'

'So how *did* you find out?' Pippa asked, and her interest was not so much in the affair but more in how Luke had worked it out.

Even if there was no future for them, she still wanted to know more about him—ached to know more and therefore get closer to this man who enthralled her.

He always would.

Even that inward admission startled Pippa a touch. All this time she'd been telling herself she could do this—could keep things light and enjoy their time together. Yet here they were, on a night like no other, wrapped in each other's bodies, and she was asking him to confide in her.

'You don't have to tell me…'

'That's just it,' Luke said. 'I've never told anyone. But I want to tell you.'

It was the same way he'd felt the need to come here tonight— not just to apologise for messing up her birthday, but because he'd needed to see her. And that was a very unfamiliar feeling, but one he'd chosen *not* to push aside tonight.

'I always get my parents theatre tickets for Christmas— well, I used to,' Luke explained. 'That year I'd got them tickets for *Hamilton*. Anyway, one morning I heard him humming a song from it in the changing room. I didn't have time to give it much thought. I had a big case that I was rushing to get to.'

'How long after Christmas were the tickets for?'

'March,' he said. 'I'd pretty much forgotten about it till I heard him humming, and I made a sort of note in my head to ask him if he'd enjoyed it. But then I remembered that my mother had been away with friends that weekend. I guess I figured they must have changed the tickets. To be honest, I didn't dwell on it. Shona was scrubbing in for me that morning, and I just asked her how come I hadn't seen her recently. Had she been avoiding me? That kind of thing. It was just a joke, but she went so red...'

Pippa was listening intently, and he was enjoying the closeness they shared as he told her his story.

'Then, a little while into the operation, someone asked her if she'd enjoyed *Hamilton* on Saturday. It all just clicked—his singing, him being in a good mood around Theatre more.'

'What did Shona say?'

'Nothing. She was passing me forceps and her hand froze. I looked up from the patient and saw she'd turned scarlet again.'

'You were certain just from that?'

'Shona couldn't even look at me. I realised that she really had been avoiding me—a guilty conscience, I guess. And I found out I was a really good surgeon that morning, because I just got on with the operation.'

'What about Shona?'

'She said she felt unwell and scrubbed out.'

'What a mess...'

He nodded. 'Once the patient was in Recovery, I went to the break room. She followed me in and started crying, grabbing at me and pleading with me not to say anything. Her husband's a senior nurse on the orthopaedic ward. A great guy. She was saying it would break his heart, and I was telling her she should have thought of that before...' He gave her a mirthless smile. 'You know my junior?'

'Fiona?'

'She was a med student then. She, along with a couple of others, walked in on us arguing. I just left. But, given that Shona was standing there crying, they thought I was breaking up with her, or whatever—that it was the two of *us* having an affair. It was a natural assumption, I guess, given that we're closer in age. My father's in his mid-fifties.'

'Gosh. Why didn't you…?'

Pippa's voice faded. The answer was obvious, perhaps, but to her it seemed so unjust that he'd taken the hit.

'I spoke to my father and told him exactly what I thought of him. My leaving wasn't about taking the blame for him, or anything like that. I just couldn't stand to be working along-side him, and nor did I want to work with Shona and face her husband every day, knowing what I knew, but not being able to say anything.'

'Is it still going on?'

'No idea. I haven't spoken to her since, apart from profes-sionally, and nor do I want to. That call earlier was about work. She's on the ICU now.'

'Did you tell your mother?'

'No. I'd already tried that once.'

'It wasn't your father's first affair, then?'

'It wasn't.' He was silent for a long moment before answer-ing. 'I stayed out of it this time.'

'I'm sorry I said anything.'

'It's fine.' He shrugged and sighed. 'The rumours are ev-erywhere. I'm no saint, but I told you, Pippa, that I'd never get involved with someone who was already in a relationship.'

'I know you did.'

'Why do you think I never want to settle down? Or get overly involved with anyone? I trust people, but I don't trust couples. I don't want the hurt or the lies that come, or how people pre-tend things are fine when they're clearly not.' He looked at her. 'I swore off serious relationships and marriage before I'd even made it to medical school—'

He stopped abruptly, as if the memory was something he did not want to revisit.

'Is that why you want to get out of London?' she asked.

* * *

Luke was about to nod, but he knew it wasn't really an honest answer, and it seemed they were all about honesty tonight.

'It certainly factors into my decision not to go back to St Bede's,' he said, then hesitated.

His decision to leave London had been set in stone when he'd returned from the States—sell and get out. Yet now, having told Pippa, he realised that saying everything out loud and having her react so calmly had honestly helped. And, despite the gossip at The Primary, he was enjoying his time there.

London no longer felt like the closed-in, locked-down world from which he'd been so pleased to escape.

Pippa broke his silence. 'You'll be in Scotland soon,' she said. 'Well away from it all...'

'Why don't you come?' He saw her eyes widen. 'I mean, for a visit.'

'Why?' Pippa smiled. 'Because you'll be sex-starved in your little stone cottage?' she teased. And they laughed as they moved in closer to each other. 'Or so you can stand me up in Scotland too?'

'You're not going to let me live that down, are you?' he said, pushing her hair from her face. 'How long did you wait at the restaurant?'

'Half an hour.' She smiled. 'Okay, forty-five minutes, maybe? It was excruciating.'

'Why?' He pulled her closer to him. 'I often eat there alone.'

'In a new dress and dangly earrings at a table set for two?'

'On occasion,' he teased, his hand coming down to her bare arm.

'Did you really buy a new dress?' he asked.

'I did,' Pippa said, because making fun of being stood up in a gorgeous restaurant felt a whole lot better than everything else that had happened. 'And underwear.'

'Damn,' he said, then moved his hand to her smooth naked hips. 'And body lotion...'

'That's not new,' she said. 'I even wore make-up…'

'I'll make it up to you. Your next day off—our next mutual day off—I'll book and we can go again.'

'No way! I am never going back there,' Pippa said, laughing. 'The shame!' She thought of the awful waiter and then she met his eyes. 'It honestly doesn't matter.'

'It honestly does.'

Sometimes his kiss felt like an escape, a fantasy come true, or even a delicious glimpse of paradise—as if their mouths mingling somehow took her to another place. Only, in this predawn morning it didn't feel like that. It felt as if she was exactly there, and so too was Luke. Both together in a place they had somehow made—a place that actually existed.

His kiss was different. Not the rough kiss of earlier, nor the decadent, sexy ones they often shared. This kiss was slower, yet deeper.

She opened her eyes and found that she was staring into his, the contact so probing and direct that she closed her eyes. She felt as if he could see right inside her soul, and if that was true then he might see that there was a place in it reserved only for him.

Yet even as she broke eye contact, still there was nowhere to hide in this bed, where deeper intimacies were being shared.

His hand moved behind her head, with a slight pressure that felt exquisite, and Pippa put her hand on his chest, feeling the soft mat of hair. Then she explored the side of his torso, running her hand down to his waist and relishing her slow perusal of his body as their tongues mingled.

They were soon wrapped around each other, and when she rolled onto her back it was so mutual that Pippa wasn't sure if it was his command or her body's beckoning. His thighs nudged hers apart and she lifted her knees. In her cold bedroom, the warmth they made together felt essential.

Pippa heard her own soft moan as he squeezed inside her. Luke had propped himself up on his elbows, but she could still feel his delicious body pinning her to the bed. He moved, slowly at first, but so deeply that she felt a tightening low in her stomach. Her thighs parted further to allow for more intensity.

'Pip…'

For the first time she didn't object to the shortening of her name. There was no breath left to waste on such irrelevancies anyway.

His pace did not increase, and yet with each measured stroke Pippa felt as if she was falling apart. Even as she tightened beneath him and turned her head from his kiss he would not let her hide, and he moved her head to face him. Pippa put up her hand to bring his head down, but he removed it and pinned her arms behind her head, then looked at her as he moved deep inside.

'Pippa…'

He was up on his forearms, and she knew he was asking her to look at him. She knew that even if she kept her eyes closed she would still be letting him in to that place reserved solely for him.

She was coming undone, starting to cry, sobbing his name, and still he did not relent—he only thrust deeper. His breath was hot on her cheek as he finally increased his speed, suddenly moving too fast for her to think. She was always thinking—but for a second all thought stopped. Her hips rose in an urgent and involuntary motion as she climaxed and felt him still. Then came his breathless moan, and as she ached with the end of her orgasm he took her straight back there again, reviving her intimate pulses as he came deep inside.

She could feel the sheen of sweat on his arms as he collapsed onto her, and the coolness of her own tears on her cheeks. She was silently appalled at her capitulation…at the fact that she'd let go as much as she just had.

And now her mind was back, trying to count how many times they had made love in their short time together. She scanned her memory…

Then she heard the bleep of his phone, and as he rolled off her Pippa knew, with absolute certainty, that she'd just made love for the very first time.

* * *

As his phone alarm demanded they part, Luke hit snooze for the first time since they'd been together.

'Pippa…?' He too sounded as if he had found himself in an alien world.

'What?' Pippa asked, perhaps a little abruptly. But she was trying to catch her breath, and was terrified by what had just happened between them.

He was going to tell her that things had got too intense, she was certain. Had he read in her eyes or felt in her body the love she'd been trying to hide? After she'd sworn not to love him.

'Pippa,' he said again. 'We didn't use anything.'

Oh, was that all?

In the grand scheme of things, it didn't seem as earth-shattering as her most recent realisation, Pippa thought. He was probably panicking in case his bachelor life was over.

'It's fine.' She looked back at him. 'I'm on the Pill.'

'Even so…'

'Luke, you're on call.'

It wasn't like ward round mornings when he could risk being a bit late. The pagers would be handed over, and it wasn't fair to anyone if he wasn't there.

'You need to get ready.'

He nodded and, like the secret soldier she had begun to suspect he was, he rolled out of bed. Thoughtful as ever, he turned on her electric blanket before heading to the shower.

Pippa tried to correct her thoughts. It couldn't be love because that took two, she reasoned. Still, it had been intense, that sudden move from safe sex—both figuratively and emotionally—to soft, slow sex.

She lay there as he used her tiny shower, feeling the tension that had lived in her for ever starting to return.

She was falling deeper into this man, when she'd honestly hoped that this month together might break the spell of him. Always before the gloss had worn off…always she'd backed off because they'd got too close…

This time, though, *she* was the guilty party.

Oh, where is my casual lover mask? Pippa thought as he came out of the shower and started to dress.

'We need to talk, Pippa,' he said as he knotted his tie. 'Look, I'm sorry I didn't take better care this morning. It hasn't happened before—I always wear protection—but I'm happy to go and get checked if it makes you feel any better.'

'Checked?' Pippa frowned and, despite the blanket starting to warm up, she felt the same goosebumps she had last night.

She felt a sudden sense of panic, as she wondered if he was asking if she carried the CF gene, and what his reaction would be if she told him she did.

But that wasn't what Luke was asking.

'If you're worried I've got anything…' He was matter of fact. 'Though I'm sure there's no problem.'

No problem? It wasn't the unprotected sex that was the problem…

She could deny it no more.

Luke Harris was back in her life and again he was taking over her heart.

CHAPTER TEN

SOME DAYS, PAEDIATRIC nursing was the best job in the world.
Others…

Evan was dealing with the awful practicalities that death brought, while Amber was in with the child psychologist, working out the best way to tell Darcy about his twin.

Pippa was just clearing his IVAC when the question came.

'Where's Hamish?'

'Why don't I get Mummy…?' Pippa started, but was saved from having to avoid the issue by fetching his mother because Amber had walked in.

'Darcy was just asking where Hamish was,' Pippa explained.

'Were you, Darcy?' Amber said as she limped over on her booted leg, taking a seat in what must be an extremely painful position on the edge of her son's bed.

'Would you like me to leave you?' Pippa offered, but Amber shook her head.

'Stay,' Amber said, and then took a deep breath and gently told her son the simple truth. 'Hamish has died, darling.'

'So when is he coming back?'

Pippa put her hand on Amber's shoulder to support the poor mother as she tried to do what was best for her remaining child.

She answered his question as simply as she could. 'He won't be coming back.'

'Ever?'

'Ever,' Amber said.

'Like when Yoyo died?'

'Yes,' Amber replied gently, stroking his hair and talking to Pippa. 'Yoyo was the boys' budgie.'

'Will Hamish go in a box in the garden too?'

'No. There's a special garden for people.' Amber's voice was shaking, and yet she was being so tender with her explanations. 'And when you're well enough, we'll go and visit the garden.'

'Is he there now?'

'No, not till next Friday,' Amber told him. 'Mummy and Daddy are going to go and say goodbye, and when you're well enough, and ready, we'll take you too.'

'You're crying, Mummy,' said Darcy, and his little hand went to her cheek.

'Because I'm sad. You'll be sad at times too, but that's okay. We'll look after each other and give each other cuddles... Can I have one now, please?'

As Darcy wrapped his arms around his mum's neck she hugged him back hard and then quietly addressed Pippa.

'Thanks,' she said. 'I think we'll be fine now.'

Very few things made Pippa cry. Actually, until Luke had brought her undone last night, nothing really had. But hearing Amber being so gentle with her son brought a rare flash of tears.

She sniffed them back and went to tell Nola, along with Luke, who was updating his notes, that Darcy had now been told about his twin.

'Amber was really good with him,' Pippa said, and repeated what Darcy had said and his concept of death. 'He knows that his brother's...' She felt the unfamiliar sting of tears threaten again, and excused herself.

'You okay?' Luke checked, when he found her back in her default position of pouring boiling water on a teabag in the break room.

'I'm fine.'

'It's tough.'

'Yes,' Pippa agreed, unsure why she had used that tone of voice when he was just being nice. 'I'm going to have tea.'

She added sugar and pulled out the teabag, and then added too much milk.

'Pippa,' he said, halting her, 'it's fine to be upset.'

'I know.' She nodded but then, desperate to escape his scrutiny, she walked off.

'Pippa!' he called her back. 'Can we talk about last night?'

She felt her back stiffen. It was as if last night she'd revealed a glimpse of her soul, and now she truly wished he hadn't.

'If there are any repercussions...' Luke said. 'I know you said you're on the—'

'Luke!' Her eyes flashed a warning. 'We're at work.'

'No one can hear us.'

To make extra sure, he closed the door.

'Someone might come in!'

'What? And catch us *talking*?'

He walked over to the large kitchen table and took a biscuit from a packet before leaning on it.

'Let's give them something to talk about. *Ooh, Luke Harris was eating a biscuit,*' he mimicked, *'and Pippa Westford was drinking tea.'*

She let out a soft laugh and knew she was being paranoid. And it wasn't her colleagues she was worried about catching them.

She was worried that Luke might see into her heart.

'You were upset when I mentioned getting checked. Did you think I meant for CF?'

He was trying to have a very sensible conversation, she knew. And because he was a doctor, and knew about Julia, he was facing it head-on.

'Is it a concern?' he asked, and she knew he was asking if she was a carrier of the gene.

'Luke, I've told you—there's nothing to worry about. My sister died of a congenital illness. And as if I'd leave contraception up to a guy...' She watched his eyebrow rise as she hit a little below the belt.

'Have you been tested?' he asked.

'I'm not going to have this conversation—and certainly not

at work. Why would I open up with someone who won't even be here this time next week?'

'Pippa, I always said I was leaving.'

'You always did,' she agreed.

'It's actually next Saturday that my contract ends. I'm not flying off on the first plane out, but even so, it's best we address this now.'

She simply did not know how to be close to someone—to a man—and certainly not to one who was leaving. They were only ever supposed to be temporary. She took her Pill religiously, because she carried the gene, and the only person whose business that was, was hers.

'There's nothing to address,' she told him.

'Good,' he said, and turned to go.

But as he reached to open the door Luke apparently changed his mind.

'For the record, you haven't opened up at all...'

'Why would I?' she asked. 'You probably wouldn't remember if I did anyway.'

'Am I sensing some resentment here? Because I don't remember a conversation fourteen years ago?'

'Of course not!' she attempted, but she knew she'd raised the subject once too often, and this time Luke didn't let it go.

'Am I being chastised because I didn't fancy you when you were sixteen? That's not very MeToo of you...'

'Stop it!' She actually laughed. How was he able to do that? To make her laugh on what was a very sad day? In a way that made a harsh world a little softer somehow?

For both of them.

Luke knew she'd been in with Darcy, and that this morning would have been very hard, so he reeled in his own frustrations.

'I'm sorry I don't remember,' he said.

'It's fine. You told me you wanted to be a drummer...'

'I think you're mixing me up with someone else,' he said with a frown. 'I've never even played the drums.'

'It was definitely you. You'd been crying that day. Your eyes were all red.'

'Probably because I'd been swimming.'

'No.' She shook her head. 'You had double sport later that afternoon.'

'What? Do you have a super-memory, or something?'

Only where he was concerned, she thought ruefully.

But rather than admit to that, she shrugged.

'I don't know. Maybe I am mixing you up.'

She forced out a smile and remembered that they'd agreed upon fun times only. She'd told him and herself that she could do this...

She just wished she could convince her heart, but it was still busy furiously objecting.

CHAPTER ELEVEN

THEY TRIED TO get back to being casual lovers, but the genie refused to return to its bottle.

'Here,' Pippa said, as she entered his flat the next night, holding the massive pot plant. 'I've brought you a present.'

'Please, no…'

'Well, it was you who suggested I come straight here after my late shift,' Pippa reminded him. 'Anyway, it would take up half my flat. She does this every year.'

'Your aunt?'

'Yes, and every year I have to rehome a plant.' She deposited it in an alcove by the fireplace in the lounge. 'It looks nice.'

'I'll kill it,' he warned.

When he looked at the vast pot plant his smile faded as he realised why her aunt did this each year—no doubt to prompt her colleagues, or to push the reticent Pippa into revealing that it was her birthday.

It made his heart constrict, and he looked from the plant to her, but Pippa was all smiles.

'You said we had to walk the puppy.'

'So I did.'

It was frosty outside and Pippa said that she thought they might get snow.

'It's too soon for snow,' he said, as the little dog shivered, and pawed at Luke's legs every time he tried to put him down on the pavement.

He sighed as he gave in and picked the puppy up, and they walked around the corner to a small park, where they sat on a bench, hoping Sausage would wee on the grass. But still he scampered to be picked up.

'How was Darcy?' Luke asked.

While usually he tried to leave work at work, he couldn't help but enquire about this patient.

'He's drinking a little bit.'

'Still not eating?'

'No.'

'Is he talking?'

'Not really,' Pippa said. 'I think—' She halted.

'Go on.'

'He's just hurting.'

'Have you spoken to him?'

'Of course.'

'I mean, about losing your sister?'

'I'm hardly going to unburden myself to a five-year—'

'Pippa,' he warned, halting her prickly reply. 'We both know you're not going to *unburden* yourself to Darcy. Have you spoken to him?'

'No.'

He left it there, and watched as Pippa stared into the night.

'Are we okay?' he checked.

'Of course.'

'Did I scare you by asking you to come to Scotland?'

Gosh, Pippa thought, she really must be playing it cool if he thought *that* was what was on her mind.

'Nothing like that,' she said. 'It's a nice offer. I just...'

She flailed about for a reason to explain why she was stalling. How to explain without fully revealing that saying goodbye next week was going to be hard enough.

'The off-duty roster isn't up yet.'

'Fair enough.' He nodded at her casual reply. 'Good boy!' Luke cheered as the puppy finally did a wee, and then added for Pippa's ears only, 'Mind you, he squats like a girl.'

'I don't think they lift their legs until they're older.'

'The things you learn...'

And they were back... Back to protected sex and laughter... back to cramming everything in.

Jenny had had some spare tickets to an interactive theatre production which Pippa had bought from her.

'I have no idea what it's about,' Pippa told Luke as they were admitted.

'I'd better not get tickets to this for my parents,' Luke said jokingly as they walked from room to room, watching the most torrid scenes.

There was an awful lot of nudity—full-frontal and everything.

'Good heavens!' Luke exclaimed as they stepped back into the night. 'Are you trying to corrupt me, Pippa Westford?'

'Blame Jenny,' Pippa said.

They stood facing each other and she put her arms up on his shoulders.

'It was fun,' he admitted. 'Though I'm not quite sure what it was supposed to be.'

'Maybe you *should* get tickets for your parents...'

'Maybe...' He gave a half-smile. 'Did I tell you my father called me? That he wants us to go for a drink?'

'No.' Pippa shook her head. 'Will you go?'

'I don't know.' Luke shrugged.

Try as Pippa might, she still couldn't get the genie back in his bottle. And sometimes she forgot to keep things casual.

'I'd kill for my mum to call me and ask me to go for a drink,' Pippa admitted. 'Luke, he clearly cares about you.'

And sometimes Luke, too, forgot not to go in too deep. because as they stood outside the theatre, instead of kissing her, or hailing a taxi to take them back to his flat, he asked the question that had plagued him for years.

'Then why does he play Russian Roulette with his marriage?'

'It's *his* marriage he's dicing with,' Pippa said. 'You'll always be his son. Talk to him.'

'We'll see…' He looked right at her. 'Have you ever told your parents how you feel?'

'No,' Pippa admitted.

'Isn't that a little hypocritical?'

'True.'

She laughed, and so did Luke.

They were safely back on track…

Bound for nowhere.

CHAPTER TWELVE

KIM WAS GIVING the night hand-over.

'Luke suggested that the parents bring in his favourite take-away for Darcy.'

Pippa raised her eyebrows, because she'd rather thought she'd gleaned his stance on that a few weeks ago. 'Did he eat it?'

'No.' Kim sighed. 'Well, one little French fry. But he wasn't really interested. The parents have to go and meet with the undertakers this morning. They want to do that together, but they're worried about leaving him.'

Nola looked over to Pippa. 'Can you special him today?' she asked. 'I'll give you Cot Four as well, but she's got her mother with her and is due to be discharged. I won't give you anyone else—well, not if I can help it...'

Darcy had refused breakfast and much to his mother's upset didn't seem remotely fazed when she kissed him goodbye before going to meet her husband.

'I can help Darcy with his lunch,' Pippa said to Amber as she filled a bowl from the sink to wash him. 'If you need a little longer.'

'Thank you,' Amber responded anxiously, and then gave Darcy another kiss before leaving.

Pippa followed her outside. 'I'll call you if he needs you, I promise, so take all the time you need.'

'What time are you on till?'

'Four,' Pippa said. 'I can push it till five, though, if necessary.'

'We have to take in an outfit...' Tears started streaming

down Amber's face and Pippa guided her into one of the side rooms. 'I can't bear it, Pippa.'

Pippa put her arms around her as she wept for a moment.

'I don't want Darcy to see me like this.'

'I know,' Pippa said, admiring Amber for being able to cry gently with her son, but not so much that it scared him.

'I feel like I've lost Darcy too,' Amber sobbed. 'He barely speaks...'

'It's early days,' Pippa soothed.

But then she thought of what Luke had said and knew—or rather felt—that it was right for her to step up. As well as that, she had her second interview for the PAC Unit tomorrow, and wanted to test out if she could bring her very private past into work.

'I lost my sister,' Pippa told Amber, and she felt her go still in her arms. 'I was much older than Darcy, and we weren't twins, but there's such a bond...'

'Was it sudden?' Amber gulped—polite responses were forgotten when you were drowning in grief.

'No.' Pippa shook her head. 'But I remember being seven and nearly losing her.' She looked at Amber. 'Do you want me to try talking to Darcy? He might be scared of upsetting you.'

'Please,' she said, shivering. 'But only...'

'I'll be gentle,' Pippa reassured her. 'You go and see Hamish.'

Pippa was washing Darcy from top to toe.

'Your bruises are turning yellow,' Pippa said as she rinsed his little back. 'You look like you've been fighting with paint!'

She turned him onto his back and knew her light-hearted chatter wasn't helping. She tried to remember being five, but it was all a bit of a blur.

She'd loved nursery—that she did remember—and she recalled coming home and finding her mother crying in her bedroom...and her selfish wish that she'd still be able to go to the nativity play that night. That her mother would stop crying and that things would be okay...normal...

Whatever normal was.

It was lunchtime, and Darcy was gagging on a spoonful of mashed potato, when Pippa put down the spoon and spoke to him.

'I'm so sorry you're hurting, Darcy.'

He looked down at the dressings on his tummy.

'I meant here,' Pippa said, and tapped his little chest. 'Your heart's hurting. That's how I felt when my sister died.'

He didn't answer, but his big grey eyes didn't pool with tears, and for the first time they properly met hers.

'You're going to be okay, Darcy,' Pippa said, gently but firmly, in case he was scared that he might be about to suddenly die to.

Then she thought of what she'd used to wish for most in the world—Julia too.

'Mummy and Daddy are going to be okay, too. They're very sad, but they will be okay.'

She knew in her heart that in Darcy's case this was true. His parents were doing everything they could to take care of both their little boys.

'They love you so much.'

And then he said some words that cut through her heart. 'I want Hamish.'

'I know you do.' Pippa nodded. 'I wanted Julia—that was my sister—so badly after she died. She was the only person I could really talk to. She was my best friend.'

Darcy nodded, as if she'd finally said something he understood.

'I was so sad, and I needed her so much, but she wasn't there any more.'

He started to cry, and Pippa cuddled him and let him weep.

'You can always tell Mummy and Daddy when you feel sad.'

'But then *they'll* cry.'

'And that's okay,' Pippa said. 'Mummy has said to you that you can all be sad together, but I promise you will smile and laugh too, even if you can't believe that now.'

Darcy pulled back, and Pippa thought that she herself was

going to cry when he picked up his teddy bear. 'I want Hamish to have Whiskers.'

'What about Coco?' Pippa carefully asked, referring to his brother's bear.

'I want Hamish to have Whiskers *and* Coco.'

She held on to the teddy for a moment and looked at the bear's glassy eyes. She knew this was something for Amber and Evan to negotiate.

Then she looked at Darcy who, now he had cried, was ready to sleep. 'Why don't you cuddle Whiskers for now?'

'And then Hamish can have him?'

'No!' Amber was aghast at the idea.

She'd returned from the undertaker's holding Hamish's bear, Coco. Nola was there, and Luke, who was writing up some notes on another child, just happened to be in the office. He had put down his pen and was listening.

Amber was adamant. 'I've brought Hamish's bear for Darcy to have. They should be together.' Her eyes flashed at Pippa, loaded with accusation. 'What on earth did you say to him?'

Luke watched quietly, wincing inside when Amber reared, but Pippa took it well.

'I told him how I felt when I lost my sister.' Pippa had already reported back on the conversation she'd had with Darcy, and she responded calmly. 'Giving Hamish his own bear was Darcy's idea.'

Evan took his wife's hand. 'Darcy wanted him to have it even before Hamish...' He couldn't complete the sentence.

'But he might regret it.' Amber looked to Nola, who gave a small nod, and then to Luke, who opened his mouth and then closed it again.

'What if he changes his mind?' Amber demanded. 'What do I tell him then?'

'He wants to do this for Hamish,' Pippa reiterated. 'He's going to be sad and upset, whatever you decide. He's always going to miss his brother.'

'I don't know what to do,' Amber sobbed into Hamish's bear.

'Pippa's right,' Evan said.

'There's no right or wrong in this situation,' Pippa said, and took a breath. 'But I think Darcy wants to do something for his brother. Why don't you go and see him with both bears, and talk to him about it?'

Nola stood. 'I'll take you to him.'

Nola helped Amber stand, and Pippa watched as Evan pulled some tissues from the box on the table and wiped his eyes before putting his arm around his wife as they headed off to see their son.

'Thank goodness you answered,' Luke said, taking up his pen. 'I had no idea what to say.'

'They're so good with him,' Pippa said. 'In all their grief for Hamish, they still think of Darcy every step of the way.'

'They do,' Luke agreed. 'What were your—?'

He halted, knowing this wasn't the time or place—especially when the ever-indiscreet Jenny came in.

Then again, Luke thought, it was never the time or place when it came to Pippa…

'Nola's crying her eyes out in the loo,' Jenny informed them.

'Yes,' Luke responded gruffly, feeling a bit choked up himself. 'We've just had the Great Teddy Bear Debate, so go easy on Nola.'

'I know,' Jenny said, pulling some tissues from the same box that Evan had used and blowing her nose. 'She told me…'

To Luke's surprise, the formidable Jenny sat on one of the chairs and started to cry.

'I might crochet something,' Jenny suggested. 'For both of them.'

'That's a lovely idea,' Pippa said, and went and sat on the armrest. She shot Luke a quick *yikes* look. 'But I think that's something for the parents to work out.'

She gave Luke a small smile as she put an arm around Jenny, and it hit Luke then that he still didn't get Pippa. Okay, he didn't know Jenny's past, and he understood that Nola might be emotional…but, hell, even the hardened Luke felt moved by the parents' plight. Yet the one member of staff who should be dissolving, wasn't. The person who had lost a sibling, and who had dealt with Darcy's questions, as well as the distraught parents, was sitting on an armrest, comforting Jenny, when surely she must be in agony.

'Go home,' Jenny said to Pippa, while blowing her nose. 'You're supposed to be finished. You're off tomorrow, aren't you?'

'Yes,' Pippa said. 'Then back for nights.'

And Luke was stuck here.

'See you,' she said, and smiled at him just as she would if it were Martha, or Nola, or anyone else sitting in the office.

He nodded, and when Pippa had gone he flashed a smile to a still watery-eyed Jenny. 'I'll give you some privacy...'

Luke caught up with Pippa at the elevators. 'Are you okay?'

'Of course.'

'Amber didn't mean—'

'Luke, I do know what to expect from grieving parents.'

'Of course,' Luke said, but he knew how tough it must have been. Still, clearly Pippa didn't want to talk about. 'I've booked the restaurant for Saturday.'

'What restaurant?'

'The French one.'

'No way!' Pippa shot out a laugh.

'Well, I might have something to celebrate. Your pot plant seems to be working. I've got a couple coming back for a second look on Friday.'

'Fingers crossed,' Pippa said, wishing her lift would hurry up and arrive.

She was still in the land of teddies, and not up to being flirty and fun—and as well as that she had art class tonight, and was really not in the mood.

'What are you up to tonight?' she asked him.

'I might go for that drink with my father,' he said. 'Can't keep putting it off.'

'Well, I hope it goes well,' Pippa said as her elevator arrived. It didn't feel quite enough. 'He is clearly trying...' she started, but then she reminded herself that what they had was fun, casual, flirty, and most of all temporary. Instead, she only said, 'Good luck.'

'Thanks,' he said. 'Enjoy your class!'

Tonight it was guided art, and they all attempted to follow the teacher and paint a view of Santorini... Only Greek islands and oil paint weren't the best mix for Pippa's dark mood.

The scent of paint and turps reminded her so much of art class back when she was at school, and how she'd mourned not just Julia but also Luke. And the thought of hurt soon to come turned the gorgeous Aegean Sea an ominous grey, and made the little fluffy white cloud over the domed buildings dark...

'Wow,' Cassie said as she came round to inspect her work. 'There's some storm brewing in Santorini!'

There was.

Taking her painting home, she was ridiculously desperate to stop at Luke's. She wanted to make a stupid joke as she handed over her painting...only she couldn't pretend for much longer that she wasn't falling apart on the inside.

She wanted to tell him her fears about the interview tomorrow. And to sob her heart out about Darcy...to be in Luke's arms when she told him how hard it had been to relive the confusion and terror she'd felt as a child.

But he was leaving soon...

And, no, she didn't want a couple of weeks in Skye to visit him and prolong the agony...

He might be trying to get closer to her, but Pippa was certain that if Luke knew the magnitude of her feelings he would break the sound barrier running away.

Pippa loved him.

She didn't feel sixteen all over again, when she'd felt so lost and alone.

Pippa felt thirty and adrift...

And dreadfully, scarily in love with Luke.

CHAPTER THIRTEEN

'PIPPA!' LUKE SMILED in recognition and then, looking at her unusually smooth hair, all neatly tied back, he frowned. 'You look very smart.'

'Thanks.'

'I'm guessing you're not up in Human Resources to sort out your leave or your pay?'

'Sorry…?' She frowned. and then gave a small shake of her head. 'Oh! No, I'm not.' She glanced up at the time. 'I really have to go…'

'Good luck,' he called.

Pippa swung around and frowned.

'For your interview.'

Pippa gave a wry smile. 'Has Nola been gossiping again?'

'I don't think so. At least, she didn't say anything to me.' He put his head on one side in a knowing gesture. 'Just a guess. I know interviews for the new wing are taking place at the moment.'

He looked down at the grey dress she had worn on their first date, now styled more formally with heels and such.

'I'm surprised you didn't say anything.'

'I haven't got the job yet. I messed up the first interview.'

His eyes widened. 'So this is your second?'

'Yes.'

'Yet you never mentioned it?'

Pippa knew it was quite an omission, and she could see he was a touch offended—possibly even hurt.

'We're not a couple,' she pointed out. 'You said at the start—'

'That was at the start, Pippa! Things have changed—or at least I thought they had. We were talking about Scotland…or I was… Hell, I've told you things I've never discussed with anyone—ever. And you've told me…' He looked upwards then, as if scanning back over all their conversations, their moments, their time. 'Nothing.'

'That's not true.'

'It's close,' he said. 'Because if I hadn't already known about Julia you'd never have said anything.' He took a breath. 'Look, I'm not going to get into this discussion now, because you've got an interview. Is it for Nola's job?'

'No.' She raked a hand through her hair. 'It's for the PAC Unit. Paediatric—'

'I know what PAC stands for.' He nodded, and then, because he did know about Julia, he seemed to understand immediately why she might want to work there. 'You can't have done that badly if they've called you back.'

'Believe me, I wasn't expecting them to. The first interview really was a bit of a disaster. I just…'

'What?'

'Clammed up,' Pippa admitted, 'and gave bland answers.'

'Of course you did.' He gave a wry smile.

'What does that mean?'

Her voice was defensive, she knew, but then her shoulders dropped. Because she also knew he was speaking the truth.

'I'm scared of saying the wrong thing,' she admitted, but it was only half an admission. 'I'm dreadful at conflict.'

'Good!' Luke said, and made her blink. 'Do you really think they want to hire someone who thinks they're brilliant at conflict? That's a red flag if ever there was one!'

She gave a reluctant smile. He made a very good point.

'And you are good,' he added. 'You stood up to Jenny when she was being mean about a mum…'

'That's not conflict.'

'It doesn't have to be a boxing gloves situation to be considered conflict.'

He'd made her feel better—at least, he'd stilled her racing heart enough for her to admit her greatest fear.

'I'm worried I might get overly emotional if I…'

'Pippa, I can't even imagine…' He paused, looking around him. 'How long till the interview?'

She glanced at her phone. 'Fifteen minutes.'

'You're early for once! You must really want this job?'

'Yes.'

'Try opening up a bit, Pippa.'

'I don't know how,' she admitted, but then she shook her head. 'I can't do this.'

'Yes,' he said, as if he'd decided that it had to be now. 'You can.'

He steered her out of the main traffic of the corridor and to the side of some vast noticeboard displaying plans for the new wing of the hospital.

And maybe it was because she really wanted the job, or perhaps because Luke Harris was so incredible that he could somehow manage to stop clocks as well as her heart, she decided that he was right, and maybe she could share a little of her fear.

It was more terrifying to be here than in the interview, standing in front of Luke, about to admit a deep and painful truth.

'Everything leads back to Julia…'

'Of course it does.'

She blinked at his matter-of-fact response, but then shook her head. 'I don't want to walk into an interview and get upset, or…'

'Show yourself?'

'I didn't say that.'

'No, *I* did. Pippa, it's not just in interviews. You hold back all the time.'

Luke was wondering if now really was the right time for this conversation. He knew she held herself back. In truth, her reluctance to get emotionally involved with anyone had appealed at first. After all, wasn't that perfect for a temporary relationship?

Only he felt that now he had become emotionally involved, perhaps more than he wanted to be—or more than Pippa wanted him to be. He'd seen her. He'd seen the Pippa behind the barriers she put up—or perhaps it would be more accurate to say that he'd *glimpsed* her at times. Not just in bed, but sometimes when she looked up and smiled, or when they sat waiting for a puppy to wee... And the real Pippa, when she wasn't hiding, was so direct and so stunning that she really had blown him away.

'I know why they called you back,' he told her.

'Why?' Pippa frowned.

'Because they saw that there was more.' He thought for a moment. 'Of *course* everything goes back to Julia. How could it not? The things that happen to us—'

'Define us?' She almost sneered. 'Shape us?'

'No.' He shook his head. 'But we learn from them. Why do you think I've sworn off relationships and refuse to rely on anyone else?'

'That's not learning, Luke.' She gave an impatient shake of her head. 'Your parents' marriage makes you swear off relationships for life. That's hardly learning...'

'I'm just trying to say...'

He closed his eyes in frustration—not only because she was right, but also because she was wrong! Lately, thanks to Pippa, he *was* learning that things weren't all black and white.

'Okay, I'm not the best example, but you have learnt from your family—'

Pippa cut in with the truth then. 'I'm scared I'll break down.'

'Okay...'

'I haven't cried...not really. Not since...'

'Since...?'

'I honestly can't remember. Since I was four, maybe, or five,' she admitted. 'And I don't want it to be at work, and I certainly don't want it to be in there.'

She pointed to the interview room and Luke looked down the corridor. He'd known she was closed off, but hadn't realised just how serious it was.

She hadn't cried since she was four or five?

'You could postpone the interview,' he suggested. 'I'll even write you a doctor's note!'

'I don't want to postpone it.'

'Okay…' He had a think. 'You did well with Amber and Darcy.'

'Because I was worrying about them—not me.'

'Okay, worst-case scenario, maybe you'll cry a bit if you talk about Julia. Just don't boo-hoo.'

'That's far from my worst-case scenario!' she dismissed. 'Thanks for the sage advice, Luke.'

'Pip, listen to me.' He touched the top of her arm. 'You can talk about your sister if you're up to it, but the moment you've had enough, you stop it right there.'

'How?'

'Oh, what did you say to me?' He smiled. 'That night in The Avery? Something like, *"I don't want to talk about it."* It doesn't matter if it's an interview—you still get to say that.'

She chewed her lip doubtfully, but Luke had enough confidence for them both.

'Look how you've helped Darcy and his parents.' He gave her a soft smile. 'The teddy debate…'

She nodded.

'I had no idea what to say.' He was shepherding her towards the interview room now. 'I doubt many would.'

'There's no right or wrong…'

'Sometimes there is,' Luke said, thinking of his own ineptitude when it came to certain conversations. 'You're good at knowing it.'

It was Pippa who frowned now, but as they reached the bench where she was to wait, he snapped his fingers to get her attention back.

'You could help guide them because you've been there.'

'I haven't lost a child…'

'You were speaking up for Darcy,' he said. 'And you were good at that.'

'What if I—?'

'Worst-case scenario?' he checked.

'What if I lose it?'

'If you're really about to crack, then say one of your contact lenses has fallen out and excuse yourself,' Luke suggested. 'Though I doubt it'll come to that.'

She nodded.

'Okay. Just go in there and show them the real Pippa...'

'Philippa.' She gave him a wry smile. 'They keep calling me Philippa. It's very off-putting!'

'Then tell them you prefer Pippa.' He gave her a squeeze on the arm. 'Best wishes, Pip.'

'Not good luck?' she checked.

'It's not luck you need. Just be yourself.'

'What if they don't want that?'

'Then it's their tough luck.'

'Come through, Philippa.'

It was quite a panel that Pippa found herself facing, but before taking her seat in front of them she took a breath.

'Actually, most people call me Pippa.' She sat down. 'Except my parents when they're cross.'

She was prepared for all their questions, and she also went through her nursing experience and said how keen she was to be part of the start of a new venture.

'Yet I see that you only applied recently,' one of the directors interrupted. 'We've been advertising for some time.'

'I wanted to be very sure,' Pippa admitted. 'There was an Acting Unit Manager role on my ward. However, I realised I didn't want to apply for a caretaking role. If I'm going to be a unit manager, then I'd want to make the role my own.'

'It would be a demanding role,' the director said, and then quizzed her on what she'd achieved in her previous roles relating to standards.

Pippa had practised, so she answered more smoothly this time. Then came the awful conflict question again.

'How do you deal with it?'

'I try to avoid it,' Pippa admitted wryly, and instead of it being the completely wrong answer she saw that a couple of them smiled. 'It's probably my weakness—personally, that is—but professionally, I know there are times when you can't avoid it.'

'What about angry parents?'

'Most of the time they're more upset than angry,' Pippa said. 'Or frustrated. Or scared...' She spoke from the heart, rather than from the cheat sheet she'd memorised. 'I think moving them away from the child—'

'That can be hard to do.'

'Not usually.' Pippa shook her head. 'I've generally found that if you tell the parent that a conversation might be better had away from their child, most agree, and then you can hopefully address whatever it is really concerning them.'

'Okay.' It was Miss Brett's turn now. 'What would you like to see implemented on the PAC Unit?' she asked, then took off her glasses and stared at Pippa. 'If you were given carte blanche, and could do anything at all?'

Pippa thought of Luke, urging her to be herself, and it made her feel brave enough to answer once again from her heart.

'I'd have a study area,' Pippa said, 'for siblings.' She saw Miss Brett blink. 'And a lounge, perhaps. Somewhere they can charge their phones, take a break, be apart but not far away....'

'A study area for siblings?' Miss Brett frowned, but it wasn't a dismissive frown, more an interested one. 'Why do you suggest that?'

'I had a very ill sister,' Pippa said. 'She died when I was sixteen.'

'I'm so sorry,' Miss Brett offered, and there was moment of silence, but not a strained one, as Pippa nodded to her offer of water.

'Thank you,' Pippa said.

'Do you mind us asking how old your sister was when she died?'

'Eighteen,' Pippa said. Her voice wavered, but she chose to push on, ready to talk a little about Julia. 'She'd just been accepted into St Andrew's to study History.'

Pippa gave a fond smile, but as she thought back to that time she found it was a double-edged sword. The fond memories of her sister were tinged with her own private heartache that she'd hidden so fiercely until now. She thought again of what Luke had said, about showing her true self, speaking up…

She felt a pinch in her nose that signalled tears. 'Excuse me,' she said, and took out a tissue and blew her nose, then forced herself to speak on. 'I didn't do very well at school—at least not as well as I'd hoped to.' She wanted to explain better…to speak honestly about that time. 'I was always behind with homework and catching up. My sister's illness took precedence—of course it did.'

'How were your parents?'

'Julia was their world,' Pippa said. 'She still is…'

Miss Brett gave her a long, assessing stare. 'They haven't got over it?'

'No. There was bereavement counselling offered, but they never…' She couldn't quite go there, and neither did she want to. 'I really don't want to go into that here,' Pippa said.

Luke was right—she didn't have to.

She turned the conversation back to the interview, though with a personal slant. 'I don't know if there's anything the hospital staff could have done to change the trajectory for my parents, but I do know how the kindness and thoughtfulness shown to me by them meant the world.'

'It's very easy for the well sibling, or siblings, to get lost,' Miss Brett said, nodding. 'Overlooked…' She paused and thought for a long moment. 'A study area for siblings…' She turned to another member of the panel and asked to see the floor plans for the unit, then looked back to Pippa. 'Their own locker, perhaps? Or at least some stationery supplies.'

'And a printer,' Pippa said, and felt her heart start to hammer as she realised her suggestion was being taken seriously.

Then they moved on to speak about their prospective patients, the variety in their ages and conditions. How teenage boys with fragile bones who shouldn't be getting into fights all too often did. How an appendix didn't care if you were already a cancer patient—it just flared up.

It didn't feel like an interview any more, more like an exchange of ideas, and when it concluded Pippa felt that even if she didn't get the position there might still be a study room for siblings incorporated into their plans.

And birthdays would hopefully be remembered.

'How did it go?'

Luke was waiting for her outside.

'It went well, I think.'

'Did you tell them about…?'

'Luke!' She put her hand up to stop him, still attempting to hold herself together.

And then she remembered something she hadn't asked him earlier because she had been so focused on the interview.

'How did things go with your father last night?'

'They didn't.'

'You cancelled?'

'I never asked.'

'But—'

It was Luke's turn to raise a hand, warning her to leave it.

'We should apply for jobs as traffic controllers,' Luke said, and made her laugh. 'Let's go to The Avery.'

They went to the bar this time, rather than the restaurant.

'What do you want?' he asked.

'Champagne,' Pippa said.

'Celebrating?'

'No, I'm just spending your money while you're still here,' she teased.

'Pardon?'

'It was a joke!'

'I didn't hear what you said.'

She went on tiptoe and got an extra dose of his citrussy scent. 'I said…' She cupped her hand and whispered into his ear, 'I'm just spending your money—'

'Enjoy!' Luke said, laughing. 'That dress is making me think unholy thoughts,' he told her, and looking down she saw it was starting to gape. He picked up a strand of previously straightened hair, which was now starting to curl. 'We could take a bottle to yours…'

'I like it here,' Pippa said.

Nice loud music…where you almost had to shout to be heard. So loud that if she blurted out that she loved him, or begged him not to go, he'd put his hand to his ear and ask, *What did you say?*

Safe.

CHAPTER FOURTEEN

'No way that's Santorini.'

Luke was ready for work and pulling on his jacket while looking at her attempt from art class the other night.

'It's like a Goya painting,' Luke went on, referring to an artist known for his rather morbid paintings. 'Thank goodness I didn't give you free range on decorating the apartment.'

'I like it,' Pippa admitted.

'I'll see you tonight at work?'

'Yep.'

Luke peered out through her flimsy curtains at the grey sleet and shivered at the dismal sight. 'What a horrible day for a funeral.'

Was there ever a good day to have one? Pippa thought, but didn't say.

When he'd gone, she turned her blanket up to high, set the timer for six hours and deliberately went back to sleep.

It was exhausting being an upbeat, casual lover.

There was pall hanging over the ward when she arrived for her night shift.

The children and babies were oblivious, but Hamish's funeral had been held today and there was an air of sadness amongst the day staff. Pippa could feel it when she stepped into the office for hand-over.

Pippa was in charge of the night shift, and after taking hand-over, even though Darcy wasn't her patient tonight, she popped her head in and saw that he was asleep. In place of Whiskers there was a tatty purple dinosaur. Amber was sitting in the recliner, staring at nothing.

'Hi, Amber.' Pippa went over and sat on a stool by the chair. 'Is there anything I can get for you?'

She shook her head.

'I've made up a bed for you in one of the offices,' Pippa told her. 'If you need a break…'

'I want to be here whenever he wakes up.'

'I know you do, but if you or your husband want to take a short break then at least you'll have somewhere private. Do you want me to show you where it is?'

Amber nodded and hauled herself up from the recliner, and they walked in silence past the nurses' station and down the side corridor.

'It's tucked away,' Pippa said, opening up the door.

'I might lie down for half an hour,' Amber said. 'I've got the worst headache…'

'Of course.'

'Evan's coming in a bit later. He's with family at the moment.'

She was in a daze, and looked so utterly drained that when she sat on the low bed Pippa lifted her legs for her and helped Amber to lie down.

'Hamish has Whiskers and Coco. I think it was the right thing to do.'

'I do too,' Pippa said, and sat on the little bed. 'You listened to Darcy, and that's the most important thing for any child.'

'I'm sorry about your sister.' Amber looked at her. 'I didn't it say before.'

'I know you are.' Pippa gave her hand a little squeeze. 'I'll come and get you if Darcy wakes up.'

She flicked off the light and the door had barely closed before she heard deep sobs coming from the grieving mother—the saddest sound in the world, and one Amber had fought to protect Darcy from.

Pippa wanted to cry too.

She wanted to curl up and cry—for Hamish and his family, for her sister, and also because Luke would very soon be gone. Tonight was his final shift, and Pippa knew that soon she'd have to reset her heart and start all over again.

'Hey…' He came down to the ward about eleven. 'How are they all?'

'Amber's asleep in one of the back offices,' Pippa said. 'I think Evan will be in soon.'

'How's Darcy?'

'Worn out,' Pippa said. 'He had some supper, though.'

Luke checked the labs on a couple of patients, then stopped back at the nurses' station and leant on the desk overlooking her.

'Do you want a puppy?'

'My mother warned me about men like you.' Pippa laughed. 'Seriously…?'

'My neighbour has decided that Sausage is too much responsibility. She's taking him back to the breeder.' He gave her a smile. 'Maybe we're kindred spirits.'

'Maybe.' Pippa smiled back, but it faded when it dawned on her that he was suggesting that he and his irresponsible neighbour were the kindred spirts, not him and her.

'Come over in the morning?' he proposed, but Pippa shook her head.

'I'll be tired.'

'Later, then? I still owe you a dinner…'

'French champagne to toast your last shift here?' she said, and hoped he missed the slight twist to her words.

'I think I can manage that. Then we can go back to mine for a proper celebration—and no having to get up at the crack of dawn to make the bed!'

'You've sold the flat?'

'Tentative offer.' He smiled, but she didn't quite know how to return it.

All his loose ends were being tied up and he would soon be gone. How could she toast that with champagne? Could she really keep up the pretence of not being emotionally involved until he left?

She needed to stay strong.

'I don't know if I can. I promised my parents I'd go over—'

'Pip,' he interrupted, and at the pursing of her lips checked himself. 'Pippa. If I remember rightly—and I do—you were lying to avoid your parents on the day we first met. Don't do the same to me. What's going on?'

Pippa closed her eyes and took a breath, then opened them. 'Okay, then. I don't like goodbyes.' It was only the tiniest fraction of what she was feeling. 'I don't know if I can sit there, raising a glass…' She tried to keep to the deal they had made. 'We've had a great month…'

Luke saw that she didn't meet his eyes.

He came around the desk and took a seat next to her. 'I'm not on the next plane out of here. In fact, I asked you to take some time off and join me.'

'I know you did.'

'And you still haven't answered.'

'What's the point, Luke?'

'Time away from here?' he suggested. 'A holiday?'

'And then what?'

'Pippa…'

'What if we don't work out?'

'I'm asking you for a holiday, Pippa, not a lifetime commitment!'

'I know that,' she snapped. 'I told you at the start that I'm not brilliant at long-term relationships.'

'It's just a couple of weeks in Scotland,' he pointed out.

'For you, maybe!' Her chair scraped as she pushed it back. 'I'm going to do the meds.'

Luke's mood wasn't great as he headed for the on-call rooms.

He knew he was changing the rules by suggesting a holiday, but he was changing too. He wanted more—and that was new to him. Usually he was more than ready to walk away.

Not now.

But what did he have to complain about? Luke thought, when he saw Evan sitting in the near-empty canteen.

And, yes, he was changing—because rather than walking on by he took a breath and forced himself to walk in.

'Hey.' Luke went over to Evan. 'Taking a break?'

'Yes, I'm just...' Evan stared at his uneaten roll. 'I don't know if we should show Darcy the recording of the funeral service or talk to him about it...'

Where was Pippa when he needed her? Luke thought. He'd been hoping to offer his polite condolences, even answer some medical questions, but this was much harder.

'I don't doubt you'll make the right choices with Darcy,' he said.

Evan nodded wearily, but then a look of agony flashed across his features, so acute that he might just as well have been punched, and as he folded over, Luke was certain he was reliving his choices that fatal morning.

Luke knew he was a good surgeon, but in this department he didn't exactly excel. Then he thought again of Pippa...how her words had brought comfort that night when he'd been berating himself for not transferring Hamish to be with his twin.

'Evan,' he said, placing his hand on the man's shoulder. 'I know you're questioning your decision not to leave the twins at home that morning.' He felt the man's grief beneath his fingers. 'But I've seen the consequences of that far too many times.'

Evan wept.

'I have,' Luke said. 'I've had to sit with parents who *have* made the wrong choices on many occasions. And I am telling you now, you did the right thing.'

'Thank you,' Evan said.

But Luke wasn't finished. 'May I say...?' He took a breath. 'May I say that I'm in awe of the two of you and how you've handled things with Darcy.'

He carried on comforting Evan as best he could. And afterwards, instead of heading to the on-call rooms, he went back up to Paediatrics.

To see Pippa again?

He didn't know why.

To say what?

He wasn't sure of that either.

He just knew that he could not leave things as they were.

He was used to dealing with the usual sulks after a break-up, but he'd asked her to join him in Scotland and he couldn't make sense of her reaction. He was still trying to keep things light—he'd told her he wasn't proposing marriage!

Then he stilled.

There she was, sitting at the desk with the lamp on. She was wearing a cardigan to keep out the chill, and he realised that her contact lenses must have been irritating her eyes because she was wearing glasses.

Suddenly, he was transported back to a day many years ago...

Philippa.

Who'd liked French and Art and...

It was coming back to him now.

Cake.

Philippa—which it turned out she didn't like to be called...

Julia's sister Philippa.

And now he knew her better, he could guess why she hadn't revealed the connection that day.

He watched her reach for a box of tissues and blow her nose. He wasn't vain enough to think it was to do with his leaving.

But he was sure enough in himself to know that it played a part.

A bigger part than he'd ever considered...?

Was Pippa actually...in love with him? And if she was, how the hell did he feel about that?

'Hey,' Luke said, walking over, and she blinked and looked up. 'You do have a super-memory.'

'Do I?'

He nodded. 'It *was* me in the library.'

'Told you.' She smiled.

'You were right—I had been crying that day.'

'So you do remember?'

'I'd just gone home to get my swim kit and caught my father cheating.' He gave a grim smile and then came around and took a seat beside her. 'I insisted that he tell my mother. I thought I was doing the right thing...'

Pippa looked at him.

'She didn't take it well, to say the least.' He exhaled sharply. 'She had a breakdown and ended up in hospital for a few weeks. I thought I'd killed her.'

'I'm so sorry,' Pippa said. 'No wonder you messed up your chemistry exam.'

'Bloody fragmentation.' He rolled his eyes. 'That's why I stay out of people's personal lives,' he said. 'Why I don't do long term...' His eyes never left her face. 'What about you?'

'Oh, I'd love to do long term,' Pippa readily admitted, but then hastily retracted. 'Maybe someday.'

'Yeah...'

'Thanks for remembering,' she said. 'It's silly, really, but it meant a lot to me at the time. I hated it that you'd—' Pippa pressed her lips together.

'Forgotten?'

She nodded. 'It doesn't matter now.'

They stopped talking as Evan came onto the ward and asked about Amber.

'She's asleep,' Pippa told him. 'Do you want me to show you where she is?'

'Let her sleep,' Evan said. 'I might go and lie down with Darcy.'

'So,' Luke said, when they were alone again, 'am I booking the French restaurant? I'll be barred if I cancel on them twice...'

'I don't think so.' She shook her head. 'No.'

Luke checked no one was around and leant in. 'You don't want champagne and a lot of sex?' he asked, feeling the heat from her burning cheeks. 'One more wild night...?'

'I'd rather give it a miss, thanks.'

He was dismayed, but he noticed what it cost her to force out a smile.

Liar!

He didn't say that, though.

As he walked across the ward, he glanced through the glass

and saw Evan giving Darcy a drink with a straw and pulling a funny face to make his son laugh.

His own father had done that for him when he'd had his tonsils out. He'd come down from Theatre to check on him in the night, and persuaded him to take some fluids.

Luke didn't care that it was three a.m. He fired his father a quick text before he could change his mind.

Do you want to meet for lunch?

Matthew Harris didn't seem to care about the late hour either. Perhaps he was on a night shift himself.

Does midday work?

It did.

Luke looked back at Pip, who was carrying an angry toddler, bringing him to sit with her at the desk.

Pippa, he amended.

Yet he saw Philippa.

And he actually ached for all she'd been through.

She hadn't just been forgotten by her parents.

She had never really been loved.

Julia wasn't the ghost in that family. Pippa was.

Then, hearing a tap on the window, he turned and saw Darcy in his father's arms, smiling.

For the sake of his son, Evan was too.

As Darcy waved though the glass, so too did Evan, and of course Luke waved back, then gave a little thumbs-up to Evan.

What a brave man, Luke thought, and he realised that the Williams family were going to make it.

Despite all that life had thrown at them, they would get through this.

In their own way...

CHAPTER FIFTEEN

PIPPA WOKE AT two in the afternoon, completely at sixes and sevens.

She wanted to see Luke, of course she did, but she honestly didn't know if she could get through a romantic dinner without falling apart at the seams.

Let alone sex.

And yet she wanted him so badly.

Luke's re-entry into her life had indeed muddied the waters, and there wasn't a soul she could discuss it with.

Well, maybe one soul...

Pippa had never really found any comfort from going to the cemetery.

Julia's was possibly the best-kept grave in the place, given that her mother was here most days.

Today, though, Pippa had it to herself. She took off her coat and placed it on the ground then sat on it. Staring at the grave she looked at all the little things her mother brought and frequently rearranged.

'I wish I could talk to you,' Pippa said suddenly, her own voice surprising her. 'We always could talk.'

It was true.

She and Julia had tried not to upset her mother, but they had been more honest when it was just the two of them.

'Luke's been working at The Primary,' Pippa said, and realised that on top of everything else she felt guilty. As if she were stepping into her sister's life or her dreams—except that

Julia and Luke had never really existed. 'We've been seeing each other. Just a casual thing,' she added hastily. But there was no reason to lie. 'Well, according to Luke… He's asked me to visit him when he moves Scotland, but there's no point.' She voiced another thing that scared her too. 'Can you imagine Mum's face if I told her?'

But in the past trying to protect her mother hadn't solved anything. Pushing down her feelings…even the fact of her existence…

'Pippa!'

She turned at the sound of her mother's voice, and saw that she carried the gardening basket that she always brought to the cemetery.

'I wasn't expecting to see you here!'

'Hi, Mum.' Pippa stood to give her mother a kiss, but it was a haphazard one as she was pulling on her gardening gloves at the same time. Then she put a little mat onto the frosty grass to kneel upon. 'I just thought I'd come… Have a few moments…' Pippa said falteringly.

'That's nice.'

'I was just telling Julia…' she took a breath '…that Luke Harris has been working at The Primary for the past month.'

'Oh!'

That had got her mother's attention.

'We've been seeing each other…'

'Pippa!' Her mother's eyes darted to the grave. 'Not here.'

'Then where?' Pippa said. 'Julia can't hear, Mum, and if she can, well…' She took a deep breath. 'If she can hear then it's nice for me to have someone I can actually talk to about myself…about how *I'm* feeling…'

Her mother stood up and pulled off her gloves. 'The one little relationship Julia had!' she hissed. 'Of all the men in the world, you have to take the one that she cared for the most.'

'Of all the men in the world,' Pippa shouted, 'he was the one *I* cared for the most!'

She took a shuddering breath and felt the sting of tears as

she admitted out loud the truth she'd been fighting not to reveal, even to herself.

'He was the one. Even back then.'

She stormed off.

'Pippa!' her mother called out.

'What?' Pippa turned around but did not retrace a single step. 'What do you want?'

'I had no idea about—'

'How could you have? The only thing we ever talk about is Julia! It was my birthday last week. My thirtieth!'

'I know that. There's a card and—'

'I don't *want* a card!' Pippa was too upset to even shout any more. 'Or money. I wanted you to remember…to make a fuss. Just for once not to make me feel guilty for existing.'

'Pippa!'

'You don't have room for me in your heart.'

She felt tears splashing down her cheeks, and she didn't know if she was crying for Julia, for her lost relationship with her mother, or even for Luke, who surely didn't want her desperate love either.

'It's true…'

'Pippa!' Her mother's voice was shocked. 'I did my best…'

'Well, it wasn't enough.'

She practically ran from the cemetery, gulping back sobs as she hurried into the Underground, desperate to make it home…

And there she cried like she never had before.

She had hidden her tears from Julia, and later from her parents, and in the end from herself too. Now Pippa curled up on the bed and cried, and it sounded so much like Amber sobbing her heart out that at the thought of that little family Pippa only wept harder.

It didn't help, though. Because she wanted Luke's arms to be holding her. She wanted the one thing he would never give, and she couldn't put herself through this any longer.

Yes, Julia had been able to laugh and squeeze every ounce out of her life, but she wasn't here any more. Her advice had run out.

Pippa really was alone.

She gulped as she admitted the truth to herself: she was scared.

Scared of being in love.

Scared of being left behind.

Scared of being forgotten.

As Pippa's sobbing slowed, it felt to her as if her sister was in the room. It truly felt as if she could hear Julia's breathless voice…as if Julia was stroking her hair.

'Pip, everybody gets scared at times. I just tell myself I'll let myself be scared tomorrow…'

It had made little sense at the time, but it made every sense now!

Before she could change her mind, Pippa called for a taxi. She had precisely fifteen minutes to transform her red and swollen face into something French-restaurant-worthy.

She slicked on some lipstick and hoped her wild hair would cover the worst as she pulled on the lilac dress he'd stood her up in once already.

Then she pulled on heels and took the Santorini picture from the ledge.

She was ready.

Ready for one final night with Luke.

Then she'd tell him what he could do with his emotionally uninvolved relationships and walk out of his life.

Whatever the day brought—or the night—Pippa vowed to deal with it by telling herself she could be scared tomorrow. Just like Julia.

It only dawned on her as she buzzed his intercom that she'd told him not to book the restaurant.

'Pippa!'

He buzzed her up and stood at the door, wearing the bottom half of a suit, naked from the hips up and holding a glass of wine. She could hear music in the background.

'I thought you weren't…'

'I'm intruding,' Pippa said, suddenly worried that her replacement was already in situ! 'I should have called first.'

'Of course not.' He held the door open. 'What's this?'

'The Santorini picture you liked.' She gave him a wicked smile. 'It might help clinch the sale.'

'Or have the buyers running for the door. Are you okay?' he checked.

Perhaps he'd noticed that she looked a bit off.

'Contact lenses!' Pippa said. 'Allergies.'

'Goodness,' he replied, and poured her a glass of red. 'You're not allergic to this, I hope?'

'No, that would be lovely.' She took a rather hefty gulp. 'I had a row with my mum,' she admitted.

'Bad?' he asked.

They certainly weren't playing traffic controllers tonight, because she didn't put her hand up to halt him. 'Dreadful. I think I said too much.'

'Well, I can't really imagine you doing that,' Luke admitted, 'but even if you did, there's a lot of hurt and trauma there. Some things have to be said.'

'Yes.'

'If it makes you feel better, I had a row with my dad,' he told her. 'I took your advice and went for lunch with him.' Luke sighed. 'We started arguing in the car park, before we'd even gone in.'

'Oh!'

'But then we actually managed to eat lunch. I don't understand the details, and frankly I don't want to.' He rolled his eyes. 'We've called a truce.'

'That's so good.'

'Thanks to you,' he said. 'Look, I wouldn't want their marriage—but then I don't have to live it, do I?'

'No.'

'Oh, and I told him I'm getting them tickets for that interactive theatre thing for Christmas and that he's to take my mother this time.'

Pippa laughed, and it was a real laugh. Because that was what he did, even on dark days: he made her smile. No, she would never regret this crazy month.

'Is it too late to book the restaurant?'

'Sorry.' He shook his head. 'Not a hope on a Saturday night.'

'Oh, well,' Pippa said. 'Just sex, then...'

'Wow!' he said, blinking.

'Look, I know I've been a bit difficult. But I did warn you I was lousy at relationships.'

'You're hard work for a fling.'

'Yes.'

'But more than worth it.' He placed down his glass and then took hers too and pulled her into his arms. 'How did you leave things with your mum?' he asked.

'I don't know,' Pippa admitted, feeling his naked chest against her cheek and allowing herself the bliss of being held in his arms. 'I can smell baby powder...'

'I like it,' he said. 'I bought a can of my own...'

'You didn't!' she said.

'No, I pinched one of yours for work.' He lifted her face and gave her a soft kiss. 'I'm so glad you came.'

How close she'd come to missing this... Pippa didn't even want to consider it. She could lose herself in his kiss for ever, and she loved the easy way he dealt with her dress, lifting her arms and pulling it over her head.

Taking her hand, he led her to the bedroom.

'Excuse the mess.'

She didn't care if the bed was unmade, especially when he was pushing her down onto it. She let go as he slid her knickers off and delivered the bliss that only he could with his mouth.

'Sorry, Pip,' he said, just as she was about to come. He left her on the edge of heaven as he unzipped and then, patient and tender no more, he was inside her. 'I couldn't wait.'

She wrapped her thighs around him and clung on, because, in truth, neither could she. A rollercoaster called Luke had thundered back into her life, and now he was looking right at her as he took her, and she was looking back at him.

Until she couldn't any more. And then she closed her eyes to the bliss and the noise of them coming together.

'Damn, Pip,' he said as he lay on top of her. 'You've messed up my plans…'

It had been the most rapid, intense sex of her life. She resurfaced, a little bewildered, not just by his words but because all the familiar landmarks were missing.

No cushions.

No rugs.

No ugly pictures on the walls.

'That was unexpected!' he said, as she lay staring at the ceiling. 'I hope the estate agent doesn't bring someone to view—'

'Stop!' She was startled by the horror of that thought. 'I thought it was under offer?'

'Not any more.'

'Did they withdraw?'

'Please don't talk about withdrawing,' he said, and with his hand sliding between her thighs it was indecent with meaning.

'I told you. I'm on the Pill. I take it religiously. I've got the—' She took a breath and then just said it. 'I'm a carrier.'

'Well, thankfully I'm not.'

She frowned. 'How do you know?'

'I got a test. That's what I was trying to discuss.'

'Why would you go and get tested?'

'Because I felt bad for being careless that morning, and I guessed there was a reasonable chance you had the gene. If there were consequences… Well, that would have been one thing we'd have needed to know.'

'You went and had a test?' Her voice was incredulous. 'You did that?'

'I was hardly strapped to monitors and asked to run for an hour with a mask on. It was a cheek swab.'

'But…why?'

'Because I care about you, Pippa. Because we'd have needed to know.…'

He said it so calmly, and in such a matter-of-fact voice, when all she'd ever known was panic and fear around the subject.

'Come on—get dressed. We need to eat. Chicken Provençal is waiting.'

'But you couldn't get a reservation.'

'No, but I could get them to deliver. I just need to warm it. We're not eating dinner naked.'

'Why not?'

'I have standards.'

He pulled a shirt out of its plastic bag and retrieved the bottom half of his suit from the floor, then went to select a tie.

'Are we seriously dressing up?'

'Yes,' Luke said. 'We're celebrating.'

Remembering her vow to face anything now and be scared tomorrow, Pippa retrieved the clothes she'd so hurriedly taken off and went into his bathroom.

He'd spun her completely!

But she was going to be brave and fearless...

'Dinner!' he called.

She walked into the living room and found that he'd set the table. There was even a candle stuck in a wine bottle.

'This looks incredible,' Pippa said as he brought over two plates.

'Never tell Anton that I microwaved it,' Luke said, laughing, and he let her take a gorgeous herby mouthful. 'Or that we had red wine with it...'

'I won't,' Pippa said, and didn't add that she'd never get the chance to now. She was through with sniping and being insecure. Instead, she would enjoy the gorgeous food and wine, and of course the company too.

'Pip...' Luke said, and she looked up at his serious tone. 'I haven't been completely honest...'

'That's okay,' Pippa said.

After all, she hadn't been completely honest with him either. He'd have run a mile, Pippa knew, if he'd known the strength of her feelings for him.

'The thing is,' Luke said, 'I need a break...'

'I get it,' Pippa said. 'This has been great. It really has—'

'Pip!' he interrupted. 'I mean from work.'

'Oh.'

'I'm not going to Scotland for work,' he told her. 'I had a

great mentor in Philadelphia, and he was very insistent that it's important to take a break and get away every so often. He goes fishing...'

'You're going fishing?'

'No.'

He was very serious, Pippa realised, and she put down her cutlery.

'I need a month or two away from broken bodies,' he said. 'I scoffed at Carl at the time, but I can see now he was right. I love my job, and I'm going to keep doing it, but I'm going to make sure I take my breaks more seriously.'

'And not take on a month's casual work while you sell your flat?' Pippa said, and raised her glass. 'I'll drink to that!'

'Come with me,' Luke said. 'I know the off-duty's tricky, and that you may have a new job soon, but...'

Pippa was determined to be the bravest she'd ever been. And instead of declining, instead of running from potential hurt, she followed her heart and nodded. 'I'd love to come to Scotland.'

'You're sure?'

'Very.' She gave her bravest smile. 'Can't leave you sex-starved in your little stone cottage.'

'I'll get dessert,' he said, and looked at her. 'What are you smiling at?'

'You,' Pippa admitted. 'How you can just end a conversation—an important one—as if you're calling for the bill!' She even laughed. 'Will you wave me off in the morning?'

'I hope not,' Luke responded, and disappeared into the kitchen.

He came out with a cake, lit with one long, slender candle.

'You didn't have to do that...' She laughed, but there was a lump in her throat that he was trying to make that awful birthday up to her. 'I told you, it was no big deal...'

'It's a very big deal,' Luke said. 'Because as well as asking you to join me in Scotland, I *would* like a lifetime commitment.'

He put down the cake.

And it was not just any cake!

'You deserve cake on your birthday. I'm so sorry I added to

the misery of this year's. Now, I was going to make one myself, but in the end I left it to the experts,' Luke explained to his stunned audience. 'Smoked almond praline and chocolate.'

But Pippa wasn't interested in the ingredients, no matter how delicious they sounded. Neither was she interested in the pale white candle, with its twitching flame. She was only interested in the appalling piping that looked so at odds with the exquisite, delicate cake...

Surely they'd delivered the wrong cake. Because instead of *Happy Birthday* it read: *Marry me.*

'I decided not to attempt a question mark,' Luke joked. 'There wasn't room.'

'I thought they'd delivered the wrong cake...'

'It's the right cake. Well, it's certainly the one I piped.'

'*You* piped this?'

'Much to Anton's scorn.'

'Why?'

'It's the little things,' he said, as she had to him one day. 'Though, before you say yes or no, in the interests of full disclosure...'

'You have an ex-wife?' Pippa checked, and he shook his head.

'Children?'

'Close,' Luke said. 'A puppy with bathroom issues.'

'You're taking Sausage?'

He rolled his eyes as he nodded. 'I have to walk him in an hour and then drag all his stuff over here. Oh, and I've taken the flat off the market.'

'Why?'

'I want your dark art on my walls.' He took her hands. 'I don't want to a be a lone wolf. I don't want my parents' messes and mistakes to serve as my lessons in life. I love you, and I think you might have a little more than just a crush on me...'

He knew! Pippa realised.

But he couldn't know just how deeply she loved him.

'I love you too much,' Pippa admitted, and then she looked over to him, wanting to make sure he knew how big her love was. 'I made a heart in art after the library that day. I painted it Kobicha-brown with russet and copper flecks. It was the closest I could get to the colour of your eyes.'

'Gosh…' He pondered that for a moment. 'Have you still got it?'

'Yes…' There was more. 'And I fantasised about you a few times…'

'That's fine.'

'No…' She flushed with guilt. 'I mean, when I was with someone else…'

'Well, I'm glad I could help!' He laughed.

'Luke, I love you, and I think I always have.'

'And I want your love. I want you to hole up with me in Scotland. If you can get time off, that is. And I'll talk to your parents.'

'Let me,' Pippa said. 'Luke, you're still on their mantelpiece. A picture of you and Julia.'

'I understand.' He nodded thoughtfully, then said, 'I don't particularly want our parents at our wedding…'

He held her hands, but it wasn't enough contact so she came around the table and sat on his knee.

'Look, I get that it might not work for you. They've only got one child. So if you think we ought to—'

'Just us,' she said.

'Just us?' Luke repeated. 'Is that a yes?'

'You didn't need the question mark, Luke.'

He'd had her heart since she was sixteen years old.

'It's always been a yes.'

CHAPTER SIXTEEN

IN FEBRUARY SHE would be starting her new role at The Primary, and Luke had landed a plum consultancy job at a famous teaching hospital—one without the shadow of his father hanging over it.

'Six consecutive weeks off each year...'

It was written into his contract, and even though Pippa didn't have quite enough pull to get it written into hers, she had told Miss Brett that she'd be taking the same.

As for Pippa's parents...she'd told them that she was serious about Luke.

At least they were talking...

And the picture on the mantelpiece had thankfully been taken down.

But right now, it was their wedding day.

Pippa wasn't even nervous. How could she be when she felt as if this day had been etched into her lifeline—as if they'd been destined for each other and finally the world had caught up with what had been written in the stars.

As well as that, she was grappling with new underwear, as Luke watched on.

'We're not having sex again until we're legal,' he told her.

'Then hurry up and make me your wife!' Pippa laughed as she pulled on a gorgeous jade dress. 'My favourite colour...'

She looked down at her stunning engagement ring, which sported an emerald with every shade of captivating green— even army-green. She loved it so much.

'Here,' he said, handing her a small box. 'Your flowers.'

Heather and thistles.

Spiky and soft.

A lot like life.

And—also a lot like life—very beautiful too.

Luke picked up Sausage, who was dressed in a tartan bow for the occasion, and they headed off to be wed.

The Wee Neuk was the smallest wedding venue in Edinburgh's City Chambers, and for Pippa and Luke it was the perfect venue for such a special day.

The celebrant greeted them warmly, along with their two witnesses. Their hands were wrapped in silk rope, and they exchanged the traditional handfasting vows they had chosen.

'Do you, Luke, take Philippa to be your wife? To be her constant friend, her partner in life, and her true love? To love her without reservation, honour and respect her, protect her from harm, comfort her in times of distress, and to grow with her in mind and spirit?'

'I do,' Luke said in a confident, clear voice.

And those vows, those words, meant everything to Pippa. She took a breath, and the celebrant asked her the same questions.

'Do you, Philippa, take Luke to be your husband? To be his constant friend…?'

Till then, Pippa had done all she could to hold it together. She'd never thought it would be Luke's eyes that would fill with tears.

Of course she knew that he loved her, but it was then, in that moment, that she understood just how much, and what these words meant to him.

'…and to grow with him in mind and spirt?' the celebrant asked.

'I do,' Pippa said, and then she looked at the man her heart loved, and reiterated, 'I really do.'

And with the rope removed, and their promises still hanging in the air, he pulled her into his arms and held her.

Pippa felt a moment of bewilderment and wonder. 'We're family now.'

'We are,' Luke agreed. He looked at the white-gold ring she'd placed on his finger, and then back to her, and said, 'You've got me now.'

And it wasn't said in an arrogant way. He wasn't teasing her for her devotion. He was gently addressing the fact that she'd never really been loved. Well, apart from by one other person...

'Are you ready?' he asked, when the paperwork was all done.

Because there was one more place they needed to be before they headed to a beautiful hotel for the first night of their honeymoon.

And then off to Skye...

Luke held her hand as a driver took them on the hour and a half journey to St Andrew's. There was a light snowfall, and Pippa looked out at the North Sea, which was churning and grey, and then to the gorgeous buildings dusted in white. She gasped at the splendour of the university.

'They won't mind?' she checked.

'I told you—I've made all the arrangements.'

As she stepped out of the car a piper was playing—by chance, Pippa thought at first. But then he walked ahead of them, leading them to the chapel.

'Amazing Grace' had been played at her sister's funeral, but it sounded so much sweeter now, and this time around she was free to cry, even on this, the happiest day of her life.

'I came,' Pippa said, recalling one of her conversations with Julia, when her sister had asked her to visit St Andrew's in her place. 'Thank you,' she said.

And she laid her little posy on the steps, because without her sister's brave spirit spurring her on she might never have had the courage to risk her heart and say yes to Luke's proposition. Even if they had only lasted a month, Pippa knew it would still have been worth it.

'I love you, Julia.'

She always had and always would.

Then she turned to Luke, who was holding Sausage, and took his hand as they walked back to the car. 'I wish she'd been here today.'

'You'd have been fighting like two cats over me...' he teased.

'Stop it!' She nudged him playfully, and then, in the midst of her tears, she started to laugh. And it was so nice to actually laugh as she spoke about her sister. 'You're so sure of yourself!'

'Oh, I am today,' he said.

So sure of their love.

* * * * *

HEALING THE BABY DOC'S HEART

FIONA McARTHUR

MILLS & BOON

Dedicated to Jodie and her babies.

PROLOGUE

Vietnam, the first of May

ISABELLA HARGRAVES PULLED aside the curtains and looked down to the waking Hanoi street, seven floors below.

Warm air swirled around her fingers as she cracked open the window, yet the sky still radiated a pink glow from dawn. Her favourite time. Another hot day was coming.

An elderly vendor peddled below on a push-bike laden with multi-sized straw hats. These conical woven workers' hats could be seen in fields, sampans, on cyclists, and on the heads of tourists. On this pushbike, the towers of plaited straw rose behind the rider and out sideways, so he was encased in a cage of hats. He'd be on his way to sell them in the old quarter of the city.

One of Isabella's highlights for people-watching in Vietnam was noting the piles of drums, ladders, picture frames—in fact anything—on the back and front of push-bikes. Once she'd even seen a cow on a trailer pulled along by a motorcycle.

Nine million people and three million motorcycles. Such a crazy, wonderful place to live and work.

Of course, if you wanted to cross the road only a percentage of traffic would stop, and you needed to take your life in your hands. The trick, she'd found, was to walk slowly—no dashing—hand out, eyes open, and *voila*, the traffic avoided you. That was the local theory, anyway, and when she followed that it seemed to work.

From her window she could just see the pink sky lighting Hoen Kiem, the Lake of the Returned Sword, where an emperor had been said to use a magical sword to defeat the Ming Dynasty from China. The legends here fascinated her.

In this story, after victory, the Golden Turtle god had returned the sword to the bottom of the lake, and today the Turtle Tower stood on its own tiny island, on guard, as if to keep an eye out for the endangered turtles that were swimming in the lake.

Isabella pulled on her runners so she could circle the expanse of still water in the early morning before she went to the maternity wing of the Old City Hospital.

Circumnavigating the lake on the winding paths at daybreak had become Isabella's favourite start to the day. The streets were quiet, and the pleasure of watching groups of women on the grassed foreshore, line-dancing to boom boxes, bickering over which song to play and the exuberance once decided, seemed to bring some of their infectious joy her way.

She and her partner Conlon had another month of secondment here. She'd loved every second so far. Loved sharing it with Conlon. She'd even begun to hope she'd found a partner in life after she'd been alone for so long. Conlon had suggested she should become a full-time academic instead of fitting her research in blocks between her nursing work as an intensivist.

Her mood dipped. Yesterday's emergency in the neonatal intensive care unit—or NICU—had required all her skills to assist in saving the firstborn son of a woman she'd befriended, and though she'd been present in the unit only for research, it had been her skills from the other part of her life that had helped to save the baby.

Isabella, an expert in the field, had been invited to participate in a study of neonatal outcomes for premature babies. Conlon, an ambitious lecturer at Sydney University, had been so eager to co-author the paper she was writing that he'd asked to join her. Their relationship had become more than collegial, and he now shared the flat she'd rented.

She was still getting used to the fact that Conlon had said he was there for her. It seemed hard to believe when she'd been let down so often by her father's work priorities while she was growing up. It had felt as if every single time she'd needed him that her father had been elsewhere, working.

Her phone rang and she glanced down to see the caller ID. Speak of the devil. Her brows furrowed. Dad? Six a.m. here… It would be nine in the morning in Australia.

Suddenly she felt as if she were a motherless seven-year-old seeking an elusive hug, not a woman of twenty-seven.

She could count on the fingers of one hand how many times her father had rung her in the last year. Messages were usually sent via his very busy secretary at the Sydney Central Neurology Department.

A feeling of foreboding crept up her neck and circled her throat—because the last time he'd phoned had been to tell her about her brother-in-law's car accident, six months ago.

'Dad?'

'Isabella. I have bad news.'

No sugar coating. No, *How are you*? No, *I'm sorry to say this*. Not from Dad.

She felt her stomach roil with sick fear.

Was her widowed sister sick? Was it Nadia's pregnancy? The baby?

'It's your grandmother.'

Gran! The woman who had made up for the loss of her mother so long ago. The loss of her father, too, really. Because he'd morphed into a machine after Mum had died, and had only become more mechanical in his affections.

No. It couldn't be. Not Gran.

'An accident. Hit and run in Coolangatta. She's unconscious,' he went on. 'I don't believe she'll wake.'

Isabella closed her eyes as horror and the wash of devastation began to saturate her insides along with cold fear.

'Isabella? Hello? Are you there?'

She jumped at the tone in her father's voice. 'Yes, sorry. I'm just trying to take it in. I'll come home, of course.'

'What?' she heard him snap. 'Why? There's nothing you can do.' His tone disbelieving. Sharp. Emphatic. 'No need. No. You must finish your work.' She heard the cold and clinical man for whom the god Work meant everything.

Her grandmother lay dying. Unconscious in hospital. Isabella wasn't leaving her alone.

'Of course there's something I can do. I can be with her. And with Nadia.'

Her father hmphed with exasperation. 'Your grandmother's not going to know you're with her.'

There it was. The impatience she'd grown up with. The inhuman being who was her father. He was probably already thinking about his next task.

'She's comatose. It's very sad. However, as I've said, it's unlikely she's going to regain consciousness.'

'I'm coming home.'

Or at least not home. Not to the cold, empty mausoleum her father lived in.

'I'll go to the Gold Coast. Be with Nadia. Stay at Gran's flat.'

I will talk to my grandmother even if she's unconscious.

It might help. Her grandmother might hear her at any point. Isabella would be there when she woke up.

Oh, Gran.

He huffed. 'You do what you need to do—though I can't imagine Conlon will be happy if you leave.'

She tilted her head at that. 'Conlon will come with me. Be with me. He'll support me.'

'Really? You both went there to do a job. Conlon knows your work is important and it's not finished. You should both stay.'

'We'll go back to Australia early. Come back to Vietnam later.'

Of course he'll come with me...support me.

God, she wanted him now, his arms around her, but he was already out jogging around the lake.

'I don't think you should. Nadia's there. She'll keep you up to date.'

She could almost imagine her father looking at his watch. Thinking he'd wasted enough time on this call.

'Thank you for ringing.'

And not getting your secretary to do it.

Isabella's fingers felt numb. Her lips clumsy as she said goodbye.

Gran...

A flash of sympathy for her father pierced her before he could hang up. 'Dad. Are you okay? Gran's your mother...'

'I'm sorry it's happened, of course.' He was silent for a moment. As if he was actually going to say he was upset. But no. 'There's nothing we can do. Your grandmother is eighty. She's had a good life.'

And then he was gone.

At first Isabella walked around the room in circles, picking things up and putting them down, trying to work out what to do. Trying to grasp the enormity of Gran lying in a hospital thousands of miles away. Alone. Possibly dying.

She thought about how much life, and love and laughter her grandmother had left inside her. Gran *had* to wake up. She couldn't bear the thought that her grandmother wouldn't be there. Wouldn't see Nadia's baby born.

The Sydney flights didn't leave until six p.m. from Hanoi to Singapore. And then a few hours later from Singapore to Sydney. They'd have to catch a domestic flight from Sydney to Brisbane and hire a car to drive to the Gold Coast. She'd arrange for her own car to be shipped up.

She thought of her sister. Alone in this. Poor Nadia... Six months pregnant and now she'd be losing two people she loved. Nadia needed her, too. No. Gran wouldn't die. She'd phone her as soon as she spoke to Conlon.

The door opened and Conlon breezed in from his run,

bringing the heat from the pavements outside. His jet-black hair lay plastered to the sweat across his brows, which creased when he saw her face.

His long legs crossed the room to her quickly.

'What's wrong?'

She wasn't alone. Too many times in her childhood she and her sister had been alone...until Gran had stepped in. Thank goodness Conlon was here.

'My grandmother. She's in a coma. Hit and run in Coolangatta. We'll have to go back to Australia.' She reached forward and took his hand. 'We have to go home.'

He stared. 'I'm sorry... Run that by me again?'

How could he not have understood her?

She tamped down her impatience. 'My grandmother has been involved in an accident. I have to go home. I'll tell them we have to postpone our study. Put a hold on the paper.'

'Of course you have to go. But what do you mean, we have to postpone? We need to finish the project.'

He shook his head.

'I'm going home.'

'I know. I heard that. Your grandmother. You're fond of her.'

Fond? The word sat oddly.

'I'm terrified my grandmother is going to die,' she said slowly. Familiar dread was coiling inside her chest. 'I need you right now. You'll support me...?'

She hadn't meant to make it a question but it was too late now. She trailed off, looked at his face. Saw the truth. The distance that had grown between them in just minutes. That's all it took. Saw the selfishness she'd tried to ignore in all those little daily moments. Saw her father.

Conlon was looking past her, his gaze shifting away. He gave a more emphatic shake of his head this time.

'I'm not going to be any help. I'll stay and finish the project.'

This wasn't happening.

'They'll understand...we can come back. You don't need—'

He cut her off. 'No, it will only take a month for me to finish it. You go. Do what you have to do. Then come back if you can make it in time. If you can't, I'll tie it all up.' His chin went up. 'I'll still add your name on the paper.'

She shifted again at that. It had been her paper and she'd invited him to join her. He'd asked her to let him join. Now he was going to 'add her name' on it when she'd done eighty percent of the work?

She shook her head. Stung. Disgusted, actually. She narrowed her eyes as he avoided hers. But that was just work. Stuff to think on later. Later—when Gran was well. This was not important now.

Isabella shook her head. 'You're not listening to me. I want you to come and be with me. Support me. What if she dies?'

She knew she sounded forlorn and lost, and she hated it.

His face was screwed up, incredulous. 'You've flown alone more than I have. You'll be fine.' He waved a hand and glanced at his watch as it moved past his face. 'I'd better get moving.'

Isabella felt sick. And stupid. 'I don't want protection. I want support. There's a difference.'

'I would. If this was finished. But this work is too important, Isabella.'

She winced. Hurt. 'And I'm not?'

He'd already turned towards the bedroom. 'Don't be petty. Of course you're important. But I think you're not thinking right. Not thinking of our work. You're prioritising all wrong.'

Had he really just said that? Red-hot anger flooded through her. She could almost imagine her blood boiling like lava. Her father's favourite word all through her childhood. At school events and award nights. He was unable to come because he was 'prioritising'.

Conlon turned back briefly, oblivious to the fact that he wasn't in the right. 'Ridiculous for me to come with you. We're so close to finishing. This will be a breakthrough paper. Give us excellent credibility behind us.'

Through gritted teeth she whispered, 'My grandmother is dying.'

Oh, God. She saw it then. Why? Why was she attracted to these men who put work in front of everything? Like her father. She'd thought Conlon was safe. He was an academic, so at least he had no urgent calls taking him back to the hospital night after night. She'd thought—foolish her—that during every event or crisis, he would be there. For her. Would want to be.

If it hadn't been for Gran, she and Nadia wouldn't even have had a childhood. They would have spent their holidays locked in the house with part-time servants instead of going to visit Gran and flying up to her at the weekends when they were older.

And she'd thought she could make a life with Conlon. Thought they wanted the same things. Thought they'd be a caring family.

Idiot.

She'd have spent her life waiting for scraps of attention that didn't involve work. Just like in her childhood.

But she couldn't think about that now.

She said dully, 'You go and shower. When you come home I'll be gone.'

'Of course. That's fine. I'll give you a ring.'

Wow. So generous. Thoughtful.

Very quietly and clearly she said, 'No, don't bother.'

Conlon's dark brows drew together. He was irritated. His turn to be impatient. 'You're being foolish. We're good together. Our work is amazing.'

'*My* work is amazing.'

Because she was the one who found it easy. Made the connections and garnered the interviews that clarified the answers. She had a way with equations, and probabilities, always finding the right questions and writing everything down in the right words.

Conlon had let her down.

Hell, he couldn't even take the time to give her a hug of sympathy. What had she been thinking to attach herself to a man who was so like her father she'd have been starved for affection for the rest of her life?

Her heart wasn't broken—bruised, maybe—but her pride had taken a blow that had left her reeling.

She'd loved her time in Vietnam, had been honoured by the openness of the midwives and neonatal nurses she'd interviewed for her thesis. She'd ached over their stories, and enjoyed learning about a culture that was so different from her own. But she'd been here with Conlon and had thought something had been growing between them.

He'd been so enthusiastic about her scientific paper, and his handsome face had promised her a wonderful future at home and at work. She'd not seen what was now so obvious—that the man was selfish and egotistical.

Wow. Remembered his comment about the paper. Seemed he thought it was generous that he'd let her share credit for her own thesis.

She'd almost loved him—or the man she'd thought he was—but now, as he turned to shower and change for the hospital, she felt as hollow and cast off as she'd felt as a child, when her father had immersed himself in his high-powered job.

She'd thought she'd got over that. Her gran would have scolded her for being dramatic. Would've said Conlon had done her a favour, exposing his shortfalls before she'd done something worse—like marrying him.

But after that Gran would have lovingly offered her a shoulder to cry on. Conlon hadn't.

It would take her twenty-four hours, but Isabella would be by her grandmother's bedside until she woke up. And Gran *would* wake up. She had to.

Alone, seven floors above the Hanoi street, Isabella said quietly, 'I'm coming, Gran...' To her sister whom she'd ring shortly, she promised silently, *Nadia, I've got your back.*

She'd find a job at the nearest hospital, visit Gran, be there for Nadia in the last months of her pregnancy. She'd get back to doing what she needed to do. Caring for those who loved and wanted her. Working with babies. She would leave behind Vietnam…this foray into academia… Conlon. Leave behind any silly little girl fantasies that men could be relied on.

She'd learnt that lesson. Oh, yes.

CHAPTER ONE

Three weeks later, Gold Coast, Australia

NORMALLY DR SIMON PURDY, senior consultant paediatrician at Coolangatta Central, wouldn't notice a new nurse in the neonatal intensive care unit.

But today wasn't normal. Because seeing this new nurse hit him like a wrecking ball and he actually staggered. Mayhem exploded in Simon's chest and gut, and he could barely shift his gaze from the stranger across the room as he found his balance.

The unfamiliar sensations had begun when he'd seen her smile as she chatted with a newborn in an open cot—as if the baby could answer.

The tiny patient had done something that had made the nurse's mouth stretch softly until her whole face lit up with mischief.

She was so vibrant—good grief, she hummed with it. Visibly pulsing with life and vitality that made him see, and feel, the depth of his own emotional emptiness.

Now, suddenly and rudely awakened, he remembered he was alive. A man. A broken one. But still a man.

Then all he could think about was his inability to keep those he'd cared for safe. He didn't want to look at that frozen guilt that had been a part of his life for so long. His failure. His culpability that those he'd dared to love were dead.

Thankfully he'd made it to a dimmer corner of the clinical

area before he'd been stricken by this strange paralysis and he'd had to force his hand up just to loosen his irritatingly constricting too-tight Tigger tie.

The new nurse, just for a moment, had looked like an angel. Blonde and gentle. Bathing him with healing light.

And then she'd turned side-on, and those curves had not made him think of his lost wife or celestial chastity. She was tall and strong. Like some goddess he had no right to covet. Someone else he would lose if he let himself care. Her thick plait of sun-and-sand-coloured hair swung and danced, with the end of the plait pointing to her backside like a neon arrow, as she floated across the polished floor checking the cots.

'Can I help you, Dr Purdy?'

Simon blinked. At least his eyelids worked again. He swivelled his head—though not his taut body—and looked at Carla, his good friend, and the neonatal nursery's unit manager. The woman who'd nagged him to get on with his life.

She'd spotted him and had her list of patients prepared for him, as usual, in order of urgency. But right now her head was tilted to the side and her eyes twinkled.

'Do you need help?'

He did. But nobody could help him. Where was his usual wall? His defences?

'No.'

The word came out unexpectedly. Just as the woman across the room was unexpected. He blinked again. 'Sorry, Carla. I'm off in another land. Thinking about a patient,' he lied.

Why did he lie? He never lied. Apparently he wasn't very good at it, either.

Carla snorted. 'That's Isabella Hargraves. Very experienced neonatal nurse. Her dad's Professor Piers Hargraves, the neurologist.'

'Head of Neurology at Sydney Central? Chair of Neurology Australia?'

Hopefully she was a socialite, then.

He was dreaming, A quiet, insidious voice inside his head whispered, *But maybe a one-night stand?*

'The same. Isabella's a midwife and neonatal nurse who loves babies. That's what she said when she interviewed. But she's also worked in retrieval, has five scientific papers to her name and has great experience across diverse units. She's moved from Sydney to here to be with her sick grandmother and pregnant sister.'

Simon shook himself.

Loves babies? Good sister? Caring granddaughter?

Despite her stunning looks she was a family girl. Not for him, then. Danger with a capital D. Nothing to fancy there. He liked surfing alone, working hard and staying too busy with other people's babies to think about having any of his own.

That woman there could break hearts and he was not going there. Damn her. He'd already had more heartbreak than he could deal with. He turned his back on the unit. For some bizarre reason it made him angry with the newcomer.

'Let's see your list, Carla.'

Carla eyed him shrewdly. Handed over the patient list.

She murmured, 'I saw your friend Malachi Madden the other day. He even made a joke—a funny one. Seems having a family suits him.'

Simon raised his brows and side-eyed her without lifting his head.

'And your point?' he asked.

Carla pushed up one shoulder, her mouth kinking with amusement as she winked at him.

'Does there have to be a point, Simon? Could you perhaps think of something other than work? Just for a moment?'

CHAPTER TWO

IT WASN'T UNUSUAL for Isabella Hargraves to feel a stranger's gaze, so she didn't take much notice of the tall man in the corner. Although she had to admit that he wasn't a bad piece of eye candy—despite the scowl.

She'd eased so joyfully back into working with babies in the NICU that it would take more than some random non-admirer to divert her from her tasks.

When the apnoea alarm sounded from Baby Jones she was at his open cot in an instant. Checking the time. Checking the monitor. Watching for breaths as the heartbeat slowed with a brief dip into bradycardia before righting itself as he eventually took a breath.

'Good boy,' she murmured.

She silenced the alarm, and by the time she lifted the chart to record the time and duration of the bradycardia, Carla and the tall man were next to her.

'Isabella.' Carla indicated the man beside her. 'This is Dr Simon Purdy.'

Ah, Dr Purdy... Isabella connected the name with the cot cards. She lifted her head and smiled. 'Nice to meet you, Dr Purdy.'

This man's name sat on the identification cards of nearly every open-sided cot in the place. Obviously, here stood the favoured paediatrician. She'd heard the staff rave about his thoroughness, dedication and diagnostic abilities since she'd arrived here.

Up close? Oh, my… He was more than just eye candy. Broad-chested and broad-shouldered with tanned, handsome features and a crop of wayward golden hair. He was the full sweetshop. His eyes were the blue of the Coolangatta waves across the road from the hospital, but for some reason his gaze pierced her with surprising harshness. Her smile dimmed. Even his sinful mouth had been pulled into a taut line.

He nodded his blond head briefly—his face all carved cheek bones, patrician nose and strong chin—but his cool eyes swept away from her to the cot.

Obviously, he'd found her lacking in his previously extended perusal. 'Nurse Hargraves.' His voice was deep and dismissive.

Her brows furrowed. *Nurse?*

So, he was doing titles. Everyone else here was on a first-name basis. But he could call her what he wanted. She was actually a doctor of midwifery. She had a PhD. She gave a mental shrug. She could use professional focus against rudeness.

'Self-righting apnoea?' he questioned. Curt and clipped. Cool, even. Barely courteous.

'Yes. Self-stimulation. Sixteen seconds duration. Heart rate dipped to seventy beats per minute.' She handed him the chart.

Baby Jack Jones, his parents having only yesterday decided on his first name, was ten days old and had arrived six weeks before his due date. He lay pink and placid in the cot in front of them.

Jack's heart rate monitor read one hundred and twenty beats per minute—directly at the lower end of the perfectly normal range.

'When was his last feed?'

Although a full tummy often caused a baby's heart rate to drop post-feeding, Dr Purdy's tone seemed taciturn for a man so many had raved about. Still, a chilly tone wasn't Isabella's problem, or even interesting.

She leaned forward and touched the chart, pushing his long, elegant finger aside to lift the top sheet. The feed chart lay underneath the observation chart. But he'd know that. So why ask her the question?

'Thirty minutes ago,' she told him.

'No problems during the feed?'

'No.'

She glanced at Carla, surprised to find a glare in her boss's eyes that was certainly directed at Dr Purdy. Carla's brows were crinkled and her eyes narrowed.

Was he acting out of character? And if so, why?

Did she care?

Nope.

Isabella smiled and moved away from the ward round that she would normally follow with attentiveness. Dr Purdy didn't like her for some reason, though how that could be when they hadn't met before, she didn't know. It was not something that happened often, she realised, giving herself another mental shrug.

She glanced up at the big ward clock. Almost time for Baby Timms to be tube fed.

Cosette Timms was the smallest baby in the unit at the moment, weighing in at seven hundred and thirty grams. She'd been born premature at twenty-nine weeks, thanks to her mum's eclampsia, but had passed the fifteen-hundred-gram mark now.

Isabella would warm expressed breast milk from the fridge and prepare syringes to feed Cosette.

Carla had mentioned that Ellen Timms, Cosette's mum, phoned every morning and evening to check on her daughter.

Isabella had taken the phone call this morning. Mum wasn't coming in. She normally managed the three-hundred-kilometre round trip from the family farm twice a week—even with her other children and her husband's disability after a farm accident. But she couldn't make it today because of a home drama. There was plenty of frozen expressed milk, prepared by Ellen for just such an occasion.

Not at this feed but just before the next one, it would be

Cosette's weigh time, and the baby would have to be stripped off and redressed for weighing. Being handled too often tired the premature infants—so it coincided with bath day. Isabella had plans to sending cute bath and weigh-in photos to Ellen from the ward's mobile phone.

Isabella pictured the mum's delight at receiving the pictures as she bustled around the milk room, preparing the feed. She checked the labelled container against the chart, hailed one of the other passing NICU nurses to confirm and countersign the chart, and withdrew the correct amount of milk into the syringe to heat up.

'Isabella?' Carla called out to her.

The nurse who'd co-signed the chart with Isabella reappeared and gestured to the apparatus in her hands.

'Carla said I should take over. She's got another job for you.'

'Oh...' Isabella put the syringes and the bottle of milk down and nodded. 'Okay. Thanks.'

She washed her hands, a small frown crinkling her brows until she let it go. Hopefully, she'd still get to bath Cosette later.

She crossed the room to where Carla stood with Dr Purdy and tilted her head. 'Do you need me, Carla?'

'Yes. I've been called to a managers' meeting and Dr Purdy wants to re-site Jack's IV cannula. You know how unstable Jack can be, so I'd rather you assisted here for the moment.'

'Of course.' Isabella glanced around until she spotted the trolley they used for procedures and Jack's chart. And anything else she might need.

Dr Purdy glanced at his watch.

Isabella raised her brows at him before saying placidly, 'Give me a moment to set it up, Dr Purdy. Then I'll be with you.'

He seemed to drag his eyes away from his expensive diver's timepiece and nodded. Thankfully, he then turned to the last cot and picked up the chart.

Well, at least he wasn't going to stand there and watch her while she made everything ready. That was a good thing, but Isabella was way past worrying about nervousness with new doctors.

They came in such variety. She'd dated more than a few herself before she fell for Conlon, though most seemed to be obsessed with their own importance.

Probably Freud could have told her why she'd gone for those doctors. Daddy complex. It was a terrible thought.

But now? Hah! No more doctors or lecturers for her. She'd given up the idea of expecting anything from them except self-absorption and egotism.

She knew that was perhaps unfair. But she'd been to so many boring medical fundraising dinners with her father, and playing hostess at her father's house, she'd met many impatient doctors like Simon Purdy.

Most seemed to be in awe of their own intelligence, without observing that Isabella could have run rings around them. Though that didn't matter because she'd chosen midwifery and neonatal nursing.

She liked the hands-on patient care. She didn't want to sit all day in consulting rooms, only being allowed out for surgeries or emergencies—which mostly came during family time if her childhood had been anything to go by.

She wanted continuity of patient care. Being somewhere like here at the NICU, watching tiny newborns struggle, change and finally grow into good health. This was what she wanted to do.

That first rotation through a neonatal nursery had changed her life. She'd found her calling and taken herself to the top of her game as a neonatal intensivist. She'd been asked to join the neonatal emergency retrieval consultancy board, and through that had met neonatologists from all over the world. Which had led to her writing her thesis in Vietnam.

Conlon had jumped on board, seeing an opportunity to advance his own career by sharing the scientific paper she'd spent a year preparing.

She wasn't going there.

Deftly, she completed setting up for the procedure. She had at hand two different types of intravenous fluids, in case Dr Purdy wanted to change the intravenous concentrations. She washed her hands again.

Dr Purdy wasn't obviously looking at her, but she still felt his scrutiny despite that. It was as if he couldn't grasp something he should be able to see.

Well, she had things to do.

'When you're ready, Dr Purdy...'

CHAPTER THREE

SIMON WATCHED NURSE HARGRAVES out of the corner of his eye, refusing to think of her as Isabella. Although, grudgingly, he had to admit it was a beautiful name.

He couldn't help his strange fascination, or being impressed by her. She moved gracefully, efficiently and without hesitation as she gathered supplies and opened them onto the sterile field. Her obvious experience seemed to be at odds with her apparent youth.

Maybe she wasn't as young as she looked—but she was younger than him. And she was full of life and energy. Unlike him. She made him feel old.

As he glanced at her long, graceful neck, his breath caught again, until he had to force his eyes back to the chart that he hadn't even read once.

He wasn't that old. Just sleepwalking through life…until now.

What was it about her?

Dispassionately, you might say her eyes were too big—yet they shone like pools of jungle-green and gold, like a lioness guarding her small cub. Her nose was too straight. No, not straight…refined. It suited her face perfectly. Darn it, he wasn't going to say her mouth was too big…because seriously that mouth was to die for.

Was he sixteen years old?

'When you're ready, Dr Purdy…'

He'd sworn he would never be ready again. He wasn't ready now. He wasn't.

His mouth felt dry—parched, like the sand across the road at the beach. And he swallowed once before he answered, 'Thank you.'

Simon's critical gaze skimmed over the dressing trolley that looked to include anything he could possibly want. Forcibly, he cleared his mind of everything but the task at hand. He lifted Jack's tiny hand and studied the translucent skin and the tiny, thread-like veins beneath.

Simon noticed Nurse Hargraves had the tips of her fingers very gently resting on Jack's foot, as if reassuring him. He'd forgive her the disruption to his world for that.

'Thank you. Everything looks perfect.'

As they worked, she seemed to know what he'd ask for next. They didn't speak and, though they were both unhurried, the procedure was completed smoothly and successfully within minutes.

He frowned at the dexterous and innovative way she wrapped the insertion site.

'That's different. And better than the way I do it. Can you show me again? Please.' He handed her a small splint to mimic a baby's arm and opened another canula packet and held it up to her. 'On this?'

He poked at the facsimile.

'I like the way you've taped it down. Without any strain. And yet so secure. Teach me?'

Simon had forgotten for the moment that he was bizarrely attracted to her. His mind wanted to know how to perform this technique that looked far more comfortable for the infant.

'It's a trick I learned in Vietnam,' she replied.

He watched her fingers while she dipped and circled the cannula, then secured the tape to the imitation arm. Absently he asked, 'When were you in Vietnam?'

'Last month. Helping out in a neonatal unit in Hanoi on an

exchange organised by the university in Sydney for a paper I was writing.'

Simon nodded as he began to wrap Jack, who'd fallen asleep. When the baby was secure, Simon tucked him gently back into his open cot, then ensured all the alarms for the monitors were switched back on.

'What's the paper on?' he asked.

'Outcomes in neonatal nurseries in Vietnam, and how to raise Vietnamese community awareness for screening and neonatal care for congenital abnormalities.'

She reeled it off as she worked, cleaning up as fast and efficiently as she'd prepared. She seemed to know where everything was in the unit already as she slipped things they hadn't used back into their correct place. She'd only been here a day. He knew that. He came here every day. Many times. He would have noticed her if she'd been here longer.

He liked her forethought in learning the layout of the unit—she'd ensured that she'd be ready for emergencies. Impressive.

Lots of things about her impressed him.

Stop it.

He murmured, 'I've never been to Hanoi. How was the unit? The staff?'

'The unit's not as high-tech as this one. But the staff are amazing. The aim of my study was to encourage more antenatal attendance with the advantage of picking up potential problems before they happen.'

'Sounds like an interesting study.'

'It was.'

Something in her voice said she wasn't happy with how it had ended.

Then another apnoea alarm began to chime, and she turned and calmly walked across the room to observe and record the event. The alarm stopped.

Simon glanced around the unit. He knew all their patients were stable for the moment. He also knew that he should get to his consulting room for the morning's appointments, but he felt strangely reluctant to leave. Which reminded him: he was supposed to be distancing himself from this woman. Their conversation had pushed her even further under his skin. He needed to stop that. Back away. Fast.

That might have been why was curt as he said, 'I'll be in my office if Carla needs me.'

She lifted her hand but didn't turn around. He guessed he was dismissed. But for some absurd reason he could still see her in his mind.

CHAPTER FOUR

THE FOLLOWING MORNING the sun offered Isabella a pastel bouquet for breakfast—along with a text from Conlon, which she deleted unread.

On the horizon, the guava-pink sky hung with eggshell edges, and where the ocean fell off the edge of the world it turned strawberry around the glow in the east.

'Red sky in the morning,' Isabella murmured. 'Got the warning.'

And it's nothing to do with my new job, the swanky and cranky Dr Simon Purdy, or anything else. Not today. No, siree.

After Hanoi—and the disappointment caused by her ex—being back in Australia with Gran felt right. Her grandmother's condition had been labelled 'stable', but she was no closer to waking.

Isabella had found her sister Nadia to be well, and the promise of Isabella surfing just outside her door made this place feel like an adventure she wanted to live through every day of her life.

Except for Dr Simon Purdy.

Rainbow Bay, so aptly named, had settled into her mind as a sandy paradise. The ocean vista waved and frothed ahead of the break wall of rocks that lined the eastern edge of the beach and greeted each wave.

This is the best place to be, she mentally reassured herself.

No Sydney traffic snarling her up on the way to the beach. No disappointment waiting for her—like Conlon, who was still oblivious to his disloyalty. No daily hurt caused by her father's dismissal because he was far away in Sydney.

Gran's apartment, just a few steps to the beach and one floor from the top, gazed across the bay towards the tall skyscrapers of Surfers Paradise in the distance. The same skyscrapers that right now were blazing windows of blinding gold reflecting the sunrise from across the waves.

The drone of a plane rose above the din of the surf for a moment, until the plane disappeared behind the hill of apartments to her left to land at the hidden airport.

Why on earth hadn't she thought to come to the Gold Coast earlier, instead of working in Sydney? Why hadn't she stayed close to Gran—the most important woman in her life? Because now it might be too late.

She should have had more quality time with Gran. Especially now her widowed sister had bought a tiny courtyard apartment in her grandmother's small block facing the beach. The ground floor apartment seemed perfect for when the baby was born.

Isabella had moved into her grandmother's spare room in a bittersweet temporary arrangement while Gran lay unconscious two kilometres away, in the hospital's critical care unit. Isabella visited every day.

This morning, day two of her new job, she sat on Gran's balcony, watching the ocean and the world awaken. Drinking green tea with jasmine, she studied the water and tried not to think about the irritating Dr Purdy, who'd gone back behind his grim rock façade after the brief period of rapport they'd had while re-siting Jack's cannula.

She just wished she could remove his annoyingly handsome face from her mind, but he lurked and aggravated her like a jagged splinter in her finger. Maybe if she scraped him out and examined him under the light like a wood shaving the annoyance would go away.

Nope. Not going there.

As if to distract her, the currents and swells ebbed and

flowed, whispering their secrets, and hidden rocks showed themselves briefly. Peace—at last— seemed to soak into her, like a rock pool into a sea sponge, until her disquiet eased.

As the light grew, she watched the first surfers run to the water. Watched a lithe and powerful man run out to the back of the swells, catch a monster of a wave and ride it like quicksilver skimming the crest.

Nice.

She watched the foamy lines of rips. Looked for the best places away from the rocks and the longest rides into the beach. She worked out where she wanted to take her first surf on Rainbow Bay, tomorrow. Then she rose to get dressed for work.

'So, Gran. Today was my second day at the hospital. I think I'll really enjoy working in the unit here.'

Her grandmother's chest rose and fell.

'Carla, the unit manager, is the best kind of boss. Calm and sensible, with one of those honest faces I really like. You know that she's really *seeing* you.'

Isabella glanced across the sheets to the wrinkled face so dear to her. Gran, who had always *seen* her and Nadia, giving boundless love without coddling them.

But Gran's eyes were shut now. The wrinkled lids hiding the faded green of her irises, probably like Isabella's would in fifty years. Gran's eyes were closed as they had been since the accident, when her head had suffered the blow that had silenced her. But Gran's chest rose and fell in those shallow breaths that Isabella tried to tell herself were good enough. At least she was breathing for herself and not through a machine.

'Anyway… The unit is state-of-the-art. There are babies in there I adore already. There's this little girl—Cosette. Her mum lives an hour and a half away. She runs a farm, but still comes to visit and drop off expressed breast milk three times a week. Her husband was disabled in a farm accident, and she has three other kids. I can't wait to meet her. She sounds like a champion.'

Isabella watched the red electronic trace of her grandmother's heartbeat on the monitor above the bed. Rarely, there was a variation that suggested she might wake. But there were no signs that Gran could even hear her.

Isabella's father—expert neurologist that he was—had reminded Isabella that the longer the oblivion continued the less chance there was that her grandmother would ever wake. So clinical, even when it was his own mother he was talking about. She'd wanted to hit him.

Even more so when he'd said, 'Or if she does wake, she will most likely be in a vegetative state.'

It had been three weeks and three days since the accident and her father had given what scarce hope he ever had, away.

Lately, even Nadia seemed to be accepting that Gran was gone. But Isabella couldn't.

It was Isabella who had begged her father to request that Gran stay here, in the high-dependency unit at the private hospital, which was not quite critical care but still well-watched, for another month before they transferred her to a long-term facility.

Isabella would come and talk to Gran for as long as it took. She knew that the last sense to go in an unconscious body was hearing. She came every day for at least half an hour, either before or after work, depending on the shift, and shared the events of her day.

'There's this paediatrician—Simon Purdy. I loathe him. Don't start me on him. If he wasn't such an excellent neonatologist…'

She frowned at herself.

She *thought* she loathed him.

'Actually, he's too good at intubation and cannulation with tiny babies for me to loathe him. He managed to intubate this twenty-nine-weeker today, in less time than I had to think about it. And he got the cannula in on the first attempt. Pretty incredible. But he's still a pain.'

There—that sounded right.

'But I'm not wasting any more of our time talking about him. I had my first surf this morning.'

Gran had taught her to surf.

'You would have loved this big wave I caught...'

On Thursday Gran's heart rate had risen by ten beats per minute. Isabella checked her observation charts. There was no sign of a temperature, and even her respirations had increased in depth.

Was she getting better? Closer to surfacing? Or was Isabella dreaming?

This was a good sign, wasn't it? Or was it an infection?

'How are you, Gran?' Isabella picked up the limp, age-spotted hand and lifted it to her cheek. 'Are you okay?'

Gran's hand was cool and dry, so Isabella squeezed her fingers softly and lowered them to the bed as she sat.

'Well, this week flew by, with busy shifts at work. But these daily doses of Simon Purdy are getting harder to take. Remember I said that first day he'd started cold and then got almost civil after Jack's cannula re-siting? Well, since then he's barely said a word to me.'

Her grandmother breathed. In and out.

Isabella sat silently for a bit.

'It's weird... It's as if I can feel his eyes drilling into my back every time I turn around. Like he doesn't want me to catch him looking. But if I turn, he's spinning away. What's with that?'

She frowned at the monitor as she thought about it. And the heart rate rose for a few beats and then fell.

Isabella turned back to her grandmother and looked down at the small hand in hers. 'And of course he's as nice as pie to everyone else in the unit. So why am I getting the silent treatment? What did I do to him?'

She felt her own heart rate speed up as she thought of the unfairness of Simon Purdy's behaviour. Felt her eyes narrow. She'd like to kick him. Which was so unlike her she almost gasped.

Gran's chest rose and fell. The line on the monitor didn't change again. But it was if a thought had wriggled into her brain from the pillow beside her. Almost as if her grandmother had answered.

Isabella said slowly, 'Me being there must be doing something to him. But what?'

Of course she hadn't done anything. But the thought sat there. Hanging. Germinating.

Isabella's brows drew together again. 'Seriously, Gran. The man doesn't seem to have a life outside the unit. He's never impatient to leave or to go home. He was there every morning before I got in this week, and still there for the afternoon shift.'

She'd thought it often enough, and finally she said out loud,

'He reminds me of Dad. Spending his life at work. I pity his poor family.'

She sat back in the chair and thought about that. She could actually imagine a quarter-sized boy, the image of Simon, with the same ocean-blue eyes and full mouth, blond hair and scuffed knees. A little boy waiting for his father to come home. It made her sad for that little boy...

She refocussed. Sad for an imaginary little boy? What was wrong with her?

'Does he even have a wife?' she wondered aloud.

She'd been there a week and she still didn't know. Well, she'd know if she let people tell her. But for some crazy reason she kept holding up her hand when any colleague—and there were a couple who loved to gossip—started to wax lyrical about Simon and his life. She didn't want to know.

Why was that?

Friday dawned with another perfect daybreak in paradise, and Isabella needed the cool water in the bay to wake her after an unsettled night. Her feet slapped rhythmically on the cool sand as she ran towards the surf. Her board lay tucked securely under her arm and her anticipation rose, like the waves out there, as she carried it across the cool pre-dawn beach towards the water.

'Morning,' a chic, elderly woman called out as she passed, lifting her hand as her cavoodle chased seagulls at the edge of the water.

'Best time of the day!' Isabella called back.

The woman, Elsa Green, lived two floors down in the apartment building. She was a friend of her grandmother's.

Isabella's run to the surf slowed, as if a sea fog had rolled over her, as she remembered the cheeky, wise woman her grandmother had been for both her and her sister before that horrible day everything changed. She'd been such a loving set of soft arms when her father had been immersed in work. A rock in their childhood until she'd moved north to Rainbow Bay.

It was tragic. Unfair. But when were accidents ever fair?

She lifted her chin. Catherine Goodwin Hargraves would wake up.

Moving here had been one of Isabella's best ideas. And Nadia selling her ostentatious and heavily mortgaged house to buy the apartment under Gran's was a great move. Meanwhile Isabella could stay and mind Gran's apartment upstairs, so it would be perfect for when she came home.

And Gran *would* come home.

Isabella was already helping Nadia in the last months of pregnancy. Which only bolstered her need to be close to her sister and Gran. Rainbow Bay worked perfectly. Isabella could surf and Nadia could photograph endlessly. And soon there would be a baby—Nadia's baby. And Isabella wouldn't be in her sister's pocket because they had the separate apartments. She might even buy her own apartment in the block if one came on the market.

She just wished Gran was there with them...

The first wave slapped her knee as she jogged deeper into the breaking wash. The water soaked her thighs and waist and she sucked in a breath at the delicious coolness.

Her gaze scanned the distance and she let thoughts of the past and the present fade. She observed about two dozen riders out there with the waves, but she was concentrating on the swells. Rollers that were big enough to give a nice run in towards the beach but with no need to concentrate excessively on avoiding others with her unsettled mind.

It was Simon Purdy who had caused all this twitching and turning through the night. It didn't matter which shift she worked, he turned up at least three times and never seemed to be in hurry to leave.

He took up so much space—and not all of it physical. Though his shoulders and big bronzed arms could block the light, his hands were always gentle and capable.

She could almost see the way his mind zeroed in on their small charges, making him aware of the status of every baby in the unit. She could see it because she did the same.

An ill baby could keep him there for hours. And now, for some illogical reason, he'd apparently decided he needed Isabella as his private assistant for the trickier procedures. Even when she would have preferred not to be called upon because she was doing something she particularly enjoyed.

Especially as he still didn't talk to her.

If he hadn't been so good at what he did she'd have lost patience with him long ago, but she wanted those babies to be well as much as he did.

It was the fact that he talked to everybody else except her that made her seethe. He treated all others with friendliness and respect, while she got the serious looks, the furrowed brows, the unsmiling mouth and gestures rather than words. Hand signals. Head-nods. It wasn't fair. And, if she was honest, it was more than a little annoying.

Yet at other times she caught his glance on her and felt his attention on her back. It was as if he didn't trust her. Which was ridiculous when he'd said himself she was easily the most experienced neonatal nurse in the unit alongside Carla. What was there not to trust?

A wave slapped her in the face—she hadn't seen it coming. And there he was again, intruding on her special time. *Grr...*

Isabella put her head down and paddled, her hands digging into the water, shooting past other surfers as she arrowed through swells and crests and pushed for the back of the sets. She was using up the energy that seemed to be zinging around her body like some electrical conduit of annoyance.

She looked up. There was just the ocean in front of her, all the way to New Zealand, and she finally stopped. As she sat back on her board, legs dangling in the clear blue water, she twisted to face the beach a couple of hundred metres away, then looked back to the far horizon.

She was alone, except for the guy to her left with his back to her, who seemed to be checking out the route to New Zealand as well.

But there wasn't time to think of him. The largest swell she'd seen this morning was rolling towards her and she lifted her feet and pressed her belly and breasts into the board and began to paddle, timing the connection.

Out of the corner of her eye she saw the other surfer shift to do the same. Plenty of room between them. This wave was a monster—one of those walls of water that people didn't notice but came every couple of sets and washed fishermen off rocks. The type of wave that gave surfers the best rush. A wave that reminded her that the sea was royalty and she just its subject.

The power and height of the wave surged swiftly and smoothly and she did the same, springing to her feet and tucking her board on the shelf of water like the bow of a boat. Wind dragged at her hair. Her eyes watched the water shoot below her and around her.

Blue everywhere—above her and beneath her. The sky, the wind... The world was condensed into this ride along the shoulder of a magnificent wall of myriad coloured water.

Her feet danced as she adjusted angle and weight, almost flying as she shot faster and closer to the beach, until the water monster collapsed under her and she slid out at the back and surfaced in a wash of foam and clinging magic.

Isabella lifted her chin, tilted her face to the sky and whooped.

She turned to see if the man at the back of the waves had made it, to share the moment, but he was already paddling away. He must have made it, because he was close, but she had been in a world of her own.

CHAPTER FIVE

SIMON HAD NOTICED the glorious woman before she'd entered the water. Hell, every man out at the back of the waves had noticed her in those bikini bottoms under a short-sleeved surf shirt. Her board sat under her arm as if it was a flimsy paddle-pop stick, rather than a finned, fibreglass weight. Her long, luscious legs bronzed by the sun, glided smoothly as she ate up the distance between the sand and the launch point.

She hadn't been looking his way—her eyes had been fixed on the sets of waves, the wash, the horizon—but he'd been drawn, then, to her face.

His stomach had twisted as if a shark had come up from beneath him and chewed on his intestines.

Not happening. Couldn't be.

His breath had hitched as his chest went tight. It was *her.*

He'd almost fallen off his board—not something he would have lived down with his peers—but he'd stopped himself wobbling in time to absorb the shock. Might as well have been slapped in the nose by a neighbour's board. But his eyes had stayed glued to her.

Isabella Hargraves had run into the waves and launched herself on top of the board and then begun to paddle towards him, squashing her beautiful breasts. Which had meant the taut globes of her tanned buttocks had been there for all to see as her strong, feminine arms arrowed through the swells towards the quieter water.

The force of the biggest wave in the world couldn't have stopped him watching.

Me and all the rest of the guys out there, he'd thought sourly, as he'd glanced around.

Yep. She was poetry in motion. And the last thing he needed to see. Or feel.

But, dammit! This was *his* beach—*his* sanctuary— and now she was here to destroy the peace he'd fought for all week.

Another ghastly thought intruded.

Was he going to bump into her every morning when the surf was up as well as at work?

This was wrong. Already she was taking up too much head-space just by him seeing her in the NICU. He didn't need her glorious backside and her long, lean legs to kick him when he was down.

Since that first day he hadn't been able to ignore her, no matter how hard he'd tried. And he had tried. He'd managed to shore up his defences by barely speaking to her, so that he didn't get any closer, but he couldn't keep his eyes and his thoughts away.

Thankfully, his ridiculous fascination had kept his mouth shut. But, bizarrely, his brain kept going back to that brief rapport they'd had that first day, and how she'd felt like the easiest person in the world to talk to. How much more he'd wanted to know about her... How he'd wanted to lose himself in her fiercely intelligent eyes and revel in the elusive dream he'd vowed would never be his again.

That was when he'd really panicked.

Carla was on his case for giving Isabella the cold shoulder and apparently singling out a staff member she really, really wanted to keep, so he'd agreed yesterday afternoon that he'd try harder to be civil to Nurse Hargraves.

But his whole psyche had screamed *danger* right along with *hot, hot, hot* when he looked at Isabella.

Simon would not let anyone close again. His own mother had died giving birth to him. And he would not put himself out there to risk the grief, the loss and the monumental guilt he still carried from three years ago when he'd lost his wife.

Louise had been his first love, the first woman he'd allowed to get close to him. He'd sworn to protect her and keep her safe.

Probably another guilt trip left over since his seventh birthday, when his father told him that *he'd* been the reason his mother had died. A fact that his older, medically trained self knew was spurious, but it was still so hard to convince the seven-year-old kid inside him.

Then Louise and their son had died. When he had been absent—working. And despite his best friend—his wife's doctor—telling him that nothing would have changed the outcome, Louise's death had damaged him. Adding to the loathing his father had heaped on him in the dark times of his childhood.

In short, he was not going down the route of attraction, falling in love, planning a life together and then losing the one he'd pinned his future on ever again. *Ever.*

Never.

No matter how glorious Isabella Hargraves was. No matter how much poetry in motion he saw in her.

He just wasn't sure how he was going to stop himself.

CHAPTER SIX

WHEN ISABELLA WALKED into the unit later that morning, the ferocious glower she received from Simon Purdy could have shrivelled her on the spot.

She froze. Stared. Glared back at him.

The calmness and tranquillity from her amazing surf this morning seemed to trickle away like seawater down her back, leaving her cold and chilled. And then red-hot with fury. She was *so* over this.

Isabella marched across the unit. Stopped in front of him and asked very quietly, so nobody else could hear, and very clearly, so he would understand, 'What is your problem?'

'You,' he replied.

His blue eyes were stone-hard and his mouth was a thin line.

She narrowed her eyes at him. It was a measure of the build-up of tension over the last week that she allowed her hands to come up to her hips.

'What have I done?' she shot back. 'Or did you just get out on the wrong side of the bed? *Again.*'

Before he could answer, Carla glided up and stepped between them. 'What's going on?' she asked them both, but she was looking at Simon.

Isabella said quietly, and with impeccable calm, 'I don't care if Dr Purdy is the best paediatrician this side of the equator. I expect to be treated with the respect I deserve and the politeness he so easily gives to everyone else in the unit.'

Carla nodded. 'Fair call, Isabella. Simon…?'

Isabella's and Simon's eyes were still locked—neither had looked at the unit manager. Isabella held his gaze—his hard and blue, hers determined not to give in—until he flinched.

She heard his breath heave out and for some strange, stupid reason she actually felt sorry for him.

What the...?

'You're right,' Simon said.

He lifted his chin. Straightened his shoulders. Stared at the wall past her head.

'I apologise, Isabella. Something happened this morning that I shouldn't have brought to work.'

His gaze drifted briefly to Isabella's face. She saw the briefest flicker of searing pain there until he looked away to Carla.

'I'll do better.'

Then he walked out of the unit, leaving Isabella staring after him, still not understanding why she wasn't angry any more and confused as to why on earth she was wishing she hadn't said anything.

Carla must have read her expression. Or else she was prescient.

'It needed saying. And he wasn't listening to me,' Carla said as she patted Isabella's arm. 'He knows he wasn't being fair.'

'Hi, Gran. How are you today?'

As Isabella leaned over and kissed her grandmother's soft cheek she inhaled the faint, sweet rose scent. Gran still smelled the same as she had for as long as Isabella could remember and the fragrance always made her feel hope that her grandmother would wake up.

That was why Isabella replenished Gran's favourite soap when it shrank, and why the nurses promised to continue to use it during her care.

Isabella sat down. 'Work was fine...'

Gran's chest rose and fell.

'Although this morning, when he came in, Simon Purdy was in a foul mood.' Isabella scoffed. 'He actually glared at me as if I'd done something wrong. So I confronted him. That's not like me, I know, but I was so over the dirty looks. He did apologise. But he looked strange…'

She shook her head.

'I still have no idea what his beef is, and if he wasn't one of the best neonatologists I've ever seen I'd have made a formal complaint. Still, maybe he'll be better now.'

She listened to herself. Gran did not need to hear this.

She blew out a breath. 'Luckily, I had such a great surf before work. So it was like water off a seagull's back. You would have loved this huge wave I caught. It was so good…'

It had been an amazing start to the day.

And then that man… Her mind drifted back to Simon Purdy. It was disconcerting. She'd never had someone take an instant dislike to her before. And then there'd been that look of agony she'd seen.

Gran didn't need to know about that, either. But she felt agitated at the thought of him, and grimaced.

Isabella leaned forward and opened the drawer beside the bed. Her fingers found the tube of rose-scented hand lotion and she reached to pick up her grandmother's hand. She squeezed the tube and gently swirled the lotion onto the papery skin of Gran's hands.

Isabella did this often—sat and gently massaged the long, thin fingers of Gran's hands with the lotion while she talked. As always, a sense of peace settled over her.

'Anyway… Nadia's been getting headaches. I don't think it's pregnancy-related, but her next antenatal appointment isn't until next Wednesday. Hopefully she's going as an outpatient today to get checked, as I suggested, but you know what she's like. Stubborn.'

As Gran breathed in and out her heart rate did that little rise and fall thing again, but Isabella was used to it now.

'You always said we were both stubborn, but I think Nadia's more obstinate than me. I'll find out whether she went when I get home.'

Home. To Gran's apartment without Gran. It was getting harder and harder to imagine her grandmother ever being there when she came home from work. She hated that and hoped she wasn't losing faith like everyone else.

No. She wouldn't. She'd use some of her own stubbornness to stay positive.

'Your flat's looking fine. I haven't killed all your plants.'

Yet, she thought ruefully. Most were drooping, and she didn't know if she was giving them too much water or not enough.

Or maybe they needed more sunlight?

'I mentioned my concerns to Mrs Green…'

Isabella thought about that, and a smile tugged at her mouth.

'So cool that her name is Green and she's good with plants.'

She waited for her grandmother to smile, but of course she didn't.

She shook her head at herself.

'Mrs Green said she'd use her spare key and come up and water the plants on the veranda every other day, when she knows I'm out. She always asks about you. I keep telling her you'll be home soon.'

Gran continued to breathe. In and out.

The monitor continued to trace her heart rate.

By the time Isabella parked her car under the apartments it was nearing four-thirty. Instead of pressing for the lift she climbed the stairs, turned left, and knocked on her sister's door.

When there was no answer, she knocked again. And again. Until she heard Nadia's voice inside. Faintly.

'I'm coming… All right… Give me a minute.'

A cold flicker of worry ignited in Isabella's chest at the dull timbre of Nadia's voice. But at least the shuffling noises were coming closer, and finally the door opened.

Her sister leaned against the door frame like a droopy sun-flower, with her yellow hair falling over her face and her long neck bent as if she could barely hold the weight of her head up. Let alone the big belly out front.

'Isabella. It's you.'

Who else would it be?

Isabella pushed the door open and gently turned her sister, nudging her back into the lounge room and into a chair. 'You look terrible.'

'Gee. Thanks, Sis.' Nadia's voice trailed away listlessly.

'Did you go and get checked out today at the hospital?'

'Didn't have the energy.'

'How's your headache?'

'There all the time. All over my head. It's weird…' Nadia lifted a tired hand to rub her scalp.

Isabella peered down and examined her sister's ankles. No, they didn't look swollen. But oedema could happen quickly.

'Are you going to the toilet as much as you normally do?'

Nadia sighed. 'Probably not. But then I'm not drinking or eating either, so there's nothing to pass. I'm a bit sick in my stomach.' She rubbed her abdomen under her breast. 'Probably picked up a bug from somewhere.'

All nebulous symptoms, but worrying. 'I want to take you in and get you checked out in Maternity.'

Nadia shook her head—gingerly. 'Not now. I've just taken two headache tablets. I'm going to go and lie down.' She closed her eyes, as if the light was too bright. 'I was lying down when you knocked.'

'I don't like the look of you… Really. Something's not right.'

Her sister made an effort to sit straighter in the chair. Forced her eyes wider. 'You're a worrywart. How about I have my sleep, then you come and see me in a couple of hours? Use your key so I don't have to get up. If I'm still no good, I'll go then.'

'I'd be happier if you went now…'

Nadia waved her away. 'But it's not about *you* being happy, is it?'

Time for the big guns.

Isabella's instincts were screaming.

'No. It's about keeping your baby safe,' Isabella said quietly. Her voice was firm and she watched her words finally sink in.

Understanding flooded Nadia's face. And then her green eyes widened in fear. 'Yes. It's about the baby. I'll go now.'

Half an hour after they arrived at the hospital Nadia began to see flashes of light in front of her eyes, and then she started to seize uncontrollably.

Suddenly the clinic was full of people and Isabella retreated to the back of the room. She gave thanks for the hospital policy of one support person being allowed to stay at all times where possible.

Then a tall, dark-haired doctor suddenly strode in and organised everyone in seconds, giving quiet orders that were instantly obeyed.

Isabella's terror receded as Nadia's hypertensive crisis was brought swiftly under control and a care plan commenced.

The new doctor turned to her and introduced himself. 'I'm Malachi Madden, the consultant obstetrician on call today. You're Nadia's sister? And a midwife?'

'Yes.'

'Excellent. So, Nadia has eclampsia—you'll know what I'm talking about. We'll keep her in under one-on-one observation for the next twenty-four hours. If she settles on the medication, we'll see how long we can prolong the pregnancy. Thirty-two weeks is not a great stage for birth, but sometimes it's necessary. We'll start steroids now, to help mature the baby's lungs, with the probability of delivery in the next forty-eight hours.'

His manner was brisk and blunt—which she appreciated—and decisive.

He went on, 'With eclampsia, there's really not much benefit to prolonging the pregnancy, because the environment becomes dangerous for the mother and is no longer optimal for the foetus.'

'I understand. I work in neonatal intensive care.'

'Do you? That's handy.' He smiled at her and, unexpectedly, his smile was sweet and sincere. 'My wife and I have one-year-old twins, and I know babies do give you interesting moments. Your sister will be glad of your advice.'

CHAPTER SEVEN

AT FIVE-THIRTY THE next morning Simon's phone buzzed. He rolled out of bed to sit up and answer the call.

Years ago, as an exhausted med student, he'd learned not to lie down and take phone calls. Though he knew at this time of day he wouldn't fall asleep, because the sun would be up soon and he'd be planning on hitting the beach.

In five out of the last six days he'd been called out before sunrise and had had to go to the hospital instead of enjoying an early-morning surf.

The only day he had made it, his longed-for peace had been slapped for six by a blonde bombshell in tiny bikini bottoms.

He glanced at the caller ID. His registrar. Not surprising. Henry was the most likely person to ring him at an ungodly hour, though he only phoned when he needed advice or help.

'Morning, Simon.' Henry's cheerful voice came down the line. 'Got a new prem. Thirty-two weeks. Female. Two thousand grams. Born an hour ago due to maternal eclampsia and requiring CPAP at the moment, plus a cannula that's proving tricky, but otherwise she's stable.'

'Nothing you can't handle. So what's the problem?' Simon didn't believe in babying his registrars. Because they were the next generation and one day, unimaginable as it was at this moment, he would retire.

'I've had two goes at inserting the line without success, and the baby's auntie said I had to get you.'

Simon's brow furrowed. 'Come again?'

He couldn't think of any of his friends due to have a baby soon. Though it sometimes happened with hospital staff. People recommended him for their grandchildren or asked him to be in charge of sick nieces and nephews. And he always agreed. There had to be some perks for these staff who cared so diligently for others. But those requests usually came when he was on duty. At handover or in normal working hours.

'She said I'm not allowed to try the cannula again.'

Simon mentally shrugged. He was awake anyway. 'Who's the auntie?'

His registrar lowered his voice. 'That new neonatal intensivist… Isabella Hargraves. She said if the kid wasn't her niece she'd put the line in herself.'

Any lingering drowsiness in Simon's mind disappeared like mist in the sun and he remembered that first day, with Carla telling him Isabella had moved here to be with her grandmother and pregnant sister.

'Ahh. Her sister. I'm coming.'

The first person Simon saw when he entered the unit was Isabella, and his gaze stuck on her like a seagull spotting a lone potato chip. He forced himself to look away as he washed his hands at the sink. Her hair had been pulled back in a blonde ponytail, she wore no make-up, and yet she still looked as if she'd stepped out of a fashion magazine. It was the way she held herself as much as what she wore.

Hell, she looked like a model even when she was in scrubs.

His gaze shifted to the cot she stood beside, and he saw the small bare limbs under the heat lamp, and the monitors and paraphernalia of a prem baby in their care. He inclined his head towards Henry and the night shift nurse as he crossed the room to them.

'Thank you for coming,' Isabella said, her voice softly hesitant.

He wasn't surprised to see uncertainty in her eyes, as if she was not sure of her reception. Yesterday had been a day of fireworks, and they'd been careful to avoid each other since her accusations and his apology.

But it wasn't as if he would ever have declined the request. He realised he hadn't been particularly friendly, but...

'Of course I'd come.'

There was no missing her relief. Though it was a surprise that she'd want him looking after her niece. And even more personally noteworthy that he found he didn't want anyone else doing it, either.

'Thank you for trusting me.'

He turned to Henry.

'Run me through the history.'

Henry did, and when he was finished Simon nodded. Then another thought intruded.

He looked at Isabella. 'Where's your sister? Is she okay?'

The beautiful woman in front of him sagged a little, and he wanted to put out a hand in sympathy. Badly. But his sense of self-preservation wouldn't let him.

'Nadia's still in Recovery. She had a caesarean section after escalating eclampsia. But she should improve soon, with the end of the pregnancy.'

He could see the concern in the creases of her brow. It must be a big worry for her to carry, and he wanted to ease that burden. He felt the urge to reassure her. Comfort her. Dammit, he wanted to help her in any way he could.

'I'm sorry to hear she's unwell. Who's her obstetrician?'

'Malachi Madden.'

She searched his face for reassurance, and he felt the consolation of being able to give it freely. Relief expanded inside him. His long-time friend was the best.

'Ahh. Great. Excellent choice. He's sharp. He'll look after her.'

'And you'll look after Kate?' she asked.

He could see she'd recovered her usual calm façade, as if he had already helped with his endorsement of Malachi.

'I will,' he told her. 'Absolutely.'

Simon was soon feeling along the edges of the tiny baby's body, skimming the abdomen and watching the equal rising of both lungs.

'Her mum had called her Kate? Great name.'

'Named after my grandmother—Catherine.'

He looked up and saw her gaze had clouded again.

'Gran's not well either.'

He nodded. Said sincerely, 'I'm sorry to hear that.'

Then he shifted his gaze down again. 'Let's have a listen to this little lady.' He raised a brow at Henry. 'You go. I'll stay.'

'Thanks, boss. Been a long night.'

The young man lifted one finger to his forehead in a salute to Simon and tipped an imaginary hat to Isabella. He was grinning as he strode away.

Simon positioned the buds of his stethoscope in his ears and examined his new patient.

He said quietly to the night shift nurse waiting, 'Do we know how the placenta looked? Was it failing? Were all vessels present?'

'The theatre notes haven't arrived, yet.' The nurse was young, nervous, and kept darting glances between Simon and Isabella. 'I'll let you know when they come through.'

'Maybe give them a ring now?' Simon suggested mildly, but the nurse got the message and took off.

He looked at 'Auntie Isabella'. The thought made him want to smile, but there was nothing funny about what she was going through.

'Is there any history of pre-eclampsia with your sister?' he asked.

'No.'

She shook her head and her ponytail flopped over her shoulder. He could see more clearly that she looked tired and a little strung out. Not surprising. And no thanks to him.

In a flash of insight, he regretted the barriers he'd been putting up since he first saw her. She was new to town. She needed kindness, not his prickly defences, and she had a lot going on in her life. He hadn't realised how much. He'd been an arrogant idiot, only thinking about himself and his own insecurities. His own demons. Which wasn't like him.

So why was that? Why act so much out of character? And why had he targeted someone he knew didn't deserve it?

He was afraid he knew why. Fear. Of himself. For himself. And, riding on the back of that, fear for her if she relied on him.

He had a sudden urge to reach out and touch her shoulder… apologise. Hell, he wanted to pull her into his arms and give her a hug. Of course he couldn't do anything so stupid. But he could breathe in the scent of her. Could watch the expressions cross her face as she looked at Kate.

Thankfully, her eyes were fixed on her niece, not on him.

'When I got home yesterday afternoon Nadia was complaining of a headache,' she explained. 'She looked so unwell I dragged her into Maternity. She started seizures half an hour after we arrived.'

Close call. And scary. She had to be imagining other scenarios.

'Lucky you did what you did.' His voice was soft. He understood the fear of others. He'd been there in the worst way. 'That's nasty. Dangerous for both Mum and baby.'

She started, as if surprised. For a horrid moment he thought she was going to cry. And then she lifted her chin.

'Yes.'

He dragged his eyes from her face, glanced towards the desk, but the young nurse was still on the phone.

'She's in the best place now. Let's have a look at this cannula…'

'Want me to help?'

Isabella had already begun to douse her hands with the cleanser clipped to the sides of all the cots.

Of course he wanted her help. She was the best to work with. But it wasn't fair when it was her own niece.

'You're okay with that?' he asked.

'As long as you don't mind that I called you in.'

He did smile at that. 'No. Never. Though Henry probably would've got the cannula in on the third go.'

'I wasn't willing to risk his next attempt.' She narrowed her eyes. 'Send him to me next week and I'll adjust his technique.'

'I'll do that.'

Simon laughed. Something he hadn't done for a while, except maybe with his friend Malachi and his wife, Lisandra. Henry did tend to rush when he was nervous. Isabella might have made him nervous. Hell, she made *him* nervous—but for a different reason.

That thought sobered him.

'If Kate was my niece, I probably wouldn't have let him try again, either.'

'Yes… Thank you for coming.'

'You're welcome. She looks good, Isabella.'

Suddenly it was easy to talk to her. Like back in the beginning, before he'd put up his great wall. It was something he'd been avoiding thinking about like the plague, because that one time he'd listened, he'd been drawn to her so strongly. He'd backed away in an absolute wild panic, and hadn't wanted to repeat the experience. It hurt too much to care for people and then lose them. So, he'd vowed to keep that wall way up during work—to make it unlikely he'd do anything stupid.

Anyway, she was experienced enough to know what he wanted during procedures without him having to use words. All it took was a lift of his brow and she knew what he wanted. Which made it easier. And harder.

Aside from that, the more he discreetly watched and listened to her, the more he suspected she might be one of the smartest people he'd met.

But now she was a concerned relative. And he talked to her because it was part of his job. She needed to hear what was going on. He passionately believed in not holding back information from those who had the right to be told.

'She's got a heart murmur. Did you hear that?' he asked her.

Isabella had a stethoscope around her neck, and he assumed she'd have listened to her niece's chest.

'I did. Sounds like a PDA. Hopefully, because she's prem, her patent ductus will close as she grows.'

'My thought too.'

Ha! He known she'd pick that up.

'And we both know that children born after twenty-eight weeks of pregnancy, and with a weight like this little lady, have a big chance of having no long-term problems.'

'We know eight out of ten do,' Isabella corrected him.

He smiled to himself, and didn't look at her as he studied the lack of creases on Baby Kate's feet and the cartilage growth of her ears.

'But she's a good weight for thirty-two weeks, so the pre-eclampsia hasn't been a long-term issue she'll have to recover from.'

Her shoulders rose and fell in a sigh. 'When it's your own sister's baby, she looks more tiny and delicate than everyone else's baby. I'm used to seeing babies without toenails and hair, and she has both, but she's so fragile. What do you think of her breathing?'

'I think she's doing well for the day she's had.'

'I know. Don't tell me.' She waved her hand at him, apparently aware he'd been about to say something reassuring. 'Albert Einstein was born two months premature and look at what he achieved.'

She smiled, and he couldn't help smiling back. He'd bet she'd heard that so many times. They'd dined on that story in med school, and he suspected midwives did too.

'Exactly. We'll get her started on some broad-spectrum antibiotics. Do you know if Nadia's going to breastfeed?'

He saw Isabella was looking better for their conversation. More herself. Not so shattered.

'She intends to.'

'Great. She'll have you to help her.'

CHAPTER EIGHT

SIMON PURDY WAS being nice to her, and now she felt like crying. Felt like burying her nose in his big, beautiful chest and sobbing. Of course it was just emotional overload from the last twelve hours. Her sister and niece could have died—highly unlikely in the modern day—but the risk had been there.

And then Isabella had demanded they get Simon. She didn't know how it had happened, and she wasn't normally a pushy person, but she'd stood there watching his registrar's second attempt at placing the cannula and known he wouldn't get it.

She needed Simon on board for her niece. She didn't care if she was being demanding. Didn't care if Simon hated her guts. He was the best. This was all about Nadia's baby and Nadia couldn't be there. Isabella was. And she would be Kate's champion until her mother recovered.

And so here they were. Back to working on a baby together—although she was pretending it wasn't her flesh and blood lying there.

Her hands moved confidently, with muscle memory, as she assembled fresh equipment and Simon prepared Kate's tiny arm for another attempt at the cannula insertion.

He'd come when she'd asked, she thought. So fast. He must live as close as she did. And Henry, the registrar, hadn't been offended, which was a good thing for future professional relationships. Although, even if he had been miffed she would still have demanded Simon.

All these thoughts played in her mind as she watched his

long, slender, yet strong hands. Piano player's hands…calm, capable, hands, she thought, her eyes glued to them as they very gently tilted Kate's skin this way and that to catch the light and expose the minuscule thread of veins below the skin.

'One there,' he said, and she peered with him. She inhaled his man scent and felt her pulse jump and her heated skin react to his nearness.

She ignored the sensations. She didn't want to think about them. She returned her mind to Kate, and allowed the relief of seeing Simon's skills to flow over her.

The vein was faint, but clear to see. Henry hadn't seen that one. The tension in her shoulders and neck released. The responsibility had shifted to the man beside her.

Simon Purdy had this all under control. She could relax.

He was here and—surprise, surprise—finally treating her the same way he treated the other staff.

She thought about that. No. Actually, he was treating her as if she was the relative of one of his patients. With reassurance and an unspoken promise to do his best. And yet there was professional appreciation for her as well. She'd seen a glimmer of it before, when they were working together, but it was a little hard to feel appreciated if the person you worked with didn't speak to you.

If her niece wasn't so fragile she'd be thinking all her Christmases had come at once. But for the moment she just wanted to see this cannula in and working.

Within seconds the procedure had been completed successfully and their eyes briefly met in relief. Held for a couple of seconds longer than necessary.

She taped the tiny tube down while Simon held it still. Then they both stood back as the machine began to count the slow drops of fluid running into Kate's arm.

All tension her released and relief washed over her. 'Thank you.'

He smiled at her. His teeth white, his mouth curved and that beautiful, strangely sexy nose of his pointed her way.

'You're very welcome. As always, you're a great right hand.'

'As always, huh?' She tilted her head at him and raised her brows. Her voice just a little mocking. 'Can't say I've felt that appreciation much over the last week.'

Good grief. Not now. She closed her lips.

Not when he was doing her and Kate a favour.

But he had the grace to look away. 'Some personal stuff,' he murmured. 'Not your fault. But, yes, you copped some of the fall-out. I apologise again for that. My behaviour hasn't been fair.'

That made her blink. She had not expected a confession and another comprehensive expression of regret.

Off balance, she said quietly, 'Why were you so foul yesterday when I came in?'

Lord, it was as if her filters had been lost sometime in the long night.

It was her turn to look away. 'Sorry. Ignore that. It's been an emotional twelve hours.'

His whole body went rigid. His mouth pursed. And then he sighed. Shook his head and turned his gaze to her. He studied her face and then shook his head again. His expression was resigned...even slightly amused.

'Would you like to go for breakfast after this? I know a place that opens early. I can explain.'

And that was another thing she had not expected him to say.

She glanced at the clock. Twenty minutes until the day staff began to arrive. She was on the afternoon shift today, and she had to sleep. But...

'I guess I need to eat. I've drunk lots of coffee. But no food since lunch yesterday.'

'We'll wait to hand over to Carla...get the morning staff here first, if that's okay with you?'

'Of course. Actually, I'd prefer that.'

'Thought you might.'

He smiled, and she felt that ridiculous urge to cry again. She didn't think he would notice, but he said softly, so nobody else could hear, 'You'd be eligible for compassionate leave, you know. Next of kin. You should take a day or two, get some sleep, come and go to see Kate and your sister without having to concentrate on your patients.'

That did sound like heaven, and she was so tempted—but she was new here, and couldn't let Carla down. The unit had already been busy before Kate, and a new premmie would stretch their limits.

'I think they'll need more staff...not less.'

'I thought you might say that too.' His blue eyes were too kind. 'We'll see.'

He walked away a few steps, picked up a chair and placed it gently beside Kate's cot. 'Sit here, watch your niece and enjoy her. She's stable, if early in her adventures. I'll do a quick round to check everyone else while we wait.'

So she sat. In the chair he brought for her. And the overwhelming facts finally sank in. She was an auntie. Nadia was safe. And Simon had come to care for Kate.

They'd walked to breakfast. They went to the coffee shop that sat perched above Rainbow Bay, with its high stools and tall benches under red umbrellas, all facing the waves. Jars of pretty purple-blue knives and forks sat in the middle of the tables. Very beachy...

Simon had said he lived too close to the hospital to drive—it was only a block—so he didn't take his car to work. She said she didn't either.

Isabella hadn't realised there was a place so near to where she lived that was open this early. She studied the menu briefly—*yum*—and put it back down. Her stomach rumbled.

The waitress, a young woman with a dozen piercings and her hair shaved so close to her head she was almost bald, grinned at Simon. 'Yo, Doc. The usual?' She patted her pocket and pulled out a pen and notebook.

'Yes. Thanks, Lulu.'

He turned to face her. That lovely, debonair nose of his—

which for some reason she liked too much—was suddenly too close to hers and his face, too handsome, was filling her vision.

'You ready to order?'

Order. Right. Stop looking at the pretty man.

'Smashed avocado and eggs, thanks. Plus, your rainbow juice. No coffee. I need to sleep soon.'

'On the way,' Lulu said, and winked at Simon.

He was obviously a regular patron.

'I think the waitress likes you.'

'Lulu's the proprietor. I looked after her twins when they were born. Twin-to-twin transfusion, and the smallest one struggled a bit at first. They're both at preschool now and doing well.'

'No wonder you're a favourite. A story around every corner. Or around every cafe.' She waved her arm towards the other stools. 'Great to know this is here, though. Thanks.'

He lounged in his chair, relaxed, soaking in the sun and the admiration of passers-by like a darned rock star. Not looking as if he'd been dragged from his bed by her. Drat the man. No doubt she looked as if she'd been raking her hair and sleeping in her clothes for the whole night.

'Despite how I look now, I do like to get up early,' she said.

'Me too,' he said, with an odd tone in his voice. 'I've been surfing here for the last three years. It's where I find my peace.'

There was a definite note of pique there. Plus, a strange twist to his beautiful mouth. And why she was noticing all these masculine attributes she did not know.

That was the last thing she needed to do. She needed to eat and go to bed. And put the intriguing Simon Purdy, currently being so pleasant to her, out of her mind. Another workaholic she was drawn to. What was wrong with her?

Then his actual words sank in.

She turned to face him. 'You surf?'

'Mm-hmm,' he said, very dryly.

She crinkled her brows at him. Now that she thought about it, he did have more of a laid-back, world-class surfer look than a rock star gleam, with his blond hair slightly ruffled and his skin tanned bronze. The way his azure-blue eyes crinkled at the corners could be from watching hundreds of promising ocean swells roll his way.

And suddenly she knew.

'You were out at the back of the swells when I was there yesterday.' She should have recognised those shoulders. That hair. 'And later that was you paddling away after that amazing wave.'

'It was.'

She frowned. 'I've been surfing every morning this week. I haven't seen you...'

Then she remembered that first surfer she'd watched, and suspected that had been him as well. How could she have missed him? She couldn't believe she hadn't recognised him yesterday. She guessed on a surfboard was not a place she'd expected to see him. But surely, she hadn't missed him day after day, every morning?

'I've had a run of early call-outs that have impacted on my surf time this week.' He breathed in slowly and let it out. 'Since my wife died, and since I moved to the beach...' He lifted his shoulders, and then his chin. 'The waves and work. That's where I find my peace.'

'You lost your wife?'

Heck. That explained a lot. He was broken. He had a right to be moody.

'I'm sorry for your loss.'

'Three years ago. Louise and our baby both died. Amniotic fluid embolism.'

Disasterous. That happened when amniotic fluid crossed the placenta into the mother's bloodstream. How awful for all of them.

He was looking at her as if he didn't believe her. 'You didn't know? Hospital staff usually make sure everyone knows everything.'

She shook her head. 'I make an effort not to engage. I come from a high-profile family and I dislike gossip.'

'Yes. Carla told me about your father on your first day.' His mouth quirked. 'Apparently, I do listen to gossip. She could see you had made an impact on me.'

She had made an impact on him? When? How?

But he didn't add to the statement. Maybe she had heard him wrong.

Something else bothered her. 'You said you'd tell me what happened yesterday. Why did I get the super-snarly Dr Purdy?'

He rubbed his chin with his knuckles, and looked relieved when their drinks arrived.

Lulu stood for a minute, examining Simon's face. 'Haven't seen you for a while…'

'We've been busy in the NICU. This is Isabella. She's one of those hotshot neonatal nurses—like the ones who came in the helicopter to scoop up Lily when she was transferred.'

Lulu looked impressed and Isabella felt the heat in her cheeks. He'd known that about her, too?

'Cool.' Lulu grinned, and the tiny diamond in her tooth glinted. 'You people are amazing. I hope we see you again another day.'

Isabella smiled back, even if it was a tired smile. She could feel herself wilting.

'You will. I live around here. Or my grandmother did…' *Not did.* 'Does. She *does.* She's in hospital at the moment.'

Why had she started this? She was too tired to be sensible. 'Anyway, thanks…'

Lulu nodded and went off to answer the bell at the kitchen window. It looked as if their food was ready.

Lulu arrived back with their plates just as Simon asked, 'What's wrong with your grandmother?'

His concern warmed Isabella more than it should have, but still she felt the tug of old grief and shock. 'She was knocked over by a hit-and-run driver a month ago. She's still unconscious.'

Simon closed his eyes briefly and muttered, 'I've been stupid…' He shook his head. 'Mrs Hargraves…' He turned his shoulders and pointed to where her grandmother's apartment block was just visible through the trees. 'You're living in her flat?'

'Yes. And my sister bought one in the same block.'

He said something she couldn't quite hear, but it sounded possibly like *Fate is conspiring*.

'Sorry?'

'Nothing.' He lifted his hands and said to the sky, 'Should I just bow to the inevitable? That I'm going to see you everywhere I go?'

Isabella stifled a yawn. 'You're being annoying.'

He tilted his head as if he changed his mind about what he was going to say and gestured for her to eat. 'I'm guessing you've been up for twenty-four hours. You need a sleep.'

He still hadn't told her what his problem had been yesterday, but at that point she just didn't care. She'd got to the stage when she was almost too tired to eat, but she'd better—she'd need some energy to get home.

CHAPTER NINE

SIMON FINISHED HIS breakfast and sipped his coffee while his companion finished hers. Really, there was nothing he could do except make sure Isabella made it to her apartment.

He might as well tell her he lived upstairs, even if she was too tired to comprehend, because it would be stupid to put her into the lift and not get in after her.

Lulu brought the bill and he paid it. Isabella didn't notice as she stared unfocussed into the distance.

Yep, she'd crashed.

'Come on, sleepyhead, I'll walk you home. Can't have you falling asleep in a bus shelter.'

'I will not fall asleep in a bus shelter,' she said with just a little fuzzy haughtiness that he found surprisingly cute. She gathered her bag and slung it over her shoulder. Then she turned back and said, 'Thanks, Lulu. That was wonderful.'

He thought it sweet that she'd appreciated the service. They walked side by side along the path towards the square apartment building that soon loomed over them.

He couldn't believe he hadn't run into her in the lift. But then, he had been keeping odd hours lately. Pretty funny that he'd spent most days with her at work, though, and yet they hadn't realised they shared an address.

As they reached the ground floor entrance she fumbled in her bag and he touched her shoulder. 'I've got it.' He pulled out his keys from his pocket, opened the door, and gestured for her to go in front of him.

She frowned. 'Why have you got a key to this building?'

'Not that sleepy, then?' he said, amused by her suspicion.

She tilted her head back, stared at him with narrowed eyes. He noticed her gaze had lost its dozy inattention.

'I live on the eighth floor,' he said succinctly.

Her eyes widened. 'You're kidding me?'

'I was surprised, too, when I worked it out at the café.'

'So you know my grandmother?'

Her eyes were an incredible shade of green with gold flecks. The world shifted as he stared. His gaze drifted to her mouth, where the words had come from. So soft. Tempting. He could just kiss... And then he woke up. Hot. Bothered. Mentally smacking himself.

She said, 'Hello...?'

Simon stepped back to make more space between them.

Oh, whoa, lost it there for a second.

What the heck had happened?

He'd known this was a bad idea.

He reorganised his thoughts and played back the conversation. 'Yes. Mrs Hargraves? I've met her many times in the lift. She's a lovely lady. I was very sorry to hear about her accident.' He pressed the lift call button and stood back with her to wait.

'She's still unconscious,' Isabella said, in a normal voice.

Maybe she hadn't noticed he'd almost kissed her, he thought. Hoped.

He had almost...what?

'I see her every day, depending on my shift. I'm still praying...' Her voice trailed off.

This was not about him. This was about her world and he had no idea about it.

'You've had a tough month,' he said.

'You have no idea,' she said, as if she'd read his thoughts.

There was just a touch of bitterness that seemed very unlike her, and he wondered what else could have gone wrong for her.

He knew about ghastly times. Things had gone horribly wrong for him.

'Where there's life there's hope,' he said. A trite saying that tasted bitter in his mouth.

During his ghastly time he hadn't even had that—hope. His wife and child had both been gone within minutes. When he wasn't there. No hope. But he was finding a little more distance from the shock as the years passed. And even more since he'd met Isabella.

What?

He took another step back as the lift doors opened. He was suddenly very conscious of how small the lift was, and how close they'd be. Maybe he should dash back to the hospital to check on Kate?

'Get in. I won't bite,' she said, and the super-confident woman he'd first met was back in place.

He felt his cheeks warm. He hadn't blushed since high school. But he stepped in and the doors closed.

She pushed buttons seven and eight. 'You never told me what happened yesterday.' Her eyes widened. 'And I didn't pay for breakfast.'

'I settled the bill. You were half asleep. You can pay next time.'

Next time? Was there going to be a next time? Heaven help him.

The lift stopped and he put his hand across the doors to prevent them closing prematurely on her.

'Phone me directly if you're ever worried about Kate. I'll come as soon as I can.' He opened his wallet and gave her his business card, so she'd have his cell phone number.

Suddenly her eyes glittered with tears, and he saw her throat shift as she swallowed. She nodded. 'Thank you.' Her voice cracked. 'I appreciate that.'

'Sleep well.' He pulled his arm back and the lift doors closed as she walked away.

CHAPTER TEN

'Nadia's had her baby, Gran. A little girl.'

Gran's serene expression didn't change.

'She's called her Kate after you. Catherine and Kate. I think it's a gorgeous pairing.'

Isabella had slept for four hours. She'd spoken to her father again, as she had before she'd gone to sleep, and deleted another text from Conlon. Then on the way back to NICU she dropped in to the high dependency ward looking after her grandmother.

'You're a great-grandmother.'

Gran breathed in and out. Her eyes were still shut. Hopefully one day soon they'd open.

'I'm going to see her again now. She weighs two kilograms—that's four pounds four ounces in your terms—and she's gorgeous. Big eyes like Nadia.'

No twitch from Gran and Isabella sighed.

'Still, she's so tiny and fragile-looking. But Simon Purdy— that doctor in the unit I was telling you about—is going to look after her, so I'm happy about that. Turns out he lives one floor up from you.'

The penthouse, she guessed. Funny to think of Simon in a penthouse...

She thought about what she'd said about Simon before to her grandmother.

'And even though I was cross with him yesterday...' Had she been? Yes, actually. She'd been cross that he'd been so cold towards her when she didn't deserve it. She'd still not found out what had upset him. He'd said he'd tell her at breakfast. He hadn't!

'Anyway, he is an excellent paediatrician, and my niece—your great-granddaughter,' she added, trying to break through her grandmother's silence, 'has to have the best. Simon said he would be there whenever Kate needed him.'

She sat back and thought about the relief that gave her. And the fact that Nadia had been pronounced as 'improving' as well. Soon she'd be well enough to visit her baby. It must be so hard for her sister to be stuck in intensive care as a new mum.

'When I phoned just now they said I can see Nadia even though she's still in Intensive Care. I'll have to hurry, because I start work in an hour and a half. I'll drop into the neonatal unit first, and check that Kate's fine, and take a few more photos for Nadia on my phone before I visit her.'

She stood. Looked down at the now familiarly sleeping face.

'It's time you woke up, Gran. We need you to meet your namesake.' She leaned down and kissed the soft wrinkled cheek. 'Love you.'

When Isabella reached the NICU, she saw Simon, tall and far too eye-catching, beside Carla at Kate's cot. He looked up as she washed her hands at the sink and smiled.

Carla turned Isabella's way as well, as she crossed the room, drying her fingers on a paper towel. 'Congratulations, Auntie,' she said. 'She's beautiful.'

Isabella looked down at the baby with her nasogastric tube and IV line, and the electronic pulse oximeter sensor strapped to her foot. 'Thank you. She is, isn't she? Has she been a good girl?'

She addressed the last question to Simon, who nodded.

'She's behaving like a typical thirty-two-weeker, so she'll have her moments of unusual interest. But she's stable. Have you seen your sister?'

'I phoned the ward when I woke up. They say she's stable

and improving. I thought I'd take a few more photos before I went up. I'm allowed to see her in Intensive Care.'

'She's awake,' Simon said. 'I went up after I'd checked on Kate. I explained Kate's condition and said that we were happy with her.'

Of course he would have done that. Bless him. Not something she would have thought about Simon Purdy a few days ago.

Isabella pressed her lips together to hold back the rush of words. Seemed she was still emotional. That had been very kind, and she wasn't used to it from him.

'Thank you. She must have been so relieved.'

'She was.' He smiled, and she could see he understood she was still feeling fragile from the fright.

Carla spoke up. 'It's not sensible for you to work this afternoon. You should take the day off today—and tomorrow as well. Family and carer's leave. Though you won't get paid. If you agree, I've found someone to replace you, so no guilt trip needed.'

'Thank you. That would be...' she waved her hand vaguely '...great.' She flicked a glance at Simon and then away—had he asked Carla? 'I'll catch up on sleep.'

'Of course a substitute won't really replace you,' Simon said, and she realised, with a little spurt of shocked amusement, that he was teasing her. Now, that was a first. She furrowed her brows as he grinned and turned back to the cot.

She looked at her boss. 'Thanks, Carla. I was planning on coming in this afternoon, but it's probably safer this way, as I'm still fuzzy from lack of sleep.'

'I do prefer my staff awake,' Carla said mildly. 'No need to rush away after you visit your sister. Take all the time you need and we'll see you as a visiting auntie for the next couple of days.' She tilted her head at Simon. 'As long as Dr Purdy can do without you?

'He managed perfectly well before I came. I'm not worried,' Isabella said dryly. Though it was interesting that Simon had been the first one to suggest she have time off. For someone who had barely spoken to her, he'd made a reversal of interaction with her, even with teasing thrown in. It was all too much to take on board, but right now she didn't want to think about it, because she desperately wanted to see her sister.

Isabella snapped several photos of Kate on her phone—one accidentally, with Simon looking gorgeous in the background. She should delete that, but didn't.

She said her goodbyes, but once she was outside the unit she realised she wasn't sure which way to turn or which floor to get off the lift.

Simon appeared beside her. 'Do you know where you're going?'

'I just realised I don't. I can ask at the reception desk.'

'Follow me. If you don't mind moving fast, I'll show you.' They set off at a rapid pace until they got to the lift. Stepped in. 'I'm going to Theatre to check on a newborn. I'll drop you off on the way.'

'So many words... Who is this chatty person I've met this morning? He's quite a nice fellow.'

'Ha! Nice? I heard he's moody,' Simon said.

Isabella glanced up at him from under her eyebrows. 'Really? Imagine that... I wouldn't have believed it.'

'Cheeky!' Then his voice became more serious. 'What about your parents? Do they know?'

'I rang my father this morning, and then again when I woke up. After I'd spoken to the ICU staff this afternoon. He's flying up tomorrow. Of course he's too busy to come today.'

She heard the underlying bitterness and frowned at herself. It had been unrealistic to expect him to drop everything. She should be used to that now.

'I guess he has to rearrange his schedule,' Simon said, but Isabella could hear the surprise in his voice.

Suddenly she was defensive. 'You should talk. Being married to your job.'

'Not always. I had a life. When I had a wife.'

Suddenly Isabella felt sick. She'd known about that. His loss. His wife. What had she said?

'Heck, Simon, I'm sorry. That was unforgivable of me. But unintended, I promise.'

The doors opened and they stepped out of the lift.

'Don't worry about it. Intensive Care's just there on your left. Say hello to your sister for me.'

He strode on, leaving her feeling like a callous cow.

Damn!

She stared at his rigid back as he disappeared fast. Then looked back at the closed doors of the intensive care unit. Later she'd find him and apologise.

Again.

CHAPTER ELEVEN

SIMON WINCED AS he sped away from the truth and the pain that slithered around his body like a snake in a box.

Isabella's words had stung. Because it was true. He *had* put his work before his family when Louise was alive. Hell, he'd missed most of the pregnancy, rushing to and from work. She'd never complained. She'd been a saint. And if he'd paid a bit more attention—if he'd been there more—then maybe his wife wouldn't have died alone.

Malachi had told him time and again that nothing could have saved Louise. That it had been quick. An anaphylaxis from a bolus of amniotic fluid, later found in her bloodstream at autopsy, and the allergic response causing rapid cardiac arrest.

But she'd died alone.

And the baby?

Malachi hadn't been so sure, though his friend had said that the chance of survival would have been slim even if someone had been there.

But Simon knew. If he'd been there, his son would have had greater than a fifty-fifty chance. Simon knew that.

If he'd been there, instead of at work, his son might be alive now. They just might have been able to save him from the wreckage of his mother's body before his life was lost.

He knew Isabella hadn't meant to hurt him. But he didn't need anyone else to say it because he reminded himself every morning and every night, getting in and out of bed. The words of his father from long ago—'*It's your fault your mother died giving birth to you.*' And it was his fault for not being there for his wife and child.

Malachi had said he should let it go. And over the last day or so he'd actually thought he was. But it had all crashed back with Isabella's words. Of course he was married his job, and to saving others. He had to make up for the past.

Simon quickened his pace. That was his life. Best thing, really. He needed to work.

Simon left the operating theatre fifteen minutes later. The baby girl he'd gone to see would be transferred to the ward with her mother and he'd check on them both later. After a forceps delivery, the baby had been slow to turn pink after respiration started. But he was confident she had it all worked out now.

He guessed he could go and see Nadia, and ask if she had any questions about Kate, but in his head he knew if she had questions she'd only have to ask her sister.

Still. It couldn't hurt. Any new mother would love to hear about her baby from the baby's doctor. He couldn't avoid Nadia just to avoid seeing Isabella.

Simon felt like slapping his own forehead. He was having so many internal conversations he was twisting himself up in knots.

It all boiled down to the fact that he was being drawn like a lemming to the edge of a cliff—the cliff being Isabella Hargraves—and to the stark reality that he had nothing to offer a woman like her except a sliver of time that would never be enough. And would leave her at risk should she need him.

But Isabella Hargraves had crashed into his world. She would be there in his face at work, in the freaking surf, and even in the lift to his own apartment. The mischievous angels in heaven must be laughing their heads off.

Not his fault. It was fate. He'd tried to stay away.

He pushed open the swing doors to Intensive Care and spoke to one of the nurses there. She told him that Nadia was improving and would probably go to the ward tomorrow morning. He encouraged her to find Nadia a room close to the NICU, and when she agreed to try, he took himself to the sink to wash his hands.

Funny how he couldn't help turning his head towards the room where he knew Nadia had been put... As he'd expected, he noted two blonde heads together.

Isabella was still there. Of course she was. He'd only been gone twenty minutes.

'Here's Simon, now,' he heard her say.

Just hearing that woman speak his name made him stupidly warm.

'Spare me...' he muttered to himself. This was getting out of control. He needed to stop.

He crossed the room and kept his eyes on Isabella's sister. 'How are you feeling, Nadia? Pain under control?'

'I'm getting better all the time.'

Nadia's voice had similarities to Isabella's—he heard them—but her confidence didn't come across as much as Isabella's did.

Could be the fact that Nadia was a patient in a hospital after a traumatic illness and birth.

Or the fact that her husband had died.

He'd discovered she was a widow, and he knew all about that knocking the stuffing out of you. But he suspected it was something else. Perhaps the reason her elder sister was so protective. Had something else happened to Nadia?

He frowned at himself. What was he doing? He should back away from these women and not get more embroiled than he already was.

He didn't want to think about loss. Guilt. Or regret.

'I just dropped in to see if you had any questions. Though I expect your sister can probably answer most of them anyway.'

'None for the moment,' Nadia said, smiling wanly. 'And you're right—Izzy knew the answers to all the ones I had. I loved the photos.'

Izzy? What a travesty to shorten a beautiful name to that. Perhaps Bella? Meaning beautiful. But not Izzy. Sacrilege...

'I sent the pics to her phone,' Isabella said, and he could see in her eyes the anxiety she tried to hide as she watched her sister's tired face. 'As long as you leave it on aeroplane mode, you can look at them as much as you need—until we can get you to her.'

Isabella stood up.

'And on that note...' She kissed her sister's cheek, said softly, 'You need a snooze. I'll be back this afternoon.'

'Say hi to Gran for me,' Nadia whispered, and Isabella nodded.

Mrs Hargraves. Yes. Isabella went every day to see her unconscious grandmother. Somewhere in his chest he felt a twist of empathy that made him want to reach out to her and say he thought she was amazing. She was doing it tough but still thinking of others.

Unlike him. He suspected his attempts at selfish self-preservation hadn't helped her at all this last week. It was hard to remember that she'd only begun in the unit such a short time ago. It felt as if he'd been watching her for way longer.

Simon saw a man in the dark suit striding swiftly towards them and his mouth quirked up. One of the ICU nurses followed the newcomer, trying to catch him up with a chart.

'Malachi.' Simon held out his hand and his friend shook it warmly.

'Simon. Come to see my patient, have you?' Malachi leaned past Simon and smiled at Nadia in the bed. 'I won't stay long and interrupt your visitors,' he told her.

CHAPTER TWELVE

MALACHI MADDEN, THE man Isabella had seen when Nadia had first been admitted, was clearly Simon's friend. He looked nice, if in a hurry, and she recognised the consultant's fierce intelligence and wanted all those brains directed at her sister.

'Nice to meet you, again.' she murmured. 'Thank you for looking after my sister so well. Please don't rush—I'm just leaving.'

Before she could move past him, Simon said to Malachi, 'Isabella is one of the NICU nurses in our unit here. And a midwife.'

'Yes, I know. Nice to meet you again, Isabella.' He glanced at Simon and raised his brows, with a twinkle in his intelligent eyes. 'I've heard the team are pretty good down there.' She watched their rapport. It was easy and were obviously used to teasing each other.

Isabella glanced at Simon. 'Yes. We're very fortunate.'

Simon said, 'Do you remember Mrs Hargraves? That friend of your grandmother's who lives in the flat below me?'

Malachi frowned, and then nodded. 'She was injured in that nasty hit-and-run accident a month or so ago. Millicent was very distressed to hear about it.'

'Nadia and Isabella are her granddaughters.'

Malachi's face softened, as did his voice. 'Oh… How is she? I heard she's still unconscious?'

Isabella didn't know what to say. Why had Simon shared

this? She scrambled for a short response. 'Yes, she hasn't woken up yet. I see her every day.'

'Of course.' Malachi nodded. His face was serious. 'I would visit if it were me, too. I must tell my grandmother. You should come and meet my wife, Lisandra,' he told her, with a searching look towards his friend and then a smile. 'Simon, you should come too. Isabella, maybe you can convince him to arrive for dinner instead of dessert.'

What? Dinner? With Simon? She felt as if she'd just been steamrollered.

Malachi raised his eyebrows at his friend. 'If you're done with Nadia, trot away with Isabella so I can see my patient.'

Isabella closed her mouth on the open sag it wanted to make. 'Goodbye, Dr Madden.'

He nodded vaguely, as if he'd already forgotten her, and walked instantly over to Nadia and took her wrist.

She didn't realise Simon was behind her until she went to open the swing doors out of the ICU and he stretched out his arm ahead of her and pushed the door until she was through.

'He's funny,' she said.

'Malachi is no-nonsense and a very good friend. We went through med school together.'

She still didn't understand Simon's blurting out of information. 'Why did you tell him about Gran?'

'No idea… I'm sorry if I shouldn't have. I think maybe because I think you'd like Lisandra, and I think you need a friend right now. She's also a midwife. You have that in common. They have twin boys who just turned one.'

'Good grief. How does she manage when he works all hours as an obstetrician?'

'Lisandra is one of the calmest women I know. As well as the best thing that's ever happened to Malachi—for which I am very grateful.'

She still didn't understand why he'd shared so much about her and Nadia with his friend. 'What made you think of my grandmother when you were talking to him?'

'I remember meeting Mrs Hargraves and Malachi's grandmother, Millicent, in the lift one day. Now, Millicent…she's a terrifying lady.'

Isabella couldn't imagine Simon being terrified by any woman. But she suspected he meant the comment fondly. His eyes twinkled.

Something made her ask, 'Do *you* have a terrifying grandmother?'

'I don't have any grandmother. Or a mother.'

There was darkness there in those words. Sorrow. Regret. Something she wanted to find out more about.

'In fact,' Simon went on, 'Malachi's the closest thing I have to a relative and he's not even blood-related.'

Oh… More sadness. Simon had baggage she hadn't even considered.

'I'm sorry to hear that. My family might not win any happy-all-together awards, but at least I have them.'

'Yes—and they have you.' He cast a sideways glance at her as they walked to the lift. 'I'm beginning to see that you're the person who worries about everyone else.'

How the heck had he deduced that? It wasn't true. Was it? He barely knew her. And apart from Nadia, he didn't know her family at all.

The lift arrived and deposited them on the ground floor. 'Are you coming to check on Kate before you go home?' he asked.

And suddenly she was awkward again. 'I'd like to. Is that okay? Even though I'm not working?'

He waved her in. 'Of course. You're officially a relative. Next of kin to his mother. You can visit any time.'

It still didn't feel right to go outside of regular visiting times. 'But there are specific visiting hours for non-staff members. I don't want to be a nuisance.'

He wrinkled his brow at her, as if he couldn't believe what she was saying. 'I don't think there's any risk of you abusing your position.'

And he held the door open for her so she had no choice. Not that she wanted one.

Shoulder to shoulder, they washed their hands at the sink until Simon, who'd finished first, tore off some paper towel and then went off to see Carla.

Isabella crossed the busy unit, past open cots and rolling cots, and past the staff working on the tiny inhabitants of both, to check on Kate.

Her niece lay on her belly, leads sneaking from under her chest at each side. Her left foot now sported the pulse oximeter probe that had previously been attached to the right foot. She was sleeping and serene. Warm under her heater. Her breathing steady and sure.

Isabella's quick survey of the monitors suggested her vital signs were stable. She picked up the chart, not sure whether she was allowed to, but not letting that stop her.

She confirmed everything looked normal for the moment, though she suspected a tinge of yellowing jaundice in Kate's skin. She expected there'd be a need for phototherapy soon, to assist her body to rid itself of the extra bilirubin. And the use of purple lights to help disperse the toxic by-products.

Once born into the outside air, babies normally discarded unneeded extra oxygen-carrying blood cells. But, as Kate was a prem, her liver would struggle to break down the products left behind. Hence the build up of jaundice.

Simon didn't need her mentioning it—he'd already be on top of it all—and it was truly strange how relaxed she was feeling about Kate's progress. There were still so many obstacles that could catch her tiny niece out as she grew, like infections and breathing difficulties, or a need for nasogastric feeds of expressed breast milk—something she and Nadia had discussed and would address again this afternoon.

It was almost a shock, how calm she felt now that Simon was in charge of Kate's care. How reassured. Though his very competent registrar would have been just as good. She needed to remember that.

It just went to show that sometimes too much knowledge could be a problem.

Maybe she should go home before she said something else out of line. Again.

She would drop in to Gran as well—tell her about Malachi Madden's grandmother. Maybe that would be something that might stimulate her.

Then she'd have a sleep herself, she supposed, and she'd better polish Gran's flat and clean the bathroom in case her father decided to stay there. But knowing him, he'd book a suite at the nearest hotel, so he could be on his own. That was more his style. But maybe she'd have a chance to be his host and they could really talk.

Who knew when he would come? He hadn't known himself when she'd last spoken to him. But she couldn't help being glad that he would. For Nadia. For Gran. And for her. Because if it wasn't for Simon she would be feeling very alone amongst all these medical dramas.

Simon…the kind-eyed Simon…who was suddenly her friend.

Simon returned with Carla and Isabella felt awkward again. In the way. Superfluous. Without a real job. A third wheel because she wasn't working this afternoon.

'I'm going now,' she told them.

Simon frowned, as if he'd read her thoughts, and she saw him close his mouth as if he was about to say something.

Carla lifted her head from a chart. 'I'm sure we'll see you later.'

Isabella nodded. She glanced once more at her niece and then left, feeling suddenly rootless.

CHAPTER THIRTEEN

SIMON'S GAZE FOLLOWED Isabella as she opened the door and left. There was something about the droop in her shoulders that hinted she felt a little lost.

Funny how much that thought troubled him.

Which was a very good reason for him to turn around and concentrate on the baby in front of him.

'Do I sense a change with you and Isabella?' Carla's voice was quietly discreet, and didn't carry, yet he wished she hadn't voiced the question at all. It meant that others could see that things were noteworthy between them.

'No. Not really.' He lowered his brows at her, but she knew him too well to be bothered. 'Why would you ask that?'

'Uh…because everybody can feel the friction between you two and it would be good if you could clear the air.'

He huffed. 'I have. We had breakfast together this morning and I apologised for my moodiness with her.'

'Simon, I'm impressed.' But her eyes twinkled and he suspected she was more amused than impressed. 'That was brave.'

He pulled a face. 'That's the end of this topic. Back to work,' he mock-growled, and Carla dipped her head to hide her smile.

Simon pointed to the prem in front of them. 'I think Kate's becoming jaundiced. I'll order a serum bilirubin. Has she started on EBM yet?'

'Yes. Mum's started expressing and the ICU sent down the first colostrum. You happy for us to start that?'

'Absolutely. ASAP. The usual regime.'

Carla made a note. 'Yes, we'll gradually increase the expressed milk and decrease the IV if she tolerates it.'

'Has she passed meconium?'

'Yes. And voided twice. Clever baby.'

All looking good for the moment, then. The extra relief he felt was interesting.

'Excellent. All systems working. Let me know if there's problems. Tell the night staff to ring through straight to me for Kate.' He avoided meeting Carla's raised brows. 'Anyone else you're worried about?' he asked.

'Nope. All up to date. We'll let you know if we need you.'

'Fine. I'll head to my rooms, then. I've got appointments all afternoon, so I'll be there if you need me.'

By four-thirty Simon was with his last patient.

Young Reece had unstable diabetes. He was thrilled with his new insulin pump, which meant he could play with the other kids more than he'd ever been able to before.

Simon had known Reece for the last three years, and always enjoyed talking to the boy and his mother.

By five p.m. he was waving them farewell at the door, and he was just about to head for the children's ward when his phone rang.

'Dr Purdy.' Malachi was in good spirits, it seemed.

'Dr Madden. You sound chipper.'

'My wife requests the pleasure of your company tomorrow night for dinner.'

'Does she? Are you home from work already, Malachi? Things have certainly changed.'

Malachi had been worse than Simon for staying at work all hours.

'You should try it,' his friend said. 'The twins are waving at you. They want to see their uncle Simon.'

Simon shook his head. But he couldn't stop the big smile on his face. 'Who are you? What happened to the workaholic?'

But Simon knew what had happened. Lisandra had changed his friend's life, and his priorities, for the better. And even though the twins weren't Malachi's, he adored his new family and revelled in being a father.

Malachi said, 'I've seen the light. So, how about you shift your last appointment and get your rounds done early tomorrow?'

Simon considered that. 'My secretary hasn't left, yet. I'll see what I can do.'

'Lisandra said to bring Isabella.'

Good grief. Malachi—or Lisandra, more likely—was matchmaking, and the idea scared the daylights out of him.

'I'm not sure about Isabella's shifts.' Except he knew she was off. He'd seen the staff rota.

'How about you give me her number and Lisandra can ring her? Midwives stick together, you know.'

Malachi wasn't fazed or worried about Simon's feelings. It wasn't in his make-up—and hadn't Simon accepted that years ago?

Served him right. He'd been the one to tell Isabella she would like Malachi's wife. But now it was happening, old doubts and insecurities slithered in. Was this really a good idea? The one situation he'd thought he wouldn't bump into Isabella was socially, with Malachi. Now Malachi was changing that.

Without permission, the words slipped out. 'Seems there won't be anywhere I can go and not meet this woman.'

'Explain?'

Simon sighed. Bowing to the inevitable. 'She lives in her grandmother's flat—which, as you know, is one floor below mine. We work together in the NICU. And guess what she does in her off time.'

Malachi laughed. 'Don't tell me…she's a surfer.'

'Yep.'

Malachi laughed again. 'I can't wait to tell Lisandra.'

Simon couldn't help smiling. Not so long ago even one Malachi laugh would have been a reason for celebration.

'Tell me what…?' Simon heard Lisandra ask in the background.

'Simon's being stalked by a midwife.'

Simon grimaced as Lisandra laughed. 'I am not. She didn't even know any of those things.'

Malachi chuckled. 'Who knew Simon's relationships could be so much fun? Six p.m. You'll be kicked out at eight. You know we like to go to bed early.'

The phone went dead.

Simon stared at the receiver in his hand and gritted his teeth. Served him right for dumping all that information about Isabella on his friend. Malachi wasn't stupid—too freakin' smart. But usually not so intuitive.

Of course introducing and giving the back story on a woman was out of character for Simon.

Too late. Lisandra had the run of it now.

He shrugged and went to make peace with his secretary about changing his appointment times tomorrow, then took himself off to the children's ward.

After work that night, Simon took his car from the garage underneath the building and did something he hadn't done for a long time. He went to the cemetery where they'd buried Louise and Lucas, his son who had never breathed.

It was sunset. And between the trees lay shadows. Although above the canopy the sky was alight with an orange glow that made the headstones sparkle as the last rays sank into the sandstone blocks.

He walked to the row he needed, and six graves along, until he came to Louise and Lucas's. There. A cold stone where once a sweet woman and the promise of a young life had been.

Just twenty-eight, and so gentle in spirit had been his kind and loving wife. He'd thought that there would never be another woman for him. That what they'd had was too special. Too perfect.

But mostly it had involved too much guilt.

Because the ending had been anything but perfect.

She'd been so happy in her pregnancy. And he couldn't remember how many times since her death he'd railed at himself for not spending more time at home with her.

Three years. A long time to mourn. Or not long enough?

His friends had been pushing him to look for happiness again, but he'd felt so guilty. So disloyal. So uninterested.

Until now. When suddenly he was swamped by the feelings that were growing for Isabella Hargraves. What if he let them flower? What was his plan? To fall in love again? Have a baby again? Already his head was shaking at the thought. What if he lost another wife? What if Isabella died in childbirth?

No. He couldn't. He wasn't ready.

CHAPTER FOURTEEN

ISABELLA'S PHONE BUZZED with a text at six o'clock that evening.

Hello, Isabella. My name is Lisandra Madden. Is this a good time to call you?

Isabella read it again. Then she remembered Malachi Madden inviting her and Simon for dinner.

Good grief. They didn't let any grass grow underfoot.

She texted back.

Now is fine.

The phone rang within ten seconds.

'Thanks for the quick response,' came a lilting woman's voice. 'It's Lisandra here. I've got twin boys and they're asleep at the moment. I try to do everything in the quiet times.'

I bet you do.

Isabella could imagine. And she smiled at the thought.

'Malachi tells me you're a midwife and new to the area. He also says you work with Simon Purdy. Well, those boys are great friends, and it's always a struggle to get Simon to come out. We're having a dinner party tomorrow night. Malachi's grandmother will be there, and we'd like to invite you both as well—if you're up to it.'

Before Isabella could answer Lisandra said quickly, 'It won't be a late night. We call them "six to eight" parties.'

Isabella laughed—how funny—and replied, 'I'd probably run on the same hours if I had twins.'

She could absolutely fit that in.

'My father is flying up tomorrow, to see my sister, but he won't be here till late. I've been invited to his hotel at nine, and I was wondering what I'd do until then.'

'Good grief, we'll all be snoring by that time,' Lisandra murmured with disbelief.

Isabella laughed again. She liked this woman already. 'Then thank you. What can I bring tomorrow?'

'If you can bring Simon on time, I'd be very grateful. The man doesn't seem to know the meaning of punctuality. Everything else is covered. I'll text you the address, in case Simon gets called away. You can park underneath the apartments in the visitors' parking and then take the lift straight up—I'll send you the codes.'

'You've thought of everything.'

'Good. I'm looking forward to meeting you. I haven't had a good chat with a midwife for ages.'

'I'm more of a neonatal nurse, right now. But I look forward to meeting you too.'

'Great. Bye.'

'Bye.'

Good grief, Isabella thought as the call ended. A whirlwind had just blown past, and she'd been caught up in it. She wondered what Simon thought about going with her to dinner. Her mouth twitched.

Someone knocked on her door.

Was she about to find out?

There weren't many in the block who knew her well enough to knock on her door.

Isabella peered through the peephole and saw Simon on the other side, staring off to the left.

Yep. She was about to find out Simon's response to the dinner invitation.

While she watched, he lifted his hand to the back of his neck and rubbed. *Tired or uncomfortable?* she wondered, and opened the door.

'Hello.' She opened her mouth to say more, when a horrible thought crashed into her. 'Nadia…? Kate…?'

'Both fine,' Simon said quickly. 'If they weren't I would have phoned immediately.'

She blew her breath out. 'Of course. Sorry—mild panic attack came up out of nowhere.'

'I get it. But I'm here about Malachi and Lisandra…' He put his hand over his face as if he was embarrassed. 'Have you had the call yet?'

She opened the door wider and swept out her arm to indicate that he could come in. 'Yes, I've just finished. Lisandra's a force to be reckoned with.'

'Lisandra's a delight, but when she's determined on something, it's hard to get away.'

She chewed her lip to stop the smile. 'My task is to get you there on time,' she said.

'Well, I'm to take you and a bottle of wine.' He met her gaze fully, concern in his. 'So, you're okay with this?'

'Sure. Sounds like fun.' She smiled reassuringly at him. He looked as if he needed it. 'My father is arriving tomorrow night, and I'm to meet him at nine at his hotel. Saves me sitting here, watching the clock.'

She saw his gaze slide over the room. And the hallway beyond. 'He's not going to stay here with you? It's three bedrooms, isn't it?'

She sighed. 'Yes. And I've just cleaned in case he comes.' She shrugged. 'But no. He'll feel much more comfortable arriving late at a hotel.' She could see that he thought she might be hurt by her father's choice. 'It's fine with me. I told you we don't do *happy-all-together*.'

He nodded and she went on.

'I'm a little bit nervous about meeting Malachi's terrifying grandmother now you've told me about her.'

Simon laughed. 'Oh, she'll love you. You won't have any problems.'

And what did she do now? With Simon in her flat? Looking scrumptious. With the scent of freshly showered man, damp hair and that subtle woodsy cologne she was coming to recognise.

'Would you like a drink? Tea? Coffee?'

'Tea would be great. Black. No sugar, thanks.'

Same as her. And why would that make her want to happy dance? Weird…

She flicked the kettle on. 'Got it.' She started rifling through the cupboards. 'I think I've got some biscuits here.'

'No, it's fine. My housekeeper leaves me dinner in the fridge to heat up.'

That made her pause, her hand on the cupboard door. 'You have a housekeeper?'

'I spend a fair bit of time at work.'

He looked just a little embarrassed, and that made her smile. As if he was a bad person for not wanting to keep house.

'I'd rather surf waves than clean.'

She nodded. She thought of her afternoon of rubber gloves and bathrooms and grimaced. 'Me too. Speaking of surfing… Have you had a chance to get back out there since yesterday morning?'

'Was that only yesterday morning?' His hand pinched the bridge of his nose. 'It feels like a year ago.'

She narrowed her eyes at him. 'I've been thinking about that.' She poured boiling water into a cup. 'And I have a theory.'

'Oh, yeah?' He took the cup from her, removed the teabag and put it in the bin.

She liked the fact that he was making himself at home here, opening cupboards until he found the garbage.

'Yes, I think the reason you were bad-tempered with me at work is because I was surfing in your spot.'

'I don't own the surf.'

But it sounded as if he wished he did.

Then he smiled. Held out his hands in a *What can I do?* gesture. 'I told myself you were an incredibly intelligent woman and I'd have to stay at the top of my game.'

'True.' She nodded slowly. 'You do. Is the rest true, you were bad tempered because I was surfing in your spot?'

'I confess.'

'The ocean is big enough for both of us,' she mused.

He was watching her. 'It should be.' There was a small, ironic smile on his mouth. 'But if I want to try not to expose myself to the fact that I find my new colleague compellingly and breath-stealingly attractive, it's very difficult when she pops up not only at work, but also in the one place I go to escape work.'

She opened her mouth, but he held up his hand.

'Oh, it gets worse. She even lives in the same block as I do.'

She opened her mouth again.

He said, 'And one more thing. Let's add to that. My friends have now included her in their circle. So, I'm going to be exposed to Isabella Hargraves in every part of my day.'

'Poor you,' she said.

'Or poor you? I'm not cross any more, because I've given up fighting the inevitable.

That made her blink. 'What's the inevitable?.'

Did she sound petulant?

'Being drawn to you. Attracted. You know you're delightful.'

He must have seen her brows draw up into her hairline. Because he went on.

'And, yes, I would like to be your friend. Please.' The humour left his face. 'I need to say that because of the past I'm in no hurry to be more than that. And I think it's only fair that I tell you I live for my work.'

Wow. That was pretty brave. And a downer. Because she was attracted right back, and he was married to his work. Still, she appreciated his honesty—even if she was a little bit disappointed.

But she had the feeling this was a big admission for Simon. So she held out her hand. 'To friendship.'

CHAPTER FIFTEEN

SIMON TOOK ISABELLA'S slender hand in his and solemnly held it. Her fingers felt warm, silky, and suddenly fragile in his. He didn't want to let go. But he had to. Now. He'd ease his fingers away as soon as they weren't Velcroed onto hers.

'Are you surfing tomorrow?' he asked.

She pulled her hand away, picked up her mug and sat at the small table.

'Yes, because I don't have to go to work. Thanks to Dr Simon Purdy, who has told my supervisor that I require two days FACS leave.'

He laughed. 'I did do that.'

'Well, I appreciate it. Thank you. I would have pushed myself to turn up, but it wouldn't have been a sensible thing to do with no sleep.'

'They're moving Nadia down to a room near the NICU tomorrow. Did you know that?'

Her face lit up and he saw again her love for her sister.

'No. That's good. She's still improving, then?'

'Blood pressure is settling well.'

'And my niece?'

'I'd say she'll be under phototherapy by tonight.'

'I thought that.' She nodded and he could see she'd expected it.

'You didn't say anything.'

Her mouth kinked up and drew his gaze.

That mouth.

'I have great faith in you. But I would have said something tomorrow,' she told him.

He laughed and thought, *Oh, yeah, I'll have to watch myself, or I could fall hard for this woman.*

He was not going to do that—for her sake, not his.

At five forty-five the next evening, after he'd ensured Isabella's sister and niece were both stable and improving, and he'd dressed appropriately enough to satisfy Malachi's grandmother, Simon pressed the bell on Isabella's door.

The NICU had been busy today, with the new admission of twins at thirty-four weeks. But he'd put Henry in charge and suggested, for once, that he only be called for his own patients instead of the usual—being called by anyone who needed him for a paediatric consult.

The door opened and Isabella stood there, stealing his breath, then his words. And he hoped not his heart, as his chest felt clamped in a vice that made cardiac output difficult.

'You look beautiful…' The words escaped in an awed murmur.

And, my glory, she did. The flowing silk trousers and jacket floated over a cream blouse in soft shades of lilac that brought out the green of her eyes while they hugged and skimmed the length of her body. The feather-light material shifted alluringly as she moved.

Her gaze skimmed his outfit and then finished at his face. 'Looking good yourself, Dr Purdy. I like the Tigger tie. And you're right on time.'

She pulled the door shut behind her. He stifled disappointment. So, he wasn't going in?

'Malachi's boys like this tie,' he said, struggling for normal conversation. A 'date' with Isabella was having way more impact than he'd been prepared for.

They'd finally agreed the previous evening to go in her car, against Simon's preference. She'd argued that she was driving on to the hotel afterwards to see her father. She would drop him home on her way.

Now, as he waited beside the driver's door for her to unlock the car, she slanted a sideways look at him. 'Are you planning on driving my car?'

The lock clicked and he reached down. 'No, I'm opening your door for you.'

She lifted her head and laughed up at him. The sound was sexy as hell, and sent blood pounding all over his body in ways he'd forgotten existed.

'Well, thank you, kind sir.' She pulled her beautiful mouth into order, as if holding back more mirth. 'Do I have to come round to your side and open *your* door?'

'It would have been easier if we'd taken my car,' he said.

'But not more sensible.'

'And if I get called out?'

She shrugged, with a *not my problem* attitude he also found sexy.

He sighed. 'It's close… I can always get a taxi.'

She settled into her seat. 'Or I can drive you. Let's go.'

He closed her door, his mouth twitching, because he was so unused to this kind of rapport where she could fire back. Shaking his head at his own smitten-ness, he walked around the car. It was cleaned and polished enough to show she cared about it.

'Nice car,' he said as he climbed in.

'This is Rosa.' Isabella patted the leather dashboard. 'She's my friend. Buckle up.'

Once Simon had himself settled, trying not to deep-breathe the now familiar scent of her delicate perfume, Isabella pulled smoothly out of the garage and into the busy street.

It was still light outside, and there were families wandering across the road to the beach and people dog-walking after work. Her driving style was smooth and confident, like everything about her, and he could feel himself relax.

Maybe he could cope with her driving. Louise had been a timid nightmare…

She glanced at him. 'So how did Malachi and Lisandra meet? Was she working as a midwife?'

Simon laughed. He couldn't help it. It was funny. Though he was sure it hadn't been at the time.

Isabella turned her beautiful face his way briefly and arched her brows. 'Was it that good a meet-cute?'

Meet-cute? He'd seen that movie. Ha!

'They met in a stuck elevator at the hospital. Lisandra's waters had broken and Malachi almost delivered the twins in there.'

Thankfully they'd pulled up at a red light. Because he could see his driver was having trouble concentrating.

Something lodged in his chest as she stared at him. She looked so cute, blinking incredulous green eyes at him. Then she turned back to the road. He could see the smile on her face, and he just had to lean forward to see her full expression, not just in profile.

He felt as if he could actually see her imagining the scenario. 'Crazy, huh?'

She inhaled with amusement. 'That's different…'

'There's a long story there that's not mine to tell, but they're the happiest couple I know. Lisandra changed Malachi's life for the better, and for that I'll always be grateful to her.'

'Well, I'm sure he's changed hers too. He seems very nice.'

'He is.'

They drove through busy Coolangatta, along the beachfront and around the headland to Kira Beach. The waves rolled in as the road curved around the bay.

He pointed. 'The underground car park is up ahead. Just past the lights. Yep, turn left here.'

They pulled under a tall white building with beautiful gardens full of red hibiscus in flower.

He watched her press the code numbers into the keypad and

the boom gate lifted smoothly, so they could drive past and park beside the elevators in the visitors' parking.

'If I ever come back here to visit Lisandra, I'll know how to find the place.'

He hoped she would. 'It's easier for her to have visitors here, with the boys, than it is for them to go out.'

They went to the lifts, and he pressed in the code, and then she was next to him again in another closed space. Alone. Just the two of them. Close.

There would be time for a kiss, his crazy inner demon told him, as he stared straight ahead at the doors.

Diversion needed. His mouth dried and he had to moisten it before he could speak.

'You'll enjoy the view from Malachi's apartment.'

When the lift doors opened, they were in an entry foyer with only one closed front door. Thankfully, as he stepped out, Simon could breathe again. He took a couple of extra, subtle inhalations before he knocked.

CHAPTER SIXTEEN

A BLONDE WOMAN in her late twenties opened the door, leaned forward and kissed Simon's cheek. This had to be Lisandra, Isabella thought. She had a fine bone structure, a pink bow of a mouth and big, deep turquoise eyes.

'Simon. Welcome.' She smiled at Isabella, her face warm and happy. 'And you must be Isabella.' The woman kissed her cheek too. 'That's for getting him here on time.' She laughed at Simon and ushered them in, saying, 'It's so lovely to meet you. I'm Lisandra. Come in… Come in… Malachi is just bathing the boys.'

And after that whirlwind introduction, reminiscent of the phone call she'd shared with Malachi's wife, Isabella just knew she could become firm friends with this woman.

Their hosts' apartment seemed to stretch for ever—probably because the sea air flowed seamlessly through open sliding doors to a wide terrace instead of a narrow balcony. She guessed there was a big drop to the ground below, but in front of them the horizon stretched over the waves.

White marble tiles ran from the floor to the terrace rail, past white furniture with blue accents, a wall-length television screen and a small curved bar with stools.

'Come through and meet Malachi's grandmother, Millicent. She's out on the terrace.'

A tall woman, possibly in her early eighties, stepped away from the rail and turned their way. Not quite as tall as Malachi, she was wearing peach silk trousers and a paler peach sleeveless tunic, almost white. The silk draped softly over her reed-thin body. Her make-up glowed with perfection, and her short, curly, snow-white hair was artfully tousled. Her smile shone warm and genuine as she came towards them.

'Simon,' she said, and her voice was huskier than Isabella had expected. 'A pleasure as always to see you.'

She kissed his cheeks in the French style, but her eyes were on Isabella.

'My dear, you have a look of your grandmother—those fine eyes and cheekbones. I'm Millicent Charles. A friend of Catherine's.'

It felt so long since she'd heard someone actually refer to her grandmother by her first name and a lump formed in her throat. She swallowed and smiled. 'It's lovely to meet you, Mrs Charles.'

'Likewise. And, please, call me Millicent. I've been so distressed since Catherine's accident. Any sign of improvement? I've asked your father, but he had nothing to offer.'

Isabella tried not to wince. *Yes, that sounded like dear old Dad*, Isabella thought grimly.

'She's breathing for herself. The hospital is maintaining intravenous nutrition. And...' she spread her hands '...we're just waiting.'

'Malachi says you visit often?'

Had they been talking about her? No, probably just about Gran. And it was good to talk about her grandmother with someone who knew her.

'I visit every day. Sometimes I think she can hear me. Hopefully I'm not driving her mad with my chatter.'

Kind, yet faded eyes shared sympathy and understanding. 'I'm very sure she loves your visits.'

'Well, I told her yesterday that I would be meeting you tonight. Now I can tell her tomorrow that I did.'

'Excellent. Would you mind if I visited her as well? I didn't get the impression from your father that it would be possible.'

'He's arriving tonight. I'll make sure he knows that your

visits certainly are permitted. The staff have been wonderful at welcoming me. She has an IV, and monitors, of course, but nothing that jumps out at you too much. I think it's a lovely idea.'

Malachi appeared out of a side hallway, carrying two blonde-headed toddlers in zip-up sleep suits, one in each arm. One of the boys leaned towards Simon as they drew close, and Simon scooped him out of his father's hold and perched him against his chest.

Malachi leaned across and shook Simon's hand. He smiled at Isabella. 'Welcome to our home.'

Lisandra lifted the other little boy from his father and perched him on her hip. 'Isabella, these are our boys, Bastian and Bennett. Bennett is the one who grabbed his uncle Simon.'

The little boy had caught Simon's tie and was tugging it.

'That's his favourite tie. Simon bought him a stuffed Tigger and Bastian a stuffed Winnie-the-Pooh bear, which they sleep with.'

And there was Simon—gorgeous Dr Simon Purdy—so at ease and delighted with the little boy in his arms. Of course, he was a paediatrician, so he was good with kids. But, dammit, she could see him being a fabulous dad with a pack of his own.

Except he'd said he would never marry again or be a dad. That was sad. For him. Not for her. That tragic fact had nothing to do with her. But her heart still hurt.

Millicent had taken herself to one of the large white sofas, and Lisandra carried Bastian across to her and settled him in her lap. His grandmother tucked her chin down to talk to the boy, and for a minute Isabella thought she was going to cry.

That was what she wanted Gran to do. She wanted Gran to be there for Nadia's baby, like she'd been there for Isabella and Nadia. Like Malachi's grandmother.

Why couldn't her grandmother be here, too? She'd already lost her mother. She wasn't ready to lose Gran.

Isabella felt a sympathetic touch on her shoulder. A touch that filled her with comfort and strength. Then Simon lifted his hand and let it fall. He had followed her gaze. As if he knew what she was thinking. She shoved the emotion away. He couldn't have. But she glanced at him with gratitude because that touch had helped.

'Come through to the kitchen, Isabella.' Lisandra intruded on her thoughts as well, and she was glad to step away from the sadness. Maybe not so glad to step away from Simon's side...

'I'd love to. What can I do to help?'

And that was how the evening went. Every time she felt even a tiny bit sad, or a little out of place amongst these people who knew each other so very well, Lisandra was there to bring her into the conversation or ask her a question. Or Simon would catch her eye and smile. Touch her briefly. Make sure she didn't feel as if he didn't understand.

When the meal was over, Isabella helped Lisandra stack the dishwasher while Malachi and Simon took the boys to their bedroom to read them a story.

'There's no excuse for you not to visit me,' said Lisandra. 'You know where I live and now you know all the codes.'

'And I have your phone number,' Isabella agreed, with a grin.

'While the boys are little, I'm not thinking about going back to work.' She dropped the volume of her voice so she wouldn't be overheard. 'Malachi would be happy if I never went back to work, but I loved being a midwife.'

'It is special,' Isabella agreed.

Lisandra shrugged. 'No rush. I'll get there. Malachi says you work in the neonatal nursery?'

'Yes, with Simon. He's very good. The unit's excellent.'

Lisandra's bright eyes closed briefly. 'It is. And I know. We had a scare with Bastian and Simon was there for us.'

'I'm sorry to hear that.'

Lisandra glanced towards the bedrooms. 'We try not to think about it.'

'Then don't.' Isabella changed the subject. 'Simon's looking after my sister's prem baby.'

'That's right. You're an auntie. First time?'

'Yes. And a first grandchild for my dad.'

She hadn't really thought about that, and wondered if there was any chance Kate could change him into a more human, human being.

'You said your father's arriving tonight?'

'Nine o'clock,' Isabella confirmed.

'I won't even be awake to think of you.' Lisandra mimed sleep.

'Yes, but you're a lot busier than I am.'

Lisandra shrugged. 'I'm not working… Malachi tells me you surf?'

'Yes, I've just found out Simon does too.'

There was a definite sparkle in Lisandra's eyes. 'I know… Are you good at it?'

Isabella knew she was good. But she didn't boast. 'Good enough to enjoy it.'

'Will you teach me?'

Ah… Hence the questions? 'Of course. I'd love to. My grandmother taught me.'

Lisandra looked ridiculously happy. 'That's a date, then.'

Malachi and Simon returned to sit with Millicent in the lounge room, and the women joined them there. Lisandra touched her husband's arm, her fingers resting lightly on his shirtsleeve, and they shared a smile. The look of connection in their faces made Isabella look away. She wanted that too. Connection. Silent communication.

Her thoughts stilled. Narrowed. Wasn't that what Simon had been giving her all night?

Dimly she heard Lisandra say, 'Are the boys asleep?'

'Out for the count.' There was a satisfied smile in Malachi's voice.

'Then I'm going to show Isabella the angels through the doorway.'

Lisandra took her arm, and they turned left up the corridor

to where a door stood ajar at the end. Soft light spilled into the hallway. It had an odd bluish tinge.

Isabella leaned her head around the doorway and could see a blue nightlight shaped like a fishbowl, with tiny imitation fish swimming in a blue ball. The light allowed her to see two blond heads on the pillows in twin beds. One tiny boy was tucked under his cover with his Tigger, and the other had already thrown his quilt off, one arm flung out, holding his Winnie the Pooh.

Isabella stepped back. Mouthed, *They are gorgeous.*

Lisandra smiled and drew her back down the corridor. She sighed theatrically. 'Even more so when they're asleep.'

It wasn't much later when Simon stood up. 'Gone eight o'clock. Looks like it's time for us to be kicked out.'

Malachi glanced at his watch. 'Oh, you sneaked in an extra five minutes there. Luckily someone was watching.'

Simon laughed. 'Did you bring your car, Millicent, or would you like a lift?'

Isabella lifted her head to smile.

Simon put his fingers over his face and dragged them down comically. 'I mean would you like a lift in Isabella's car, because she won the discussion on who was driving tonight.'

Millicent smiled approvingly at Isabella. 'I have my own vehicle, thank you.' She nodded. 'Always good to keep them guessing who's boss.'

'It's a democracy,' Simon said dryly, and shook Malachi's hand.

Millicent laughed.

'Dinner was wonderful, as always.'

Simon kissed Lisandra's cheek and stood waiting patiently for Isabella to say her goodbyes.

It had been perfect, Isabella thought. Not a boring dinner party at all like her father's events.

Everything had been a pleasure, and she thought Lisandra might be one of the luckiest people she knew.

'Thank you so much for a wonderful evening.'

'First of many, hopefully,' Malachi said briskly.

Lisandra hugged her. 'Ring me when you're ready for a surf on a weekend. Malachi and Simon can mind the boys.'

Suddenly she and Simon were standing close together again, in the lift going down to the car park. She felt as if she'd glimpsed a family the like of which she wanted so badly her heart and arms ached with emptiness. But it did feel like that warmth would never be hers.

'Did you enjoy that?' Simon asked, and Isabella turned her eyes to him.

She couldn't articulate how much. Instead, she nodded and asked, 'Did you?'

His tie looked crumpled, where Bennett had mashed it with his pudgy fingers and Simon had tried to straighten it. It needed an iron. She leaned across and tugged it, to pull the creases out, and then stepped back. That had brought her very close to him. She probably shouldn't have done it.

He was looking at her quizzically, and she hurried into speech. 'It was a wonderful night. I love your friends—and Millicent is wonderful.'

Two 'wonderfuls'? Brain, brain...where is my brain?

She concentrated on the evening, because that was safer than dwelling on the fact that the lift was slow, and that they were alone in the small space. And that she'd just touched him without invitation.

His shoulders loomed next to her but it wasn't just his big body taking up space—it was his personality. The one she'd seen tonight. The friend. The uncle. The charming escort. The man who cared if she felt sad. She almost couldn't believe that side of him.

Thankfully the lift had arrived at the underground car park, so she stepped out, unlocked her car, slid past Simon's door-opening arm, and sat behind the wheel as her mind mulled over the conundrum of her thoughts.

Earlier, she hadn't noticed being overwhelmed by Simon in the car because she'd been driving. But watching Simon tonight, listening to his jokes with Malachi, seeing his kindnesses and the way he'd handled the little boys, as if they were the most delightful thing he'd seen all day, it was hard not to be awed by him. Not to want to hug him. To feel his arms around her, too.

This was the Simon Purdy she'd hoped would be inside him. Tonight she'd seen the real man. Why on earth was this glorious nurturer standing behind his decision not to embrace life and a family? Yes, he'd lost his wife, but… There had to be another reason she didn't know.

But, again, like his tie, Simon's life wasn't hers to straighten. *None of your business, Isabella.*

If she started on trying to convince him she might cry.

Instead, she talked about her family. 'It was good to talk about Gran. Even for a little bit.'

He nodded thoughtfully as he slid into his seat belt and snapped it shut. 'Must have been.'

He tapped his watch. A high-pitched electronic voice said, 'It's eight-fifteen!'

She pushed back in the seat and turned her head briefly. 'What was *that*?'

He laughed. 'Mickey Mouse. The boys love it when I change my watch to Mickey.'

'You have a Mickey Mouse watch?'

'I'm a paediatrician. Of course I do.' He grinned at her amused face. 'I meant to change it back to silent when they went to sleep.'

'You're full of surprises.'

'You have no idea…' He waggled his brows. 'It's still early. Would you like a drink at the hotel bar until you see your father? I can just get an Uber home at nine.'

She'd like that. She wasn't sure how sensible it was, because the way she felt towards Simon Purdy right now she needed to take two steps back before she did more than straighten his tie.

She started the car and drove out of the car park towards the airport.

'Company at the hotel sounds good. If you don't mind? I'd love that. Saves me sitting by myself, watching the clock. You could even come with me to see my father, if you don't want to wait for an Uber. I'll only be there half an hour. If that. I'm sure he'll be interested to hear straight from a paediatrician about his new granddaughter. But he'll be keen to get back to work on his computer.'

'Easily done,' he said, and turned his head briefly to study her face. She felt his gaze on her. 'Barring Henry calling me,' he added.

Oh, heck. She'd forgotten about Henry. About Simon's world. Being on call. She'd lived with being on call with her father. Even been on call herself when she'd worked for retrievals. She remembered how much that impacted on life—more than expected.

That was why she'd gone for an academic, like Conlon. No on call. No emergencies. No need to be constantly aware and ready to go at a moment's notice. Being there when families needed you.

Right… And how had *that* worked out for her?

Not so good. She'd deleted another text from Conlon today without reading it.

'Dad's at the airport hotel. We can park underneath. Apparently, there's a bar on the top floor with excellent views, open till eleven tonight.'

'Perfect. We'll wing it when your father arrives.'

'Was that a pun?'

'I'm a funny guy.' He smiled at her. 'You just haven't met him yet.'

And that was how she found herself on the top floor of a beach-themed hotel, looking over the lights of the Gold Coast with Simon Purdy. On the horizon, the lights of ships glowed as they chugged up and down the coast. Behind them the planes were coming in to land.

Simon put two steaming chai teas down and slung his big frame into the high stool.

'You're buying for me again. Thank you.'

'You're welcome. You've had a big week with your sister. So Kate's the first baby in the family?'

She took a sip of the tea. Hot and soothing. 'My niece? Yes. I've only the one sister. Our mother died when we were young.'

'Like Malachi and me. Both our mothers died early too, and if it wasn't for Millicent, Malachi would have had no warmth in his life at all. That's why Lisandra is such a joy.'

'Makes sense.' Isabella huffed a sad laugh. 'Sounds like my world. My father was too busy for either of us after my mother was gone. If it wasn't for my grandmother...' Her words trailed off as she thought of Gran then and Gran now.

'That must make it doubly hard for you to see her so ill.'

Simon's words were quiet, not over-sentimental. It was as if he knew not to be too sympathetic or she might cry.

The thought eased the tightness in her throat caused by his words.

Isabella lifted her chin and looked at him. 'We went to boarding school, but Gran was the one who took us on holidays. Made sure we knew about cuddles and hugs. She's the person I love most in the world.'

'I bet she has some stories about you.'

Isabella surprised herself when she laughed. He had such a way of lifting her up. 'She does. But what about you? You lost your mother? What was your childhood like?'

His face closed. 'No memories of my mother. She died when I was born. I don't think my father ever forgave me for that.'

CHAPTER SEVENTEEN

SIMON COULD NOT believe he'd just told her his deepest secret. Malachi was the only other person who knew. And probably Lisandra now, because Malachi would keep nothing from his wife.

Hopefully, Isabella would let it go.

'I'm sorry, Simon. Did you have any mother figure who gave you hugs? At least I had Gran.'

He sighed. Nope. She wasn't going to let it go.

'There were housekeepers. My grandmother died not long before my mother.'

'Well, you wouldn't know it from the way you interacted with Malachi's family. You look very balanced.'

'Do I?' He smiled at her. 'Diplomatic… Especially after the way I treated you last week.'

'We'll come to that—but not here. Ah…here comes my father. And soon I'll introduce you to my grandmother.'

'It is unlikely your grandmother will wake, Isabella.'

Simon heard the voice behind his right shoulder. He stood, sliding to the left and moving closer, instinctively, to Isabella, as if to offer her protection from the coldness in the man's words.

Isabella stood up as well. 'Good evening, Dad.' She inclined her head.

There wasn't even a hug between them. It had to be the coldest father-daughter reunion he'd ever seen, and Isabella wasn't a cold woman. He'd known that from the first moment he'd seen her. In fact…

No, he didn't want to go there.

Maybe her dad had realised his lack of warmth would reflect badly, because the man stepped forward and touched Isabella's shoulder. 'I'm aware how fond you are of your grandmother, but you need to be realistic. I spoke to the staff yesterday and there's no change. That's not good.'

Isabella ignored his comment and turned to Simon. 'Dad, I'd like to introduce you to Dr Simon Purdy, a consultant paediatrician where I work. Simon, this is my father, Professor Piers Hargrave, Director of Neurology at Sydney Central.'

Simon put out his hand to the older man and Piers shook it briefly, but Simon was marvelling at the strength and composure in the woman beside him. He could only imagine the distress her father's comments would have caused her. Good grief! Had he heard the man actually say he knew Isabella was *fond* of her grandmother, when anyone could see she adored the woman?

'Are you the consultant for my granddaughter?'

It looked as if Piers Hargraves had finished on the topic of his mother. Maybe that was for the best.

And Simon could do composed, too. 'Yes. Kate is as stable as any thirty-two-week prem can be. At the moment, we see no reason to expect more complications as she grows. But of course everything is fluid.'

'More complications?'

The question was fired at him.

'She's undergoing phototherapy at the moment. But has successfully commenced EBM through her NG tube. We're pleased that she doesn't require supplemental oxygen or respiratory support now.'

Piers nodded at Simon and then looked at Isabella. 'How's Nadia?'

Nice that he'd asked, thought Simon—but maybe he was doing the man a disservice.

Isabella remained steady. 'We expect her to be discharged from Intensive Care tomorrow morning and transferred to a room near the NICU. Her blood pressure is coming down. It was a rapid onset of eclampsia, as I said on the phone. Dr Madden is the consultant looking after her. He seems happy with her progress. You should call him tomorrow.'

'Excellent. Thank you for the update.' He glanced at his watch. 'I expect to be here until the flight out tomorrow afternoon. I'll see Nadia and...' he hesitated over his granddaughter's name '...Kate.' He looked at Isabella. 'Is that her full name?'

'Yes. Though it is a derivative of Catherine.'

He frowned. 'Right... I imagine I'll see you tomorrow, Isabella?' He inclined his head at Simon. 'Dr Purdy.'

Then he was gone.

Isabella watched him go and then Simon heard her say softly, 'And that stellar conversationalist was my father. All warm and fuzzy, as usual.'

Simon studied the expressionless face beside him and his mouth quirked. 'As you say, I need to meet your grandmother. Because you are nothing like *him*.'

Isabella turned her face to his, and despite the tinge of sadness in her eyes he saw her lips twitch.

'Apparently, I have his brains. But I refused to go into medicine when he wanted me to. Things got even cooler then.'

She looked a little lost, and he didn't want her father to do that to her. 'Nursing's gain and medicine's loss. Now, would you like another drink? Maybe a stiff one? Or would you like to go home?'

She laughed. Which surprised him and possibly her, too.

'Thank you, Simon. For being here.' She raised her brows at him. 'Actually, I'd like to go home and have a stiff drink.'

That was dangerous, but wild horses couldn't drag him away from such an idea.

'Let's do that.'

Isabella drove. He'd opened her door for her, then strode

round to the other side to climb in. Neither had said anything but they'd both smiled.

He watched her handle the car beautifully, slipping through the traffic and down into the parking garage as if the car was on rails. When she'd pulled up they sat there for a few seconds, letting the engine tick as it cooled down.

'Your place or mine?' he said as he looked across at her from the passenger seat. She looked small and tired. And a little bit wounded. Which was a contrast to the confident woman he'd seen in the rooftop bar, talking to her father.

He felt the privilege of her allowing him to see her distress. He didn't want to take advantage. But he also wanted to be there for her. So the dilemma... Too much or too little being there for her? That was why he'd passed the decision to Isabella.

She said quietly, 'I'd like you to come up. To Gran's apartment. With me.'

Simon nodded. 'Stay there,' he said, and slipped out of the car and went around to her side and opened the door.

'You don't have to open my door.'

'It gives me pleasure.'

And it did. He wanted to protect and nurture her, despite the complex, rippling ramifications of that. What he didn't know was what *she* wanted.

She shrugged and slid gracefully from the vehicle. 'Feel free.'

She smiled, and that smile shone a little more vibrantly than before.

Pleased, he walked with her across to the lifts and used his key to let them in. He stretched out his arm across the doors as she stepped through and then followed her.

He could see she wasn't thinking about the present moment, because she didn't even move to the buttons they needed to press.

He pushed seven. The doors closed.

'We've done a lot of lift travelling today, haven't we?'

There's a conversation, he thought. As a starter, it was pretty useless.

But she lifted her head. Glanced his way.

'We have.'

And there was something there, at the back of her voice, that he'd like to know more about. Follow up. Explore…

The lift stopped before either of them said anything else. Again, he put his arm in front of the doors as she walked past to her grandmother's door. Yep. Protective. He could feel his own need. It had started.

She used her key and didn't wait for him. Just left the door open behind her.

Simon followed and closed the door to temptation behind him with a click.

His heart went thump at that same moment.

CHAPTER EIGHTEEN

ISABELLA PUT HER leather clutch down with tingling fingers. Her whole body was warm from standing next to Simon in the lift. She slipped out of the silk jacket she'd had tailored in Vietnam and took it through to the hanger in her wardrobe. The jacket and trousers had been one of those indulgences she'd promised herself.

Tonight, she'd dressed for dinner with friends, but the choice of outfit had been for her father more than Simon. Really it had. Of course, dear Dad hadn't noticed or commented on it. Though, she could tell Simon had admired it.

When she came back into the sitting room Simon still lounged against the door. Waiting for permission to enter further?

He said softly, 'You looked stunning tonight.'

It was as if he'd heard her thoughts. But he couldn't have.

'You still look stunning. That colour is amazing on you. I've never seen anything quite like it.'

The way he'd said *'never seen'* was almost as if he meant he'd never seen anything quite like *her*. And it was a very nice balm for her apparent insignificance to her father.

She rubbed her arms, because the warmth increased and suddenly her skin felt super-charged as he looked at her.

She could almost hear Gran scolding her for feeling slighted by her dad. *'Drama, drama, drama!'*

She tried to let it go. Gran had also said, *'Thank someone if they pay you a compliment.'*

'Thank you, Simon.'

She waved him to the little bar in the corner, where the sherry and the spirits lived.

Obediently, he shifted. As she watched his muscular body ease into motion, calm and unhurried, yet eating the distance from the door, that slow, primitive warmth settled low in her belly.

Oh my. There goes a man who could help a person forget anything.

She'd enjoyed the intimate side of her relationship with Conlon, but she'd never felt this heat Simon generated just by standing there in front of her. This awareness. This lust that was coiling deep inside. Yes, Simon had annoyed and frustrated her before yesterday, but she'd always been aware of her overwhelming physical attraction to him. After tonight at the Maddens' it was more than physical. It was a little too close to consuming.

As if he'd picked up on her thoughts, his voice sounded deeper than usual when he asked, 'What's your definition of a stiff drink?'

She felt the timbre of his quiet words slide into her bones. *Oh my.* She should *not* be going down this path.

'Gran has a lovely cognac...'

It was as if they were both playing a part in a play. Pretending to be normal.

Then she thought of her father's comment.

'I'll replace it when she comes home.'

She heard the harshness in her tone when she said that. But, damn it, her father was wrong.

'As I said before,' Simon murmured as he poured, 'I can't wait to meet Catherine.'

Isabella crossed the room. Simon still had his back to her as he poured the drinks, and she gave in to the urge to slip her arms around his waist and rest her cheek against his broad back, looking for the comfort she knew she'd find there.

He was warm—hot, really—and muscularly hard. He smelled like cinnamon and the wind out on the ocean.

She closed her eyes and breathed him in. Letting go of the tension that had risen higher every day and coiled deep inside her, with Gran not waking, her sister's crisis, Kate's frailty, and tonight waiting for her father.

'Thank you, Simon. Thank you for being with me tonight. Thank you for being there during that incredibly painful five minutes my father could spare me. Thank you for understanding that I need to hope Gran will be back here.'

He put the crystal glasses down on the silver tray with a gentle *ting* that seemed to shimmer in the air like the sound of Tibetan bowls.

Very, very slowly, he unfastened her hands from around his waist, slid them to hold in his, and turned to look down on her so that the front of her body lay against his chest. He studied her face and then leaned down and kissed her lips gently, until he pulled back to stare at the spot he'd just saluted.

His gaze darkened to midnight-blue as it met her eyes. Her heart tripped. She could still feel the imprint of his mouth, hot against hers, and taste the chai on his breath.

In that deep gravelly voice that sent tingles through her, he said, 'You, dear Isabella, are very welcome.'

She loved the way he said her name. And he didn't step back. Didn't let her go. Didn't push on.

All it would take was one lift of her chin up to his mouth and she could forget. Escape from so much. Lose herself in Simon Purdy until tomorrow. She searched his eyes, but he wasn't giving her any pressure. This was her decision.

And what of tomorrow? What then? What of now? What about her needs? The comfort she needed right at this moment? Had needed since she'd landed in Australia?

Simon was offering that. *Simon*. He'd already said it wasn't a relationship thing. But he would be gentle and kind and most likely a wonderful lover.

And tonight she'd feel warm and cared-for.

She searched his face. What if Simon needed it too? How long since he'd felt cared-for? She suspected it had been far too long.

With that thought she lifted her mouth to his.

Thankfully, he didn't need to be told twice.

Simon's strong hand lifted to her neck and he tilted her head back to expose her throat. His fingers slid down her cheek, down her throat, past the side of her breast and down to the small of her back in a hot trail, coming to rest just above the crease of her buttocks.

He pulled her in against him. Gently, but firmly. He was interested, too. Very interested.

'You taste like chai and sunshine,' he murmured into her hair.

'You taste like chai and the waves out on the beach.'

'Just one night...' he murmured against her mouth as he tilted his face down at her. 'I need you to know it's just one night.'

She stared into the depths of his eyes. Saw the fear in his. The need for mutual comfort.

'One night, or one night at a time,' she breathed. 'Either is fine.'

The hand that rested in the small of her back slid down until he caught her under the swell of her hips and swept her up against his chest.

'Lucky it's Saturday tomorrow and I'm not on duty till the afternoon,' he said. 'Because I'm planning on a late night.'

CHAPTER NINETEEN

DECIDING TO SPEND the night with Simon was like surfing the first wave she'd ever ridden.

A leap of faith that she wouldn't fall flat on her face and get hurt.

And, like that first exhilarating wave, carnal pleasure with Simon had been everything she'd hoped for and more as she'd lifted her face to the sky and flew.

It had turned out to be a mutual delight and an unexpected healing. But both of them knew it wasn't happily-ever-after.

Now it was morning. The pillow was cold beside her. Like the space under her ribs as she realised he wasn't there and she didn't know why. He'd said one night but she'd not even had that. Just hours. And then he'd left.

In the early hours she'd dropped into a boneless sleep in his arms. It must have been some time after that when he'd slipped away. Had he left to avoid talking when they woke? Had she not been good enough? Or had he been called out?

This was why she didn't have one-night stands.

How had this seemed like a good idea last night?

For pity's sake. She had to work this afternoon and face the man.

What she needed was the fresh start of the ocean, but she wasn't sure she wanted to meet Simon face to face in the waves either.

His pique at her invading his surf-space suddenly became more understandable.

But maybe that was the best place to meet him. Floating on a board. A distance apart. With the excuse of looking forward as well as behind them to see a promising wave.

So that was what she did.

The sand flew cold and grainy from her bare feet as she ran towards the breakers. The seagulls were squawking, as if they knew there was juicy gossip to be had, and she squinted up at them balefully.

'Go eat a chip.'

She'd been avoiding it, but now, as she drew closer, Isabella narrowed her gaze to the waves. The space where Simon had been last time and she hadn't recognised his face.

Well, that wasn't going to happen now. She'd identify him, all right.

She'd traced the lines of his cheekbones. And his mouth. *Oh my....* That mouth could do wonderful things. She'd gripped the hard muscles of his body and...

Nope. No forgetting Simon Purdy—today or probably ever.

Her cheeks warmed even with the cool breeze on them, but her lips curved as the water sloshed up her ankles and knees and she jogged into the waves. Leaning down, she pushed the surfboard in front of her and launched herself along it, to push the water past with her hands.

Her breath caught as she saw a lone figure ahead. She wondered what time he'd come out. Because he was just sitting there. Like a lone pirate surveying the world. Now he was surveying her.

She paddled towards him, but not too close, always leaving a distance between their boards.

'Good morning, Dr Purdy,' she called as she sat up on her fibreglass island.

'Good morning, Isabella. A beautiful morning.'

But there was more in his voice than a remark on the weather, and his blue, blue eyes were looking at her as if she was the best thing he'd seen since he got here.

Her cheeks heated again, and she glanced away from him to the horizon, and the movement of water towards them.

She gestured with her arm. 'Nice swells coming in. Had some good rides?'

She did not just say that. *Shoot.* Her face scorched this time, and she spluttered and shut her mouth.

Simon was too much of a gentleman to laugh, but his eyes danced.

She turned her back on him, paddled quickly, and caught a wave, even though it wasn't as perfect as she would have normally chosen. Right now she needed space.

Surprisingly, considering the mediocrity of the ride, Simon followed her. When she slipped off the back of the wave he paddled strongly towards her, white teeth gleaming, all rippling muscles, brown skin and big arms bringing him closer.

When he'd closed the distance he paddled up beside her and murmured, 'We said it wasn't going to be awkward.'

'It's not,' she lied.

He raised his brows at her. 'Do you regret spending the night with me?'

She looked up then, and forced herself to hold his gaze. 'Do you with me?'

He laughed. 'No, gorgeous. How could I? You were amazing.'

Oh. That was all right, then.

A weight fell off her shoulders.

'Then, no. You were pretty wonderful, too.'

And suddenly the awkwardness between them slipped into the water beneath them and she smiled.

His teeth gleamed again. 'Although perhaps what we shared last night could be a little more distracting than either of us expected.'

'Sorry.'

My word, it was certainly distracting.

'I'm not much of an expert at morning-afters.' She put her head down, suddenly shy.

She heard his voice, but she still wasn't looking at him as they paddled side by side, up and over another wave.

'Surprisingly, neither am I. Henry rang me not long after you went to sleep. I left to speak to him.'

Isabella sucked in a breath.

He held up his hand. 'Not about Kate. Your niece is fine.'

And that allayed two concerns in one. He hadn't left because of any awkwardness or because he was uncaring. He'd left for work. And he'd reassured her about Kate before she could jump to wrong conclusions.

'Thank you, Simon. You're a thoughtful man.' She lifted her head and risked looking into his face. 'Race you to the back?'

When they'd surfed the early morning away, they stopped at Lulu's café for breakfast.

As Simon was off duty, and Isabella was not working until the afternoon, they had time—unless their phones rang.

Lulu swept up, pencil behind her ear and notepad in her hand, her usual exuberant self. 'Good morning, you two. How's the surf?'

'Nice swells, thanks, Lulu.'

Simon leaned back in his chair and Isabella tried not to stare at his strong throat and chest above the open neck of his shirt. It was as if everything about him had taken on colour and tactile recognition and scent and memory, but he was still talking to Lulu.

'How're the twins?'

'Full of mischief. The usual for you, Simon? And what about you, Isabella? Smashed avocado and eggs on rye? Orange juice and coffee?

Isabella smiled up at the woman. She'd remembered her name and her previous order. 'Great memory, Lulu. All of the above, but a skinny cap, please.'

'Done.' Lulu swung away with her notebook.

'Why does she carry a notebook if she remembers everything?'

'For the chef. I've seen Lulu take an order from ten people

at a table and bring out the correct food to everybody without writing a thing down. That's her superpower.'

'I think her personality is her superpower. She's amazing.' Simon was looking at her with a smile on his face.

'What?' she asked.

'Some people might judge her for the piercings and the tattoos.'

'She's vibrant and happy and amazing. All the while loving twin babies. No judgement.' Isabella shrugged. 'So, what was the problem in the unit last night?'

She could do this. Talk to Simon normally after a night of incredible, bone-melting... She didn't like to call it sex. It had been more than that. How about mutual appreciation? Tenderness? Gentleness? A little bit of wildness. And lots of healing. She felt as if every knot in her body had been undone.

'Earth to Isabella?' Simon was watching her face and his blue eyes had darkened to ocean-depth-blue. 'You might want to stop looking at me like that...'

Her face flushed. Her neck heated. She closed and opened her eyes. 'Oh, dear.' She raised her gaze to his face. 'This is your fault.'

He laughed. 'I am not taking all the blame. No way. And last night at work it was the new twins.'

Lulu brought their coffee and juice and put their cups down. She didn't say anything, but she waved her hand at her own face as if fanning it. The smile in her eyes said, *It's smokin' hot over here!*

Once Lulu was gone, Isabella said quietly, 'So where do we go from here, Simon?'

'I'll go back home. I imagine you'll visit your grandmother, get ready for work, and visit your sister before you start. And I'll run into you this afternoon in the unit. At least we have two days before Carla is back with her eagle eyes, ready to tease us. Everything will be fine by then.'

She wondered if he really would *imagine*, daydream, or think about her while she was doing all that.

'You have experience in all this,' she accused.

He'd just laid out a very sensible plan, but it was sweet that he'd paid enough attention to know what her movements would be.

CHAPTER TWENTY

SIMON WASN'T EXPERIENCED. Not with what had happened last night. He'd played around a bit before he'd met Louise, but since her death he'd been in cold storage. Now Isabella Hargraves had swooped in, and lust had taken him by dangerous and heated surprise.

Last night, while incredible, had been so momentous he knew without a doubt it had been a mistake. No way could he do that again and walk away.

Not with how amazing it had been and how hazardous it was to his resolution to stay single and safe from the type of pain he couldn't even contemplate going through again.

Isabella would want it all. She deserved it all. He just couldn't give it to her. He couldn't keep her safe.

He would remain focused on his career. He would not go down the route of falling in love.

Isabella Hargraves had all the makings of an addiction. And he knew where that led.

A place he wasn't going. Hadn't he told himself that before? Didn't matter. It had never been as important to remember as it was this morning.

They would finish breakfast and go their separate ways. And when they met in the unit he would be pleasantly friendly, because she deserved that. But he would pretend nothing had happened.

Eventually, she'd get it. He hoped.

Except he was kidding himself.

Simon grimaced into his coffee and pushed that thought away along with the cup.

The food arrived and they both tucked in.

It seemed neither of them had eaten for a week, because there was no word said as they shovelled the nourishment down. He hadn't been this hungry for years. Three years, in fact.

They sat back at the same time and looked at each other, and then looked down at their empty plates. And he couldn't help it. He laughed when she did.

'Apparently surfing works up an appetite,' he said.

She pushed her gorgeous lips together, as if holding words back, and he just knew what she was going to say.

Surfing wasn't the only thing that had given them an appetite.

He needed to run away. Tried to say, *I have to go*.

The one time he wanted his phone to ring and it wouldn't do it!

His phone rang.

Thank you, heaven.

His pulse rate settled.

There we go.

He stood up.

She said thoughtfully, studying his face, 'I'll pay for this. You go.'

And, contrarily, just for a moment he didn't want to leave.

CHAPTER TWENTY-ONE

THAT. THERE. THE TWITCH. The flicker she'd seen in his eyes. He'd wanted to get away, to get to work. That was her father all over again. She felt the knowledge slide in, felt as if she'd been stabbed with one of the happy, beachy purple knives off the table, straight in her heart.

Simon wanted to leave her behind and get on with more exciting business-like work.

It stung. She'd told herself that she was fine for a one-night stand. And on one hand it had been a good decision to sleep with Simon—apart from all the benefits of the best sex she'd ever had—because now she knew, without investing in any more wishy-washy thoughts of the future. Even after what they'd shared, Simon wanted work more than he wanted her!

Message received.

Isabella watched as Simon ate up the distance to the apartments in big strides, even more quickly than if he'd run. And, yes, it all underlined the fact he wanted to get away.

'He's a nice guy,' Lulu said at her shoulder.

'Wonderful.' Isabella sighed and finished her coffee. 'But married to his work. I had a childhood like that. Not doing that for the rest of my life.'

She wasn't sure why she'd told Lulu that, except Isabella needed to hear it out loud. Her statement solidified in her mind as she reached for her purse.

'And it's grateful I am that he is,' Lulu murmured, and there was emotion and a hint of Irish brogue under that sentence.

She got that. Oh, yes, Dr Simon Purdy was great at his job. And right now she was glad of that too. She had a niece who needed him.

'Hello, Gran. It's Isabella. I've brought you flowers. Deep purple with a subtle perfume.'

She subconsciously waited for a greeting that never came. Shook her head at herself.

'Violets. Your favourite. That's right...'

She tucked the small vase next to her grandmother on the side table and tweaked one of the blooms more upright.

'They say gently stimulating the five senses might help you to wake up.'

Please, Gran, she thought as emotion clogged.

She swallowed the lump in her throat.

'It's four weeks now, so that's enough of this sleeping for you.'

She pulled open the bedside drawer and took out the hand cream. She sat down and picked up her grandmother's thin, wrinkled hand in hers.

'Anyway, back to the five senses. I'm trying to stimulate your hearing, not drive you mad with my babble. And later your friend Millicent is coming to chat as well. Would you like that?'

That made her think about Simon.

She glanced across at her grandmother's face and for a moment she'd thought her eyes were open. They weren't. Her heart thumped faster and then settled down.

Wishful thinking.

Her brain wasn't working properly with images of Simon intruding with every second thought. She'd have to do something about that.

'The flowers are to stimulate your sense of smell...'

She began to smooth the cream into her grandmother's soft hands.

'And I'll spend a little time rubbing your fingers to stimulate your sense of touch.'

With a hint of asperity that wasn't solely directed at her grandmother, thanks to her father and Simon, she said, 'It's a beautiful day outside and you need to wake up.'

There was so much she wanted to tell her grandmother. Wanted to pour out into her ears.

But she was not going to talk about Simon. All she said was, 'The nurse said Dad has been in to see you. Did you recognise his voice?'

When Isabella walked into the neonatal intensive care unit the first person she saw, for a change, was her father. Tall and strangely gaunt-looking, and almost seeming old. She hadn't noticed that last night.

The second person was Simon, too darned handsome and full of stamina, standing beside him, talking beside Kate's cot.

Two tall men. One dark-haired, one light-haired. Both standing there with that consultant doctor attitude. An *I've studied a long time to be able to help this sick patient* look on their faces. Both married to their work. Both saving the world.

Blow the both of them.

She was early, so she had time to have a quick word before she officially started.

She put her bag away in the small staff room and crossed the room towards them.

They stopped talking as she approached. 'Hello, Dad. Simon…' She addressed her father. 'You went to see Gran? What did you think?'

She suspected he wouldn't even have said anything if she hadn't asked.

Her father's cool gaze held a hint of concern, which wasn't like him, and she focussed her attention on him while her stomach dived.

'There's a possibility she's not as deeply unconscious as she has been earlier, but I hesitate to give you false hope. Extensive brain damage is likely.'

And there it was. Did the man not have any heart?

Simon's gaze raked her face and she felt his sympathy. She didn't need it. She was becoming even more disenchanted with her father.

She narrowed her eyes at him. 'Thanks. Don't hold back. I need all the hope I can get.'

She turned to Simon before she said something she'd regret. Her voice softened and she searched his face. 'How's Kate?'

That was the question for now.

She plastered on a cool, calm expression for all to see. She looked down at her sleeping niece and asked, 'All going well?'

Simon spoke quietly. 'Kate's temperature control is erratic. We've had a couple of bradycardias and two occasions of apnoea. We've stopped the feeds for the time being.'

Stopped the feeds? Her stomach plummeted.

'Infection?' That was the most common cause of problems with premature babies. 'Her breathing?' She was certainly breathing a little faster. 'Not NEC…?'

Her brain rifled through the options. Infection they could treat with antibiotics. Kate had already been started on some. Could be anything. Worst-case scenario it could be the beginning of a Necrotising Enterocolitis, but it was very early.

She studied Kate's belly. Was the tiny tummy a little more bloated? It was the third day. That was a horrifying concept.

Simon studied her face as if he could see the thoughts chasing through her mind. 'There is some decrease in bowel sounds,' he said.

She nodded. Ignored her father. Fished her stethoscope from her pocket, where she kept it to keep it warm, and wiped the membrane and casing—the listening end—with an alcohol swab from her other pocket. When she was done with meticulously cleaning it, she looked for somewhere to put the discarded swab and debris.

Simon held out his hand. Their eyes met and she saw the

understanding in his. She settled the wrappings carefully in his palm, as if doing so equalled crossing her fingers behind her back and therefore she could keep Kate safe.

'Thank you,' she murmured, before leaning down to very gently put the stethoscope on Kate's belly to listen. She was hoping Kate's belly would gurgle. Or hiss. All she got was a tiny trickle. The rest was…silence.

She took the stethoscope away. Fear clutched her throat but she pushed it down.

'Do you think her abdomen is swollen?' At Simon's nod she asked quietly, 'How's the gastric aspirate trending? Has it increased?'

'Five mils removed last time.'

'X-ray?'

His intent gaze never left her face. 'There is a small collection of gases.'

'Treatment?'

'Change antibiotics. Nil by mouth for three days and fingers crossed.'

Okay. Standard protocol.

'When did you first notice it?'

'On my round an hour ago.'

He'd called over a radiologist for the X-ray.

No doubt he would have ordered blood tests as well.

Pre-empting her question, Simon added, 'Blood results aren't back yet. Not even the preliminary ones.'

Simon was worried—which meant she was worried.

She glanced towards the nurses' station and the staff who had gathered there. 'I'll take the handover report and come back.'

She didn't say it, but she wanted him still to be there. She glanced at her father, but uncharacteristically he didn't say anything. She nodded and left.

CHAPTER TWENTY-TWO

PIERS HARGRAVES SAID, 'My daughter was always very quick on the uptake.'

Simon heard the pride in his voice. And he guessed that he, himself, was a little impressed that he hadn't been wrong about Isabella's ability to take in the situation instantly.

'She could have been a doctor, you know. She chose midwifery.'

Simon heard the curl of disgust in her father's voice. He was liking this guy less and less.

He lifted his chin and met the man's eyes. 'I have no doubt she's an amazing midwife. She's certainly brilliant as a neonatal intensivist. We're very lucky to have her.'

'Yes, you are. Hopefully she won't stay. I'm keen for her to move back to Sydney.'

Simon hoped Isabella's father didn't mean after Piers's mother had passed away. That was just too cold.

Either way, he couldn't see Isabella leaving. Not with Nadia here. And Kate. Even though Kate's situation was worrisome, Simon was quietly confident the baby would rise to the challenge. He thought this would only be a small setback, because they'd hit the problem quickly.

No doubt Isabella would think that too.

But he wasn't saying that out loud. He wasn't going to guarantee anything or make promises he couldn't keep.

And that went for other things as well. No promises anywhere about anything.

But was that just like Isabella's father?

Simon changed the subject. 'How's Nadia?' He hadn't seen Kate's mother today though he planned to go there now. Now that he'd seen Isabella.

'The oedema is receding. And her blood pressure is stable. It appears there is no sequalae. She's said she'll try to walk to the NICU late this afternoon.'

'Of course. I imagine she's been waiting for Isabella's shift. I'll ask them to bring her in a wheelchair.'

Piers dropped his voice. 'What is your intention with my daughter?'

Simon almost said *Nadia?* just to annoy him. But he didn't. And as for Isabella… He wished he knew.

'We have a mutual respect,' he said gravely. And left it at that.

Anything else was not her father's business—especially after the cold way he'd treated his daughter in the bar at that airport hotel.

Simon didn't want to think about why he was feeling so protective.

He saw the good doctor glance across at the nurses circumnavigating the unit, stopping at each cot to discuss progress and treatment. He glanced at his watch.

Surely Piers wouldn't…?

'Let's go over and you can say goodbye. That'll be better than just slipping away. She's finding it tough,' Simon said, pre-empting Isabella's father's obvious intention of getting Simon to pass on a farewell message. Words that might sting Isabella with dismissal.

No. Simon wasn't going to let him do it.

He turned and crossed the room, and guided Piers to where the nurses were gathered to discuss their next patient.

'Sorry for the interruption, ladies,' Simon said. 'Isabella?' She looked at him. 'Could I borrow you for a moment, please?'

Seeing as he tended to do that all the time, nobody was surprised.

She detached herself and came to where he'd moved, back to Piers's side.

Her father's lips were pressed together. 'Goodbye, Isabella. You're doing a good thing, being here for Nadia. For everyone. Thank you.'

Simon saw her surprise and the quickly veiled pleasure at her father's words and breathed out a little deeper in relief, fiercely glad he'd leant on the other man to make a formal goodbye.

'Thank you,' she said quietly, and leaned forward to kiss his cheek. 'Safe flight.'

Her father nodded and strode away.

Simon saw the questioning look in her eyes. 'Yes. I'll still be here when you finish.'

It was her turn to nod, but he saw that same satisfaction flare briefly, and his own pleasure at her response sat warm in his chest.

'Thank you.'

She turned and walked back to the group and he went to the desk to call Pathology, to see if any results had come through for Kate.

CHAPTER TWENTY-THREE

IN THE END, just before tea, Simon went to the postnatal ward and brought Nadia back in a wheelchair himself, to sit beside Kate.

Isabella didn't know what he'd said to her, but Nadia looked calm and composed, and she understood that her baby had issues that needed dealing with.

For Isabella, her concern was shelved as she watched her sister reach out and touch her daughter's hand for the first time. A baby too sick to travel up to visit and a mother to unstable to be transported down from the intensive care. But Nadia was in the new room on the same floor now. Everything would be easier. That small, tentative mother's touch brought tears to Isabella's eyes.

Hospital policy made it against the rules for its staff to care for their own relatives, so Isabella wasn't looking after Kate. But while she was not responsible for her care or observations, she could—and did—keep an eye on her from her side of the unit.

Thankfully, it seemed a quieter afternoon in the unit. Nice, Isabella thought, because it meant she could slip over and talk to her sister when she had questions. Also, it would be her break time soon, and she would spend it with Nadia.

Simon had disappeared to the emergency department, to treat a three-year-old girl with epilepsy, but had promised to come back.

Her sensible brain would have preferred he went home and got some sleep, just in case he was needed for her niece...

'Has Dad gone?' asked Nadia, glancing at her watch.

Nadia. Think about Nadia. Be present.

'Yes, he left not long after I started shift. I guess that means he didn't drop in to see you on his way out?'

Nadia shook her head and Isabella could see the quickly veiled hurt.

Darn him, Isabella seethed. What would it have cost him? Three minutes? Nadia was five doors away from the NICU.

'He said he was going to see Gran today, but he didn't come back to tell me what he thought about her prognosis.'

Isabel wanted to grind her teeth. The man had real issues with being a parent, and for the first time she wondered how many times her grandmother had actually forced him to do things that they'd thought he'd instigated himself.

'Did he tell *you* how Gran was?' Nadia asked.

Isabella said gently, 'He said he thought she wasn't as deeply unconscious as before, but he's not optimistic.'

She didn't say that she'd thought their grandmother's eyes had opened. Or that their father thought brain damage would be a problem.

'Imagine that...' Nadia drawled grimly. 'Dad not being optimistic...' She glanced up at Isabella, said softly, 'I'm sorry I didn't go more often to see her before Kate was born. It just upset me too much.'

Isabella leant down and hugged her. 'It's okay. I understand. Being pregnant mucks with your emotions.'

Right then Kate's cardiac monitor alarm went off, and Isabella watched the screen as her niece's heart rate slowly dropped. She glanced across to the nurse looking after her, who nodded and slipped across to watch as well.

Isabella said softly in Nadia's ear, 'We don't want to stimulate her—we want her to stimulate herself. But we will if her lack of breath and falling heart rate goes on for longer than thirty seconds.'

Nadia paled, and Isabella squeezed her sister's shoulder.

After seventeen seconds Kate breathed in, and her cardiac output increased as her heart rate went back up.

'Good girl,' Isabella said, and the nurse next to them smiled.

'She didn't need stimulation,' the nurse explained to Nadia. 'She's managing.'

'Yes, thanks… I see,' said Nadia, but her eyes tracked back to Isabella, who nodded encouragingly.

'Jesse has this. She'll watch her,' Isabella said, and then continued, 'I'd better get back to my own babies. See you soon. Let me know when you want to go back to bed.'

Nadia nodded unhappily. 'I'll stay another ten minutes, but I'm getting sore…'

Isabella frowned. 'If you're in pain, only stay a few minutes more, while I phone an orderly to take you back to your ward. I'll come and see you in your room when I go on my next break.'

Forty minutes later, after all her babies were fed and their observations were up to date, Isabella went along to Nadia's room with the packed dinner she'd brought from home.

Nadia was just finishing off her own tray of food.

Nadia's first words—'Kate's good?'—made Isabella smile. 'Kate's good.'

'Great. And now, because I'm dying to know…' Her sister sat back expectantly. 'How was your date at Dr Madden's house with the hunky Dr Purdy?

Isabella smiled. Her sister had been very patient. 'Hunky Dr Purdy, eh?'

She was thankful this conversation hadn't come up on the unit, with everyone within earshot.

'Not my type.' Nadia tilted her head. 'But definitely hunky.'

She looked crestfallen for a second, and Isabella guessed Nadia had just remembered her late husband. The man had been not a happy partner in life for Nadia. A gambler and unfaithful. It would take time, and someone very special, for

Nadia to trust a man again. Her sister did not need to go there yet, and Isabella could sacrifice a little privacy to cheer her up.

'It was fun,' she said, pretending she hadn't seen Nadia's punctured mood. 'And Lisandra Madden is a lovely woman I hope I see more of.'

'That's nice…' Nadia surreptitiously wiped her eyes.

'Yes. And I even met Dr Madden's grandmother. Millicent. She's a friend of Gran's.'

Nadia opened her eyes wide. 'Is she?' She smiled and shook her head. 'It's like a small town here.'

Isabella laughed. 'Probably because we're all connected through the hospital. Anyway, it was a lovely dinner, great conversation, and Lisandra's twins are gorgeous.'

'I'm jealous.' Nadia sounded wistful. 'You're making new friends and I haven't made any.'

Isabella opened the tucker box on her lap. 'It will happen.' She popped a cherry tomato into her mouth.

'But what about Simon?' Her sister shifted on her pillows as if trying to get comfortable. 'Did he kiss you goodnight?'

Isabella's mind flew back to that long look in the lounge room of Gran's apartment, and the way, after that, Simon had carried her to bed. She slowed her chewing to give herself time to answer.

My word, he'd kissed her.

Her stomach curled, kicked and rolled.

She looked down at her food box.

He'd kissed her so many times. In so many places. She didn't think she'd ever forget that night. Or his mouth…

Instead of answering the question, and fighting down the heat that wanted to flood her cheeks, she offered, 'Simon and I called into the airport hotel after we left. He even came with me when I spoke to Dad. He met us in the bar.'

Nadia opened her eyes wide. 'Did he?' Thankfully she was diverted. 'That's above and beyond for Simon.' Then she frowned. 'How did Dad take that?'

'Didn't blink an eye.' Isabella grimaced. 'But then it didn't take very long. I was out of there in five minutes.'

Nadia shook her head. 'What do you think is wrong with our father? Do you think we'll be like that when we're old?'

Isabella couldn't help but laugh. 'He's not old. But no, I'm not turning into an antisocial pessimist. I refuse. And neither will you. I'm starting to think Gran is the only reason we're both turned out so well.'

That brought the mood down again. They were both thinking about Gran, lying there unconscious, her eyes closed. Not what she'd intended. But at least it diverted Nadia from asking about Simon kissing her goodnight again.

'Do you think she'll wake up?' asked Nadia.

'Yes. I do. When she's ready.'

Strangely, her dwindling hope had taken off again.

Isabella took a bite of her sandwich, because she needed to eat before she went back to work and she only had fifteen minutes left.

'Did you see Dr Madden today? Sorry I haven't asked before.'

Nadia nodded. 'Yes, just before lunch. He says I'm making good progress, but they need to keep checking my blood pressure.'

'I think you're in the golden light of Simon and Malachi now.'

And because that wasn't a bad place to be from Nadia's point of view, she smiled. Nadia and Kate needed the care.

'Also, it's great that we live close for later, as Kate grows up.'

Nadia sighed, long and loud, and then held her aching stomach. 'How long do you think Kate will be in hospital?'

That was the question most asked by parents in the NICU, Isabella thought, and her sister was no different. 'I always tell people that however early the baby is in weeks is the general length of time they're going to stay in hospital.

'It could be eight weeks?' Nadia sounded forlorn.

'Could be… But probably closer to five. There'll be ups and downs, like today, so it's hard to tell.'

She pointed her finger at Nadia. 'But her mother and her auntie will be here for as long as it takes, and the time will pass. She just needs to be well and grow up. It will happen.'

CHAPTER TWENTY-FOUR

SIMON DROPPED BACK into the NICU after the emergency department's call, hoping to catch Isabella before he went home. He'd planned to give her the pathology results personally, but she wasn't there.

He knew where she'd be.

On her break with her sister. Caring.

He should go home. The result would be in Kate's records soon, and the staff would let Isabella know when she came back. That would be in less than half an hour. He didn't need to go looking for her all over the hospital.

Except his feet carried him out of the NICU and along the corridor to the postnatal area and Nadia's room. He could hear Isabella's voice as he approached.

'It will happen.'

What will happen?

He couldn't help thinking of last night, and paused at the door to gather himself as memories tried to break through the wall he'd erected. Yes, it had happened. He squeezed his eyes shut, trying to hold back the images.

My word, it had.

He knocked. Two blonde heads turned his way, and two pairs of green eyes: one pair sleepy and owl-like because of the drugs, and the other alert, cool, and too beautiful for their own good. How did he find one of these sisters totally pole-axing and the other merely pleasant? Nadia was a beautiful woman, too, but Isabella stole his breath.

'Pathology back?' Isabella said softly as her brows rose in question.

He hadn't really noticed people's brows before, but hers were arched, darker than her hair. They drew the eye to the angles of her face. Perfect.

What was he doing? Spending seconds he didn't need to thinking thoughts he shouldn't be thinking. He should be walking in the opposite direction. Jogging? Sprinting?

The thought soured in his mind, and he pushed it away.

'Pathology? Yes. Not looking too bad. If Kate has an inflamed bowel, it's only just started, and hopefully the antibiotics will stop any spread of infection. We'll keep her nil by mouth and wait. She'll get IV nutrition.'

'Thanks, Simon.' Isabella smiled at her sister. 'That's good news, Nadia.'

Nadia breathed out a sigh. 'Wonderful. So, when will her tummy work again? Should I carry on expressing breast milk?'

He watched Isabella tweak the covers straight on her sister's bed, making sure she was snuggled in.

'You keep expressing every few hours, like you have been. We'll store the milk. There won't be much at first, but it will meet Kate's needs when she's ready. We'll sort that.' Isabella glanced at her watch. 'Thanks for the update, Simon. You going home now?'

He felt dismissed. Maybe she did have a bit of the old man in her. The thought made his mouth twitch. Isabella was nothing like her cold father.

'Yes.' He had a sudden uneasy thought. 'Did you bring your car? How do you normally get home at night after a late shift?'

He walked the block and a half home at night. The fresh air after the air-conditioned hospital felt good. But he didn't like the idea of Isabella out at eleven p.m., when her shift ended, which coincidentally was not long after the pubs shut with all the drunks and revellers emptied onto the streets.

It was dark on the road towards their apartments, even with the streetlights.

'I walk fast,' she said. 'Like you do. And I carry an alarm.'

He opened his mouth and closed it again. Fair enough. Except he wasn't happy. His neck crawled with how unhappy he was.

'She has a black belt in karate,' Nadia said with a wicked, sisterly grin. 'Which she doesn't tell anybody about.'

That made him blink. Why was he surprised? Why did that make her even hotter?

'I should ask you to walk *me* home, then,' Simon quipped, but his brain spun with relief…and maybe some graphic imaginings of Isabella flying through the air or kicking out at an assailant.

His body stirred. *Hot, or what?*

Nope. Not going there.

It wasn't strange that his mind was on alert—he had feelings for Isabella…complicated feelings. But she was a friend. They'd agreed on that.

Friend with benefits? his libido whispered.

No. No more benefits.

But maybe he'd watch for her out of his balcony tonight and just make sure she was safe.

'I'll leave you, then,' he said, wishing his phone would ring. Why was he still here?

'I'll come with you.' Isabella leaned down to kiss her sister. 'You need sleep, missy. I'm not far away if you need me.'

Ah, Isabella would want to talk to him about the results. That was why he hadn't left. He'd known she'd want that.

It was as if another Simon lived inside him—one tuned to Isabella and Isabella's needs.

He waved, and Isabella said, 'See you tomorrow, Nadia.'

He walked to the door and Isabella followed until they were out in the corridor and halfway back to the NICU. Then she stopped.

'Thanks for being here today, Simon.'

He saw her concern, her worry, and his heart ached a little

at the load she carried. But he needed his walls to stay up. Especially when she looked at him like that.

In response, he made light of his part. 'Easy done. I don't have a life.'

That was true. But the statement fell flat. She didn't smile. 'Why is that? Why don't you have a life? You deserve one.'

Her voice was more intense than he'd expected.

His brows furrowed. 'I told you why. I've had my time.'

Because I'm scared that if I allow myself to care and something happens again...

He wasn't going to say that. So he batted the question back to her. 'Why don't *you* have a life, apart from worrying about your family? Where's your home life?'

He hadn't wondered about that before, and suddenly the answer was very, very interesting.

She looked away. Which wasn't like her.

'I tried that in Vietnam. His name was Conlon. He let me down, too.'

He saw the subtle shake of her head, as if she was calling herself a fool for believing in fairy tales. She deserved the fairy tale. He just couldn't give it to her either.

The man must have been a fool. He wanted to say so, because standing there with Isabella he felt as if they were in a bubble, insulated from the world.

Except they weren't alone in the bubble.

An orderly pushed an empty stretcher around the corner and they had to separate to let him through. It broke the spell.

'I'm sorry. It's none of my business. I'd better go.'

Before he said something else stupid.

He turned and left, but he could feel her gaze on him as he walked away.

At ten past eleven that evening Simon stood on his balcony and watched the road between the hospital and the apartments.

He'd never really thought about the fact that he could see

his place of work from where he lived, but for the purpose of watching for Isabella it was perfect.

There she was. Right on time. Walking under the first streetlight with a brisk pace and a cross-body bag tucked in front of her. There was something in the droop of her shoulders that said she was unhappy.

He scanned the streets, but there was no one around. Still, he didn't like it. He wanted to slip down in the lift and stand outside, open the door for her.

Crazy on top of crazy. He needed sleep.

He stayed watching.

He'd phoned half an hour ago to check on Isabella's niece, and she'd been stable, so nothing new to worry either of them there. They should both sleep.

But why was she unhappy? Was it him? Had he done this to her?

She must have felt his attention on her, because she glanced up at his balcony and shaded her eyes from the streetlight. He reached his hand back into the apartment and flicked the light on and off.

She offered a tiny wave and he smiled. Felt his whole face crinkle with satisfaction from one miniscule hand lift. *Idiot*.

He texted her. Fingers moving before he could stop them. He hadn't even realised that he had his phone in his hand.

Do you want to come up?

And that was why he was standing there. God, he was such a fool. He hadn't realised that was what he was going to do.

She texted back.

Two minutes.

His libido whispered that he could be fast, if that was what she wanted. Against the door, maybe?

He closed his eyes.

No. No. No. He wasn't going to do this. They weren't going to do this.

He was just there to hear about her night. Be an ear and listen to her, because she didn't have anyone else. Let her unwind so she could sleep without her brain reeling in the night with suppressed conversations she couldn't have on her own.

Like he did. Nearly every night.

He went back inside to the kitchen to put on the kettle. Absently checked there was ice in the freezer in case she wanted something stronger. Put out two mugs. Threw in two sleepytime teabags.

Because then he wouldn't have to spend time in the kitchen, when really he wanted to look at her, talk to her, not have his back to her making tea.

She knocked at the door before he had time to put everything back and tell himself to stop being stupid, so instead he crossed the room in long strides.

He took a breath to fill his lungs and opened the door, so he could search the features he was coming to know so well.

He'd missed her face.

He frowned when he saw the worry in her eyes. The concern in the pull of her mouth. The weariness. He wanted to hug her.

'Come in,' he said.

She eased past him, bringing the smell of the hospital and handwash in with her.

He shut the door and followed. 'How was your night? I thought you might like a quick debrief before you went to bed.'

Her chin lifted and he saw the glitter of tears. 'Nadia had another seizure. Malachi's with her and she's back in Intensive Care.'

This time he didn't hesitate before he stepped up and pulled her to his chest, wrapping his arms around her. The hug was long and firm. She shuddered with distress under his hands.

'I'm so sorry, Isabella. No wonder you look stressed. I'm glad you came up.'

He tucked his chin on top of her head and breathed in the scent of her hair. Herbs. Flowers. And Isabella.

'What time did it happen?'

'Nine p.m. Malachi came down to see me afterwards. Very kind of him. He said she's stable now, but will have to stay in the ICU for another forty-eight hours at least.'

She lifted the back of her hand to wipe a tear off her cheek.

'I rang Dad. But he was in a late meeting, so I left a message.'

Of course he was. Useless man. Or useless to Isabella, anyway.

She pulled away and he let his arms fall so she could step back.

'Sorry.' She turned her face away. 'You don't need all this drama.'

'Hey...' He lifted a finger and turned her chin back. 'You're the lone lighthouse here, for all these people. It's tough being you. You just keep on being an incredible rock for everyone and I'll help hold up the foundations when you need it.'

She sniffed and lifted her chin, but her mouth trembled. 'I don't feel very rock-like at the moment.'

'How about you roll your rock my way?' He patted his chest. 'Let me be a refuge you can come to when you need it.' He stepped closer and pulled her in again. 'Another hug won't hurt.'

She let him, but she mumbled against his chest, her words vibrating between them.

'You couldn't wait to get away this morning,' she said.

And, yes, he had wanted to get away. He'd actually bolted. And he was ashamed of that. Yet, strangely, he didn't want to escape at this moment.

'But not now,' he said by way of apology.

Because she needed him now. And he couldn't dispute the fact that he needed to be there for her.

'Doesn't mean we're not friends. Just means I'm trying not to promise something I don't think I can give.' He dropped a kiss on her hair. 'But this is now. I can give this. The other is for the future. Would you like a sleepy time tea? Or something stronger?'

She stepped back again. When she looked up at him her mouth had firmed and her eyes were clearer. 'I'll take the tea.'

He nodded and pulled her over to the long sofa with all the cushions, and made sure she was comfortable before he turned for the kitchen.

He was back less than a minute later, with the tea poured, and a small empty bowl for the tea bag when she was happy with the strength of her beverage.

'Do you need something to eat?'

'I couldn't eat,' she said. 'I've been feeling sick since nine.'

'Understandable. But you know what? Sometimes food helps. How about I make you some cheese on toast cut into soldiers?'

She leaned her head leaned back at that, and stared up at him quizzically.

He shrugged, his face a little warm. 'Malachi made it for me after my wife died and I was doing zombie impersonations. I find it really helps when things get bad.'

She shook her head, as if she couldn't imagine what he described, but then a small smile bloomed on her beautiful mouth. 'Truly, that sounds wonderful. I'd love to try Malachi's soldiers.'

They sat together for the next half an hour, munching on crunchy toast and melted cheese, and drinking sleepy time tea as the clock ticked towards midnight. He'd dimmed the lights, so they could see out through the door towards the twinkling lights of Surfers Paradise across the wide bay.

Outside, the sound of the waves on the beach made a rhythmic hum as the traffic died away. His arm lay across her shoulders, pulling her into him, and her skin was like silk against his, warm and wonderful. Gradually Isabella relaxed beside him. His own stomach unwound as the tightness in her neck loosened and her head sank back into his arm. Good.

'I checked on Kate at half past ten and everything was fine with her,' Simon murmured quietly, not wanting to upset the mood but giving her the option to talk if she wanted to.

She shifted her head to look at him. She was so close. Kissably close.

'This is nice. I feel better,' she said, off-topic. Then, 'Yes, she looks good. I think you've nailed the danger after that first sign of inflammation. Nipped it in the bud.'

He stared back at her. Her eyes had deepened to emerald in the low light. 'I hope so. When are you on shift again?'

'An evening shift tomorrow.'

He fought with his body to lift his arm from her shoulders, because it really didn't want him to move. 'I, on the other hand, am on duty at eight. And you, missy...' he smiled as he remembered her addressing her sister like that '...need to go to bed.'

And not with me, despite how lovely that would be.

But he didn't say that out loud.

'You need sleep.'

'So do you,' she said. She turned her face and kissed his cheek. 'Thanks for the listening ear. I needed it.'

When she stood, she looked better somehow. Stronger. As if she'd regrouped. And he hoped that he had been a small part of that, even if he couldn't be anything else.

CHAPTER TWENTY-FIVE

ISABELLA'S HEARING SEEMED bizarrely attuned to hear when Simon shut the door after her. But when she got to the lift there had been no sound, and she turned back. He was still waiting.

She furrowed her brows at him. He smiled and waited until she'd slipped inside the elevator and the doors began to close before closing his own door.

That had been lovely interlude after a mad day. Simon had cosseted her. Not something she'd experienced often—someone looking after her.

Gran was bracing. Fun as she was, she expected the girls to look after themselves.

Simon making her cheese on toast soldiers, instead of Isabella doing the nurturing, sat oddly, but was warmly comforting—as it had been intended to be. There was no doubt she felt more serene than she had when she'd walked through Simon's door forty-five minutes ago.

But yes, she was tired. Needed to sleep. And not in Simon's bed. There was no future there. She wasn't going down that rabbit hole before trying to sleep. It would be too easy to get used to it.

The next morning Isabella launched her surfboard into the ocean and let the clarity of the waves wash away the fog, drama and fear of yesterday.

By the time she left the water she felt awake and alive. Ready for the day. Simon wasn't there, though. She'd spent a lot of the time looking. She tried not to worry about Kate just because he was missing. He had promised to call and her waterproof watch said she hadn't missed any attempts of communication.

She jogged back to her apartment with her surfboard under her arm, feeling her body lift and respond as if eager for more of a workout.

Nadia had told Simon about her karate. She hadn't thought about joining a martial arts class up here but that would be a great idea to give her another outlet. A place to stretch her muscles, keep fit and expend extra energy. Distract her from thinking about Simon.

Yup. She'd look into classes after Nadia was home and safe.

She'd phoned the ICU this morning. Her sister was stable and there'd been no more seizures. Kate was unchanging, according to the night shift in the NICU, though Simon's absence from the beach made that less reassuring.

She'd see Gran soon. Something about today felt positive, instead of a day spiralling down into worse and worse, and Gran was a good place to start.

'Good morning, Gran.'

Isabel placed another bowl of tiny heart-shaped purple flowers on Gran's bedside table. This time they came with succulent leaves as well.

'Mrs Green has more violets for you.'

She glanced down at the familiar face and froze.

Her grandmother's eyes were open. Isabella shut her own eyes and held them shut for the count of three. She slowly opened them, terrified of what she'd see.

Gran's eyes were still open. They weren't vague and staring. They were lucid. And warm.

Isabella's mouth opened in wonder as two single tears slid from the corner of her grandmother's eyes.

Isabella watched, barely daring to breathe, as Gran moistened her lips and whispered hoarsely, 'Bella...'

And then she closed her eyes and drifted off. But this time there was a smile on her face.

'Gran?' Isabella called, her voice frantic. Her gaze flew to the heart rate monitor above her head and she saw the rise in the heart rate begin to settle down again from the faster rhythm to the usual seventy. She hadn't noticed it when she'd arrived.

Gran had woken up.

Spoken and been lucid.

She'd recognised Isabella.

Isabella sank into the nearest chair. She put a hand to her mouth and silent tears ran down her face.

When she lifted her head there was a nurse there. Ella—the one she saw most mornings.

'What's wrong? I saw the monitor change,'

Isabella turned damp eyes to the young woman she'd spoken to nearly every day for the last month. 'Ella... Her eyes were open. And she said my name. Then she went back to sleep.'

Isabella heard herself say the words, but even she couldn't quite believe it.

Ella nodded with delight. 'They all said I was mad when I said she was less deeply unconscious than before.' Ella reached down and quickly hugged Isabella and then stood back. 'I'm so pleased for you all, Isabella. I'll phone the doctor.'

The room quickly filled with people and Isabella found herself tucked into the corner of the room, her heart still pounding.

She needed to tell Nadia.

And her father.

But, strangely, the person she really wanted to tell was Simon.

Ella said, 'They're going to take your grandmother down to have another CAT scan. Probably other tests as well.'

Isabella understood. Ella meant she'd soon be sitting in an empty room. 'I'll leave and come back on my way to work.'

Ella nodded. 'I'll phone you if anything changes.'

'Thank you.'

Her voice cracked. Time away was probably a good idea.

She walked away, her head full of improbabilities and hope and dread all mixed up so that she could barely think. When she reached her car, she sat in it, but didn't turn on the engine. Couldn't bear to drive away.

She looked down at her phone and her fingers flew as she texted before she thought too much about it.

Gran opened her eyes, Simon. And said my name.

She sent it just like that, and a text flew back within a minute.

Where are you?

She texted back.

Sitting in my car outside the hospital. I can't seem to drive away.

His reply.

I'll be there in ten minutes.

He was there in eight. He must have run to the apartments to retrieve his vehicle. He parked three car spaces down and was out of his car and at her door faster than she would have thought possible.

He opened her door and she climbed out and into his strong, warm arms. They wrapped around her. Wrapped her with kindness, understanding, and the big-heartedness she desperately needed right at that minute.

'But what if that was her last lucid moment before she passes away?' She whispered her worst fear into his chest.

He rubbed her back. Up and down, up and down, soothing her like a child with a skinned knee.

'What if it's the beginning of her waking up properly?' he said quietly into her hair. 'I think we should go for that one. Don't you?'

The sob in Isabella's throat turned into a strangled hiccup of a laugh.

'I like your optimism,' she said. 'I desperately *need* your optimism.'

His big warm hand, still rubbing up and down her back, patted her. 'Maybe she regained consciousness because she knew you'd be here, waiting for her.'

Isabella sobbed until his shirt was wet. Big, ugly, heart-wrenching sobs of relief that she hadn't allowed herself before.

As she quieted, he pushed a big, folded square of soft white material into her hand and she glanced at it. Her shaky laugh was a good exchange for the tears. 'I didn't think people carried handkerchiefs anymore.'

'I'm in a job where I sometimes need more than a tissue. Fragile paper just doesn't cut the mustard when your baby is sick.'

She sniffed, opened out the handkerchief, wiped her saturated eyes and cheeks, and blew her nose soundly.

He laughed. 'You can keep that.'

She offered him a wobbly grin. 'I'll wash it and give it back to you.'

He stepped away. The warmth of his hand falling away from her left a gap in her world and she missed it.

'Feel better?' he asked.

She sniffed again, but she felt as if she'd dropped a neck yoke and two full buckets off her shoulders.

'I do.'

Then she saw the way his damp shirt clung to the muscular ridges of his chest and abdomen, and suddenly she wanted nothing more than to trace the lines and hollows of his torso. She pulled her hand back as soon as it began to reach out.

'Um…you're wet. Sorry.'

'I didn't have time for a swim this morning. Must be my quota of salt water.' He was smiling, but there was heat there, too.

'Cute,' she said.

She eased away. Further. Until her back was against the closed door of the car. It felt warm from the sun, but not as warm as her belly. 'You got here quickly.'

'My friend needed me,' he said.

Friend. Cold water. That put out some of the flames.

'But I have to go back now. Are you going to be okay?' he asked.

She was used to standing on her own. But she appreciated the thought.

'Yes,' she said. 'I'll be fine. I'll go home now. I'll visit Gran again this afternoon, before I come to work.' Then another thought intruded. 'How's Kate? I was worried when you didn't come surfing.'

'The new twins are playing up. Respiratory issues. But I've pulled them into line,' he said with an easy smile.

Yet still his eyes remained serious and concerned.

About her?

'That's good. And I'm good. Now.' She met his gaze. 'Thank you, Simon. For coming when I needed you.'

His mouth opened and closed again. As if he'd thought better of what he'd been going to say. Instead, his lips formed different words. 'Have you called your father?'

No, she hadn't. She'd called *him.*

'Not yet.'

He smiled, and she suspected he liked it that she had called him first.

'I have to go. I'll see you later.' He turned towards his car, then spun back. 'Text me if you need to talk.'

CHAPTER TWENTY-SIX

SIMON LEFT ISABELLA at the hospital and his mind spun with what seemed suspiciously like delight.

She'd contacted him before her father.

To share her news and her fears. Because she'd trusted that he'd understand and be there for her.

She couldn't have known that he'd come, and he wondered what had been going on inside her head that had made her think texting him would help.

He lifted his chin as he drove back to the hospital. He had helped. Judging by her face. But when he'd first arrived—heavens, she'd looked like a fragile crystal vase about to smash into a million pieces.

He guessed she had finally broken against his chest, judging by the dampness of his skin. But the idea of Isabella—beautiful and tough and, yes, astoundingly fragile—needing him made him glad she'd called him.

In fact, the idea of Isabella seeking comfort anywhere else made his eyes narrow.

Simon wondered just how deeply he was falling for Isabella Hargraves…and if there was any hope at all that he could extricate himself before it was too late.

Simon should be in his office with his afternoon appointments, but his two-thirty had called to cancel. And instead of catching up on paperwork—which he always needed to do—

he was striding through the hospital to the NICU, to be there for when Isabel started work.

He watched her push through the door, totally put-together, showing no hint of the life-altering change that had occurred for her that day. Maybe there was an extra spring in her step. Certainly there was a smile in her eyes when she saw him.

He smiled back. Must be good news with her grand-mother—but he'd have to wait. She'd only just made it in time, because the shift handover was about to begin.

While he waited, he finished typing up the changes he'd made to one of the twins' treatment and checked through the notes for the rest of the tiny patients in the unit.

Fifteen minutes later the nurses had finished their walk around the patients and Isabella arrived at his side.

He was still typing on the rolling computer in front of the cot. 'Are you looking after these boys today?' he asked her.

She nodded. 'Yes.'

'Good,' he said.

They talked about the twins. Their treatment. The results of the latest blood tests. They compared thoughts on an X-ray and Simon realised he didn't even have this kind of in-depth conversation with Henry, and he was supposed to be his registrar, able to keep up.

Isabella mentioned something that might lead to a break-through.

He looked at her sideways. 'Good insight. I hadn't thought of that. Thank you.'

She lifted a hand, brushing it away. 'I love X-rays—they can show so much. So, you're welcome.'

He nodded, and knew he would think more on that later, but for the moment they had more important things to talk about. 'How's your grandmother?'

As he asked the question he studied her face and saw that her eyes were sparkling.

'She woke up again. She's incredibly weak, of course. But her doctor seems to think that because she recognised me and spoke again, making sense, she should just get better every day.'

'That's wonderful.' It was. Mind-blowing, really. 'Have you told Nadia?'

'Yes. I dropped into Intensive Care just before I came here. Malachi has her on some pretty strong drugs, so she's vague. But she's as thrilled as I am.'

'And your father?'

'My father told me not to expect too much.'

Simon was relieved to see she didn't look too disappointed. 'Of course he did…' Simon muttered. And then pressed his lips together. *Oops.* 'Sorry, that was judgmental.'

Isabella laughed. 'But true.'

He touched her shoulder. 'I'm very happy for you all.' *Especially you.* But he didn't say that out loud. He looked up as the phone rang and Carla called his name. 'I have to go. But I'll see you before I go home.'

He watched her beautiful mouth curve and her eyes lighten. Yes. She was glad that he'd said that. Which was good. Wasn't it…?

But Simon didn't make it back to the NICU before he went home because he spent the evening in the ICU with a young boy who'd came into Emergency with a severe asthma attack. It was touch-and-go as to whether they could save him. Simon couldn't leave the child until he was stable.

He had managed to lift his hand in a wave to Isabella when she'd entered the ICU to see Nadia. Isabella had waved back.

He finished in the ICU at ten-thirty that night, tired, rumpled, with his shirt slightly bloodstained from a tricky cannula.

On seeing the time, his first thought was Isabella, but it was too early to walk her home, and a bad time to talk to her as she prepared to end her shift and hand over. Instead, he decided to go to his own flat and shower. With luck he could walk and meet her on her way home.

Which was how he managed to find her under that first

streetlight just outside the hospital, in his fresh attire and with damp skin. He'd had to rush.

Isabella met his eyes as she walked up to him. 'Fancy meeting you here.' She looked him up and down, taking in his different clothes and wet hair. 'I'm guessing you had a busy night?'

Before he could speak a huge yawn overtook him and his hand lifted to hide his cracking jaw. 'I did. But the good guys won, so that's what's important.'

She bumped his shoulder with hers. 'You're the good guy.'

Nice. He smiled at her. 'Thank you. But this good guy is exhausted.' He side-eyed her and thought, *I'm exhausted, but loving the view.* 'And starving. I didn't get dinner. Fancy sharing a late-night snack?'

'I'd like that—but how about you come to Gran's apartment? I've got some homemade pumpkin soup, half a cooked chicken and some sourdough I'm happy to share.'

'Sounds even better. What shift are you on tomorrow?' It wouldn't be fair to keep her up if she started at seven a.m.

'A two-thirty start.'

'Excellent.' And he realised as he walked along the dark street with Isabella by his side that he was very, very content.

When Simon stepped inside Catherine Hargraves' apartment his eyes skittered to the bedroom he could see through the open guest room door. The bed was made. It hadn't been before. The last time he'd seen that room Isabella had been well loved and asleep amidst tumbled sheets.

His body stirred at the memories of that night, and when he looked away he saw she'd caught the direction of his interest.

Her voice conversational, she asked, 'You regretting that?'

'Lots of emotions,' he said soberly. 'But none are regret.'

'Good.' Her gaze left his and she walked into the kitchen, as if he'd given her the right answer. 'Do you want your sourdough toasted or soft?'

CHAPTER TWENTY-SEVEN

'SOFT, PLEASE.'

Isabella turned away to hide her blushes, because she had lots of emotions about that night, too. None of them regret. And none of them soft. Mainly she felt caution, the possibility of peril, and the absolute fear of never finding another man she cared about as much as Simon.

Maybe he would change his mind.

But she was trying to keep a lid on fantasising until she heard or felt something positive back from Simon.

She understood he was wounded. Battered by the loss of his wife. And probably scared of losing another someone he might possibly build a life with. She could see why. But there had to be more.

She had her own fears. She thought about Conlon. How he'd let her down when she'd needed him most. Thought about her father and how he'd let her down so many times when she'd been desperate for a shoulder to cry on. And she thought about Simon itching to get away at breakfast the other day.

But also she remembered today. When he'd come and held her while she'd been at her most vulnerable.

Had Simon changed his mind? Let himself become more accessible to her? It did look as if he wanted her to call on him if she needed support.

Or was she dreaming the fact they were getting closer because that was what she wanted? That he might reconsider them being more than friends?

Or maybe the guy just wanted more sex since he'd broken his drought.

But she didn't think Simon was shallow, and she suspected he knew she was protecting herself from expecting more than he offered.

Which left her vulnerable again.

Maybe inviting him here tonight hadn't been her most sensible idea.

Through all these thoughts and tortured paths of indecision her hands were busy heating soup, buttering sourdough and pulling the chicken from the fridge to cut up onto a larger plate. She threw on a couple of cherry tomatoes and a handful of spinach leaves, along with a baby cucumber and sweet yellow capsicum, sliced quickly. Then she gathered a knife and fork and a bottle of mayo and put the plate down in front of him at the table.

'You start on this while the soup heats and I'll butter more toast.'

He glanced up at her. His eyes twinkled and her belly kicked.

'So…you're one of those women who can make something out of nothing in less than two minutes?'

Stick to this conversation.

'I've had years of grabbing quick snacks. And I don't like commercial fast food, so I always have the makings.'

Simon opened his eyes wide. 'You don't like fast food? Wash your mouth out.' He reached for the plate and the cutlery.

He laughed and ate, and by the time she brought out the toast and soup he was scraping the plate.

'Hungry, much?'

'I have been wasting away,' he acknowledged, as she put a blue mug filled with steaming soup beside him, along with a plate holding two big slices of sourdough and real butter.

She considered his wide shoulders, gloriously broad chest—and those arms! *Oh, my.* This man was *not* wasting away.

Luckily, Simon missed her long, hungry examination as he looked at the soup with eager anticipation. 'Now I might live.'

Smiling, damping down the fire that had burst into flame in her belly, she went back into the kitchen and returned with her own soup and bread. She sat down opposite him. 'So? What happened in ICU?'

He was the one who was strung up this time. She, for a change, was feeling calm—or as calm as she could be with Simon across the table from her late at night, looking scrumptious. It was a nice change from her meltdown against that particular awesome chest earlier today.

But she had a feeling he'd had some trauma that still bothered him. Horrors lingering after the close call she'd heard about tonight, when one of the ICU nurses had spoken to her during her break with Nadia.

'Was it the young boy? Arlo? Asthma?'

Simon shook his head. 'Horrid disease. I hate it. Sometimes they get so shut down you just can't break through to their lungs.' He blew out a big sigh. 'We were lucky. We managed in the end.'

'Good job.'

He shook his head. 'I still can't believe the kid didn't even have an asthma plan for his mum to work through if he started to get sick. I'll have to contact his GP. Have a word with the practice about patient safety with asthmatics.'

She listened as he ranted a little. And then talked about the scariest bits. The fact that the boy's eyes had watched him, terrified, as he'd struggled for breath, and how Simon had thought he'd been going to lose him. And that wasn't even mentioning the distraught parents.

'But we won,' he finished, as if it had been a huge battle.

She could see that it had been. 'They were lucky to have you,' she said.

'It took a team,' he said. And looked away.

He seemed uncomfortable with the praise, and she wondered about his childhood. About his inability to take a compliment graciously. Not losing a patient seemed vitally, intrinsically imperative to him. It was the end goal for all health professionals, but to Simon it seemed more. As if his own life and death was in the balance.

'I'm lucky to have you to listen to me. And feed me. That was delicious.'

They'd both finished, and the empty plates had been pushed to the middle of the table.

Suddenly it felt as if the air had been sucked from the room. Which was crazy, because she had the door to the balcony open and the curtains were floating in a soft sea breeze.

She licked her suddenly dry lips. 'You should go to bed, Simon.' She stood up. 'You need to sleep.'

He rose, and Isabella walked towards the door. He followed her closely—which was good, wasn't it? But so was the fact that before she could undo the lock he had rested his hand on her shoulder and turned her to face him.

Yes. She wanted this.

Stepping close, he put both hands above her head against the door. Caging her loosely. But not holding her.

As he gazed down into her face she knew she should slip under his arm and away, but there was a lot of heat coming from his body that was now so close to hers. And she liked that heat. All she had to do was say the word, though, and she knew he would let her go.

But that was hard to do when she didn't want to.

'Is this a friends-with-benefits moment?'

He winced. He lowered his face, resting his forehead against hers. 'I don't know what this is.' Then he straightened, kissed her very gently on the lips before he pulled back. 'But right now I think I want to find out.'

His lips had been warm…seeking and offering. But his words stopped her.

They made Isabella lift her chin higher and move her head towards the door a little, increasing the gap between them.

She caught and held his gaze, her eyes narrowing. 'Are you sure about that Simon?'

There was challenge in her words…regret in her stomach. Because she knew how this would end. 'Because "I think I want to find out" isn't good enough.'

She scooted under his arm and put some distance between them before she did something that she, and apparently he, would regret.

'Nowhere near good enough. You should get some sleep. Goodnight.'

CHAPTER TWENTY-EIGHT

SIMON FELT THE absence of Isabella as she moved out of his reach like a gap in the universe. How had it come to this so quickly? So quickly that his head spun?

While his sense of loss urged him to answer her question the way she wanted, he knew that wouldn't be fair. Because it was true. He was still thinking about this. And he was a fool for pushing it.

'Thank you for being the sensible one,' he said.

He moved his hands from the door where she'd been. Returned them to his sides.

'Good call, Isabella. I need to sleep.'

He reached forward, opened the door, and let himself out before he could promise something he still wasn't convinced was true.

All the way back to his apartment he remembered her face, and the narrowing of her beautiful eyes as she demanded an honest answer.

She was amazing. Incredible. A way more put-together person than he was. Hell, he probably didn't deserve her anyway.

His father had said he wouldn't amount to much. And that parting sneer had driven Simon out of the only home he'd known to push himself at his studies until he could prove the man wrong.

The old martinet had died before Simon had been admitted to med school, which had left Simon a little skewed about his self-worth. But he'd hung out with the other misfit in college—

Malachi Madden—and together they'd been a force to be reckoned with. The bond that had grown between them had turned out to be rock-solid, and Malachi—the brother he'd never had—always had his back.

Was his lack of self-worth stopping him? Was that why he was holding back from Isabella? He didn't know. Maybe he'd ask his pseudo-brother tomorrow. Because Malachi had been worse at relationships than he was—until Lisandra had taken control.

Simon woke at dawn. For once, his phone hadn't gone off overnight. He jerked on his board shorts and grabbed his board. If he hadn't had two metres of fibreglass under his arm he would have jogged down the fire escape, to get a bit more exercise. But surfboards and narrow stairwells didn't go well together.

As he stepped out into the dim, cool morning, he breathed in the fresh salt air and decided to stop beating himself up about his vacillations over Isabella.

It would take as long as it took for him to get over his bereavement...be normal again.

In fact, he had come a long way towards 'normal' since Isabella Hargraves had first smashed through his barriers nearly five weeks ago.

Had it even been five weeks?

She'd been like a steamroller through the barriers that he'd thought impervious. She'd pushed through his defences as if they were putty.

And that had been just her looks.

Her brilliant brain blew him away, too.

He thought about the way they were so synchronised in their thought processes when discussing sick babies and possible prognoses. That was hot too.

Then he'd seen the big family-centred heart of her and he'd been a goner.

A goner? *Was* he a goner?

He thought about the way she caught his eye every time

she moved. He thought about the softness of her skin against his. Glorious. And she knew karate. His mouth kinked up. He wanted to explore that!

But questions and commitments and answers were all in play, and he couldn't go through another heartbreak. His father was right. He couldn't even keep the people he cared about safe. And Isabella didn't deserve the kind of person he was.

Simon walked into Malachi's office at eight-thirty, with his hair still wet from his post-surf shower.

There'd used to be days when Malachi was there at seven a.m., but family life had trained him out of that. Now the man even left before five in the evening some nights. Simon wasn't quite sure how Lisandra had achieved that, but there was no doubt that Dr Madden had more balance in his life now than Simon had.

Malachi looked up to see him at the door and raised his brows. 'What are you doing here?'

'Lovely greeting for your best friend.'

'*Only* friend apart from my darling wife.'

That was probably true. 'I've come for advice.'

The twinkle that materialised more and more often in his friend's eyes made Simon feel as if his ears were burning.

'You've fallen for Isabella!' Malachi appeared disgustingly delighted.

It wasn't a question. He hadn't even had to explain. Which was a relief of sorts.

'Not like you to be so observant, Malachi.

He shrugged. 'Lisandra told me.' It was a statement of fact.

Simon sighed. Of course she had.

'Thing is, I don't know if I want to do that whole *I would lose my world if anything happened to her* scenario.'

'You're scared.'

Malachi was known for his straight shooting. And for his ability to miss the concept of tactful advice. That was why he'd come here, wasn't it? Maybe...

Malachi sat down at his desk and leaned back in his chair. 'How long have you known her?'

'Less than five weeks.'

'Plenty,' said his now superior friend. 'Even I, stunted relationship guru that I was, only took a week to realise that Lisandra was the one I didn't want to get away.'

'You're saying take the risk? Put myself out on a limb?'

Malachi arched a brow. 'You won't be out on the limb by yourself. Isabella will be there. But you're the only one who knows whether you're ready, Simon. Lisandra says you've taken too long as it is.'

His friend tilted his head at him and shooed him out of his office.

'Get a move on.'

CHAPTER TWENTY-NINE

AFTER ANOTHER BUSY SHIFT, with two new prem babies admitted to the NICU and Kate improving, Isabella finished work and stepped out into the night with a smile. She wasn't surprised to see Simon under the streetlight outside.

'We really have to stop meeting like this,' she quipped.

It was funny, considering they'd spent about four hours together on and off throughout her shift.

'Was there something you couldn't tell me in the middle of the NICU?'

He didn't answer her facetious question. Instead, he said, 'I've started to really like this time of night.'

'Really? Angling for another invite? Well, I'm on the morning shift tomorrow. No midnight snacks for you.'

He smiled easily. Which meant he hadn't been expecting that scenario but had decided to come and meet her anyway. Curiouser and curiouser...

He glanced up at the moon overhead. 'That's okay. I just thought I'd walk you home.'

'Thank you. I may be your *friend*...' she emphasised the word '...but I don't need protecting. You know that, right?'

He looked struck for a moment, and she wasn't sure why. But then he went off on another tangent. 'I see Malachi is transferring Nadia back to the ward again tomorrow.'

She thought about her sister's excellent progress and it sat well. Such relief.

'Yes. He's pretty sure she'll be fine this time. She's still on

heavy-duty antihypertensives, but at least the blood pressure
is staying down now.'

'And I assume you'll be happy that Kate's back on oral
feeds tomorrow?'

'I am.'

She wasn't making it easy for him, which wasn't like her,
but Isabella was still a wee bit irritated about last night. Her
mind had circled around Simon's intentions. What were they
if he didn't feel that there was a relationship in the future for
them? Just sex?

Today, when they worked together, they'd both remained
very professional. Even Carla hadn't made any cheeky comments. So why was he here? Apart from his notion that near-
midnight rambling was a pleasant idea.

'I didn't get a chance to ask—how's Catherine? Has there
been more progress??'

Her crossness evaporated. She loved the way he called her
grandmother by her name. Highlighting that he saw her as a
person, not just as a patient recovering from a head injury or,
as in her father's case, a hopeless invalid. She appreciated that
subtext of support more than he probably knew.

Relief and pleasure rolled over her as she thought about
Gran. 'She was sitting up today. In the chair. Not for long,
but they've stopped the parenteral nutrition and she's drinking and eating soft foods.'

'That's amazing.' His delight seemed genuine, and she
hugged that to herself.

'That's what the doctors are saying. They can't believe how
fast she's recovering. Even Dad's gobsmacked. He's flying up
at the weekend to see her.'

'I really am thrilled.'

And his smile, which was pleased for her as well as Gran,
warmed her more.

'Nadia might even be discharged by then,' he added.

'I know. My world is changing. Things are finally going right.'

She should not have said that.

They were almost at the apartments, and up ahead she could see a man sitting on the low wall at the front of the block. She was glad that Simon was beside her.

Simon saw the figure as well, and stiffened. He stepped closer, until his shoulder touched hers.

As they neared, the man stood up. She recognised him. Though he seemed smaller. Slighter. Compared to Simon. Her light-heartedness disappeared. So much for everything going right for a change.

'Conlon. Hello. What are you doing here?'

She felt Simon's stillness. Did he remember her mentioning him?

Her ex glanced at Simon, and then back at her. His brow furrowed. 'I flew into Brisbane. You didn't answer my texts.' It sounded like a complaint not a statement.

She felt Simon relax slightly beside her.

Conlon was whining on. 'Your father said you were finishing at eleven and gave me your address.'

Still whining. Had he always whined?

Isabella closed her eyes for a moment. *Thanks, Dad.* She could feel Simon looming beside her, radiating distrust and other emotions. She wondered what he saw when he looked at Conlon. Judging by the expression on his face, not something he liked.

'Simon, this is Dr Conlon Brazier. We were working on a scientific paper together in Hanoi. Conlon, this is Dr Simon Purdy. Simon is walking me home in the dark.'

Conlon put his hand out. 'Great idea. Thanks for that.'

Simon jammed his hands in his pockets. The action quite forcible, as if had he not performed it, he might do something he regretted. 'Didn't do it for you, mate.'

Isabella suppressed a smile. 'No, you did it for me.' She looked up at him and smiled. 'Thank you, Simon. But I'll be fine now.'

She thought for a moment that Simon wasn't going to leave, but he nodded, stalked into the porch to unlock the door, and disappeared. The door didn't click shut behind him, staying open a crack. She suspected Simon was making sure Conlon wasn't going to annoy her.

She hid her smile. Her over-protective friend. That said more about Simon than he probably realised.

Had Simon been jealous? She'd think about that later.

First, she had to shake off her ex. Permanently.

'I'm on a morning shift tomorrow, Conlon. There's no need for us to talk. Anything between us is well and truly over.'

Conlon came closer. Into her space. *Idiot.*

'We had something, Isabella. We were good together in Vietnam.'

She stared into his arrogant, handsome face with a coolness she wouldn't have believed possible a month ago.

'Maybe. Briefly. But…' She shook her head as if msystified. 'It's gone now.'

She shrugged and saw him flinch. She wanted no misunderstandings. No comebacks. She doubted it had ever been more than superficial, now that she knew what real, world-shaking attraction, lust and magnetic draw was. Like she had for Simon.

She resisted a glance towards the door he'd disappeared through.

Conlon eased closer. 'I should have been more supportive. I'll try to do better. I flew all this way to see you.'

Yep. Whining.

'Conlon. Not happening. You let me down when I needed you. There's no going back.'

Isabella stepped past him—though really she wanted to push him onto his backside. Instead, she huffed out a small puff of amusement. He'd just think she accidentally shoved him. The guy was oblivious.

She said, with finality, 'It's been a big week for me, and I desperately need sleep. You can go now.'

His horrified eyes widened. 'You're just going to leave me out in the cold?'

She almost laughed. Except none of this was funny. 'It's the Gold Coast, Conlon. Twenty degrees Celsius.'

He huffed in disgust. 'I hoped you'd at least put me up.'

She teetered for a moment. Maybe she should take him in? They had been more than friends. But then common sense flooded back, and a wave of tiredness over the top of the shock of seeing him. Unannounced. Unwanted. Unsupportive Conlon.

No.

'You're a big boy. The airport hotel has twenty-four-hour check-in. That's where Dad stays when he's up here. I'm surprised he didn't tell you that.'

Conlon had the grace to look slightly embarrassed. 'He did.'

'I *would* drive you, but I'm done. Call a taxi—they respond fast here. Do you want me to wait here with you?'

'Not if you're too tired to talk to me.'

Sarcastic and definitely with the assumption that she would stay, and he'd keep trying, Isabella decided.

He'd be fine. 'Excellent. Goodnight.'

How had she ever thought she had a future with this petulant man?

She turned and left him, relief expanding inside her as she walked away. Simon wasn't behind the door inside, but the lift was still going up. He had just been there. She smiled.

Riding up in the elevator herself, Isabella felt briefly tempted to keep going all the way to the top and tell Simon that she and Conlon had no future. Ever. But Simon... Well, Simon was still *thinking* he wanted to find out what could grow between them.

Let him think about Conlon. She really was tired.

At last Isabella allowed herself to acknowledge the strain of the last weeks.

Tonight, seeing Conlon, she'd remembered the first moment her father had called her in Hanoi to tell her of Gran's accident.

She hadn't had any support as she'd rushed to Gran's side.

And she'd had to be the strong one and drag Nadia to the emergency department when she'd suspected pre-eclampsia.

It was her belligerence that had requested Simon's consultancy when Kate was born.

She'd even refused to believe her father's dire prognosis, and stayed with the faith Gran would wake.

Now that Gran was improving, Isabella wanted to stand down. Stop being the rock, always on her own against the odds.

But maybe she wasn't truly on her own anymore.

Simon had stepped up.

He'd taken over with Kate, ensuring her excellent care.

He'd been her sounding board when her father had let her down, as usual.

He'd been there when Nadia had been readmitted to the ICU and Isabella had been so scared.

Most of all she remembered him driving fast to the hospital, when Gran had opened her eyes and Isabella had melted down against his shirt.

The elevator doors opened.

There, beside her front door, stood Simon.

Despite the fact that she'd just decided he could stew in his own juices, it was good to see him. Wonderful.

She couldn't help the crooked smile she gave him. 'Fancy meeting you here,' she said, echoing the earlier greeting. She crossed the hallway to him.

'I'm sorry,' he said. 'I was a jealous idiot downstairs and I behaved badly. And I eavesdropped.'

She looked at him. Blond. Strong and beautiful. Hopefully hers.

She touched his cheek. 'Don't bother worrying. He won't be coming back.'

'Why is that?' Simon asked, but she saw that he knew.

'You were listening?'

'In case you needed me.'

'I didn't.'

'I heard that.'

The relief in his eyes shone plainly. Along with a furnace of heat.

'Because he let me down.' This was important. It had to be said. 'That's the one thing I won't have from the man in my life. Never again.'

Simon stepped closer. 'And if I promise not to let you down?'

'There's no "if", Simon. *Do* you promise that?'

His chin went high. He lifted his hand to his heart to rest on his chest. 'Yes.'

His voice was firm. His eyes held hers. There was no doubting the sincerity. The inherent promise.

'If you'll let me into your life?'

'I know—I don't *think*,' she said, using words ironically, because he'd used them last night, 'that you're already in my life, Simon. You're the one who needs to remember that I'm in yours.'

She passed him and put her key in the lock and slipped away.

The door closed behind her.

CHAPTER THIRTY

SIMON STOOD OUTSIDE Isabella's door and thought about knocking. Asking her what she meant.

He imagined kissing her.

Then he thought about the tiredness in her eyes and in the droop of her shoulders.

Shook his head. No. Not tonight.

He played back what she'd said about Conlon—that he would never come back after today. He'd heard that dismissal. *Ouch.* Okay, then. He acknowledged the fact that she was willing to trust that he would never let her down if she let him in. That she'd said he was a part of her life.

She'd also said he needed to realise she was a part of his.

Suddenly it wasn't hard to be certain that he wanted Isabella Hargraves in his life—for now and for always.

The other thing he'd come to realise—painful, but true, and just a bit enlightening—was that Isabella didn't need his protection. She would protect herself. In fact, he thought with a smile, she could probably protect *him*.

She didn't want protection. She wanted a partnership. With him. She wanted support as an individual. But with him.

His darling Louise had always been soft. Gentle. In need of protection. Thus, when she'd died, his soul had whispered that he was the one at fault for not protecting her.

That whisper had coiled around him, merged with the guilt his father had left him with, and stolen his smile. His faith in himself. He'd built up his walls so that he could never fail to protect anyone ever again. Those conjoined whispers had kept him from trusting his heart to find someone he wouldn't let down.

Isabella had restored his faith. Isabella didn't want protection. She wanted a man at her back as well as by her side. Through thick and thin. She wanted him, and he had no idea how he could have been so lucky.

He could do what she needed. Because it was what he needed too. He wanted to be there always for the woman he loved.

He loved her. She'd been a wrecking ball he hadn't expected—stealing his breath and his heart.

He'd been finding his self-esteem in protecting his patients. Being there for them twenty-four-seven at work had given his life meaning. What Isabella offered was so much more than that...so much more sustainable.

Maybe now he could understand his friend's soul-deep happiness. And his advice to get a move on.

It was time to start wooing his love. Building trust. To ensure that his Isabella knew he would always be there for her. Proud to be by her side.

The next afternoon, late in the day, as he walked back into the unit, Simon acknowledged that it had been a good day. He and Isabella had a professional working relationship that ran smoothly, and he was planning to court her with his charms when work was behind them. He even had a plan.

Nadia had moved back to the ward and was looking well. Simon felt pleased for her, and Kate, but also for Isabella, who had been so worried about her sister.

Malachi had assured him that Nadia would continue to improve now, as all her blood results had settled down—Simon had checked with him so he could reassure Isabella if she needed more.

Kate was back on tube feeds, and had had her first skin-to-skin kangaroo care with her mother, tucked under her mum's shirt against her bare skin.

He'd gone down to the unit for the event, and had smiled with everyone else when Kate was settled, with her head poking out of her mother's shirt. He'd been watching Isabella the most, and the joy he'd seen on her face had warmed his heart and filled him somewhere he hadn't realised he'd been empty.

There'd been three babies discharged from the unit as well, going home happy and healthy.

With those babies gone suddenly there was time to breathe—until the next rush of patients arrived. These moments gave the dedicated staff time to be satisfied with the job they were doing, caring for their tiny charges.

He'd timed his return to the unit now for just before Isabella walked out through the door. He caught her as she was saying goodbye to her niece and she didn't see him coming.

He touched her shoulder. 'I know you don't have to see Big Boy Conlon when you finish here...'

She flashed a grin at him, remembering that she'd told Conlon he was a big boy and could find himself somewhere else to sleep. 'Funny man...'

He smiled. 'Well, I used to be a funny man. And I'm finding humour again. Because there's this woman I fancy so much that I'm willing to change. And Carla tells me the sadness I've been wallowing in has grown really old.'

She smiled at that too. Watching his face with that careful attention she gave to anyone she spoke to.

'But that's not why I'm here,' he said.

'Goodness,' she said—a little facetiously, he thought. 'Why *are* you here?'

'Anyway,' he continued quietly, 'when you leave here, are you going to visit Catherine?'

'Yes.' Those lovely brows arched. 'Why?'

'Would you mind if I came? You could text me and I could meet you there.'

He wasn't sure what he would do if she said no.

She tilted her head at him. 'Sure. I can leave at five.'

'Great. I'll be on time.'

She looked startled and pleased. Good. He'd ticked one box on his mental list.

'And afterwards…' He tried a winning smile and her lips twitched. 'I'd like to take you on a dinner date.'

'A date?' she said. 'Haven't we moved past that?'

'Not officially.'

She cocked her head. 'We've had breakfast together… I've met your friends…we've had dinner…' She waggled her brows. 'And more!'

'Yes, but this is me asking you to dress up and come out to a flash meal with me for the purpose of getting to know each other better. With nobody else present.'

'Simon Purdy—' she started, but Carla had crossed the room to them with a small piece of paper for Simon and she stopped.

'Yes, I know,' he said. 'We'll talk about it tonight.'

He saluted her and turned to Carla.

And that was how he ended up at the hospital just after five.

Now that he really observed Catherine Hargraves, he decided she looked like he imagined Isabella would look in fifty years. Snow-white hair had been brushed back off her face in soft waves. She had a long neck, like her granddaughter, and the same angled cheekbones and the same large green eyes, though faded.

But mostly it was the bright mind lurking at the back of those eyes that made him think of Isabella.

He picked up the wrinkled hand, stroked his thumb over the soft skin and bowed over it.

'Mrs Hargraves… You're obviously made of stern stuff,' he said. 'It's wonderful to see you looking so alert.'

'As opposed to comatose?' she said, a quirk of amusement tilting her mouth.

'Isabella never gave up on you,' he said.

'No. She didn't.'

He watched Catherine Hargraves glance at her granddaughter.

'She's a strong woman. She's had to be.'

There it was. That mutual appreciation between Isabella and her grandmother. A precious thing that he envied.

'I know,' he said softly.

He squeezed her hand gently, rested it back on the covers and stepped back.

Isabella had been talking to the doctor at the door, discussing discharge dates and reminding the doctor that she lived with her grandmother and would be able to help with the heavier tasks that might be difficult for her at the moment.

When she returned to the bedside her smile was reflected in her eyes. 'Possibly Monday. How do you feel about that, Gran?'

'Sounds fine.'

'Great! I'm off Tuesday and Wednesday. I could pick you up after work Monday afternoon. Then we'd have two full days together.'

Her grandmother pretended to slump in exhaustion against the pillows. Or most of it was pretend. 'Not full days, child. Your energy would drive me batty.'

'I'll take her off your hands when she's too much, Catherine. Just let me know.'

Simon watched Isabella's face as he said it, and saw how she tucked in her chin and looked at him from under her brows.

'Will you, now?' she asked.

'Surf, sand and avocado on rye as necessary,' he agreed. 'But now I think I've stayed long enough. I'll wait for you at your car. No hurry.'

He watched Isabella shoot a quick glance at her grandmother. 'No. I'll come too. We've both stayed long enough.'

Which was what he'd hoped she'd say. Because he knew that even in Isabella's excitement she would not have missed the droop of exhaustion in the older woman's shoulders. But he didn't think she'd mind him creating the opportunity to leave.

As they walked out onto the street, he said, 'So…? Dinner? Do you like Greek?'

'I love Greek food.'

'Is seven p.m. enough time for you?'

He couldn't wait.

'Sure.'

'I'll pick you up at six forty-five. We'll take my car.'

She laughed, and her face filled his vision. She leaned in and kissed him. She tasted of sunshine and mint. 'You haven't got over that yet. Have you?'

Her mouth against his made him melt. But this wasn't the place. Or the time.

Instead he said, 'Smart Alec.' She filled him with joy.

'I'm willing to be persuaded to take your vehicle occasionally, but you'll need a good argument,' she told him.

He wondered if even Hanoi traffic had fazed Isabella.

She patted his arm. 'You can be the driver tonight.'

CHAPTER THIRTY-ONE

SIMON BROUGHT FLOWERS. Wildflowers. Her favourite kind. A huge bunch of beautiful proteas, flannel flowers, waratahs and everlasting daisies.

The armful lay against his white shirt like a frame for his smile until he handed it over. The bouquet almost sang with exuberance—glorious and perfectly set off by native leaves and grasses.

'So beautiful... And they will still look gorgeous when Gran comes home.'

'I thought about that,' he said, smiling around his pleasure at her obvious approval.

'That's thoughtful.' He *was* thoughtful.

'Thank you.'

He had no idea how much she appreciated his kindness.

'I love them.'

And she knew, now that she'd allowed her dreams to surface, how much she loved *him*.

His expression—the tilt of his stubborn chin and the beautiful smile on his face—said how pleased he felt as he watched her reaction.

He slid a small blue paper packet out of his pocket. 'I also brought chocolates.'

This was a real date, then. The whole hog.

She widened her eyes at him. 'Thank you. I love chocolates. As long as you help me eat them later.'

His eyes said he could do more than that.

Oh, my.

His lips formed the words. 'I can do that.'

She nodded for him to put them on the table while she took the flowers into the kitchen and hugged them to herself. She breathed them in to steady the excitement that had ramped up since he arrived. Her date really was pulling out all the stops. She wondered if she should thank Conlon for Simon's over-eagerness to pursue her and suppressed a grin.

She pulled the largest vase from under the sink and filled it with water. 'I'll pop the whole lot in here until later, and sort them out when we come home.'

She heard the echo of those words...*when we come home.* Presumptuous—maybe ambitious—but her belly kicked in anticipation.

Simon must have caught on to the concept, too, because his eyes darkened. 'We should go now...'

His voice had dropped to that deeper, hungry, gravelly tone she was coming to recognise.

'Or we'll be late.'

She glanced up at him. Saw the craving, heard the unspoken *really late*, and smiled as she grabbed her small clutch with her keys inside.

She said a little breathlessly, 'Coming.'

They didn't speak on the way to the restaurant, but the car simmered like a pot on the stove with the unspoken heat between them. His shoulder and hers were close, and buzzing even without touching.

The restaurant had dressed itself in blue and white, which was funny because Simon was wearing a white shirt and she was wearing an Aegean-blue trouser suit in silk.

'You look beautiful,' he murmured. 'Did you get that in Vietnam?'

'Thank you. And, yes, I did. My friend is a tailor there, and she kept pushing them on me after I nursed her son. We're very colour co-ordinated in here.'

He lifted his glass to her.

They'd ordered two flutes of sparkling Greek rosé and they clinked crystal in a toast.

'To the future,' he said.

'The future…' she murmured.

That was…unexpected. And bold. She met his eyes and sipped. She tasted the explosion of fruit in the underlying rose petals and set the glass down.

'Lovely wine.'

'Malachi tells me it's Lisandra's favourite. I thought you might like it.'

'I do.'

So he'd discussed this dinner with his friend. Interesting… Very interesting.

'What else did you discuss with Malachi Madden?'

'Apparently, Lisandra told him I was taking too long to make a move on you.'

Isabella spluttered, glad her wine was on the table. 'Did she, now? I'll tease her about that when I see her next.'

His hand reached across the table and captured her fingers in his. 'I was a fool the other night. I don't want to be a fool again. I'm moving now. Forward, I hope. Not letting go.'

The dinner passed in a blur of heated glances, brushing fingers and hot knees touching beneath the table.

Isabella didn't remember much about the food. She remembered the wine, because the cool touch of the glass against her lips put out some of the heat from Simon's gaze. His hot, hungry gaze that rested so often on her mouth…

When she opened the door to her grandmother's apartment, he backed her into the room and pulled the door handle from her fingers gently. He didn't turn on the light, letting the glow from the moon be the only illumination in the room.

She'd left the curtains open and moonglow spilled across his face. It turned him into a silver god, and her into a woman so very willing to surrender.

His hand captured the back of her neck, warm and possessive. The other cupped her cheek as he leaned her against the wall.

'Do you have any idea how much I want you?'

His words caressed her skin, murmured against her throat, heating her nerves from throat to toes. His dark, dark eyes drilled into hers with such awe and possessive need. She hadn't dreamt that so much wanton, fiery desire would ever be directed at her.

She waved her hand in front of her face. 'There's a lot of heat coming from you,' she whispered. 'Perhaps we'll both burst into flames.'

The idea had merit.

Simon growled, 'I'd like to find out. You know I'll want you for ever? You up for that?'

'I was hoping…'

And that was the last almost full sentence she managed to utter for a very long time.

CHAPTER THIRTY-TWO

Three months later

ON THE MORNING of Simon and Isabella's wedding, Isabella watched the last of the wedding preparations from her bedroom in Gran's apartment. The temporary lights set up on the beach allowed the wedding planners to scoot around and set up before sunrise.

The path to the beach held an avenue of tall white wedding flags with silver hearts dangling from their ends. Isabella would walk through them and the newlyweds would return that way.

The sand hadn't found its sunlit gold yet, and the still, indigo ocean lay flat, a lazy mini swell all that hinted at the possibilities Lady Ocean could offer. Later she would glitter and spin with the sunlight under the gentle breeze.

Down at the water's edge and to one side, a huge white circular umbrella gently flapped, tipped with the same silver hearts dangling from each flag. The umbrella was planted above a white table covered in the same material, flanked by potted palm trees. Two pristine deckchairs waited for after the ceremony, when Simon and Isabella would sit and sign the marriage certificate.

Five rows of white chairs, four each side of the aisle, waited for the guests. More palm trees in pots graced each row on the outside edge.

The whole thing was like a tiny chapel at the edge of the sea.

Isabella blinked back unexpected prickles in her eyes. *Stop it. No time to redo mascara.* But the setting below had sprung up even more beautifully than she'd imagined, and would look wonderful when the sun rose.

'Isabella? Darling, nearly time to go.'

Her grandmother stood at the door in a pale turquoise sheath. Her eyes were clear and bright. She had recovered most of her vigour and all of her sharp wit.

'You look beautiful, Gran,' Isabella said as her grandmother came into the room.

Gran's make-up lay perfectly, and her white hair, professionally styled, was soft about her face.

Isabella knew that Lisandra had been the instigator of quite an organisational campaign in the early hours, from five a.m., when a team of stylists and make-up artists had arrived to prepare the wedding party.

Catherine murmured, 'You look beautiful in white, darling. You should wear it more often.'

Isabella glanced down at the floor-length sheath, studded at neck and hemline with the luminous pearls that her seamstress friend from Hanoi had wanted to sew on as a gift.

'Thank you.'

The long slit that ran to Isabella's tanned thigh would make her walk up the sandy aisle easy. Her feet were encased in tiny silver slip-ons which she would leave at the edge of the sand and go barefoot—she and Simon wanted to be the only ones who would go unshod.

'I never imagined myself in a white wedding dress, Gran...'

'And why not? Today is the start of your beautiful life with Simon. Mutual love such as yours should be celebrated with distinction.'

Distinction? Yes. Her gorgeous, generous Simon deserved distinction. Their joy in each other had grown and spread like foam on the ocean, diffusing through their world and reaching out to bubble into everything. And everyone. Even her father looked happier sometimes.

She loved Simon so much…admired him, delighted in his brilliant brain, and in his quirky sense of humour that still caught her at unexpected intervals and seemed to grow each day. She loved him so much she couldn't imagine not having him by her side. At her back. In her bed. For ever.

Two more figures crowded at the door. Nadia in cornflower-blue and Lisandra in lapis lazuli. Her three matrons of honour matched the shifting blues of the ocean. Each carried a small spray of multi-shaded blue flowers, with baby's breath backed by blue-green gum leaves, and wore silver slip-on sandals like Isabella's.

She'd wanted to be there before dawn, when the beach colours were the most ethereal, but they'd compromised for the non-morning people and had gone for sunrise instead.

It had taken three months for Catherine Hargraves to re-establish her strength well enough to be able to enjoy a wedding as a principal player, and Isabella and Simon had waited patiently for her grandmother to be one of the bridal party.

Now it was time.

Professor Piers Hargraves appeared at the door, with a serious face that said he couldn't see any good coming out of this match. The women in the room glanced at each other and pressed their painted lips together.

'For goodness' sake, Piers! It's a wedding, not a funeral. Smile!' his mother ordered.

Isabella had to stifle a laugh. The more time she spent with Simon, the less her father's dourness affected her. Simon had helped her realise that her dad's emotional distance was his default. And not her fault. It didn't matter. She still loved him, despite all his doom and gloom. But that didn't stop her winking at her grandmother.

Simon stood barefoot at the edge of the water, watching the path through the flags for the woman he loved.

'She'd better hurry or we're here early for nothing and we'll miss the sunrise,' Malachi murmured sagely. He had shoes on.

Simon shook his head. 'She won't be late.'

Just then the music began—gentle flutes playing the 'Bridal March' in the morning air, the notes soaring and sweeping like the gulls above.

The first of the bride's attendants swayed into view and he heard Malachi suck in a breath. When he glanced at his best man, he saw Malachi's attention was focussed fully on his wife. Lisandra swayed onwards, in a dress coloured with the shifting, vibrant blue of a lapis stone.

'So beautiful...' his friend sighed.

There was an amused huff from Simon. 'You're supposed to be supporting me.'

Malachi flicked him a glance, and then his gaze ricocheted unerringly back to his wife. 'Don't need to. I'm surplus. You've got this.'

Nadia sashayed into view. Isabella's sister looked so good in a dress the paler blue of a cloudless afternoon sky.

Then came Catherine, slow and gracious, in her dress which was the turquoise of ocean shallows in the sunshine.

Isabella had told him she'd chosen the colours because those were what she saw when they were out on their boards. So fitting. So beautiful. So deep and thoughtful, his Isabella...

Catherine looked well, and the rosy bloom of her now healthy skin colour made him think briefly of the unexpected delight of his being treated by her like a favourite grandchild.

But the sky was getting lighter.

Sunrise was approaching.

And finally he saw a figure in white. His Isabella. His future. The woman who held his heart in her sure hands and promised him a partnership he'd never even dreamed was possible.

His chest tightened as his vibrant, joyful bride—so vital, like the first day he saw her, his Isabella—came closer. She slipped off her sandals and stepped on to the sand.

She'd said having bare feet together meant the beginning of a promise...casting off the world to come together bare of protection, open to the sand below their feet. Connected to each other and only each other, with their bare feet joined in the golden grains that had been there for millennia.

He loved her so much.

Emotion swelled. His eyes prickled and he blinked away the sting of tears at the memory of her serious, heartfelt explanation.

Their gazes met and she smiled just for him, her face lighting with love and excitement and the *joie de vivre* that was so much a part of the woman he'd fallen in love with that first day.

He reached out his hand and finally her precious fingers slid into his palm as they entwined their fingers and their lives for ever.

* * * * *

COMING SOON!

We really hope you enjoyed reading this book.
If you're looking for more romance
be sure to head to the shops when
new books are available on

Thursday 28th March

To see which titles are coming soon, please visit
millsandboon.co.uk/nextmonth

MILLS & BOON®

Coming next month

FORBIDDEN NIGHTS WITH THE PARAMEDIC
Alison Roberts

He wasn't about to put any pressure on her, but he wanted Jodie to know that, if he had seen behind her mask, she could trust him not to use it against her or even mention it.

That she could trust *him*.

Maybe his lips curved, just a little, but it was Eddie's eyes doing most of the smiling and Jodie caught her bottom lip between her teeth.

Eddie was still holding her gaze. Or maybe Jodie was holding his. Maybe it didn't matter because something bigger was holding them both. The air in this small room with its shelves so tightly packed with medical supplies and the heavy, security door firmly closed seemed to be getting heavier. Pressing down on them.

Pushing them closer together.

Neither of them said a word. They didn't seem to need to. By whatever means, whether it was body language or telepathy, apparently the desire was expressed, permission sought – and granted.

Jodie slowly came up onto her tiptoes. Eddie bent his head just as slowly, turning it in the last moments, just before he closed his eyes and finally broke that contact, so that his lips were at the perfect angle to cover Jodie's with a soft, lingering touch.

When he lifted his head, he found Jodie's eyes were open before his. Maybe she hadn't closed them at all? Because of their soft, chocolate brown colour, he could also see that her pupils were getting bigger fast enough to tell him that she had liked that kiss as much as he did. That quick intake of her breath suggested that she wanted more.

Eddie had played this game often enough to be an expert. He knew there was an easy way to find out…

This time, the kiss wasn't nearly as soft and her lips parted beneath his, her tongue meeting his almost instantly.

Oh, yeah…

She wanted more.

So did Eddie. But not here. Not now. Not just because they'd be breaking all sorts of rules and it was a bad idea, anyway. No…he had a promise to keep to someone else and Edward Grisham never broke a promise.

He broke the kiss, instead.

'I have to go,' he said.

Jodie's gaze slid away from his. 'Me, too. We're done here.'

But Eddie was smiling as he turned away. He spoke softly but he knew that Jodie would be able to hear him perfectly well.

'I'm not so sure about that,' he said.

Continue reading
FORBIDDEN NIGHTS WITH THE PARAMEDIC
Alison Roberts

Available next month
millsandboon.co.uk

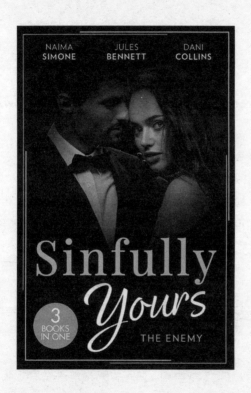

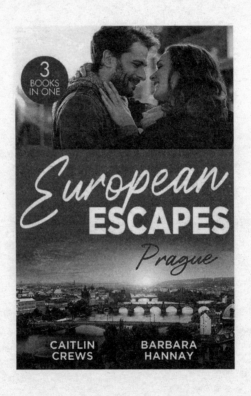

OUT NOW!

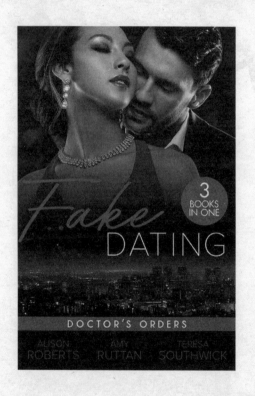

Available at
millsandboon.co.uk

MILLS & BOON

LET'S TALK
Romance

For exclusive extracts, competitions
and special offers, find us online:

f MillsandBoon

X @MillsandBoon

⊙ @MillsandBoonUK

♪ @MillsandBoonUK

Get in touch on 01413 063 232

MILLS & BOON

THE HEART OF ROMANCE

A ROMANCE FOR EVERY READER

MODERN
Prepare to be swept off your feet by sophisticated, sexy and seductive heroes, in some of the world's most glamourous and romantic locations, where power and passion collide.

HISTORICAL
Escape with historical heroes from time gone by. Whether your passion is for wicked Regency Rakes, muscled Vikings or rugged Highlanders, awaken the romance of the past.

MEDICAL
Set your pulse racing with dedicated, delectable doctors in the high-pressure world of medicine, where emotions run high and passion, comfort and love are the best medicine.

True Love
Celebrate true love with tender stories of heartfelt romance, from the rush of falling in love to the joy a new baby can bring, and a focus on the emotional heart of a relationship.

HEROES
The excitement of a gripping thriller, with intense romance at its heart. Resourceful, true-to-life women and strong, fearless men face danger and desire - a killer combination!

From showing up to glowing up, these characters are on the path to leading their best lives and finding romance along the way – with plenty of sizzling spice!

To see which titles are coming soon, please visit

millsandboon.co.uk/nextmonth